CANDLESTICKS

OTHER FIVE STAR TITLES BY SHARON ERVIN

The Ribbon Murders
Murder Aboard the Choctaw Gambler

A JANCY DEWHURST MYSTERY

CANDLESTICKS

SHARON ERVIN

FIVE STAR
A part of Gale, Cengage Learning

 GALE
CENGAGE Learning·

Detroit • New York • San Francisco • New Haven, Conn • Waterville, Maine • London

GALE
CENGAGE Learning

LIBRARY OF CONGRESS CATALOGING-IN-PUBLICATION DATA

Ervin, Sharon, 1941–.
   Candlesticks : a Jancy Dewhurst mystery / Sharon Ervin. — 1st ed.
      p. cm.
   ISBN-13: 978-1-59414-876-7 (alk. paper)
   ISBN-10: 1-59414-876-7 (alk. paper)
   1. Women journalists—Fiction. 2. Oklahoma—Fiction. I. Title.
PS3605.R86C36 2010
813'.6—dc22   2010007280

First Edition. First Printing: June 2010.
Published in 2010 in conjunction with Tekno Books.

Printed in the United States of America
1 2 3 4 5 6 7 14 13 12 11 10

To Bill,
always my hero

ACKNOWLEDGMENTS

I owe special thanks to:

Connie Kiesewetter and Debra Powell, excellent critiquers, always looking out for the best interest of the manuscript.

Jane Bryant and Ronda Talley, for friendship and their ability and willingness to do eagle-eye editing.

Oklahoma State Bureau Supervisor Tommy Graham, retired, and Christopher Elliot, able research gurus.

CHAPTER ONE

Wire Service Bureau Chief Duke Mallory didn't look up even though I was standing right beside his desk. I'd asked him again to let me cover this story on my own. Duke was old, but I didn't think he was so old or crusty that he didn't remember the want-to.

I tried to be still but gyrated a little, rocking from my heels to the balls of my feet, biting my lips to keep from repeating the same old arguments.

Mallory himself admitted I had plenty of savvy for twenty-four. He said he hated to toss me into battle, hustling against seasoned news hounds for that elusive byte no one else had. He kept saying he knew I could do it, just before he assigned me another rewrite or a celebrity obituary we wrote in advance to keep on file for the eventuality. He insisted that was the usual drill for American Wire Service interns, but how long did he expect me to endure like this? I'd indulged his protective fantasies for the six weeks I'd been in San Diego, which was plenty of time to learn my way around and find out who the main players were.

His smoker's cough emerged as more of a growl as he finally slouched back in his chair and glared at me. I couldn't figure why he was so reluctant to turn me loose. I had my degree. I'd worked two years as a reporter on *The Bishop Clarion*. I knew the score.

Waiting for him to say something made me crazy. I ran my

hand around the waistband of my slacks, tucking my shirt for the third time. My slacks bunched under the belt I'd cinched another notch.

"You know, for as tall as you are, you're getting too damned thin," he said.

I stared at him. Weight didn't have anything to do with a person's ability to report the news.

He shook his head. "You're real pretty, Dewhurst, but you don't take enough trouble with yourself."

My dark, blunt-cut hair got shampooed every morning. It was easy to keep. I just never thought about combing it during the day. Most of my clothes were wash and wear, so I didn't iron. I didn't polish my shoes, but who polished sandals? My only other footwear was a pair of sneakers, which I washed periodically. Besides, grooming wasn't exactly Duke's area of expertise either. He went around most of the time looking like an unmade bed and smelling of nicotine and stale booze.

He noticed right off that I "didn't miss much," which is really any reporter's greatest gift. He bragged about me to other people in the press room—behind my back, of course—but they repeated those things to me from time to time. He said all the best interns he'd trained had been alert and observant, but none had been any better than I was. I needed to hear that.

He told Ivy Work that the kids the wire service sent him were Double A players called up to the majors, still wet behind the ears, eager to strut their stuff, prove they could play in the big league. He said he didn't remember any of the others being quite as green as I was, or "quite as cute either," Ivy said. I was amazed and asked if she agreed with him.

"Hell, no," she said. Another veteran of the journalistic wars, Ivy said instead she assured Duke he was just getting old and forgetful.

My hair swished in time to my twitching.

Finally, Duke chose to speak again. "I guess there was a time, Jancy, when I wanted in this business as badly as you do, but I'll be damned if I can remember it."

"So?"

"Okay," he relented. "It's yours. You're on your own." He shifted in his chair, rocked back, and locked his hands behind his head. "Get out there amongst 'em and show us what you've got."

I gritted my teeth to swallow a rebel yell. I could shout later, when Mallory wasn't kicked back smirking right there in front of me. At the moment, I needed to get out of there before he changed his mind.

I had asked him to let me cover the first burglary in South Beach two weeks before. I had pleaded after the second and groveled after the third, genuinely annoyed that he couldn't see we needed to be covering this ourselves instead of leaving it to local reporters who fed their work into the AWS computers. The local guys were missing something. I could feel it. I could find whatever it was. All I needed was a chance.

Now, with a fourth burglary, Mallory finally blinked. We were going live and the story was mine—solo.

"Man, oh man," I whispered, biting back another whoop. I grabbed a steno pad, returned Mallory's smirk, mumbled, "It's about time," and darted out the fire exit, leaving my mentor alone in the pressroom—in the building, as far as I knew.

I bolted up the stairs and out to the deserted parking lot with a surge of confidence that fairly burst with another positive thought. Thad Bias was probably working the case.

Sure he was. It was the Friday after Thanksgiving. Single like me, Thad caught most of the holiday duty.

I liked Thad, of course, which made it easier to cultivate him, make him my primary news source inside the police department.

I clambered into the mid-size junker, the courtesy car provided by the wire service to its visiting interns. Moments later the obstinate vehicle squealed into traffic and shot down the boulevard toward the Elbert Ketchum residence on Dillon.

"What was the house number?" I asked out loud. It didn't matter. I hadn't driven in San Diego much, but I knew Dillon. It was close. I would cruise until I saw a police car.

I was surprised to find that a TV relay truck and crew, two police cruisers, and sightseers had pushed parking into the next block by the time I got there. Why was a garden-variety house burglary attracting so much attention? It must be a super slow news day. I pulled to the curb a block down. Jogging back, I slowed as I elbowed my way in, swimming through the neighborhood curious.

The uniformed patrolman shook his head, even when I flashed my press pass, denying me entry. "They've got too many reporter types in there already," he said.

"Bias!" I shouted at the house from behind the perimeter tape. "Thad Bias! *Thad!*"

At my third shout, the police lieutenant's lanky form appeared in the doorway of the residence. He looked out, scanning for me. Thad usually grinned when he saw me. This time he didn't. I waved.

Looking grim, Bias waved back and motioned the patrolman to let me through. I hurried.

"Sorry," I said quietly as I caught up with Bias inside the front door of the house. "Hope I didn't ruin your day." At five-foot-seven, I felt comfortable standing straight beside Thad, who towered over me.

"You're too late for that." He shook his head. "This is not an investigation. This is a joke and O'Brien's an idiot." He glowered and took a deep breath. "The biggest mystery in this town is not these burglaries. It's how that clown ever made captain.

And all the TV news people showing up like this . . . it's a damn frenzy."

I needed to get him focused on the case, not encourage a lot of nonproductive grumbling. "Did you get any fingerprints?"

"Hell, no. The lab people didn't show for two hours. It's a holiday. They're working a skeleton crew, got one team covering the whole metro. You have to take a number and wait."

I flipped open my spiral notebook. "So, what happened?"

Grasping my upper arm firmly, Thad guided me down the hall, away from the heavily populated living room. Voices came from further back in the house. Bias kept his low.

"You know I investigated the other three, so they gave me the call. When I got here, I calmed Mr. and Mrs. Ketchum down and put them on the sofa there in the living room." He nodded toward a doorway. "I wanted to preserve the scene so I kept the uniforms out, had them establish the perimeters, and I looked around." He held up his hands, displaying long, thin fingers that matched his body. "I followed procedure. Kept my hands in my pockets."

Cramming his hands in his pockets to demonstrate, he took a series of slow breaths, obviously trying to keep the lid on his percolating anger. Bias's boyish smile was buried somewhere deep within his freckled face. I actually thought Thad might be handsome, if it weren't for his nose, which resembled a hawk's beak. The absent smile was definitely his best feature. It usually made his bright blue eyes sparkle. At that moment, those eyes were thunderstorm dark. I had never seen Bias angry. I kept quiet, hoping to encourage him to talk.

"There was this water glass by the kitchen sink." Thad took a hand out of his pocket and ran his slender fingers through the thatch of strawberry blond hair, which tumbled down over his forehead. Realizing he had made several strands stand on end, he flashed me a sheepish look and used both hands to smooth his hair flat again over the top of his head.

"I looked at that glass and I got this feeling. You know, a hunch. I knew it was optimistic, but stranger things have happened. Burglars know not to leave fingerprints, but prisons are full of smart guys who weren't quite smart enough. Of course, this nitwit pitting himself against O'Brien . . ." He grimaced. "I'd call it even money."

He put his fists on his hips, drawing the sleeves of his sport coat higher, exposing skinny wrists and forearms.

"Anyway, I figured if this guy wore gloves, he might've taken them off to get himself a drink. Also the lab people now can get a DNA read from spittle on the side of a glass. I mean, forensic science can do amazing things these days, if we give them half a chance."

I glanced toward the living room, tempted to interrupt, but Thad, peering at my face, anticipated my question. "I already asked the Ketchums. She's the kind who doesn't like anything out of place. The glass wasn't theirs.

"Man, I was tickled. I just kept walking back to the kitchen checking on that glass, protecting it."

Thad's shoulders slumped and he folded his arms over his chest, shaking his head. "Then O'Brien and his mob came rolling in, sirens screaming, lights flashing, big show. He'd called the TV stations. It must have been a tortoise-slow news day. I mean, everybody came.

"I met him at the door, told him the lab team hadn't signed off yet and I thought we ought to stand clear.

"He ignored me, of course, brought all those movie star media types swarming through the whole damn house." Bias's jaw clenched and unclenched. "You know how he is. He invited them all. God, he's a great host. Congenial as hell. The poor old Ketchums, the victims, just sat there stunned, watching strangers snoop, open drawers and closets, everything. O'Brien gave them the full tour.

"On the q.t., I told him my theory about the drinking glass in the kitchen. So what'd he do? He led them all in there. There must have been a dozen people."

I groaned, indicating sympathy. Thad seemed to appreciate it.

"Anyone who watches TV knows more about forensics than O'Brien does. He crammed his big, beefy hand inside the glass and picked it up. It still had moisture on it. He asked someone to get him a plastic bag.

"I asked him to at least use a paper sack. He waved me off, put the glass in this used plastic bag, lecturing the whole time about preserving evidence, obviously a subject completely foreign to him. While he was talking, he clamped his pudgy paw around the bag, smearing it over the glass inside, and stuffed it in his coat pocket. You can probably guess what contaminated plastic does to prints, probably even DNA."

I hissed, inhaling through my front teeth. "No more chance for either one, I suppose."

"Right." Thad fisted his hands and stared at me.

"So, has the lab crew still not gotten here yet?" I asked.

"Been and gone. I caught them at the front door, told them what O'Brien had done."

"Whose team?"

"Custer's."

"Whoa. I heard she flayed O'Brien in front of everyone at the Earlys'."

Thad shook his head. "Today she just got this pained expression and ordered everyone out. She was not polite about it. O'Brien started to say something but Custer shut him up with a look. Those TV people can smell bad blood. They kept their cameras cranking.

"O'Brien took his lead from Custer and ran everyone back out behind the tape. Of course, by then it was too late.

"After the lab crew left, O'Brien called the press back inside. And here we are, partying."

"O'Brien didn't call us," I said, picking up on that one item.

"I guess he didn't think you'd want it. Your wire service didn't cover the first three."

"We used local coverage. Most of these press people are contributing members of AWS."

"Then what are you doing here now?"

"I'd been begging my boss to go live. He apparently figured a house break-in or two was not hot news, but a series might merit our personal attention."

I'm pretty sure Thad shivered. I figured he was just letting go of some of his righteous anger. I patted his arm. "I wish I could help."

He gave up a half smile before his eyes narrowed. "Maybe you can. Come here. Meet the Ketchums. They're good people. Maybe they'll think of something they forgot to mention before."

He put a hand on my back and nudged me into the living room, directing me toward a couple sitting quietly on one end of a long sofa. The throng of people in the house was beginning to thin out. I acknowledged the introduction and asked the Ketchums what was missing.

"Assuming," Thad interjected, looking around, "that all the sightseers are honest folks."

"This is the silliest thing I've ever heard of," Mrs. Ketchum said, speaking to me. "South Beach is quiet. We're mostly retired people. Oh, most of us are comfortably fixed, all right, but not rich by any means. We have a good little neighborhood watch association, too. Meet once a month, in each others' homes."

Mr. Ketchum interrupted his wife. "Ms. Dewhurst, we're having an emergency meeting tonight at six, right here. Come on back." He smiled at his wife. "The ladies bring desserts. We have some real good cooks."

I thanked them for the invitation. They seemed to be brightening up and feeling better about things.

In a tag-team way, they told me basically the same information they had given Bias earlier until Mrs. Ketchum paused. She regarded me thoughtfully, as if she were looking through me. "There is one strange thing," she said, puzzling.

The three of us waited. Mrs. Ketchum frowned at her husband. "Elbert, my brass candlesticks are gone."

Mr. Ketchum's expression turned to genuine sorrow and he took her hand. "Sweetheart, I'm sorry." He looked at Thad and me. "Our son sent those to his mother from Vietnam. He came home a month later in a body bag."

I put a star in the margin of my notes right there.

"Are you coming tonight?" Thad asked the question casually as he walked me to my car.

"I think I will. After all, they are serving refreshments." I liked the Ketchums.

"Do you want me to pick you up?"

"No, thanks. I'll drive."

Thad's blue eyes glittered as he closed my car door. "You're not afraid to ride with me, are you?"

I allowed a throaty chuckle. Not that I intended to flirt with him, but I liked Thad a lot. "No, thanks. You know I'm engaged. I need to keep my head on straight."

His playful grin broadened and he arched an eyebrow. "Meaning something about me might muddle your thinking?"

I didn't look directly at him. "Probably not, but I've been here six weeks now, and yesterday, well, being away from home on Thanksgiving and all, I'm a little homesick, a little wobbly emotionally."

"Missing your boyfriend or your mamma?"

"I'm even missing my two little brothers." I sputtered, a half laugh, half cough. "That's how bad it is."

"I've got a brother, a year older than me," he said. "I'd have to be pretty desperate to miss him."

I smiled. "Exactly."

"Jancy, are you sure you're ready for this marriage bit?" Thad suddenly sounded serious.

I couldn't look at his face.

He rested his arms on the car door and lowered his voice. "Sometimes I get the feeling you'd like to bail on that."

"No, I wouldn't. Really. I love Jim." A blush warmed my face. "I just . . . well . . ." I didn't know how to explain what I didn't exactly understand myself, a vague feeling of unease. Thad was watching too closely for me to get my thoughts in order at that moment.

When I didn't say any more, he stood upright again and let me off the hook. "You might rethink it. You've got options, you know. There's one standing right here in front of you, in case you hadn't noticed."

I couldn't think of anything to say. Awkward seconds ticked by before Thad spoke again. "Just wanted you to know. Anyway, I'll see you tonight."

"Right."

I drove to the office, chiding myself. I felt like a bum—disloyal to Jim, if nothing else—for being giddy and a little too pleased at the prospect of seeing Thad later. Was his question valid? Was I completely happy with the idea of marrying Jim Wills on December twenty-second?

Absolutely. I was just lonesome and Jim was thirteen hundred miles away. It was easy to get confused, especially with Thad so cute and making noises like he might be interested in dating me. Another thought nibbled at my conscience. I hadn't mentioned Thad to Jim and I wasn't exactly sure why I hadn't.

Shoot, I didn't need to be thinking about any of that. I had crimes to solve.

Mentally I tried to review everything I'd observed, things the Ketchums had said, and news stories of the earlier thefts.

My story was written and filed long before deadline and with nothing better to occupy my time, I drove over to the Ketchums' early. I was there as members of the neighborhood watch association filtered in the front door. They brought food and consoled their hosts by apologizing.

"It's not our fault," one man told me as he eyed the array of desserts covering the dining table. "We're protecting the neighborhood the best we can. Security's not really our job. The problem's the police. They're never around when you need them, but tap a little heavy on the accelerator through a school zone and they're all over you. They need to be chasing criminals, not harassing solid citizens."

He selected a raspberry tart, got a cup of coffee, and ambled away, momentarily appeased.

The meeting lasted two hours and consisted mostly of neighborhood gossip. Thad was a no-show and I was annoyed with myself for being disappointed.

Mallory edited my account of the series of burglaries to a scant twenty lines, then tagged it with my first syndicated byline. I had gotten my degree, worked two years on *The Bishop Clarion*, and six weeks in San Diego anticipating that byline, a hard-won trophy.

I checked newsstands late. Only a handful of member newspapers carried the story. Of those, some had dropped the byline. Most readers didn't notice bylines, but over the weekend I received calls of congratulations from my parents, my grandparents, and Jim, all back in Oklahoma. They echoed my hope that this byline was the first of many.

Monday morning, I went over news clips and copies of police reports on the four burglaries, all committed in South Beach: the Earlys on November thirteenth; Paula Hudson, November fifteenth; Sean Smith and the Ketchums both last week.

I called and asked for an interview with the Earlys, the burglar's first victims, who lived on Arcadia Street, less than a half-mile from the Ketchums.

"We don't have any idea why they chose us," Mr. Early said, referring to their break-in. The couple had taken me to a deck where the three of us settled into lawn chairs to talk.

Mrs. Early shot her husband a significant look. "They probably picked us because we don't have a security system."

Mr. Early glared back at his wife. Obviously, security systems were a sore subject in the Early household. "Neither do most of our neighbors."

"The people over there," Mrs. Early said, speaking to me, disregarding her husband and indicating the house east of them, "are on a cruise. They'd been gone nearly three weeks when we got burgled. We pick up their mail and their newspapers and turn their lights on and off every evening so no one will know they're away."

Mr. Early picked up the story. "The couple two doors west was in Oregon that week. Hell, they're gone again now. Do they get burglarized? No. Us? Our daughter called that night, spur of the moment, asked us to babysit the grandkids. We stayed over. We were gone one lousy Monday night and this happens. Who the hell could have known we were gone?"

I was back at the office when Thad showed up late in the morning with a bouquet of flowers and a banner that read, "First Byline, Congratulations!"

I smiled happily into his eyes and blushed as several co-workers in the press room erupted into catcalls and applause. I had made a mental note not to question Thad about his absence from the Ketchums'. The flowers made up for the slight.

Self-consciously trying to redirect Thad's attention, I asked if he knew about the absent neighbors in the Earlys' neighborhood.

"No." His smile faded and he eyed me curiously.

I told him about my interview with Mr. and Mrs. Early. He used the phone at my desk to send a unit to check the temporarily vacant houses. A patrolman called back twenty minutes later. Neither of those houses had been disturbed.

That afternoon, Thad drove me to Balboa Avenue to meet Paula Hudson, the second victim.

Mrs. Hudson, a petite, elderly woman with pale blue eyes, told us she had completed her Christmas shopping early and had the gifts wrapped when, during an unplanned absence, the presents and other valuables disappeared from her apartment. She discovered her loss after noon on Wednesday, November fifteenth.

"I have one of my headaches," Mrs. Hudson said before I could question her. "I'm going to have to take my medicine and lie down now."

"Will you make us a detailed inventory of items that are missing?" Thad asked as he and I moved toward the door. Mrs. Hudson picked up a grocery store tape by the phone. On the back, she had written down the stolen items, the original list she had composed and then copied for the police. We both thanked her.

Sitting in Thad's car at the curb outside Mrs. Hudson's apartment, I read over the list. Except for the gifts, it was like the Earlys'. Missing were cash, credit cards, and small silver pieces, no appliances or large items. Then one entry leaped off the paper, capturing my full attention.

"Thad, look at this. Candlesticks. Again. Small, sterling silver candlesticks. Isn't that odd?"

"What do you mean?"

"This thief is very selective. Why take candlesticks?" I looked up to find my companion staring at me. He grinned, quickly covering the somber stare.

"You sound like you're trying to understand this perp. You aren't starting to like this guy, are you?"

"The thief?"

"Yes, the thief."

I shrugged. "Or her. It could be a woman."

"Maybe, but I don't think so. Why are you so fascinated with this . . . ah . . . this person?"

"I don't know. I guess he's getting familiar."

"Like a friend?" Thad snorted a skeptical laugh.

I laughed companionably, puzzled by his question. "I guess."

CHAPTER TWO

"It was the worst damn week of my life," Sean Smith, the burglar's robust third victim, complained when I went to interview him by myself in his condo on Coastal Way.

Thad had gotten another call. He had argued, but the dispatcher said Captain O'Brien personally insisted Thad take that particular call.

"Why?" Thad asked, practically yelling into the radio in his car.

The dispatcher lowered his voice. "He knows that reporter's with you."

Thad nodded and terminated the call. "O'Brien's afraid I'll scarf off some of his press." He dropped me by the office to pick up the courtesy car.

Smith's place had been burglarized early Thanksgiving week. He had been away from home both Tuesday and Wednesday nights. Because he was a bachelor, I didn't want to ask where he had spent those nights.

The burly man paced and snapped his fingers as he talked. I sat in a straight-backed chair taking notes.

"I should have known. Monday night was bad. The Chargers lost. Cost me a bundle. My place got tossed, then to cap it, my mom died Thanksgiving. Man, I hope I never have another week like that."

Speaking quietly in an effort to calm him, I asked if he had a list of missing items. Smith handed me a copy of the one he had written out for the police. I copied it off, writing quickly.

Smith was still blustering as I left. I checked with individual policemen who had canvassed neighbors that day around South Beach. It had been a holiday, one officer reminded me. "People saw several strange vehicles in the area, but folks have company on holidays. No one remembered anything that helped. No one saw flashlight beams at night anywhere, inside or out. No dogs barked more than usual. No alarms went off. The guy came and went like a phantom."

Working on a story capsulizing all four burglaries, I noted similarities. The thefts were all in South Beach, all apparently in the early morning hours, all in temporarily unoccupied homes. The culprit rifled desks and safes for cash, jewelry, credit cards, bank card information, coin collections, some silver, took only items that were easy to carry.

Something nagged in the back of my mind. I was forgetting something. What was it? Reviewing my notes, stars in the margins reminded me of the candlesticks. I made two quick phone calls then, cackling quietly, more than a little pleased with myself, I wrote a new lead.

"Candlesticks, regardless of their value, were stolen in all four South Beach burglaries in the last two weeks."

Before the story was broadcast or published, I wanted to talk to Captain Murray O'Brien.

At the police station, I hailed O'Brien in the hallway outside his office. He stopped as soon as he saw me and waited. We exchanged the standard pleasantries before I sprung the question that had brought me.

"Captain, did you know the South Beach thief has stolen candlesticks in every one of those burglaries?"

O'Brien looked stricken, but quickly regained control of his facial expression. "Ms. Dewhurst, do you imagine our investigators would have overlooked something as obvious as that? Give me a break."

I would have bet money he was bluffing. I waved my copies of the police incident reports in his face. Blustering, he opened the door to his office. "Come on in. I can spare a minute or two to help you."

Inside, he closed the door, took the incident reports, and looked them over, ignoring me completely. None of those reports included the complete lists of items taken. Missing candlesticks appeared only on the Ketchums' report, penciled in by Thad's bold scrawl.

O'Brien blustered. "These are only the incident reports. No one can blame you for missing it. You people aren't allowed to see the investigator's write-ups. That's where we record the significant stuff."

I opened and tossed folded copies of the investigators' reports on the desk in front of him.

O'Brien's face grew stern as he glowered down at the sheets. "Where'd you get these? These are for department eyes only."

I gave him a wry smile. "Like I said, Captain, candlesticks are only in the Ketchums' report." I glanced at my notebook. "I show he took matched brass candlesticks from the Ketchums, a crystal set from the Earlys, sterling from little Mrs. Hudson, and a pewter wall sconce from Mr. Smith."

He gave me a belligerent scowl. "A macho guy like Smith noticed he was missing a candlestick? I don't believe you."

"He didn't realize it. I called him back to double check. He had to go look."

O'Brien glared at me a long moment before he said, "Congratulations. Great work, Detective Dewhurst." His tone dripped sarcasm. "Any other little thing?"

I bit my lips. "Yes."

He continued his murderous scowl, waiting.

"The streets."

"What about the streets?" His voice was a sneer.

"Don't you find it odd that the burglaries occurred on streets in alphabetical order? Arcadia, Balboa, Coastal Way, Dillon."

O'Brien set his jaw like a bulldog, staring at me a long moment before he retrieved the abandoned incident reports and thumbed through them again.

I stood and moved quickly, wanting to be well out of earshot by the time O'Brien verified my little observation. As I told Thad later, I didn't know if the information mattered or not but I felt it my civic duty to call it to the captain's attention.

What began as a trickle of mirth burst into a cascade of unbridled laughter as Thad threw back his head, his prominent Adam's apple bobbing up and down, and guffawed.

"I'd give nearly anything to have seen O'Brien's face at that moment. You are an amazing woman, Dewhurst. A remarkable piece of work." He gave me a slow, admiring look and sobered. "You are, you know. Really something."

Duke Mallory decided it was those same observations in my by-lined story that prompted the first threat.

The anonymous call came on the pay phone in the hallway just outside the press room. Ivy Work stepped out to answer the insistent ring and yelled to say the call was for me.

The caller spewed profane, descriptive epithets and ordered me to turn my investigative talents to other pursuits "or suffer the consequences," which he itemized in terms involving various and specific parts of my anatomy. Then he hung up.

I didn't want to tell anyone about the call. First off, I didn't want to repeat the caller's vile threats, not even to Mallory, who had a broad, colorful vocabulary of his own. Somehow, I thought repeating the words might give them credibility and I darn sure didn't want to do that.

After some ruminating, I decided the call was a prank. But a day or two of mulling it over and three hang-ups on the office line had me jittery. I felt oddly isolated and a little frightened. Coward that I am, I'm easy to scare.

I doubted Mallory would appreciate my sharing, but I finally decided I probably should tell someone.

"Mallory, did you ever get threatened?"

I had Mallory pegged as hard-bitten and self-centered, too egotistical to take any interest in personal information regarding someone else. He was darn sure too private to reveal any about himself, particularly his age. I figured he probably was between fifty-five and sixty. He was five-foot-ten or so and two hundred pounds, give or take. He drank excessively, chain-smoked, and picked up women in the local bars—explaining there were four women to every man in town and he wanted to do his part. His wardrobe was composed primarily of double knits, circa nineteen-seventy. Not a particularly neat dresser myself, I thought "disheveled" was too kind a term for Mallory. "Seedy" was probably more accurate.

At my idle question, Mallory looked up from the newspaper he was reading and regarded me oddly. "Any journalist worth his salt's going to hit a nerve now and then. Was your caller male or female?" Ignoring hypotheticals, he had leaped to the point in a hurry.

"Male, I think. I'm not sure."

"What'd he say?"

Mallory's usual smirk became a scowl. Keeping my eyes on the floor, I repeated the caller's exact words. Mallory grunted, indicating he had heard, and went back to reading his newspaper without comment.

Hoping for more input, I told my fiancé, Oklahoma State Bureau of Investigation Agent Jim Wills, long distance, about the call.

He sounded grim. "Probably just a crank, but keep your eyes

open, Jancy. Be aware of the people around you, especially on the street."

"You sound so stodgy." I appreciated his taking it seriously, but I tried to make light of it.

"We're four weeks away from our wedding, sweet thing. I don't want some California kook taking liberties with you until I've worked you over myself."

"Nice talk." I couldn't help laughing.

"If you think that's bad, you should hear what I'm thinking." His tone deepened. "I'm serious. Keep your eyes open. Be careful."

Despite Captain O'Brien's beefed-up surveillance and additional patrols in South Beach, a fifth burglary was reported there Tuesday, November twenty-eighth. I asked for the assignment, arguing that, after all, the burglaries were my story.

After contemplating my argument a long minute, Mallory agreed.

When I got to Dennis Harrison's condominium on Palmdale late that morning, the boisterous, fifty-two-year-old bachelor was railing about the arrogance of the police captain in charge. O'Brien had badgered Harrison about the fact he lived on Palmdale, that his condo was not on a street beginning with the letter "E."

"What is that idiot's problem?" Harrison asked moments after I introduced myself.

I felt a little guilty for having suggested the alphabetical street sequence to O'Brien. "Up until now, Mr. Harrison," I said, "the burglaries have occurred on streets in alphabetical order. Your being on Palmdale ruins that theory."

Harrison snorted. "I'm sorry as hell about being the victim who ruined that bozo's idea of things, but I expect professionalism from the police, not complaints." He thumbed himself in the chest. "I'm the injured party here."

Harrison had been away from home all night Monday.

"Do you work nights, Mr. Harrison?" I asked.

"No."

Again I was reluctant to be too inquisitive about a single guy's overnight whereabouts.

Finally, I asked the question I was itching to ask. "Mr. Harrison, do you own any candlesticks?"

He regarded me oddly, waggled his head from side to side, then stopped and said, "Yeah. One. A little wicker job. Matches the tissue holder in the front bathroom." He smiled crookedly. "My sister gave me the set. She's into cutesy." He shrugged, obviously embarrassed. "It was a housewarming thing."

"Will you see if it's still there?"

"Hell, what do I care?" Harrison jutted his chin looking belligerent. In a minute, his shoulders rose and fell as he drew and released a deep breath, pursed his mouth, turned on his heel, and marched to the front bathroom.

The small wicker candlestick was gone.

Harrison exploded out of the bathroom and stormed through the apartment looking for O'Brien. "I'm gonna sue your ass."

O'Brien yelled back but his bravado was no match for Harrison's indignation over a possession that had suddenly become important. It took Thad's soothing to finally quell the resident's thunderous complaints.

"Who yanked his chain?" O'Brien asked Bias later.

Thad flashed me an apologetic look. "Jancy asked him if he had any candlesticks missing."

O'Brien turned a hard stare on me. "The guy would never have noticed if you had kept your big mouth shut, Dewhurst."

I didn't try to defend myself.

Wednesday afternoon, November twenty-ninth, I was moving my final story for the evening papers when correspondent Billie

Stone, two cubicles over, slammed down her telephone, leaped to her feet, took two quick strides, then doubled back to retrieve the sweater dangling from the back of her chair.

I swiveled. "What's wrong?"

"They think Mark's arm is broken. I told Ben six-year-olds shouldn't play soccer." Staring at the floor, Billie jingled her car keys in her hand, looked around the room and then back at me. "They're not even supposed to practice on Wednesdays. The worst thing is: I wasn't there." Shaking her head and hurrying to the fire door, Billie stopped to cast a woeful look back at her computer. "Damn, I didn't shut down."

"I'll do it," I said. "Go."

Billie hesitated, frowning first at me, then at the machine. She drew a deep breath and shuddered.

I stood and walked over to nudge the troubled mother toward the back exit. "Where can they reach you?"

"St. Simeon's. Ben said to meet them at the emergency room."

"I'll close down and tell Chambers what's happened."

"Only if he asks." Billie's voice was strained.

"If he asks."

"I don't want him to hold this against me at Christmas."

I nodded again, took Billie's arm, escorted her to the exit, and pointed her toward the fire stairs that led up and out to the parking lot behind the building.

The heavy fire door swung shut behind me as I slipped back into the office.

With Billie's abrupt departure, the press room seemed eerily silent. No keyboards clattered, no reporters bickered, no smoke curled from either Edison's pipe or Derringer's multiple cigarette butts that rimmed his ashtray when he was present.

Leaning my backside against a desk, I locked my elbows to brace myself and surveyed the room. In the seven weeks I had worked in the disorder affectionately known as "The Hole," I could not remember ever having been there alone.

Press accommodations were located in what Mallory described as "the allegedly refurbished" basement of what had once been a post office. Conveniently, it was adjacent to the county courthouse.

Bureau Chief Duke Mallory, my mentor and cubicle mate, had been mostly absent all day. The wire service big wigs coddled Mallory. I figured they were trying to delay his impending retirement; impending, I'd learned, for nearly three years.

Looking around, it was hard to realize that achieving a desk in this shabby place had once been my greatest goal in life, a major step on my stairway to success.

Were there nine desks in the room? Impossible. I recounted. Nine. Nine indistinct areas cordoned off with temporary dividers and shelves cluttered with books, manuals, and directories, some upright with junk stuffed in on top of them, others leaning like indolent workers. The nine areas housed representatives of the three wire services, correspondents from five area newspapers, and the current AWS intern: me.

The room's cramped space allowed no real separation, no privacy to permit a reporter exclusive claim to a tip by phone or e-mail, not unless the tipster sent his furtive information by snail mail. Even then, some missives turned up mysteriously "opened by mistake."

A dozen tangled utility lines crisscrossed the floor, like giant webs waiting to ensnare the distracted pedestrian. Amazingly, people rarely stumbled. When they did, they mumbled quiet profanity, if they noticed at all; certainly no one bothered to ask for a change.

"An odd bunch," I whispered.

I had told Jim my co-workers at this lofty journalistic level seemed to be generally intelligent, quick-witted, caustic, and mostly misfits. The majority of them were precise when gleaning information or turning a word or phrase, but otherwise inclined to be indifferent, even slovenly.

I looked down at my own body lounging against the desk and scowled at the still-visible salad dressing dribbled at noon. I grinned, glad Jim couldn't see me.

"And here I am, right at home among 'em," I said to the empty office.

Pushing off from the desk, I strolled to Billie's computer, tapped the appropriate keys, and doused the power, silencing the hum. Returning to my own peculiarly defined area, I repeated the shutdown process on my machine.

There was a queer silence. I felt like a thief left alone with the loot. I basked in the quiet, in the stale smells, as another woman might have luxuriated in a sable coat. I loved the lingering aroma of pipe tobacco, which contributed substantially to the haze intertwining the pipes near the ceiling high overhead.

Strolling, I pilfered a late edition of the *Post* from Ivy Work's desk and sidled back to Duke's worn leather chair. I slipped out of my shoes and pulled the back of my skirt forward, clamping it between my knees before I kicked back and propped my feet on the only bare spot on his desk.

I opened the newspaper and immediately wished I'd gotten a bottle of pop from the vending machine before settling in. I glanced in the direction of the ancient vending machine, dismissed the idea as having come too late, and began scanning headlines.

I found what I was looking for. "O'Brien Baffled By Burglaries in South Beach." There it was again: my byline. The *Post* had run the whole seven inches.

The sight of my name right there in bold print above the story made me shiver. Was that caused by a draft in the room, excitement, or . . . fear? Duke didn't seem concerned about the threat. It was probably safe to ignore it.

He had used the anonymous call, however, as an excuse to rip Captain O'Brien royally, in the rotunda, in front of everyone. I couldn't help a smile as I savored the memory of Mallory's verbal assault on the pompous policeman.

CHAPTER THREE

Vain, garrulous Police Captain Murray O'Brien pandered to the press, striving for the catchy sound bite that would earn him exposure on the evening news or a printed line anywhere.

I speculated that O'Brien, nearly forty and inarguably inept, had deftly tiptoed his way through law enforcement to his current rank. He fancied himself a ladies' man. Stocky, dimpled, attractive enough, I guess, until he opened his mouth. O'Brien frequently spoke in clichés. And he bragged.

Newly divorced from his third wife, the captain was actively shopping for number four. Ignoring my engagement ring entirely, he confided to the population at large that I "could be in the running," if I played my cards right.

O'Brien's chronic stupidity and his inflated ego would have been enough to deter my interest, even if Jim Wills did not exist. Still, I trod a thin line with the captain. O'Brien could be a valuable news source. I couldn't afford to alienate him. At the same time, I didn't want to encourage his amorous interest. The man seemed frustrated enough. O'Brien considered the burglaries in South Beach a personal affront.

As I told Thad during one of our bull sessions, "It's not likely that the perpetrator's purposely targeting O'Brien."

Thad bristled a little. "Yeah, well, the thefts keep happening and it's no place else but right under O'Brien's nose."

"Yours, too." I hadn't intended that to come out quite the way it sounded.

Thad turned chilly and I wondered if this time I had actually offended him.

O'Brien had formulated and discarded several theories about the first few cases. He'd cornered me occasionally to describe each new hypothesis in excruciating detail, as they ebbed and flowed.

"The thief goes in where people turn on their porch lights before dark," the captain explained with exaggerated gestures. "By doing that, the victims themselves signal they'll be gone until after dark."

That theory washed. Twice.

His second theory, widely broadcast, was the one he had adopted from me. "The thief chooses homes on streets in alphabetical order." He scrapped that one after Harrison was hit on Palmdale.

Theory Number Three was O'Brien's own: that all of the burgled homes had the same brand garage door opener. He disregarded the two victims who had no garages, and ignored Bias's reminder that there was no evidence the thief entered any of the subject homes through a garage.

"We've nailed his hide to the barn door this time," O'Brien told me with blustering confidence that particular afternoon. "All we have to do is track down the guy who installed them."

Further investigation revealed that three different dealers sold and two different installers had placed the openers. Mr. Ketchum proudly admitted he had installed theirs himself.

In spite of O'Brien, I loved covering the burglaries. I liked the bylines, and I liked having an excuse to see Thad, who was balm for my loneliness.

I started when Mallory blasted into the newsroom, interrupting my thoughts and my browse through the *Post*. I pulled my feet off his desk and rocked upright in his chair. He waved me back when I started to stand.

"Stay where you are." He tossed a small package onto the desk in front of me. It was addressed to me at the wire service post office box. There was no return.

Smiling under Mallory's curious eyes, I stripped off the brown wrapping, opened the box, and joyfully dug through tissue to find . . . a rubber finger, with red droplets painted on the side. It appeared to have been part of a Halloween costume.

My eager anticipation deteriorated to puzzlement. Searching further, I found a note scrawled on a piece of standard-sized copy paper folded at the bottom of the box.

"You've been warned. Keep it up and the finger in the next box will be yours. How good can you type with nine?"

My tremulous smile dissolved to a frown.

Mallory yanked the paper out of my hands, scanned the writing, looked at the finger, then reached in front of me to pick the container up carefully, using a thumb and index finger. He placed the box and its contents in a sack left on his desk from lunch.

"Probably some wise ass idea of a joke."

I thought of the faces of the pranksters in the newsroom. No, I didn't think the culprit was one of them.

"Stay here." Mallory picked up the sack. "I'll be back in a little while." Abruptly, he stormed out the back door through which he had arrived.

Duke returned in forty minutes without the sack. During the time he was gone, I paced, flipped through pages in another newspaper, tried to straighten our work area a little, and paced some more. Mallory insisted on following me home.

Having trailed me all the way into the parking garage, he accompanied me into the Chestnut Hotel, through the lobby, and even rode the elevator with me to the ninth floor. He remained at my side all the way to my room.

He didn't say much until I was unlocking the door.

"Is your boyfriend's brother still around?"

"No. They finished the job. He's gone back."

Mallory nodded. His face was uncharacteristically grim.

"Some people in the newsroom try to one-up each other being clever," I told Jim on the telephone that night, describing the incident. "I figure it's probably a gag that went sour. Didn't turn out to be as funny as the joker thought."

"Probably." He sounded serious. "Have you got a file on the burglaries?"

"Yes."

"Why don't you fax me copies of that stuff in the morning."

"That isn't necessary."

"Can't hurt."

"Jim, there's too much of it to fax. Besides, you have your own cases. What about the Glass thing?"

"Wrapped up. I'm schooling witnesses and tagging evidence."

"You're not taking me to raise, you know. You don't have to solve all my problems for me."

"Jance, crime solving is what I do for a living and as a hobby. Some people fool with puzzles in their spare time. I follow felonies. You don't want me bored, do you, more restless without you than I already am?"

I really wanted his help but felt foolish. "Okay," I muttered finally. "I'll mail the stuff."

"Everything," he prodded. "Overnight it."

"Okay."

"I love you." His words came in a throaty whisper.

"Sure you do, when you get your own way."

He laughed suggestively. "Not to be contrary, but if you'll remember, I haven't gotten my own way with you on a lot of more significant issues than this, and I love you anyway."

When I hung up the phone, I paced. I wanted to go downstairs, have something to eat, but I was afraid to venture out, even to the coffee shop. Shoot, I didn't even want to risk room service.

"Too many James Patterson novels," I chided myself out loud. "You're here on an adventure, maybe the last solo adventure of your whole life. How do you think you would manage in these same circumstances in an overseas bureau where the threats might not even be in English?

"Face it, Dewhurst, you are a wuss." My debilitating fear irritated me. "You big sissy, running to Wills for help like Pauline in peril." I glowered at my reflection in the bathroom mirror and picked up my toothbrush.

Still, I had to admit, it was nice there was a strong, handsome hero to whom a girl could turn. I brushed my teeth vigorously, putting that scathing energy to use.

Dabbing my mouth with the towel, I felt refreshed and reassured. I hadn't scrapped my plans for a career as a wire service correspondent overseas, but this little sojourn on the West Coast, my apprenticeship miles from home and family, had taken a lot of the romance out of my original notion.

In the beginning I had been trying to establish an identity of my own. No longer content to be the Dewhursts' little girl, tagging along with my younger brothers like chicks trailing the mother hen. I had formulated my plan, my dream, and pursued it with determination. Pursued it, that is, until State Bureau of Investigation Agent Jim Wills appeared, dapper, efficient, watching me, tracking me with the determination of a hound on the scent.

Early on, Jim was only a distraction—handsome, funny, easygoing. He made no demands, seemed content with the time and attention I was willing to give him.

But gradually, almost insidiously, he had grown intense, wanting more. I struggled to maintain my independence but he was persuasive, cajoling . . . kissing . . . touching.

"Damn," I said out loud.

I had told Jim ours was a Br'er Rabbit/Tar-Baby relationship. Like the rabbit, I was happily on my way. All I intended was to say a polite how-do-you-do. Suddenly, I'd "gots my hands and feets so stuck up wid dat Tar-Baby, I couldn't get a-loose."

Not a romantic picture, I admitted, but bull's-eye accurate.

At the office Thursday morning, I collected every news clipping, every police report, and every cryptic note from my interviews with the victims, made copies of some of it for me, stuffed the originals into a large envelope and mailed it.

Admittedly, Jim was a good investigator, nearly five years with the state bureau, but no one could expect him to track a culprit or even to develop a definitive theory of the crimes long distance.

CHAPTER FOUR

Jim called mid-morning. He sounded businesslike, formal. "Jancy, if there are more burglaries and you do the stories, I want you to omit your byline."

"What?"

"I know how you feel, but I think we need to do what we can to get this bird focused somewhere else. Will you do it?"

I thought about it a while before I exhaled a big breath, mostly for effect. "Okay." If I did this for him, maybe he would return the favor. "Do you want clips and notes on any new ones?"

"Yes."

"Did you get the stuff I sent? Are you able to make heads or tails out of it?"

His laughter burbled from the telephone and I was glad to hear him loosening up. "Yeah, I've gotten a whole new perspective on you from the contents of this envelope. I'm amazed you can take that hodgepodge of chicken scratches and partial sentences you call notes and produce a news story that makes any sense at all. It's obvious that you are even more gifted than I realized."

I laughed dutifully but didn't say anything.

"You still missing me?" he asked quietly.

"Yes."

"Is this Candlesticks guy going to steal your heart and break mine?"

"Not a chance. Did Kellan get measured for his tux?"

"Yes." Jim's voice changed to a tone of incredulity. "That's just about all we have time for around here anymore—getting ready for your wedding."

"I'm working on it from this end too. I sent the patterns for the bridesmaids' dresses to Mother last week."

"I know. Amanda's flower child dress . . ."

"Flower girl," I corrected.

". . . flower girl dress is made. Beth took her by the folks' house last night to model it. Mom said Amanda looked very grown up for five. Amanda's concerned she'll look prettier than the bride. I'm glad I wasn't there. I wouldn't have known what to say without offending someone. This wedding stuff makes pretty tricky footing for guys."

I chuckled, seeing his point.

After a moment, Jim continued. "My dad went through weddings with two of my sisters, Veronica and Beth. He says weddings are a female thing. He advised me to do what you tell me and not make any suggestions. He said every time he tried to express any interest by giving an opinion, he made somebody cry. I told him you'd given me a list."

"Speaking of which . . ." I interrupted.

"All three of my brothers have been fitted. We snagged Kellan and the five of us drove up to Carson's Summit Saturday to check out the church and arrange the rehearsal dinner at Dolly's Restaurant. Dolly's is okay, isn't it?"

I choked a little, conjuring a familiar mental image of the most posh restaurant in my little hometown. "Yes."

"Greg and Tim met us at the church, introduced us to Father Gilstrap. He took us through the drill. Paul's best man. He and Kellan lined up at the altar with me. Peter, Andrew, Greg, and Tim learned more about ushering than they ever wanted to know.

"Father Gilstrap and I had kind of an informal counseling session while the guys played ping-pong in the parish hall. He said he doesn't usually marry people until he's had sessions with them together, but since he knows you, he said he just wanted to get better acquainted with me.

"He likes that I'm Catholic. He thinks it's important for me to keep you in church somewhere, mine or yours, either one.

"I had called your folks Friday night to tell them we were coming and to ask if Greg and Tim would meet us there. Your mom insisted we eat lunch at your house afterward.

"She put on a great spread. Fried chicken. She was the only female on the place. She obviously felt outnumbered. I probably should have taken Mom or one of my sisters along, or Amanda." He hesitated and there was silence. "Jancy?"

I had a hard time speaking around the lump in my throat. "I wish I'd been there."

Jim lowered his voice, I supposed out of deference to the emotion in mine. "Maybe next time. I've been to Carson's Summit twice now. You haven't been there either time."

"Do you like the town?"

"Yeah, it's friendly. Remember, I like small towns."

"How did my mother look?"

"The usual. Something like you. Shorter. Heavier. Same rosy face, chocolate brown eyes. Her hair's lighter than yours. There's an old saying among bachelors. If you want to see what your honey will be like in twenty years, take a look at her mom. I like what I see."

I snorted, suddenly annoyed. "Darn you, anyway, Jim Wills, you know I'm homesick. This isn't helping." I waited but he didn't speak. "I can hear you smiling. Stop it."

He allowed a mellow chuckle. "That's the progress report on my list. How are you coming with yours?"

"Okay, but there are sure a lot of little details."

"Like what?"

"I have a doctor's appointment this afternoon."

"For a blood test?"

"That, too, I guess. Mother asked if I had started taking birth control pills yet."

"Oh."

"You have to have a prescription, which means a physical. Mom thought it was a good idea anyway, so I'm going."

"Let me know if you pass."

"Wills," I said, pretending a threatening tone, "the dress has been paid for and altered. The invitations go out Monday. No matter what my medical condition is, you can't bail out."

He chuckled, then cleared his throat. "You're going to think I'm nuts," he said quietly, "but I'm jealous of your doctor. How old a guy is he?"

It was my turn to laugh. "Real old. I'll call you tonight."

"I love you, baby."

"I sure hope so, but I'm afraid that now I love you more than you love me."

"You know that's wrong."

I frowned at the phone as I said good-bye and cradled it carefully.

"You look terrible," I told Billie Stone when the woman walked into the press room just before noon.

Billie had on the same clothes she had worn the day before. Her brown hair hung limp and dull and her eyes were bloodshot.

Ivy Work, Bruce Edison, and Chris Derringer were the only others in the press room. Bristling, the two men both talked at once as they argued loudly about the labels "Far Right" and "Christian Coalition."

"We had to spend the night at the hospital." Billie's words, a tone beneath the argument, were easily audible, despite the noisy pair nearby.

"Was Mark hurt badly?"

"He has a broken arm. They set it. He'd taken a pretty good lick on the head. They wanted to keep him overnight for observation. A safety precaution. They had a bed available.

"Ben and I camped out in his room in chairs that made into cots. The springs in mine were stiff. If I moved wrong, they would spring and try to snap the whole thing back to sitting position with me in it. I finally figured out how to distribute my weight and dozed off when the nurse popped in and turned on all the lights. Said she had to check Mark's vital signs. She came every hour. I can tell you, if you need rest, don't go to a hospital."

I laughed dutifully, but before I could come up with anything encouraging, Billie's phone rang.

Covering the mouthpiece, Billie said, "Did Rick ask where I was?"

"He never came back."

Billie smiled her approval, then said "Hello," into the phone. She said, "Yes," then listened intently. I watched her expression wilt. "What's missing?" I heard a man's angry response rumbling through the receiver.

I assumed Billie was talking to her husband, Ben. I had never heard Ben anything but soft-spoken with his wife. Of course, he had been at the hospital all night and had, maybe, assumed some guilt for his son's injuries. Now apparently, he had gone home to discover some new problem.

Billie glanced at her hand, crooked her head sideways to brace the phone between her jaw and shoulder, and fingered her watch, her wedding band, and the diamond engagement ring on her left hand as she listened.

"I'm wearing all that," she said. "What about grandmother's tea service? Good! I guess it was too big. The coin collection?

Oh, I'm sorry, Ben. But nothing really valuable?" Again I heard the man's angry voice.

Billie glanced at me, did a double take and her eyes widened. "Ben, what about the cut glass candlesticks on the dining room table?" Billie didn't take her eyes from my face. "Do me a favor and look, will you?" There was a delay, then the drone again over the phone. "Damn!" she breathed.

"I have to go," Billie said to me after terminating the phone conversation abruptly. "I think your 'Candlesticks' creep has expanded into Brentwood."

I just nodded as Billie Stone, for the second time in eighteen hours, grabbed the same sweater off the back of the same chair, tossed it around her shoulders over the same clothing, and dashed out the fire exit.

I walked over to the city map mounted on the wall in front of Mallory's desk, picked up a red plastic thumbtack, and squinted hard to locate the general location of the Stones' home. I inserted the tack, the sixth red one on the map, then studied the design.

The Stones lived on Louisville. It was not remote enough from the others to make it distinctive. But Billie and Ben Stone had a modest home. Theirs definitely was more a middle-income area than upper middle.

Like the others, however, no one had been at home when the burglar struck and, also like the others, their absence had been neither a planned nor a routine one.

How did the thief know who would be home and who would not? I turned around, trying to concentrate, and walked back between the bickering journalists.

"Will you guys shut up," I said softly. They both stopped mid-sentence and turned to stare at me.

Seated at her own desk near the hall door, Ivy Work peered my way over her eyeglasses but remained mute.

"What's going on?" I muttered.

"What's up?" Edison and Derringer asked in unison. I ignored them. Instead, I opened my bottom right-hand drawer and took out the black binder that contained copies of the material I had sent to Jim.

Ten minutes later, I turned off my computer and trotted out to my car.

I spent the early part of the afternoon trailing Thad and a police team through the Stones' home, observing, making notes of their findings, and ducking to avoid being alone in the same room with Captain O'Brien.

CHAPTER FIVE

Having completed the required insurance paperwork, I sat in the doctor's waiting room yawning. The wall clock said three forty-five.

I usually yawned when I was nervous. It was probably due to breathing too shallowly, not supplying enough oxygen to my system.

The office was nicely appointed and well located in the doctor's building adjacent to St. Simeon's.

Forty minutes after the time for my appointment, the nurse who had periodically appeared at the doorway of the inner sanctum with charts, reappeared, and this time called my name.

I measured five-feet-seven inches tall, weighed one-hundred twenty-two pounds, had a normal body temperature, and a blood pressure reading of one hundred ten over sixty-eight as I was processed into Dr. Wayne Linquist's office.

The doctor was not as old as I had hoped.

Linquist studied my chart. He peered at it from behind horn-rimmed eyeglasses, glanced briefly at my face, and asked if I was having any problems. I supposed he was referring to my physical condition.

"No, sir."

"If everything's normal, I'll write you a prescription for the birth control pills. You can pick it up at the front desk on your way out."

His words seemed a formality and he, preoccupied. I nodded

and tried to stifle another yawn and supposed I should appreciate his being so impersonal.

He didn't look up. "The nurse will show you to the examination room."

Without a word, I followed the nurse to the adjoining room where, left alone, I followed instructions, slipping into the indicated hospital gown, which seemed to be constructed of some inferior brand of paper toweling. I then sat perched on the examination table yawning and trying to keep myself covered with the shredding gown as I waited in the chilly room for what seemed an interminable length of time.

The nurse followed Dr. Linquist into the room, where she helped him into a fresh pair of gloves. Doctor and nurse spoke only to each other, ignoring me entirely as they proceeded through what appeared to be a routine physical exam.

It'll all be over soon, I told myself as Linquist mashed and listened to my body from throat to shins. To occupy my mind, I tried to visualize the way out of the building and back to the car.

As I had parked the courtesy car, I had wondered idly where Billie Stone parked when she was in that same parking lot the night before and wondered, too, if the lot had anything to do with the burglaries. It was an open, public lot. There was no attendant.

"Deep breath," the doctor said, the stethoscope on my back. When he had heard enough, the nurse put a sheet across my lap and told me to lie back and place my feet in the stirrups.

The team seemed to be finishing up when the doctor attempted to insert a metal contraption, causing so much discomfort that I flinched. He hesitated a moment then tried again, the second time more gently but with no more success.

Standing up straight, Dr. Linquist peered at me over my sheet-shrouded knees. It was the first time he had actually looked at me. He said something to the nurse under his breath; then, looking my way again, with the same incredulity, he abruptly peeled off the gloves and hurried out of the room.

"Get dressed," the nurse instructed in an imperious tone.

"Am I through?"

The nurse smiled, obviously a rare concession. "No," she said pleasantly, "you'll need to go back to Doctor's office."

"What about the blood test?"

"Oh, yes." The nurse seemed distracted. She hurried out and returned quickly, carrying a caddy of vials and syringes. Wrapping an armband around my upper arm, she wiped the target area with alcohol, then said, "Make a fist." Expertly, she inserted the syringe, told me to open the fist, filled two tubes with blood, released the band, placed a small, round tape over the wound, loaded up her caddy and left.

I dressed quickly, glad to have that over, and returned to wait in the doctor's private office. Moments later, Linquist entered, eased into the chair behind his desk, leaned on his elbows, and regarded me seriously. He didn't speak at first, but removed his eyeglasses and the somber look gradually was replaced by a tolerant smile.

"What is it?" I asked, beginning to feel concerned.

The nurse stepped into the office behind me. When the doctor's eyes met hers, his smile spread to a broad, silly grin. The nurse, seeing the grin, giggled slightly.

"What's so funny?" I asked uncertainly, ready to enjoy the joke with them.

Linquist sobered a little and shook his head. "It's been a lot of months since I've seen a twenty-four-year-old virgin." With that, he and the nurse both broke into quiet, embarrassed laughter.

But their hilarity struck a harsh chord with me and my glare effectively silenced their mirth.

"It hasn't been a lack of opportunity!" I sounded defensive and a little waspish.

Sobering quickly, Linquist straightened in his chair and looked as if he'd been slapped. "Oh, I'm sure it hasn't. You are a very attractive young woman."

"Thanks a lot."

"I just understood that you were about to be married."

"That's correct."

"Ah . . . well . . . I can't help wondering about your young man. Is he ah, well. He is a young man, is that correct?"

"Yes, why?"

"Well, it's unusual—more than unusual really, more like rare, I'd say . . . I was just a little curious about . . ."

"About what?"

"Well, I was just wondering if your fiancé's experience has been as, ah, as limited as yours."

I heard the nurse twitter again and turned. My cold stare silenced the outbreak. "I don't think so," I said, turning back to confront Linquist.

"You mean you don't know?"

"I mean I don't want to know. I think it's better if I don't know details of the extent of his experience with women. He doesn't have to know a lot to know more than I do, right?"

The doctor risked a cautious smile and nodded. "The only reason I asked," he said, reclaiming a certain level of professionalism, "is that the natural barrier inside a woman toughens with age. You are older than most . . . ah . . . beginners. It could pose a problem. We can help you with that, if you want us to. We can do a little surgical procedure right here in the office, break through that barrier, make it easier for you—or both of you." He hesitated as if he expected me to say something, but I just sat there looking at him.

"Why don't you talk it over with your fiancé," he continued

eventually. "Let me know if you'd like some help. You may want to try to work it out by yourselves. After the honeymoon, if there's a problem or if you have any questions, drop by or give me a call. I'm not likely to forget you, Miss Dewhurst." He gave me a genuine, fatherly smile.

I nodded politely and stood. I saw no reason to mention that I wouldn't be back in California after the wedding. "Am I supposed to pick up my prescription for the birth control pills at the desk?"

"No. That was before." He lifted a piece of paper up from his desk. "I have it right here." He, too, stood and then leaned over the desk to hand me the prescription with his left hand. At the same time, he offered to shake hands with his right.

Forcing a frosty smile, I took the paper and shook the offered hand.

"It's been a real pleasure meeting you, Miss Dewhurst," he said emphatically.

I nodded. "Thanks."

I couldn't help wondering as I headed for the car. I hadn't considered my virginity an affliction. If it was, it obviously was a handicap not discussed much in polite society. It certainly had surprised Dr. Linquist and he was a gynecologist, a medical doctor who examined females all day, every day. Maybe I should be concerned. Of course, this was California. In Oklahoma, a virgin of my advanced years might not be such a phenomena.

What about Jim?

I smiled thinking of my sexy fiancé, wooing me, aggressive, his beautiful man's body always at the ready, ever eager for me.

No, I didn't think Jim would have any problem breaking either the physical or the psychological barriers. Besides, I liked the idea of Jim's guiding me through this uncharted territory.

The only problem I foresaw at that moment was in telling

him about the doctor's concern and Linquist's offer of assistance.

Starting the car, I tried to think of a delicate way to broach the subject. Jim probably wouldn't tease me about it . . . at first . . . but it wouldn't take long. I giggled, dreading and at the same time anticipating his reaction.

CHAPTER SIX

The telephone receiver propped against his ear, Duke Mallory swiveled in his chair to see who had entered the press room so late in the day. When he saw me, he waved me in, then covered the mouthpiece with his free hand.

"You've had several calls. Same person. Husky voice. I think it's a guy. Persistent. Wouldn't leave a message. I didn't know you'd been back. Where've you been?"

"Blood test, remember?"

"Oh, yeah. Why'd you come back?"

"I thought you'd want me to make up the time."

"No. They'll get more out of you in the long run than you'll ever get compensated for, I guarantee. Go on home."

Duke Mallory had been through the wars, figuratively and literally. He still used a manual typewriter, which he found best for his two-finger typing style. Someone else, currently I, had to rekey all his copy onto the computer to send. The extra step was only one of the concessions the wire service made to hang onto its prize staffer.

When Ivy Work, the *San Marvel Globe* correspondent, dean of the press room, and the third woman in the office, complained about Mallory picking his nose or scratching himself with those same two fingers when he deemed either of those functions necessary, despite the rank or sex of those in his company at the time, he turned on her, all wide-eyed innocence.

"That just shows how much you know," he said loudly. "I

53

only pick and scratch with my pinky when I'm in the company of ladies. I'm crass when it's just guys. If you want to see me get really down and dirty, you'll have to catch me home alone. Do you want to drop by tonight?"

Ivy whooped a laugh as loudly as everyone else within earshot. From then on, resident news personnel used the term "gettin' down and dirty" when referring to one another's gross behavior. I found Mallory generally easy to work with and for, unless we were on deadline, at which times his mild Dr. Jekyll facade fell victim to the unpredictable and sometimes even predatory Mr. Hyde. Despite his age and mileage, Mallory was a ferocious competitor. He insisted on having the most accurate information first and held his interns to that standard.

When our boss, Riley Wedge, called from D.C. to check on me, he cautioned me to adopt only Mallory's able journalistic habits. "Your copy's improving, getting more succinct," Wedge said. "Your vocabulary's expanding."

"Thanks."

"Are your personal habits deteriorating as quickly under his tutelage as your writing is improving?"

I didn't answer.

"Jim Wills is kind of a classy guy. You don't want to offend him by turning out like Mallory. When's the wedding?"

"December twenty-second," I said firmly. "That's the fourth time you've asked. Write it down somewhere, will you?"

"I keep hoping you'll cancel."

"Wishful thinking on your part. Am I going to have a job someplace?"

"Where?"

"I told you, anywhere you want me."

"And Wills?"

"He's promised not to interfere."

"Yeah, right."

54

I tried again. "Where are you sending me?"

"We'll see."

Mallory, too, complained about my marrying. Although he had never married, nor had he met Jim Wills, Mallory pronounced my fiancé unworthy.

"You are rare, sweetheart," Mallory proclaimed in one of his sentimental moments. "I hate for you to waste it on some muscle-bound oaf who won't appreciate what he's got."

"You don't know him," I countered.

"I know the type."

"He's not a type."

"Is he good looking?"

"Yes, but he's not pretty. Beauty's in the eye of the beholder, you know."

"Meaning I won't think so?"

"What I'm saying is, if he were a type, Mallory, he wouldn't be your type."

"Does he work out?"

"Yes."

"Is he a sissy boy?"

"Mallory," I groaned with disbelief, "he's muscular and wise and clever and funny and he's even a licensed attorney."

"A politician, huh?"

"He's more than an image. He's the real thing."

"Honey, you don't have to sell me on the guy. Who're you trying to convince, me or you? My opinion doesn't matter. If you like him, that ought to be enough, don't you think?"

I grimaced and went back to work.

"Maybe not," Mallory added, under his breath.

He is hopeless, I thought. Still, he had planted a seed of doubt I definitely did not want to cultivate.

I was already in the hallway on my way home when the office telephone rang. I hesitated. The ringing stopped. There was a little delay, then Mallory bellowed, calling me back. My persistent caller was on Line Two.

"Dewhurst," I said as I picked up the telephone, pressed the button opening the line, and moved a notepad over in front of me.

"Curiosity killed the cat," a husky voice rasped.

"What? I'm sorry, what did you say?"

Mallory looked at me curiously, then picked up the extension to listen.

"Curiosity killed the cat," the raspy voice repeated. "Unless you have nine lives, you'd better start minding your own business, bitch!" The line went dead. Biting my lips, I frowned at the receiver and replaced it carefully.

Mallory hung up with an expletive. "Who the hell was that?"

I shrugged, but I felt my mouth twitch.

"What'd he say?" he pressed, seeking verification of what he had heard.

I repeated the caller's words, trying unsuccessfully to give them some other meaning.

"Who was it?"

"Didn't say."

"It was a man, wasn't it?"

"You heard. Your guess is as good as mine."

"A crank," Mallory declared and turned his face from my scrutiny. "You get those when you're meddling. You're getting too close to somebody's secrets. Have you been poking into anything besides the burglaries?"

"No, that's the only story I'm following regularly."

"Is this the same one who called before?"

"Maybe."

"The one who sent you the finger?"

I just looked at him. "I guess so."

"You didn't have a byline this week, did you?"

I shook my head. "Only on the bridge dedication story, not on the burglary. I guess he recognizes my stuff or maybe he just guessed. I don't know."

"Don't get spooked now. Have you told O'Brien about the threats?"

I rolled my eyes. "Mallory, O'Brien's a politician. He's not a real cop. He's around for photo ops and sound bites, not for solving crimes."

"Bias seems like a sharp enough guy and he's your buddy, right?"

"Thad's doing his best, but he's still inexperienced."

"You know a real cop though, don't you? One who can actually solve a crime?"

I smiled. Yes, I knew a great cop and, as it happened, he already had the evidence in the burglaries. "But he's thirteen hundred miles away," I said softly.

"Will he come if you ask him?" Mallory's tone carried more sincerity than I had heard in his voice before. I stared at him in disbelief. Mallory shrugged. "I'd like to get a look at this guy anyway, before you go making a bunch of promises."

I remained mute, too surprised to respond.

"Hell," Mallory said finally, "I'll even spring for the plane ride."

Struck dumber still, I began nodding as an unbelieving smile crept from my heart and apparently commandeered my face.

"Will he want to bunk in with you?" Mallory asked.

"No."

Mallory looked mildly surprised. "Okay," he grumbled, "he can stay at my place for a couple of days, but if it goes extra innings, he'll have to spring for a room of his own, understand?"

I smiled, wildly relieved at the unexpected turn, then I swiveled back to the telephone. I glanced at the clock. It was after five, making it past seven in Bishop. Mrs. Teeman and everyone else would be gone. I dialed the office number anyway.

"What are you doing there?" I asked when Jim answered.

"Mopping up."

I heard his chair creak as it did when he leaned back.

"Just finished the Mason case in Connor County and I'm putting the loose ends in writing. Remember? A confidence guy, scamming old folks. I told you about it. What's up?"

"You've got vacation time coming, right?"

"Yes." He answered slowly, the smile in his voice replaced by concern. He didn't remind me that he had saved three weeks for us, time for the honeymoon and settling me into his condo.

"Mallory wants to meet you. He said he'll even buy the plane ticket. How would you like a few days away from the sleet and snow, basking in the warm California smog?"

"I'd like that." He hesitated. "Did you get another threat?"

"Sort of."

"It even got Mallory's attention?"

"Apparently so. He says you can stay with him."

"I'll call you back. Where are you?"

"Here at the office for a while, I guess." I glanced at Mallory who nodded.

"I need about thirty minutes," Mallory said in a stage whisper. "I want to follow you, make sure you get home safe."

"I'll be here for the next half hour, then fifteen minutes after that I'll be home," I told Jim.

"I'll call you back before you leave the office."

He did.

There was a noon flight out of Dominion that would put him in San Diego at one-forty P.M. California time. He would catch a cab to the office. I repeated the schedule as Jim reeled it out. Mallory nodded approval.

"Bring the packet I sent you," I reminded him.

"Tell Mallory I appreciate his letting me stay at his place. I'll pay for the plane ticket myself."

Again Duke followed me home, parked, went inside and all the way to my room, insisting he wanted to make sure I was secure for the night. I had barely put on the security chain when the phone rang. I picked it up slowly.

"Are you okay?" Hearing Jim's voice, I relaxed.

"A little jittery. How are you?"

"Calm, cool, eager. What's going on?"

"How can you always tell?" I marveled at his instincts.

"It's easier when I can see you, but it's getting so I can hear you fretting, even over the telephone."

"Phone companies advertise you can hear confetti fall, but they didn't mention hearing brows furrow."

"I can hear yours. Now, what's the problem?"

"Nothing, really. I'd rather tell you in person."

"Okay, then tell me what the doctor said."

"Well, that's kind of a good news/bad news thing," I hedged. "He said I'm fine but I may be getting too old to have sex."

Jim chuckled. "Very funny."

"I'm not kidding. That's sort of what he said."

"Jance, you're twenty-four years old, for crying out loud."

"He said he thinks the 'natural barrier' inside me is pretty tough, that I might need minor surgery before we can have sex at all. He said it's a simple little office procedure."

There was only silence from the other end of the phone. "Oh," Jim breathed finally.

I gritted my teeth. "Darn it, Jim, you can hear my brows furrow; I can hear you grinning. You know how that irritates me."

He allowed a little rolling laugh. "Tell you what," he said, making an obvious attempt to quell his mirth, "let's put 'consummate' on my list of things to do and you don't worry about it. Okay?"

"No surgery?"

"I've got a little procedure of my own I'd like to try first. We'll have plenty of time. I think we can manage. You just worry about getting the things on your list done. Leave my areas of responsibility to me."

"You sound awfully confident."

"I think the operative word here, honey, is 'cocky.' "

I allowed a little laugh. "Jim," I said quietly.

"Yes."

"Will you please not tease me about this?"

"No, I will not tease you about it."

"And will you not tell anyone else?"

"Who the hell would I tell?"

"Promise."

"Okay. I promise I won't mention it."

"Not even to your dad?"

"Not even to my dad. It'll be our little secret, yours and mine."

CHAPTER SEVEN

No one looked up when the stranger walked into the press room on the early deadline—noon—on Friday, until he spoke.

"Dewhurst?" he said to Ivy Work, who was busily typing in her appointed space, the first desk inside the front door.

Ivy glanced up, frowned over the rims of her granny glasses, which had slipped and clung precariously to the bulbous end of her long nose. She glowered. A smile enhanced his dark good looks and she almost smiled back, but instead turned her head slightly, without taking her eyes off his face.

"This guy wants Dewhurst!" she called to the room at large.

All five male co-workers present looked up from their tasks, every face adopting Work's glower. The stranger kept his eyes on Ivy. No one spoke. A presence stepped up behind the stranger and cupped a large hand over his shoulder.

"Who wants her?" Years of smoke and whiskey had given Mallory's voice graveled authority. The visitor, several inches taller, several years younger, and obviously in much better shape, turned beneath Mallory's mitt to size up his challenger before offering a conciliatory smile.

"Duke Mallory?" the stranger asked, squinting at the older man.

"Yes," Mallory said and the frown deepened. "And who might you be?"

"Jim Wills."

The hand clamped on Wills's shoulder relaxed and Mallory

announced Wills's identity, waving his hand at the room full of news people who, after giving Jim a thorough onceover, turned back, as if on signal, to their tasks.

"You're not supposed to be here until this afternoon," Mallory said. "The girl took an early lunch to get her hair curly and her fingernails painted. She doesn't do all that stuff for us. She won't be back 'til one. I'm free now. Why don't you and I go grab a sandwich."

Mallory's eyes followed as Wills glanced down at the suitcase and the briefcase on the floor beside him.

"You can stow those over here." Mallory indicated Wills should follow him.

At Mallory's desk, Jancy's mentor shoved the two cases underneath, dusted his hands, caught Wills's elbow, and turned him back toward the door.

As they walked the half-block to The Town Tavern, Wills said airline reservations had called with a seat available on an earlier flight. That opening was followed by appropriate comments on the mild California weather.

Mallory said he preferred Oklahoma, Wills's part of the country, where seasons were better delineated, but he had developed an almost irrational aversion to cold weather.

The tavern was impressively dark after the midday sunlight. Mallory led them to an empty booth in a still darker corner.

"Do you like corned beef?" Mallory asked. Wills nodded. "Karen, bring us two specials and a pitcher."

Wills didn't object.

"Okay, ask away," Mallory said, turning his full attention to his guest.

"Do we need to be concerned about her physical safety?" Wills said, knifing right to the point. The lines in Mallory's face deepened and he shook his head uncertainly.

"I don't know. She's been doing a head's-up job. She got into step real quick. She's smart, has a lot of savvy. But she's green. She still trusts people. Everyone. People tell her what they want her to know. She goes along most of the time and, most of the time, it doesn't hurt her.

"But she's got this stubborn streak." Mallory gave Wills a hard look. "Do you know about that?"

Wills smiled and nodded. Mallory plunged ahead.

"And she's always so damned sure she's right about things."

"That, too." Wills nodded knowingly.

Mallory continued. "Most of the time she reads people pretty well and quick, too. But crazies are hard to figure and they won't always stay in the category you put them in. Do you know at all what I'm talking about?"

Wills nodded as the barmaid set their order on the table. Mallory poured beer from the pitcher into the two frosted glasses and shoved one over in front of Wills.

"Part of Jancy's allure," Wills said, taking his turn to talk, "is that naiveté. Her being so trusting makes people trust her. All kinds of people. She attracts them, especially the crazies."

"Yeah," Mallory agreed. "Like I said, she was doing good work, caught onto things quick. When I saw how she was, I slacked off, unloaded some of my responsibility on her. She's a hell of a lot more reliable than I am, always where she's supposed to be and always on time."

"So what's your read on this?" Wills asked. "Is it the burglar who's threatening her or is it someone else, some crackpot. And is he dangerous?"

Mallory grimaced. "That's what I don't know, and not knowing scares the hell out of me. As far as I can tell, the burglar's never run into anyone at home. I don't know what he's capable of doing, don't even know if he carries a weapon.

"Anyway, this police captain handling the case, Murray O'Brien, is a windbag. He has a hard time finding the urinal in the men's room, much less a burglar in the population. He's such a screw-up, I thought he was on the take. I've watched him work. I don't think he's got enough sense to blow a case intentionally.

"But O'Brien is sharp at spotting talent and motivating gifted people, then running in to take credit for their success. He's got this young guy working for him who's a go-getter. Thad Bias is a good kid, smart, soft-spoken, thorough.

"And, of course, O'Brien latched onto Jancy like a duck on a June bug, as they say back in your part of the country. Between the two kids, Thad and Jancy, they may wind up making O'Brien look like a hero."

The corned beef was tender. As he chewed, Wills expressed appreciation for Mallory's lunch choice and for his familiarity with Southwest idioms, but then pressed for more of the newsman's observations on the threats against Jancy.

"O'Brien's been feeding her information." Mallory licked greasy mustard dripping from the backside of his hand. "It was pretty obvious, the way he baited her, like a fly fisherman snapping the lure back into the same spot over and over again to get the trout's attention. She nibbled at the first and second hits, liked seeing her byline. After the third burglary, she bit hard. On the fourth, I let her have her head."

"Couldn't you have warned her off?"

"Didn't want to. Once she was hooked, I didn't think she'd listen to me anyway." He eyed Jim as he said, "That stubborn streak we mentioned?"

Jim nodded.

"Besides, I really wanted to see her in action, wanted to see that mind go to work.

"It was obvious O'Brien didn't have the brain power to figure out the burglar's pattern, whatever it was, and wouldn't give Bias enough space to do it for him. Like I told you, O'Brien himself can't analyze salt.

"I also looked at what getting into it did for her. It stimulated her juices, kept her from mooning around here homesick or lovesick or whatever. And it earned her some bylines, which means nationwide credentials. On top of all that, I thought she might damn well solve the thing."

Wills frowned. "Didn't you realize it might call the thief's attention to her?"

"Hell, no. Whoever looks at a byline, except people in the business? Criminals don't know or care who's writing about them. All they care about is seeing their names in print."

Wills stopped chewing to study Mallory. "But this one is different?"

"Like I said, who knew? I've written millions of words, covered hundreds of trials and never once, not even once, has any regular criminal ever threatened me. Granted, I've had some rough conversations with some of your political types, criminals of the white-collar persuasion, but not with any run-of-the-mill riffraff."

"Jancy said you took the dummy finger to the police."

"To Thad Bias. The kid was born to law enforcement. Of course it doesn't hurt that he's crazy about Jancy. Thad hand-carried it to the lab. If there'd been something to find, he would have come up with it. The fact that he's got such a case on Jancy made him just that much more interested in the results."

Focused on his sandwich, Wills didn't take the bait Mallory was laying out for him. "What'd he get?"

"No fingerprints anywhere, even inside the box, except Jancy's. It'd been mailed locally. That was right after Halloween and stores had sold thousands of those fake bloody fingers all over the country. There was no way to trace it."

"So, what happened yesterday?"

"She got another call." Mallory repeated the caller's words, with the same tone and inflection. Wills frowned but didn't comment.

"Another thing limiting any official police activity," Mallory continued, "is that no crime has actually been perpetrated against her. It's not like they have a reason to put men on the street looking for someone harassing her."

"Right."

The two companions ate quietly for a long minute.

"Are you smart enough for her?" Mallory asked finally.

"Maybe. Maybe not. Why?"

"How do you have the balls to take someone like her all for yourself?"

Wills laughed. "I hadn't thought of it quite that way. I chased her hard; caught her, finally, because I have something she needs."

"What's that?" Mallory asked grudgingly. "I mean besides the obvious. I'll admit you are a nice-enough looking guy, probably handsome even, all things considered, but the way she is . . . well, Jancy seems like a person who has a lot to give—I mean, to give the world—not the kind of person who should limit herself to just one significant other."

Wills laughed derisively. "Like I said, I have something she needs and she trusts me to provide it."

"And, like I said, what is that something, exactly?" Mallory squinted at his companion.

Jim sobered. "She needs someone who'll give her a protected playing field but who won't crowd her, who's willing to give her room to reach for her potential.

"She thrives on praise. She's extremely sensitive to criticism. It undermines her. Because she meets people easily, most of them see her as confident. They don't see her uncertainty. Some don't want to see it. They like believing she's the daredevil she appears to be. Others see her need, but they either can't or don't want to meet it so they just take as much as she's willing to give.

"Other people want her to be as strong and smart and independent as she looks. She's all three most of the time. Every now and then, however, she gets a serious shot to the ego. It's usually when she overlooks something obvious. It makes her doubt herself and she wilts. Are you following this?"

"I think so," Mallory growled and sipped his beer thoughtfully.

Jim nodded. "I've seen all her moods, her strengths and weaknesses. She knows I know her well, and she knows I want her, just like she is, want her so much I'll take her on any terms at all.

"When she's strong and smart and independent, she knows I'll give her space. Riley Wedge, the wire service, can send her anyplace. If she wants to go, I won't interfere. But when she stubs her toe, all she has to do is call. She doesn't have to ask. I'll be there in a heartbeat. Or here, as it turns out."

"Kind of like Mighty Mouse swooping in to save the day," Mallory mused. "And you don't mind?"

"You know her. Would you like for her to need you?"

"Don't be an idiot."

"I mean it. If I told you Jancy could work with you from now on if you'd meet certain conditions, would you haggle about the terms?"

Mallory tossed his head. "I'm a little old or maybe I just don't have enough imagination." He focused hard on Jim again. "So you're actually willing to let her traipse in and out of war zones, no strings attached?"

Wills returned Mallory's stare and raised his eyebrows. "The longer we're together, the more often she needs me. With me, she can relax, let down her guard. I reassure her. When she squirms, I don't try to hold onto her. Consequently, she comes closer and closer, like a moth to a flame."

"And now she's going to marry you?" Mallory said with disbelief.

"Right."

"Isn't this moth of yours about to singe her little wings?"

"Not if I can help it. I want her to want to live with me full time, but I'm not pressing for that. Getting her under contract will be enough for now."

"Do you know what a marriage contract is worth these days?"

"Statistically speaking, yes. Jancily speaking, I think so and, as I see it, they are diametrically different. Jancy's got integrity. That's unusual in today's women. She's reliable and truthful, also rare in women and men."

Suddenly Mallory looked at the clock over the bar, which read 1:05, glanced at the three quarters of a pitcher of beer, then regarded Wills with some amazement.

"I'd say you are kind of a rare bird yourself," Mallory said, "a real boy scout."

Wills winced. "Thanks."

"I mean that in a good way. I've interviewed a lot of people. Not many made me forget a pitcher of brew. That wasn't sarcasm. You probably just never thought of yourself that way."

"The 'boy scout' comparison's come up before. Those times, it was demeaning."

"Well, I meant it as a compliment. Our little conversation's eased my mind about your being good enough for Jancy. Now I'm wondering whether she's woman enough for you."

Wills chuckled and stood, pulling bills out of his pocket for the tip. "Take my word for it," he grinned, "she's everything I ever wanted in a woman and is definitely all I can handle."

CHAPTER EIGHT

Working, I glanced frequently at the door to the press room. I had gotten back to the office at twelve-forty-five to reports of the arrival of Jim Wills, described in glowing terms, and of Mallory's spiriting him off for lunch.

Mallory usually frequented The Town Tavern. Eager to see Jim, I could have gone looking for them, but I restrained myself. I settled instead to typing up notes on Billie's burglary, again searching for common denominators that would link the victims.

How were the burgled homes selected?

I figured there was a hub into which the spokes of all the burglaries ran, but prankishly it eluded me.

It was one-ten when I heard Mallory's voice in the hallway. I drew a deep, deep breath, sat up straight, and looked toward the door, my fingers poised over the keyboard.

Mallory entered the room first, then stopped. My attention flitted to the form behind him. I didn't flinch, except for a smile I couldn't swallow.

Jim's dark, probing glance settled on my face as he stood listening patiently to the conclusion of Mallory's old Bosnian radio story. Jim didn't interrupt or even move. Instead, he stood gazing across the roomful of people—a room filled with clattering keyboards and ringing telephones and muted voices and an occasional cough—straight into my eyes.

Glancing up from her keyboard, Ivy Work followed his stare.

I felt the heat of a familiar flush, smiled self-consciously, and glanced back at the keyboard for an instant, then at Jim, unable to quiet the joy simmering to a boil inside me.

I looked his solid muscular frame up and down as if I were seeing him for the first time. As I looked at him, I stood but I didn't advance. I just stood there admiring his dark, close-cropped hair, his well-formed head, his thick neck constrained by the buttoned collar lashed in place by a paisley tie. His square shoulders were enhanced by the navy blazer. The gray slacks ended at the predictable sheen of the polished black oxfords.

When I teased him about being such a meticulous dresser, Wills explained that as the third of seven kids, he mostly wore hand-me-downs until he began earning his own money.

Oblivious to either Jim or me, Mallory continued his epic account. Noticing the contrast between the two men, I could barely stifle a giggle.

Mallory's unkempt hair was barbered so extra length on one side could be combed over to cover his balding pate. He wore a Hawaiian-design dress shirt pockmarked with tiny cigarette burns. His trousers had, as usual, slipped well below his waist and the cuffs were filthy from dragging the floor behind him. His aged brown loafers were run over at the heels. At that moment, the two men appeared to be an advertisement for the "before" and "after" look in a men's clothing ad.

I forced my attention back to the computer screen and closed down the machine before I walked as nonchalantly as I could through the maze of desks and people.

Jim watched my approach, his expression pleasant, his eyes drinking me in as if slaking a thirst. Mallory continued talking.

The pounding in my chest became a jungle beat that accelerated as I got close enough to catch the familiar scent of my fiancé. Mallory chose that moment for a pull on his ever-present cigarette.

"How are you?" I breathed, slipping the words into the break in Mallory's narrative. Mallory glanced at me, obviously unaware of the exhilaration in my ordinary greeting; unaware, that is, until he looked back at Jim.

Our visitor's gaze feasted on my face as a hungry man regards steak.

"Better," Jim said softly, but the utterance shot an electric current that recalibrated my heartbeat.

Ivy and other observers diverted their stares, their usual sarcasm stilled. Although Jim and I didn't touch physically, the rush of pleasure between us appeared to silence even the most jaded newsman—Mallory—who abandoned us without another word.

I decided the ritual of private, physical salutations should be postponed. Instead of leaping into Jim's arms, I drew a calming breath and turned to follow Mallory and lead Jim—who appeared to follow my thoughts rather than verbal directives—back to our workstation.

Mallory retrieved Jim's briefcase from under the desk and handed it to him. Jim nodded his thanks and took the chair I offered. Mallory eased into his own seat and I scrounged an available straightback. Nobody said anything.

Balancing the briefcase on his lap, Jim opened it to produce the envelope I had sent.

He laid out sets of information in neat stacks on top of papers covering the surface of my desk, slightly less cluttered than Mallory's.

"I did this to give us something to work from," Jim said, producing a printout that showed groupings of the items each burglary had in common. Mallory and I glanced at the sheets. I actually pretended to be interested as an excuse to move closer to Jim, fill up on his scent, and enjoy the raw power he exuded.

His tally sheets listed the cash and jewelry taken from each of the six homes; sterling silver items taken from three; coin collections from two; guns from two.

Every victim reported desks and safes ransacked, all of which contained records of credit card and PIN numbers, insurance policies, deeds, birth certificates, vehicle registrations, etc. The Earlys were missing a collection of belt buckles. Jim listed candlesticks in a separate category.

Both Mallory and I complimented him on the thorough inventory and Duke wondered aloud if Captain O'Brien had a list like it.

"Probably not," I sighed. "I hope all the victims have notified their credit card companies."

"And changed those bank account numbers," Mallory added, obviously getting interested. "But where's the thing that ties them together?"

Jim smiled.

"Except the candlesticks, of course," Mallory added as Jim and I both started to speak at once. The addition silenced us.

"Neither the news stories nor the police reports say where the residents were when their homes were broken into," Jim said.

I looked at Mallory, who returned my unspoken question with a shrug.

"I wondered about that," I said, "but it wasn't in the police reports so I assumed it didn't matter."

Jim smiled straight into my face. "That's not like you, bulldog, to wonder about a thing and not dig for an answer."

Mallory looked from Jim to me as if searching for an answer from one of us. While he was thinking, we both turned our questioning gazes on him.

He shrugged. "I just didn't think of it."

"It may not be pertinent," Jim said, "but then again, it may."

Mallory and I agreed with solemn nods.

"I'll find out," I said, suddenly needing something to do.

Glancing at the front of one folder for a phone number, I picked up a phone and began dialing.

Jim stood and stretched, looked at his watch, then pushed his chair a little and nodded, indicating I should move into it from the straightback, which would put me closer to the telephone.

Mallory began trying to clear his desk. Finally, he scooped the scattered papers into one pile, opened the bottom desk drawer, and swept them into it.

"Mrs. Ketchum," I said to the answering machine, "this is Jancy Dewhurst. I need to know where you and Mr. Ketchum were the night your home was burglarized. Please call me back at 555-8200. If I'm not here, leave a message. Thanks." I glanced at Jim's curious expression and grimaced. "Answering machine."

He nodded as I dialed another number.

Sitting again, this time in the straightback, Jim divided his categorized reports into three stacks, one for each of us as I continued making calls with little success.

Grimly, we each began sorting through our assigned array, reviewing information we had all covered at least twice before.

Gradually, as the afternoon slipped by, other news people in the office left, one or two at a time. Finally, Ivy Work, Jim, Duke, and I were alone in the pressroom.

"Let's talk about where the victims might have been," Jim suggested again finally. "You probably know about some of them."

"The Earlys were after the Ketchums and I know where they were," I muttered without looking up or noticing how late it was getting. "At their daughter's house, babysitting their grandchildren."

Jim jotted something in his notebook. "And Sean Smith?"

"I know where he was too," I said, looking up at him. "His mother died the next day. He was at her bedside all night that night."

"Which hospital?"

I didn't know. I peered over at his face. "Why?"

"Your friend Billie and her husband spent the night at St. Simeon's the night the burglar hit them, didn't they?"

Excitement leaped in my chest. Maybe we had a lead. "I'll find out." I felt a rush of new energy and fresh determination.

Mr. Smith still did not answer the phone either at his home or his office. I left messages again on machines at both places.

Next I tried Mrs. Hudson's. Still no answer and no machine.

"I've gotten fond of answering machines," I said as I hung up.

"I was helping a friend," Dennis Harrison explained when I reached him, still in his office at 5:30.

"Where were you?" I pressed. He was reluctant to answer, but I was beginning to get an urgent feeling. "It might be important."

"A gal here at work," he said, whispering into the mouthpiece. "She's here right now, has the desk next to mine. Her husband's dying of cancer. She sits with him all night, every night. I wanted to give her a breather. I had to beg her to let me sit with him, give her a couple of nights off. She doesn't know about the break-in at my place and I don't want her to find out. She'll blame herself and she's got all she can handle right now."

"So, you spent Tuesday and Wednesday nights at a hospital?" I asked, trying to quell the excitement that put an involuntary quiver in my voice.

"Third floor East," Harrison said. "St. Simeon's."

I sat straighter, suddenly on full alert. I was astonished and amazed and puffed up with unbridled admiration as I turned to look at Jim.

"Thanks, Mr. Harrison," I said breathlessly. "You've been a big help."

"I can call St. Simeon's to find out about the Smiths," I told

Jim, riding the crest of our new success.

"Do you know Sean Smith's mother's name?" Jim asked and smiled knowingly. I shook my head. My shoulders slumped and my excitement faded.

"Probably Smith," I offered lamely. He nodded. "But the common denominator might be St. Simeon's. That looks like the one thing they all have in common!" I exhaled, deflating again. "Except . . ."

"How does that help us?" Jim supplied when I hesitated. I guess my face reflected my bewilderment.

"Maybe it points to someone at St. Simeon's," he continued. "An employee. When did the burglaries occur? Let's recheck dates and days."

I rifled through my notes.

"Ketchums, the first one we know about, was on Monday the thirteenth," I offered.

Jim jotted it down.

"Earlys was the second one, on Wednesday the fifteenth," Mallory said, caught up in our fresh surge of enthusiasm.

Mallory, Jim, and I burrowed through the pages of information like pirates digging for buried treasure. Mallory jabbed a sheet into the air triumphantly.

"Smith, Tuesday, November twenty-first!" he said loudly.

"Hudson, Monday again, the twenty-seventh," Jim said without looking up.

"The story on Harrison ran on Thursday, the thirtieth. It happened Tuesday or Wednesday," I said and regarded Jim curiously. "And the Stones discovered theirs on Thursday the seventh," I added softly. "Is the burglar gaining momentum?"

Jim arched his eyebrows. "Maybe he's just gaining confidence. He's being pretty brazen. Notice, we have break-ins early Monday through early Thursday, but none on the weekends."

"Which tells us what?" I asked.

"Maybe he works at the hospital and is off weekends or has custody of kids. Something. Whatever it is, it looks like he's not available for burglarizing Thursday, Friday, or Saturday nights."

"That doesn't tell us how he knows when people aren't going to be home." I leaned back, folded my arms across my chest, and stared at the floor, hoping the answer might magically pop up there.

"I guess," Mallory said, "he cases the neighborhood."

Jim glanced at Mallory, started to speak, then hesitated, holding back. He had a theory but was waiting for us to wriggle our ways to the same bottom line.

"What neighborhood?" I asked, setting my eyes on his face. "The Stones live in Brentwood, outside his usual haunt."

"Maybe he's afraid the police and neighbors are too alert now for him to keep working the same territory," Mallory guessed.

"But he's struck three nights in a row," I countered. "That hardly shows a lack of confidence."

Looking puzzled, Mallory glanced at his watch, then around at the deserted newsroom. "It's nearly six o'clock. Let's turn on the answering machine and knock off for supper.

"Hey, Ivy," he called across the room, "come have a steak with us. I'm buying."

Ivy looked at Mallory, then back at her computer screen, nodded, and turned off her machine.

"We can swing back by here later," Mallory said to everyone in general, "see if we have any messages before we call it a night. What do you say?"

Jim looked at me for our answer. I could guess he wanted us to have a little time alone. "Is that okay with you?" I asked.

Jim smiled gently and nodded. "Sure."

Ivy, who seemed to know the eatery Duke had in mind, said she would meet us there.

Although I had been in California since mid-October, I had yet to experience The Town Tavern. Insisting they had "the best steaks anywhere," Mallory hauled Jim and me back to their luncheon site for supper.

It was early but the tavern was crowded. I saw several people I knew as Mallory led, elbowing his way through bodies to a small table already overpopulated with news people, two from the office, others from local TV stations and newspapers. I was surprised Mallory seemed so popular with broadcast news people, whom he often and loudly berated as movie stars rather than journalists.

Already settled, Ivy Work looked up and gave Mallory a token smile, but the smile deteriorated when she saw Jim and me trailing him.

Ivy was probably fifty years old, her face long and pinched. She wore very little makeup, paid only cursory attention to her hair, and rotated her wardrobe among identical navy blue, black, or maroon slacks and an assortment of blouses and sweaters that had all become hauntingly familiar.

Ivy had plowed new ground when she arrived at the press room fifteen years earlier, newly widowed, a seasoned reporter with respectable credentials. She became the mother hen of the press corps. She had a vast vocabulary and allowed her co-workers occasionally to pick her thesaurus brain when we were on a deadline.

As one of only two females in the office, Ivy welcomed me eagerly as a third before we had hardly been introduced. After assessing my work, she told Riley Wedge on the q.t. one afternoon that I made it look like he knew what he was doing. Ivy said Wedge assured her my potential was obvious.

While neither Ivy nor Riley publicly mentioned their nice appraisals of my skills, I felt their approval in the way they treated me. It built my confidence on my job and in the pressroom to have the unspoken backing of those two distinguished veterans.

"Don't you think they might like to have a little time to themselves?" Ivy shouted at Mallory over the din of the tavern's jukebox. Jim and I pretended not to have heard her.

"They don't go in for that touchy feely stuff," Mallory shouted back, wagging his head back and forth for emphasis. Their exchange was getting embarrassing.

"They might if they didn't always have an audience," Ivy shot back without lowering her voice even though he and she were closer.

"Nah. They're friends, not lovers." He glanced back at us. "He's staying at my place. Their idea."

Close behind Mallory, I gave Ivy an unsteady smile, a wave, and a blank look as if I hadn't heard their entire conversation. Ivy looked back at Mallory and shook her head.

The noisy music persisted, one selection after another, making conversation difficult as Mallory and Jim confiscated spare chairs from other tables and situated them in the midst of the cluster of news people.

By the time we settled, I was disappointed to find Jim several people away, at the nearest, separated by Mallory, Ivy, and Bruce Edison. He gave me a reassuring smile, mimed drinking, and raised his eyebrows, asking wordlessly if I wanted a drink. I nodded. He looked around for a waitress but they were overwhelmed.

Jim waggled his index finger to get my attention, then stood and began working his way through to the bar, glancing back to make sure I saw where he was going.

The crush of people waiting for drinks at the bar was three deep. Gradually, Jim eased forward until he had cleared leaning space, then he stuck his hand in the air and, although he wasn't able to see me, signaled me to come.

I followed his path, weaving my way through the revelers. Jim turned his back to the bar and was facing me as I approached.

Suddenly two hands grabbed my shoulders. As I tried to see who it was, the hands shoved. I lunged forward, stumbling, then falling. Unable to catch my balance, I fell headlong. Jim reacted. He caught my underarms before I went down. I swung around, trying to recognize any of the faces in the crowd, which pressed from every direction.

"Did you trip?" Jim's mouth was close to my ear, his hands gripping my upper arms.

"Someone pushed me." I pivoted to answer but kept my eyes on the sea of faces. "Maybe it was an accident." I checked out the faces of the people closest to me. A man with a rodent's features smirked at me as if we shared a joke. Thin with a long nose, high cheekbones, and small, bright, beady, iridescent blue eyes, he vanished almost as soon as I focused on him, melding into the crowd.

"Or maybe not." I shivered involuntarily as I turned, finding assurance in Jim's bold, open features.

Suddenly I was smushed against him by the surge of people trying to reach the bar. Catching the bar on either side of him, I struggled for a moment to brace myself. I didn't want to injure him in the onslaught, but he only smiled and wrapped his arms all the way around me, clasping my body tightly against his own.

I felt him draw a deep breath and I cocked my head to one side to catch a close-up of his face. He looked happy and maybe a little smug.

"Might as well enjoy it." He spoke directly into my ear, his words easily audible over the bar noise. He nibbled my cheek.

"Welcome to California." I tipped my face, my mouth summoning his. His lips claimed mine, consuming, taking everything I offered.

I noticed a patron standing next to Jim nudge his female

companion who nudged the girl next to her and they all stood there staring at us like we were a zoo exhibit.

Back at their table, Ivy poked Mallory and pointed toward the bar. "Does that look platonic to you?"

Mallory glanced, did a double take, and frowned his disapproval.

Ivy smirked.

The bartender tapped Jim's shoulder. "Get you something to drink, buddy, or are you just here for the grope?" The bartender shouted the last part of his question just as the music ended. Bystanders laughed.

"Both," Jim said loudly, smiling down into my face. "Fix us a couple of Bloody Marys."

CHAPTER NINE

"Would you rather be the 'gropee' or the 'groper,' " I asked when we had finished surprisingly tender rib-eye steaks.

At our table people coming and going had left two chairs vacant, side by side, which Jim and I promptly filled. Jim stretched an arm across the back of my chair and I snuggled close.

"I'm ambivalent. You choose," he said.

I smiled at him. "I didn't expect you to get here so quickly. And people complain about slow police response time."

"When you request my presence, sweetheart, you get priority one attention. Always will."

"The situation here probably isn't all that urgent."

"Maybe the situation wasn't, but I was sure ready to see your face."

"Oh, yeah?" I presented my face to his. "It's only been two weeks since you were here."

His eyes swept my features and he smiled, his teeth white in the half-light and his dark eyes narrowing to slits as if to conceal thoughts he didn't want me to read. "Yeah."

There had always been magic—chemistry—between us. Trying to hide my attraction to him, I attempted normal conversation. "Your natural inclination toward crime had nothing to do with your immediate response?"

"I'm not here to commit crime," he teased, "at least not one anyone's prosecuting these days."

"What do you mean?"

"Lust, baby, an archaic term in today's crime-solver handbook. Everybody freely confesses that ancient sin now. Some even brag about participating. In fact, a person my age and station in life would probably be considered peculiar if he weren't lusting after someone."

"What exactly does that term entail?"

"Not your best choice of words." He kissed my cheek. "Since most guys today are lusting after a little tail."

"Jim!"

He laughed at my pretended shock.

Finishing my drink, I shifted to sit straighter in my chair. "It's late. I'm ready to call it a night."

"Do you want to stop by your office to check the phone messages?"

"Nah, it's too late to follow up on anything tonight. We'd probably do better to start fresh in the morning."

Jim watched me thoughtfully, as if he were picking up on my strange vibes, but he didn't appear able to decipher their veiled meaning.

I stood and started toward the door, then glanced back to see if he was coming.

"What?" he asked, stepping close behind me.

"Do you want to spend the night with me?" I asked.

"Yes."

His quick answer caught me off guard. I must have looked surprised, because he chuckled. I saw Duke glance up and start to call out something, but Ivy intercepted him.

Jim held the door, encouraging me outside. I was checking out the parking lot when he took my elbow and guided me toward my courtesy car. As usual I'd forgotten where we'd parked. He put me in the driver's seat.

"I thought you wanted to wait," I said when he was in the car.

"I was never the one who wanted to wait." He gazed steadily into my face in the semi-darkness, the only available light reflected from street lamps dotting the parking lot.

"When you were here before, you turned me down flat," I reminded him. "The words 'stud fee' and 'no free samples' come to mind."

"The circumstances were different then."

"It was only two weeks ago. It was nighttime. We were together here in San Diego. I lived alone and invited you into my hotel room. You refused. What's changed?"

He laced his fingers into my hair and pulled my head back as he continued to study my face. "You hadn't committed."

I might have jerked free but liked his firm hold on my hair.

"People don't commit like that anymore," I said finally, but for the life of me, I couldn't stop looking at him, mesmerized by his eyes, his mouth, every sexy feature about him.

"We do." He pulled my face closer to his and kissed my mouth once, soundly, then turned my head and kissed my cheek again and again, his lips sliding from my hairline to my shoulder with occasional excursions back to my eager, expectant mouth.

"You didn't require a commitment from girls you knew before," I murmured, warming to this game and kissing him back, allowing my hand to slither down his chest.

"That's right."

"Why play hard to get with me?"

He smiled, caught my wandering hand, and raised it to his mouth. His breath felt warm on my flesh.

" 'Hard' is probably an appropriate term," he crooned, and guided my errant hand to the front of his trousers. There he hesitated. "Jancy, if you're just kidding around, you'd better say so. If you change your mind in your room, it'll be too late. I promise."

"I don't know if I'm serious or not." I pushed away from him. "You've been in situations like this. Tell me what to do."

With a derisive laugh, Jim rocked back against the seat and rolled his head to look at me.

"If it's not tonight or tomorrow or this week, unmarried," he said softly, "it's going to happen in three weeks anyway. I've waited this long. I don't mind another twenty days. But my self-control is hanging by a thread. I can't be strong for both of us. Not tonight. Our limits are, as they always have been, entirely up to you—until we're through the vows. After that, baby, I am nailing you."

I pivoted to look out the driver's side window. Steam on the glass distorted my view of things beyond.

"What if it's a disaster?" There it was, out in the air, my greatest anxiety. "What if I'm a disaster? I should have had sex years ago. If I had, I'd know what I'm doing now. What if I . . . can't?"

Jim laughed up at the ceiling. "You'll be awesome. Take my word for it." His eyes narrowed. There was something in his smile I couldn't quite fathom, as if he knew things I didn't. How could he be so sure?

"Dr. Linquist . . ." I began.

". . . knows the female anatomy," Jim interrupted. "I'm sure he's very competent. But he doesn't know you, sweet thing. I, on the other hand, have some working knowledge of the way a woman's body responds to certain stimuli, and I have the advantage of knowing you real well. Neither Dr. Linquist nor you yourself know your lovemaking potential like I do. I've seen you hot and I know the buttons to push to get you there. Would you like a demonstration?"

I raised my shoulder, turning away from him. "No." Then,

whether prompted by nerves or the dare, I giggled and risked a peek at his face.

Jim grinned wickedly.

"A demonstration?" I asked. "Like what?" Suddenly I felt challenged by his scornful expression. I came from a long line of females who had satisfied husbands and had produced children. Obviously they had had instincts. I might have some of those genes.

Moving quickly, playfully, he caught my waist in both hands, turned, and lifted me toward him. My head rocked back and he kissed my throat and nibbled his way down over my blouse, his open mouth hot against my breast. I gasped.

He mouthed a nipple. I squeaked as I tried to muffle a little whine. "I see," I gasped, pushing his shoulders. "Okay. Okay. I get the idea."

"I can give you maybe a dozen examples of how I plan to school you, turn you to a writhing, pleading seductress." The wicked grin appeared again as he released me.

Flustered and fidgeting, I smoothed my clothes. "There's another drawback," I said. "If you stayed with me tonight, I probably wouldn't want to go to work in the morning."

"Wouldn't matter. It's Saturday. What I'm wondering is if a couple of weeks of honeymoon is going to be enough for you."

"There probably won't be anyone else around then, right?" It was more of a question than a statement. "Where are we going? Will you tell me now?"

He gave me an evil little laugh, raised his eyebrows up and down, and rubbed his hands together like the villain in a melodrama. "Yes, I could reveal all, my love, but it's a secret. I've told no one of my diabolical plan for the joining and rejoining of our bodies."

Catching his mood, I touched the back of my hand to my forehead, playing Pauline in Peril to his villain.

"We've had all the heroic interruptions we are going to have." He maintained an evil arch to one eyebrow. "No one will save you once we are wed, my pet."

"Not even . . . ?"

"No, not even Olivia, your fairy godmother of the uncanny timing." We both laughed, remembering his mother's arrival at his condo one rainy afternoon. I regarded him boldly.

"I don't care where we go, as long as I'm with you. But how will I know what clothes to take?"

"Clothes?" He frowned quizzically. "Most of my planned activities do not require clothing. Perhaps some modicum of apparel, seemly in case you somehow, momentarily, slip my clutches."

My spirits lifted and I giggled all over again at his affectation.

He turned, addressing an imaginary audience, maintaining the character and wheezed, "Good, she suspects nothing."

I nearly jumped out of my skin at that moment when Duke rapped on the driver's-side window, interrupting our melodrama. Struggling with jangled nerves, I turned and rolled the window down.

Duke looked sheepish. "I couldn't see you, you've got the windows so fogged up. But I figured you were in here . . . because . . . well, because the windows were so fogged up. You're not doing dope or anything, are you?"

Jim and I laughed dutifully, but neither of us said anything.

"Aren't we going back to check messages?" Mallory's words slurred. He tried to open the back door, which was locked. I reached back to unlock it.

Jim fielded the question. "We decided it was too late to follow up any leads. We thought we'd call it a night and get an early start tomorrow, if that's all right with you."

Mallory stuck out his bottom lip. "It's the shank of the evening, not even midnight." He clambered into the car, then looked uneasily from Jim's face to mine. "Sure, you're right." He settled back against the seat. "Jancy, we'll drop you, then pick you up around seven-thirty for breakfast. How's that sound?"

I half laughed, half snorted. "Mallory, how long's it been since you've seen seven-thirty in the A.M.? Besides, Jim hasn't gotten to see the Pacific. He'll love the beach. He's a dedicated morning jogger. How about if I drop you two and pick him up really early for a run, then he can go back to your place to clean up and we can all go to breakfast about eight?"

Mallory seemed deflated, but nodded agreement.

But Jim objected. "No, ma'am. I want to see you settled safely inside the hotel. Mallory and I will take your car to his place and save him the drive."

I shot a quick look at Duke. He'd obviously had quite a bit to drink. Jim continued. "I can run in his neighborhood in the morning, shower and change at his place, then we can fetch you for breakfast. We can eat at the hotel, if you want to."

It was my turn to feel deflated. I wanted more time alone with Jim, but his idea was certainly more practical, actually better for everyone. Grudgingly, I agreed.

Mallory gave me a silly grin. "Sounds good."

As I started the car, I glanced down and winced to see the wet ring on my blouse circling one breast. I tried to cover the spot with my arm and put the car in gear before I risked a look at Jim. He had noticed the telltale circle, too. When our eyes met, he winked. The sudden blush overcame my warning frown.

At the hotel, Duke moved into the front passenger seat while Jim walked me inside. On the elevator, I leaped at the control panel, trying, too late, to stop the closing door.

"What are you doing?" Jim asked.

"Someone I wanted you to meet. Thad Bias. He was in the lobby. He's a young detective. He's good. He works for this lamebrain captain who keeps trying to hold him back, but Thad's sharp. I wanted you to meet him. Actually I wanted him to meet you."

"Maybe tomorrow." Jim stepped in front of me, pressed his body against mine, and buried his face in my neck. I responded immediately, arching into him, grinding my hips in an effort to get closer.

Outside my room, Jim took the key to unlock and open the door. Holding me tightly, he planted a lingering goodnight kiss, glanced wistfully at the bed looming behind me, and rigidly did an about-face and an exaggerated goose step down the hall to the elevator. I just stood there giggling in the doorway, as happy as I had been in . . . in two weeks.

When the phone rang moments later, I thought Jim probably was calling from the lobby. "So like him," I twittered. "Ever the romantic." But I was surprised.

"How are you?" Thad Bias asked.

"Fine." I tried to sound pleasant. I didn't want Thad to detect disappointment in my voice.

"Have you eaten?"

"Yes, with Mallory and Jim. I saw you downstairs. I tried to open the elevator doors after I spotted you, but they were too far gone. I wanted you to meet Jim."

"Your boyfriend?" He sounded annoyed. "What's he doing here? You didn't tell me he was coming."

"I got another telephone threat. Jim's sensitive to that kind of thing."

"Why'd you tell him? Why didn't you call me? I would have taken care of it. You didn't say anything to me about another call."

"You weren't around."

"Your boyfriend's got no jurisdiction here. I don't know why you had to drag him into this. Doesn't he have criminals of his own to catch back in Oklahoma, or has the big hero already cleaned up the badlands?"

"What are you so ticked about?" I asked. "I'd think you'd welcome all the qualified help you could get. Actually his being here might do you more good than me."

"I doubt that. So the little perp really got to you this time, huh? What'd he say?"

"Why do you always say 'little perp'? What makes you think he's not a big guy?"

"I just don't picture him as being very big. Anyway, what'd he say?"

"Nothing all that bad really. He said curiosity killed the cat and that if I didn't have nine lives, I'd better quit writing about Candlesticks."

"And that scared you? That's why you called in the big gun? I thought you felt safe with me watching after you. You know damn good and well I'll take care of you."

"You're a real good cop, but you're hamstrung, working for O'Brien."

"I can protect you, Jancy. I wouldn't let some pervert get hold of you. You know that."

"I know you wouldn't let him get me if you could help it, but you've got 'a lot of other fish to fry,' according to O'Brien."

Thad cleared his throat. "It's more than that with us, Jancy. You're not just some regular citizen I'm sworn to protect." His voice dropped to a coaxing tone. "You know you're special. We've got some good chemistry going between us. You feel it too. I know you do." He hesitated. "I'm not just imagining that, am I?"

I drew a deep breath. "No, Detective Bias, you didn't just imagine it. We are soul mates, lined up on the same side to oppose crime and O'Brien's ineptitude. But the two of us together are not the cop Jim Wills is. He's already noticed things we missed. He'll have this guy by the end of the week. I'll bet you five bucks."

Thad muttered so softly, I had to strain to hear him. "I wish you had that kind of confidence in me."

"You'll probably be as good as Jim someday," I said, wanting to console him, "when you get more experience and are out from under O'Brien. You'll see what I mean for yourself when you meet him. Maybe tomorrow?" There was a long silence.

"I'll be out of town the next three days," Bias said, sounding very official and very brusque.

"See what I mean about O'Brien holding you back? How can you catch Candlesticks if he sends you off in the middle of a case?"

"It's a seminar. The captain was supposed to go, but he's sending me. Said it would be a good opportunity for me to meet people at the state level, give me a leg up in my career."

"And it gives O'Brien a shot at getting full credit if Jim snags Candlesticks while you're gone," I said, giving him my interpretation. "Don't you see?"

"Can I call you when I get back?"

"Absolutely. I'm leaving the nineteenth and I definitely want to see you before I go."

"Why?" He sounded like he was holding his breath waiting for my answer. I didn't want him reading more into it than he should.

"Because we're friends."

"Yeah. Good night, Jancy."

"Thanks for checking on me."

"Sure." He hung up.

I stood there staring at the phone and puzzling. Had I led him on? Had I made him think I might be available? Before Jim arrived, during my sinking periods, I might have. That was so unfair, especially to a sweet guy like Thad who had been my best friend almost the whole time I had been in San Diego. Well, the best friend I had close to my own age, anyway.

No use putting myself on a guilt trip. I wasn't available and I guess I'd made that clear this time. He'd get over it. Probably already had.

Chapter Ten

Both of the messages on the office answering machine were for me the next morning when Jim and Mallory and I arrived at eight forty-five A.M., fresh, well fed, and in high spirits. No one else was in the office on a Saturday morning.

The first message was from Mrs. Ketchum.

Although Elbert Ketchum had thought he had appendicitis on November twelfth, he actually had experienced his first kidney stone, Mrs. Ketchum's recorded voice explained hurriedly. They had gone into the emergency room at St. Simeon's Hospital about midnight. During the night he had been moved to a room on the third floor east. It had been an ordeal. Then they had returned home the next morning to find they had been burglarized.

"St. Simeon's again." I whispered the words, gazing at Jim as the three of us considered the message we'd just heard. Jim nodded.

The second message was from Sean Smith. His mother had been in intensive care until the weekend before her death, when she had been moved to a private room, third floor . . .

"St. Simeon's," Jim, Mallory, and I chorused at the same time, sort of lip syncing over Sean Smith's recorded voice.

"Third floor again," Jim reiterated.

"You had to come all the way out here to give us the very information Billie Stone gave me face to face right here in this room." I groaned and gave Jim my most apologetic smile.

Instead of being annoyed, he grinned. "It's nice to be needed."

Eagerly, I tried to call the Earlys again, and again got the machine. I left another message, this one more urgent.

I dialed Paula Hudson's number and waited. The older woman answered on the seventh ring. Caught by surprise, I identified myself.

"Honey," Mrs. Hudson groaned, "I can't talk now. I'm in bed with one of my bad old sick headaches."

"Can I get something for you? Some kind of medicine? Refill a prescription?" I asked.

"Thank you. I've taken my pill. Now I must try to sleep. Pray for me to get some relief."

"Just one question." I hurried, not allowing time for another objection. "Where were you the night your home was burglarized?"

"I don't remember." The woman's voice sounded muffled.

"Did you have a sick headache that night?" I pressed, working on a hunch. It was a shot in the dark, but I hoped it might turn up something.

"That was it." Mrs. Hudson's words were barely audible. "I did have a bad headache. I was out of my medicine. It started late, spots in front of my eyes, tunnel vision. My neighbor Ms. Madison wasn't home. I had to drive myself to the hospital. They gave me a shot. They wouldn't let me leave. Wouldn't let me drive. Not after the shot. They took me upstairs. Made me wear one of those awful gowns." Her voice was weakening, her words trailing off. "They put me to bed. The plastic under the pillowcase crackled when I lay down."

"Did you stay all night?"

There was a long pause before the older woman whispered, "Yes. I dressed early the next morning, but they made me stay until after lunch. After that they let me drive. They let me go home."

"What hospital?" I pressed, my breath caught in my throat.

"St. Simeon's. Good-bye now."

I waited for Mrs. Hudson to hang up before I cradled my receiver gently. Of course. St. Simeon's. It was the hospital closest to everyone in South Beach. So far, five out of six of the victims had been at St. Simeon's when their homes were burglarized.

"But what about the Earlys?" I wondered aloud. Then I got an idea and again began rifling through my notes.

Sitting in Mallory's chair thumbing through files, Jim asked, "What are you looking for?"

Mallory, browsing through a Dallas newspaper at Bruce Edison's desk one cubicle over, flipped the corner of the paper down and regarded me curiously, his expression effectively echoing Jim's question. "Want some help?"

"I have the Earlys' daughter's name here someplace." I didn't look up. "Her parents were at her house babysitting the night their house was burglarized. I want to ask Mrs. Early who knew that."

Wills nodded. "Good thinking."

I tossed pages and scraps of paper into a jumbled stack until it was there, the bit I was looking for. I dialed the telephone.

"Mrs. Leverett?" I identified myself, and plunged. "I was just wondering how your parents happened to be babysitting for you the night their home was burglarized." I listened intently as she explained. Jim and Mallory kept their eyes on me.

"Oh? Well, congratulations," I said. "Yes, I'll bet you are. No, I don't need to talk to her. Just one question. Where was he born?"

Jim and Mallory looked at each other and grinned.

"St. Simeon's." I stalled a minute, trying to read the question Jim was mouthing.

"What floor was that?" I asked after I'd deciphered his signal.

"Maternity's on three. I see. Thanks, Mrs. Leverett, you've been a big help. Yes, I think we may finally be on his trail. Thanks very much."

I hung up the phone and turned to stare at Jim, who was leaning back in his chair, his hands locked behind his head, grinning.

"Guess I'd better pack my bag," he said. "You've about got this puppy under control."

I jumped up, jabbed both fists in the air with a victorious whoop, spun, and gave Mallory a high five.

As suddenly as I had claimed victory, I wilted and looked again to Jim. "What do we do now?"

He blurted a laugh. "Not quite ready to go it alone, huh?"

I shrugged, not wanting to admit it, but waiting for his answer.

He sobered. "We probably need to bring your Captain O'Brien up to speed."

I clamped my teeth and shook my head. "Not unless you want him to call a press conference and notify the perp that we're onto him."

"In that case, why don't we make a little trip to St. Simeon's?"

Jim guided Mallory and me directly to the hospital administrator, who was working, even though it was a weekend. After explaining the situation, Jim prevailed on the man to allow him an unofficial look at the personnel records for employees who were still on trial status. There were twenty-nine professional and hourly personnel who had been at their jobs for less than three months. To Jim's surprise, the general employees had been fingerprinted and screened far more carefully than the staff professionals—the doctors and nurses.

Jim asked the administrator not to mention the investigation, which he didn't—except to two doctors at his table in the cafeteria at lunch. "Stodgy, reliable sorts," he assured Jim later, after we learned what he had done.

Under Jim's solemn questioning, both admitted that they, in turn, had "mentioned it to a couple of other people" with whom they worked closely, "people who definitely could keep a confidence."

Word spread like wildfire among the professional staff and certain, select employees until the hospital was abuzz with embellished gossip that the notorious burglar, Candlesticks, might be one of their own.

Jim and I were at the third floor nurse's station when the revelation came. Charles (Charlie) Denim, R.N., failed to report for his shift on Sunday night, December third.

One of those rare, much-sought-after medical professionals, a male registered nurse, Denim was reputed to be efficient and intelligent. He was described by his co-workers as "nice looking," "tall and slim" with "fair skin," "sandy hair," "a long nose" and "blue, blue eyes."

"He accepts gratuities from his patients," the shift supervisor said with some disdain. "We don't allow that. We are very strict about that kind of thing, you know."

"Denim volunteered for the four P.M. to two A.M. shifts, Sunday through Wednesday," Hospital Administrator Stanley Cook explained. "We were damn glad to have him."

Denim hand-carried his letters of recommendation to his initial interview with Cook. He provided the names, addresses, and phone numbers of prior employers, all of them out of state.

"I've got shifts to fill. We're crying for nurses. I simply haven't gotten around to checking the man's references," Cook said, answering Jim's question about Denim's prior experience. "A capable registered male nurse happens into my office looking for work," the administrator said sarcastically, "like I'm going to turn him down. He was a godsend. And willing to work nights.

He said he needed the extra money we pay people to work that shift. There's no way I'd look a gift horse like that in the mouth."

I pondered the situation. If Denim were our burglar, working nights simplified things for him. Patients and their families gave detailed information he needed about whose houses might be empty. He got off work at the right time to drop by on his way home.

Jim sounded incredulous. "You didn't check his credentials?"

"I talked with a couple of nurses after they'd worked with him. They said he was not only capable, he was great. Hell, the chief of surgery raved about him. Those testimonials were enough for me.

"Besides, a man with Denim's gifts can be allowed a little latitude. I had absolutely no reason to check him out any further."

Not only listening to his words but observing Cook's attitude, I had the distinct impression the administrator would have overlooked past criminal activities, a burglary here and there, to hang onto a prize nurse.

Monday afternoon, curious and prodded, Cook did some follow-up on Denim by telephone. He was crestfallen when he discovered that not one of the four references he checked knew anyone by the name of Charles Denim.

St. Simeon's personnel office had no record of Denim's current address, only the motel he listed as his temporary residence on his application. "He lived here two nights," the motel clerk said, checking registrations. "He paid with cash and left. Didn't leave a forwarding."

The personnel clerk at the hospital could not explain how she failed to update Denim's record when he acquired a permanent residence. Nor had she gotten a telephone number for him. And they hadn't yet provided him a beeper.

Although he listed his age as thirty-one, Denim had a recently issued social security number.

"What does that mean?" I asked Jim, totally puzzled.

"It probably means that Charles Denim is not his original name, that he's assumed a new identity." Jim seemed preoccupied, poring over statements from Denim's co-workers that Cook provided.

Denim had no vehicle, required no parking permit, and had no license tag to trace. Co-workers said he rode the bus to work.

Mallory checked bus routes. "All of the homes burglarized were along metropolitan routes," he reported with a cough. "Two of them were on the same route. You think this bird rode the bus to and from the burglaries?" He rocked back and began laughing.

Jim smiled indulgently, but had me pinpoint the pertinent routes on the city map on which we had placed the thumbtacks marking the locations of the burglaries. Jim hoped to plot to a common destination.

"I'm afraid this isn't going to tell us anything," he said finally. "I thought it was worth a shot."

Still admiring the culprit's audacity, Mallory said, "Damn, this joker is full of surprises."

When Jim glowered, Mallory shrunk. "Well," he conceded sheepishly, "you've got to admit he has an original thought or two."

When the suspect failed to report for work again on Monday night, Jim said it looked as if he had been tipped to the investigation and was gone.

Continuing our probe, Jim and I interviewed patients who spoke glowingly of "Charlie, the male nurse."

He gave a ten-year-old leukemia victim five coins to start a coin collection. It was the most excited the kid had been about anything, his parents said, since he was diagnosed. Jim asked the youngster to show him the coins. They were rare, all right, described in detail in the burglary report provided by Ben Stone, part of his collection stolen when Ben and Billie Stone spent the night with their son at St. Simeon's.

"Chuckie gave me that cut glass bowl of cedar potpourri," said an elderly female patient who had had no visitors. The bowl was from the Paula Hudson break-in.

With the interviews, my mood deteriorated from quiet to gloomy to angry.

"I feel like we're dealing with Robin Hood," I said as we rode down together on the hospital elevator.

Jim sighed. "Yeah, he looks like a real folk hero. And you know who that makes us when we have to take his gifts back and return them to the rightful owners?"

"The evil Prince John?"

"The bad guys, anyway."

"But we're the good guys."

"Tell that to the kid with leukemia when we have to take back his coins and explain they were loot from a burglary, that his friend and hero is a garden variety thief."

"But we can't destroy his joy. We'll cut the hope right out from under him."

"The kid'll have to surrender the coins. They belong to someone else. Denim had no right to give them away. They're evidence in a criminal investigation."

"That bowl of wood chips is the only remembrance Mrs. Tims has gotten in ten days in the hospital. She lays on her side smiling at it. I don't have the heart to take it away from her."

"You don't have to."

"Good, because I'm not going to."

"Captain O'Brien's claiming credit for busting the case. We'll let him be the heavy."

Somehow, that made me feel better. "I see. He gets the

headlines and the credit, let him take the lumps, too."

Angry at being cast as the villain, O'Brien assigned a team to track Denim's movements, to interview bus drivers, to find where the man lived, where he shopped for groceries, anything. Twenty-two hours later, after an intensive sweep, they located his apartment—modest, partially furnished, vacant and wiped clean of all fingerprints and any trace of its recently departed occupant. A note on his door read: "Day Sleeper."

Charlie Denim was not acquainted with his neighbors. "I never ever got a look at the guy," the man across the hall said. "I didn't know he was here when he was here. I sure didn't know he was gone."

An older woman next door described him as "a well-dressed, pleasant young man, tall and slim with a very nice voice." She'd heard him singing in the shower.

"Of course, I just had cataract surgery on one eye and I'm blind in the other," she added. "I haven't gotten adjusted to the lens yet. I can't really describe him in any detail. His eyes? I'm not sure. Brown, maybe."

At Jim's suggestion, O'Brien sent a lab crew to examine Denim's locker at St. Simeon's. Inside it, they finally turned up fingerprints. The FBI computer matched them with a set belonging to Army Private First Class Carl Donnan, also known as Chester Doyle, from Wringling, Texas. Records showed Donnan/Doyle/Denim's name had been changed when he was adopted.

Although juvenile records were sealed, Jim convinced a law school buddy on the Texas governor's staff to dig up some history to go with the fingerprints. "This is a real can of worms," Jim confided as we sat browsing through files again at the pressroom.

"At least he always kept the same initials," I said. Duke and

Jim were so quiet, I glanced up to find them smiling at each other.

"That's one of the reasons we keep her around," Mallory said.

Jim laughed. "To point out the obvious."

Focused on scanning what paperwork we had, I didn't comment.

What records we could scrounge showed that Charles Denim was born Chester Doyle, in 1977, in Domino, Texas. He was given up for adoption in 1982 when his name was changed to Carl Donnan, Jr. Carl was returned to the state department of human services when his adoptive father died in 1985.

An older sibling, Lloyd (Doyle) Thatcher, was returned to the department the same year. The boys were placed in a foster home together. Less than a month later, they were labeled "disciplinary problems." Their behavior required they be separated.

Chester/Carl/Charles was in three foster homes in two years. A notation in the file read the moves had been requested ". . . following incidents."

"Set bonfire on kitchen floor," in one home (he was nine); "Drove pickup truck through barn wall," in another (at eleven); "Killed family pet," in another (thirteen).

Mallory, Jim, and I, reading the records side by side, looked at each other curiously when we reached that final notation.

I nagged until Jim again called his former classmate in the Texas governor's office. The friend reluctantly provided the name of a preacher whom Chester Doyle, at fourteen, had once designated as the person to be contacted in case of emergency.

Jim called Pastor John Wesley Lincoln in Big Branch, Texas. He introduced Mallory and me, listening on extension phones. After the amenities, Jim asked for more details of the problems

Chester Doyle had experienced while in foster care.

"Chester . . . we called him Carl then," Lincoln recalled slowly, "was fourteen years old and was all boy when I met him, a real ball of fire, just out of one scrape and into another. He was smart—clever, you might say—but ornery. It was his nature. He had a real sense of humor about him. But it was maybe more what you'd call 'dark humor.' I always thought Carl was a lot smarter than he made out."

"Can you give us an example?" Jim asked.

Lincoln paused. "I can give you one example that'll show you exactly how he was.

"Carl was in this foster home out in a rural area. The old man's name was Prophet, Edwin Prophet. Mrs. Prophet was only twenty-eight years old, but Prophet himself was as old as dirt."

Duke and I both smiled at Lincoln's colorful description. Jim allowed an appreciative chuckle. Lincoln hesitated a moment as if encouraging his listeners' enjoyment, then continued.

"Prophet was probably fifty-five or sixty. The old man saw no reason why a boy as stout as Carl should just lay up around the house when there was work to be done. He wanted the boy to help out. That was the main reason he was willing to take a foster kid, to help with chores, and he said so, right out.

"Like I said, the boy kind of had an orneriness about him. He rebelled against the old man's ordering him around."

"Did Mr. Prophet abuse him?" I asked, interrupting, trying to hurry the story a little.

"No, he didn't mess with the kid at all, he just took to beating Miz Prophet when Carl got surly."

I bit my lips to short-circuit my response. Mr. Lincoln hesitated again, maybe to allow us time to absorb the full impact of that disclosure.

"The old man had only one tender spot," Lincoln continued.

"He was foolish about this old hound dog. If he could have learned to treat human beings the way he treated that dog, things would have been peaceable. But he couldn't, I suppose.

"Well, one day things were worse than usual. Carl told me about it later.

"Prophet had Carl out helping him string fence. The boy was reeling barbed wire off a spool and the old man was nailing it to the posts. It was hot and the boy's hands were pretty well cut up and he wanted to stop. The old man said if the boy would work harder, he'd sweat more and the breeze blowing the sweat would cool him. He said the problem was not that the kid was working too hard but that he wasn't working hard enough.

"When Carl had enough, he dropped the spool and walked off, leaving the old man screaming and cursing.

"Following his usual, the old man went ranting and raving into the house and lit into Miz Prophet. Carl hadn't gone far. Hid out, he had to cover his ears to keep from hearing her screams."

"How do you know all this?" I asked, interrupting in spite of my best intentions.

"The boy himself told me.

"When she finally got quiet, the kid went through the barn, picked up an old gun they kept down there for shooting rats, and took off. He told me he'd about decided to kill the old man. He thought about it long and hard. He hated being locked up and he knew if he did a murder, he'd be in a cell for a long time. He didn't doubt he'd be caught.

"Well, he was wandering deep in the woods down by a creek thinking when he run upon the old man's hound, the one Mr. Prophet loved so well.

"That dog took one look at the kid and went to howling. At that point, Carl pretty well had all he could tolerate. Before he thought it over good, he shot the old dog dead.

"Now he knew the old man would find the dog and would see he'd been shot and it would go hard on Miz Prophet. So, the boy decided to skin the dog.

"That done, he field-dressed him like they do deer, gutted him, drained all the blood. Then he got a new idea.

"Carl butchered the dog, made him into chunks of meat."

Getting the picture, I whispered, "Oh, no."

"Then Carl went home," Lincoln continued, "told the old man he was sorry about running off when he was supposed to be helping with the fence, and gave Mr. Prophet the meat as a peace offering. Told him it was deer.

"That night they had 'deer steak' for supper. The boy said he took a lot of pleasure watching Prophet eat that meat, laughed and joked around during that whole meal.

"Mr. Prophet allowed the meat was a little stringy for such a small animal but he ate three portions. The old man saved the scraps for his hound, but the dog never did show up."

There was a long pause.

"When did he tell you that story?" Jim asked, breaking the stunned silence.

"Right after. Told half the county, laughing so hard he could hardly get it told."

"Did Mr. Prophet ever find out what happened to his dog?" I asked.

"Sure he did. I figure Carl planned it that way.

"Prophet called the boy's caseworker and kicked the kid out. The ironic thing was, old man Prophet didn't live long after that. Some say his heart was broke over that dog."

Mallory piped up. "What did he die of?"

"Don't know. He was gone two weeks before his wife told it. She said he just dropped over dead one evening and 'they' had the burying the next morning down in the woods where he was most apt to spend his time. No one questioned it. No one cared much for the old man and it seemed natural enough that his wife and whoever the 'they' was would take care of the rites themselves. The Prophets never were much to trouble folks. Soon after that, Miz Prophet sold the place and left here.

"In fact, I believe that's the last I ever heard of either her or the boy, until today. I've thought about Carl. Of course, he's no boy anymore. Probably close to thirty years old by now. But I remember him."

"Reverend Lincoln," Jim interrupted, "can you give us a description of Carl?"

"Sure. He was a rangy kid, skinny, fair with bright blue eyes. I always hoped he'd grow to fit his nose. He really had a beak on him, that kid did."

"How tall was he?"

"Maybe five-foot-eight or nine, but he was sprouting up like a weed then. I couldn't tell you where he might've topped out."

"Do you have a picture of him?" Jim pressed, "a snapshot or anything?"

"No," Lincoln drawled, as if he were thinking, remembering. "It's possible he might be in a Sunday School group picture from back then, but his attendance was spotty. It's not likely he was there when they made pictures, but it could have happened. When I get some free time, I'll look."

"We'd sure appreciate it, Reverend Lincoln," Jim said, and gave the pastor telephone and fax numbers and addresses both at the pressroom and at his office in Bishop. Obviously Jim intended to pursue the matter after he went home.

For some reason, I shivered, involuntarily. Noticing from the next desk over, Mallory frowned. Jim didn't seem to notice.

Jim thanked Lincoln for his help and then, at the pastor's request, repeated his contact numbers and addresses.

"Glad to be of service," Lincoln said. "If you find Carl, how about telling him to give me a call or drop me a note sometime.

I still think about him every now and again. Of course, if any of you folks ever get down this way, drop in and we can have a real visit."

Jim assured him we would.

After he hung up the phone, Jim walked directly to me. I was just standing there looking at him. He put his arms around my shoulders and pulled me close.

"It's rat-face, isn't it?" I asked, my mouth muffled against Jim's shoulder.

"Could be. But you said he was five-foot-eight or nine, with a beak. The workers and patients at St. Simeon's had him taller and nice looking."

"But they all mentioned that nose, and when you're lying in a hospital bed looking up, everyone probably looks taller than they actually are." I leaned back and gazed up into Jim's marvelous face.

"The description sounds awfully close to me; the age, fair hair, bright eyes, beak. Close."

Recharged by the new information, the three of us attacked the Texas files with new enthusiasm.

Chester/Carl/Charles was institutionalized after authorities caught up with him. He was placed on a mood-altering medication to control his behavior. He ran away from the institution two months later. He was fifteen. Efforts to locate him were unsuccessful, the report finished.

I had a feeling and mumbled out loud. "I wonder how hard they looked for him."

The upside to Charlie Denim's new disappearance was that the burglaries stopped. The downside for me was: (1) O'Brien called a press conference, claimed the culprit's flight was a result of his department's "tenacious diligence," and proclaimed his "successful efforts could be considered a feather in the cap of law enforcement everywhere"; and (2) Jim no longer had a reason to stay.

He left for Dominion on December seventh. He consoled me by reminding me I would be following him in "just a few days." I was scheduled to leave December nineteenth.

Jim's departure, however, signaled a new flurry of attention from Thad Bias.

Mallory teased me about it, remarking that he had not seen the handsome, attentive Detective Bias since Jim's arrival, despite the fact the pressroom had before been the man's regular haunt. I explained, more than once, that O'Brien had sent Thad to some kind of conference.

"What were you thinking, man?" Mallory taunted O'Brien later. "That was a dumb move, shipping Bias off. He might have made the collar on Candlesticks. You should have waited until he had it wrapped up, instead of hogging the limelight before the job was done."

O'Brien looked genuinely puzzled at the charge. "Lieutenant Bias took three days' leave. I thought it was odd, an eager beaver like him asking for time off in the middle of an investigation, but I figured he knew what he was doing. I thought maybe he was following some lead."

Disappointed at not getting under O'Brien's skin, Mallory thought no more about it. He didn't even mention the exchange to me, until several weeks later.

CHAPTER ELEVEN

"How's it going?" I asked when Thad strolled into the press-room late Thursday afternoon. I'd just gotten back from taking Jim to the airport and was burying myself in busywork to keep from thinking about how much I missed him already.

I just happened to glance up to find Thad gazing down at the top of my head. When he didn't answer, I frowned. He responded with an uneasy smile.

"You still getting married?"

Actually, his mouth was Thad's best feature. I smiled back. I liked Thad, thought he was wholesomely handsome, in spite of the prominent nose, which at times gave his face character. I had never been attracted to tall, slim men. Spidery-looking appendages turned me off. Other than that, Bias was attractive. Those big, innocent blue eyes, the dusting of freckles, the quick smile; he sort of personified the all-American boy. His smile made him look guileless and full of enthusiasm for life. He was smart enough to recognize and use his assets to his best advantage. He knew that insouciant way of his appealed to me. If I wanted him around, however, I must not lead him on or make him think there could be anything romantic between us. Aware of that, I could manage. I began nodding.

"Yep, I'm still in love. Absolutely."

"How about having dinner with me tonight? You can tell me everything you like about this guy."

Little warning bells went off in my head, but I disregarded

them. Alone in my hotel room, I might be headed for a real downer. It would be nice to go somewhere with someone. I could hang out with Mallory or Ivy, of course, but sometimes their jaded views of life and personal relationships got on my nerves. Thad's youth and natural optimism would lift my spirits.

I thought of Jim. Definitely not the jealous type. He wouldn't mind. He would appreciate that Thad was easy for me to talk to. Comfortable. Another look at those big blue eyes behind those pale blond—nearly invisible—lashes, blinking sincerity, and his rakish nose reassuring, I said, "I'd love to. Are you buying?"

His half-smile broadened and I realized he had not breathed as he waited for my response. The little bells sounded again in the far corners of my conscience.

"Sure enough."

"You're hooked, then."

His expression became grave as he peered into my face. "Yes, I'm afraid I am."

I waffled momentarily, but my concern vanished when he revived his broad, teasing grin.

Duke Mallory walked into the pressroom at that moment and announced to the room at large, in a booming voice, "I'm giving Dewhurst a bridal shower. It'll be at ten P.M. Friday night in the basement hallway outside the pressroom."

I heard gasps indicating I was not the only one shocked by his announcement.

"I'll provide the keg," he added, as if more information might be needed.

At her desk beside the doorway where Mallory stood, Ivy Work exploded into raucous laughter. Mallory set venomous eyes on her, but she wasn't to be squelched.

"You are hosting a keg party/bridal shower in the middle of the night in The Hole?"

Duke turned all the way around to face her angrily. "I'm also providing the barbecue."

His statement and his obvious indignation ignited whoops and cheers throughout the room.

"Gifts are required," Mallory shouted over the din, his gruff bellow directed at Ivy, who sat less than ten feet away. "And don't show up with anything cheap." He shook a warning fist at certain individuals.

The laughter continued as Mallory left to issue his verbal invitations and ultimatums throughout the building.

Ivy and I agreed rather loudly that Mallory, the man himself a walking social blunder, was showing surprising sentiment. We thought his idea "very sweet," a term we calculated he would find demeaning but humorous when it circulated back to him, as we were pretty sure it would.

As agreed, Thad picked me up for dinner at the pressroom at five-thirty. I was surprised that he was clean-shaven, had changed shirts, and smelled marvelous.

"Here you are all prettied up and I'm still sporting my usual grit and grime of the day. Did you get all sweet-smelling for me?"

He grinned and nodded and, of all things, blushed.

"When you look and smell this good," I said as we walked to the exit, "you need to be hustling someone who counts."

Thad smiled his winsome smile. The little bells jangled again. His eyes narrowed to slits, but he didn't offer an explanation.

Charlie Denim evaporated from my mind much as he had disappeared into the crowd at the Town Tavern that night; therefore, I was startled to see him again—or his image, at least—reflected in a window among a throng of Christmas shoppers determinedly marching behind us as Thad and I threaded our way through the crowd to The Steakhouse doorway.

The fugitive's beady little eyes met mine in the reflection for a fleeting moment. I don't know why I gasped at the sight of him, but I did.

Thad, his hand at my back guiding me, leaned down. "What's wrong?"

Denim disappeared by the time I turned to point him out. His bright eyes, the narrowness of his face that emphasized his long, protruding nose, burned in my memory.

"A man shoved me the other night." I stood frozen, scanning for the thief in the steady stream of yuletide shoppers. "He matches everyone's description of Charlie Denim. I thought whoever pushed me had stumbled, bumped me by mistake. But the guy stared at me. He was very distinctive-looking. A minute ago I saw him again."

"What?"

"I saw Charlie Denim. At least it's the guy I think is Charlie Denim. I saw his reflection—in the window there." I pointed to the plate-glass store front and shivered.

Bias eased his arm around my shoulders, pulling me to his side. Disregarding the move, I scowled. "I'm just jumpy." Trying to dismiss the dark image of the man and my even darker thoughts, I smiled up into Thad's face.

He gave me a squeeze. "Don't worry. I'll take care of you. I'll take care of you from here on out, if you'll let me." He turned me toward him and lowered his mouth, his eyes half closed.

Alarmed, I twirled out of the circle of his arm. I don't know how he reacted. I didn't look at him. We both covered the awkward moment by acting as if the words or our actions hadn't happened.

Later, while we were eating and I could slip it into the conversation, I asked Thad if he had a girlfriend.

"Yeah." He grinned suggestively. "But she doesn't know it. At least, she didn't before."

I blushed furiously, but Thad only smiled.

I kept the conversation after that to neutral things, like we were brand new acquaintances rather than friends. I called, "Thanks for dinner," gave him a big wave and a smile, and closed the elevator doors while he talked to one of the local reporters who'd grabbed him as we walked into the lobby. It was a perfect out. I didn't want to risk any awkward moments saying good-night at the door to my room.

Late that night, I thought the wind and the water pounding the sea wall were the culprits rousing me from a fretful sleep. My hands were clammy and I awoke with a clear mental picture of the rat-faced Charlie Denim. I shivered with an overall feeling of foreboding.

I looked at the clock. Twelve forty-five. I'd slept just long enough to be refreshed, but it was too early to get up. Unable to get back to sleep, I got up anyway. I wanted to hear Jim's voice, to have him reassure me back to sleep. I hated to disturb him. After all, it was nearly three A.M. in Oklahoma. I wanted to be as thoughtful of him as he always was of me. Finally, I made a conscious decision to be selfish and dialed his number.

After the fifth ring, his machine picked up.

"This is Jim Wills. Leave me a message." I smiled at the sound of his voice, then scowled at the clock.

"It's two forty-seven A.M. there," I said after the beep. "I don't mean to nag, but where are you? I don't really need anything. I just wanted to hear your voice. Even your recorded voice helps. Maybe I'll call back in a little while to hear it again. See you. Bye."

He might be in Dominion with his family, I thought, trying to quell my disappointment or annoyance or whatever anxious feelings his not being there aroused. I didn't dare call his parents' home at that time of night. And what if I did and he wasn't there?

He could even be in Carson's Summit with my family, I rationalized, but he hadn't mentioned plans for a trip to either place.

He might be out drinking with his buddies. That thought annoyed the bejeebers out of me. I could just see him bar hopping at the topless joints, getting hustled by the strippers, maybe even taking one home for a tumble as he faced the death knell of marriage.

"Why do you torment yourself thinking junk like that?" I asked aloud, grimacing as I tossed back the covers and got out of bed again.

My hotel room had no bar or kitchen facilities, but I had improvised. I filled a small electric mug with water and plugged it in, then dug a package of cocoa mix out of the dwindling supply in the bathroom medicine cabinet. I curled into a chair with the hot chocolate and flipped through a news magazine but nothing captured my attention. I glanced at the telephone. If he came in, heard the message, would he think it was too late to call?

Although I was staring at the phone, willing it to ring, the bell startled me nearly out of my skin. Unwinding my legs, I darted to the bedside and picked it up on the second ring.

Before I could say hello, a strange voice crooned, "What are you doing?"

In my mind I tried to make it Jim's voice, but it wasn't. "What?"

"Guess what I'm doing?" There was a playful, singsong lilt to his voice, which sounded somehow distorted.

"Who is this?"

"I'm lying here in the dark, naked and hot, so, so hot, and

I'm thinking of you lying there in your hotel room in the dark . . . hot."

I slammed the phone down.

I had been concentrating on the phone, on Jim, willing him to call. Had I somehow gotten my telecommunicative wires crossed and inadvertently summoned this dark soul?

The shrill peal startled me again. Annoyed and braced this time, I picked up.

"Baby," the singsong voice crooned, "I am burning. Let me touch your . . ."

I dropped the receiver into its cradle. Immediately, it rang again. I lifted and cradled in one motion. I followed the cord to the wall as the phone rang once more. It was an older appliance. There was no jack to unplug. I disconnected again. Then I enjoyed ten minutes of blessed silence.

Then it was a game, the victory to the most resolute. The phone rang at odd intervals eleven more times. Each time I lifted the receiver and replaced it without answering.

At three-forty the siege ended.

Cautiously, I lay back and dozed, jumping and jerking myself awake several times before relaxing enough to settle into real slumber.

I had to struggle up through layers of sleep when the telephone rang again. I was lying on my stomach. I checked the digital numbers on the clock next to me. Seven-fifteen. I picked up the phone, put it to my ear, and shouted, "What?"

"Jance?" It was Jim.

"What?"

"What do you mean 'what'? What's up?"

"Nothing."

"Are you mad?"

"No."

"I suppose you want to know where I was in the wee hours of this morning?"

"I'm not asking for explanations or excuses. Your whereabouts are none of my business."

"Everything about me is your business, sweet thing."

I rolled onto my back to listen.

"I called you back about three-thirty, but your phone was out of order or something. It would ring once, followed by a click and a dial tone. It seems to be fixed this morning." He waited, giving me a turn at the conversation.

"Okay," I hummed quietly, "where were you?"

"Foxworthy and Tinker and I were . . ."

"Out on the town?" I interrupted, scarcely able to contain my own suspicions.

"Actually, we were babysitting a witness."

"So, where are you now?"

"Relieved by the other team. I'm at home. I'm going to get cleaned up and run down to the office for a while."

Trying to relax, I told him about Mallory's impromptu, unorthodox bridal shower.

Jim chuckled. "Hope we get a bunch of loot."

"I doubt there'll be anything cheap, anyway."

"By the way, where were you last night?" He sounded casual but interested.

"Thad Bias took me to dinner."

"Did he make a last-ditch appeal?"

"What are you talking about?"

"Mallory told me the guy's sweet on you. Bias made it a point to avoid me when I was there. I figure he asked you out to take his last shot. How'd you handle it?"

"I handled it." Odd that Jim had anticipated Thad long distance when I hadn't seen it coming close up.

"Didn't drink too much, did you?" he asked. "You get affectionate when you drink. I don't want you getting affectionate when I'm not around to keep you aimed the right direction."

I laughed again but didn't say anything. Thad had encouraged me to have a cocktail before dinner and a Brandy Alexander for dessert. Aware of that "affectionate" thing, I had declined.

"What's the matter?" Jim asked, bringing me back to the present.

I thought about the annoying calls. Of course, they didn't seem nearly so threatening in the light of day. There was no need telling Jim when he was again thirteen hundred miles away. And the caller had probably given up his game long before I stopped hanging up since, obviously, Jim had been on the line some of those times.

"Nothing," I said, having pondered my way to a bottom line.

"Something embarrassing?"

"I said it's nothing. I don't want to talk about it. I stayed up too late. I had nightmares about all kinds of sinister things. I even imagined you were at a bar, drinking and watching strippers when you were actually working."

It was Jim's turn to be silent.

"Well?"

His lack of response roused my suspicions again.

"The witness we're protecting is a stripper," he said finally. "At two forty-five this morning I was drinking a beer and watching the crowd while they were watching her do her final set."

"Is she old or young?"

"Twenty-two, but she looks forty-five. She's got a lot of mileage on her."

"Is she a good dancer?"

"Gives all the guys chills and fever."

"How about you?"

"I wasn't watching her. My eyes were on the crowd. That's my job. Besides, I'm more tantalized by mental images of you peeling out of your clothes. Jancy, you don't harbor any illusions that my current chaste behavior will extend beyond our wedding ceremony, do you?"

I laughed, but I wasn't to be so easily deterred. "Does this stripper have a crush on you?"

"Yeah," he said modestly, but a self-conscious laugh gave him away. "It's part of the job. Women always get crushes on guys protecting them. It's one of the perks. They pretend the protection reflects a personal interest. They don't let themselves think that for us it's a job."

"I don't recall an Agent Tinker. Is he new?"

"He's a she, but yeah, she's new."

"Is she attractive?"

Jim laughed out loud. "What's with you today, anyway?"

"Is she attractive?" I repeated.

"In a martial arts way, yeah. She's a lifter, has nice biceps, great legs, a flat, muscular chest, and absolutely no sense of humor. She's smart. As an agent, I like her watching my back. As a man, I have no interest in getting her on her back."

"How do you know about her chest?"

He laughed again. "Don't miss much, do you? I picked her up after a competition. I got there before they finished. She won third. She was still in her competition clothes, kind of a bikini deal, shows a lot of muscle."

"And skin?"

"Skin that tight all tanned and oiled up looks like leather. It doesn't do anything for me. Besides, the oil makes her smell funny. It's just not my bag, I guess."

"You lift."

"I run and lift to stay in shape and to flex a little for you, not for an audience. These people, even the women, make me look like a wimp."

"I'd like to see the woman—or man, either—who'd make you look like a wimp."

"You don't need to be browsing. You are committed, sweet-heart."

"I'm not the one hanging out in strip joints."

He raised his voice in a mock threat. "And see that it stays that way."

CHAPTER TWELVE

Along with its other unusual aspects, my bridal shower was to begin at ten P.M., an odd hour for a prenuptial event for a bride.

Ivy invited me to have dinner and "a little girl talk" after work, five hours before the shower. Ivy also invited several other women in the building, all of whom planned to attend the shower later. The women's ages ranged from mine—twenty-four—to Naomi Tolliver's seventy-plus.

"The girls" were excited through dinner, anticipating "a little surprise" they had planned, an appropriate ending to "a real bachelorette party," they crowed. They insisted the surprise required that I have a drink with dinner. They were unanimous, so I complied.

"Bods" was renowned for its exotic male dancers. As the caravan of women pulled into Bods' parking lot, I began objecting, but to no avail.

Inside was pure bedlam as the audience of women squealed and hooted, watching a performer bumping and grinding his way around the stage. The audience howled approval as the dancer removed another essential garment.

I kept my eyes riveted on the floor as our group was ushered to a private area reserved for parties of ten or more located adjacent to the run, an extension of the stage that brought the elevated ramp out into the audience. The place was packed with women of all ages, yelling and waving dollar bills folded length-wise.

I was too embarrassed to look directly at the dancer on stage; however, as our group wound its way through the tables, I glanced at the onlookers crowding the ramp.

As the dancer neared the edge, hands holding the folded dollar bills flapped him closer to stuff bills into the waistband of the narrow red bikini scantly concealing his apparently oversized penis. He gathered the collected dollar bills with one hand, then flipped a closure and the bikini fell away, leaving him pulsating in a G-string. The move prompted a clamorous shriek of approval.

I shrunk onto a booth seat in the corner fronted by a low coffee table, as far from the ramp as possible. The music stopped, the dancer ground to a halt, and the crowd cheered wildly. The women at stage side whooped and waved their money even more frantically to get his attention.

Secluded in the darkened corner, I risked a quick peek at him.

The dancer was handsome and very muscular for a fellow as short as he was. He had a cherubic face, flashing dimples, and white, even teeth. A hardhat, a pair of work boots, and the G-string were all that was left of his original costume.

"Do not touch the entertainers!" a voice boomed over the sound system as the dancer swung himself to the edge of the ramp, knelt, and reached out to caress the face of one of his admirers who couldn't stuff money into the G-string fast enough. He gleaned the last of her currency.

"Isn't he a cute little rascal?" Ivy asked, settling onto the booth's bench seat beside me.

"The audience isn't supposed to touch the dancers, but the dancers can fondle the audience?" I asked, my mouth gaping. The young man kissed some of the women, their faces and their mouths. He caressed or whispered to others, all the time allowing them to slide dozens of dollar bills into his string.

Ivy cackled. "They don't seem to mind."

"Do you enjoy this?" I twisted so I could see my companion.

She laughed lightly. "I have a son older than he is. I just think he's cute. Don't you?"

I shook my head, signaling an uncertain no.

Hardhat left the stage as the raucous music began again for "Grady the Graduate," the next dancer, who appeared in a billowing, black graduation robe and a mortar board. As he began to peel out of his costume, hysteria again consumed the crowd. He was taller and slimmer with dark chest hair, which turned the spectators' excitement up a notch.

A smiling waiter arrived to take our orders. He was topless except for a white collar and red bow tie at his throat and white shirt cuffs at his wrists. His lower half was concealed by black trousers, cut tantalizingly low. Ivy ordered us both sloe gin fizzes. The ladies in our group gradually left ramp side and gathered around our coffee table, where they stole quick, curious glances at me and spoke in excited whispers to each other.

When Grady had revealed all that the law allowed, he was followed by "Bronco Billy," obviously a favorite, with six-guns and temporarily in Western garb.

"Doctor Dick" followed Billy as I began sipping a second drink and relaxing, enjoying the show a little more than I had.

But Doctor Dick didn't leave when he was through. Instead, he leaped from the stage and wound his way through the audience, picking up folded dollar bills and brief gropes with each step.

"The girls bought you a table dance," Ivy whispered. "They thought Dick was your type." I cringed but was mesmerized as the entertainer swam through the audience and then leaped to the coffee table immediately in front of me. A new dancer was on the ramp stage, but Doctor Dick fixed his eyes on my face as he gyrated so close that I had to sit very straight not to impede his movement.

I was perspiring and relieved when the music stopped, then horrified that the practically nude stranger knelt on the table to talk. He stroked his hard stomach with his open hand, then eased that hand beneath the G-string. The females in my group wisecracked, goading him with their glib comments.

"I'll let you see my packet, if you want to." His face was very close to mine. "We have private rooms in the back," he gestured toward the bar behind us, "for viewing the goods. It's usually a hundred bucks, but you're so pretty, I'll take you back there for seventy-five. What do you say?"

Too stunned to speak, I shook my head.

"I use the money for a good thing," he said. "I'm going to medical school, you know, that's why they call me that. I need the money for . . . you know."

"Tuition?" I risked a look at his face.

His eyes rounded. "Yeah. That's right. Tuition. Do you go to medical school?"

I smiled as I shook my head, but I was curious. "What courses are you taking? Anatomy?"

"What?"

"Are you taking anatomy? You know, the study of the human body."

Again he brightened. "Oh, yeah, we take that every day in the school I go to. How old are you, anyway?"

"Twenty-four. How old are you?"

"I'm supposed to tell the customers I'm twenty-nine, but I'm really twenty-two."

"Why are you supposed to say you're twenty-nine?"

He shrugged. "I don't know. I guess twenty-nine is sexier than twenty-two."

"You're not really in medical school, are you?"

He studied me a long moment, adjusting his G-string, exciting the onlookers. "Not really. Not yet, anyway, but I will be, as soon as I get twenty thousand dollars in the bank. I'm going to go to college then, and after I graduate there, I'm going to enroll in medical school. I heard you have to finish regular college before you can get into medical school." He frowned. "Do you know if that's right or not?"

"Yes, I've heard that's the way you do it."

"So, do you want to see what I'm packing in my pouch?"

"Not this time, but thanks for asking."

He looked sorrowful for a minute, then brightened. "But you'll be back?"

"Sure. Maybe next time I'll have more money."

He leaned closer and dropped his voice to a whisper. "I can take a post-dated check. I'd do it for you, for sure."

"That's very nice of you, but I'd probably better wait. Thanks anyway."

He smiled and leaned even closer. I turned my head just as his lips reached my face. He kissed me on the cheek, then leaped to his feet and did a bump and grind back through the howling mob, gathering dollar bills as he went, stretching the G-string, taunting the bolder women. I slumped against the seat, swigged my drink, and drew a deep breath. "Good grief!" I said to no one in particular, then I began laughing out loud for no explainable reason.

Half an hour later, having arrived only a few minutes after ten, I stood in the basement hallway of the former post office building unknowingly sipping spiked punch at my bridal shower.

The drink was fruity, innocuous, laced with gin, and intoxicating. I didn't recognize its subtlety until I began giggling, enjoying every quip and wisecrack a little too much.

Nearly one hundred people showed up, some I didn't know but who were familiar with Mallory's penchant for raucous entertaining and crashed the event, welcomed to the festivities as long as they arrived carrying the required gift.

Music produced by an unexpectedly able combo reverberated through the hallways, echoing along the upstairs chambers as well. Voices grew loud in an effort to be heard over the din. One of the news photographers milled around the room catching candid shots.

Mallory apparently noticed my inebriation as the alcohol took effect.

Thad Bias noticed too.

Thad, who arrived unheralded, stood back smiling and watching. He never took his eyes off me. I was glad to see him gradually work his way toward where I was standing. He was nearly there when Mallory heard about our trip to Bods and turned to announce it over the microphone. A roar went up. Clusters of men elbowed Thad out of the way and moved in to give me a hard time.

"Will that make Wills mad, you going to that guy strip joint?" Bruce Edison, my pipe-smoking co-worker, asked quietly when the ruckus had died down and Thad was again advancing.

"No, he won't care."

"I don't know why you'd want to look at those guys," Edison persisted. "Not any of them could be built as good as he is."

Embarrassed, I smiled and nodded mute agreement. But Edison was on a roll.

"He must have seventeen-, eighteen-inch guns. Biceps, you know."

I nodded again.

"If he ever hits you . . ."

Eavesdropping, Thad's expression turned stormy at the suggestion.

"He won't," I assured Edison. Catching a glimpse of Thad's face, I smiled to show I intended the words to allay his concern, too.

Edison raised his eyebrows. "I don't know, Jancy, you make people really mad sometimes. Even a mild guy like me's gotten madder at you than I've ever gotten at anyone else, outside my own family."

"Bruce, you haven't hit me yet."

Bias was watching us as if he were a spectator at a tennis match.

"Yes, but he might not have my awesome self-control."

I smiled secretively. "He's been pushed farther than you have and he's displayed exemplary control. Believe me."

Unconvinced but yielding the point, Edison changed subjects and targets, turning to Thad to ask about progress in tracking the elusive Candlesticks burglar.

Having escaped Edison's attention, I wandered back toward the punch bowl, leaving Thad to extricate himself from Bruce's clutches.

Thad looked as if he were only half listening to Edison's theories on the burglaries as he watched me sip a fresh cup of punch and move about the room. I stopped first at one group, then another, welcomed everywhere. I seemed to be very popular and unusually entertaining. Thad didn't butt into my conversations with people, nor did he interfere with my trips to the punch bowl.

Mallory didn't either. Instead, he frequently refilled my cup with the delicious, cooling punch. Eventually, Mallory led me to a chair and ordered me to start opening gifts. Ivy sat beside me, where she took up a pen and paper to record the gifts and the givers.

There were the usual—towels, utensils, small appliances, cookbooks, etc.—all of which drew derogatory comments and speculation about my lack of skills in the various areas. Some of the remarks were obscene, most of them hilarious. When there was only one gift remaining, Mallory ordered a drum roll, then asked the musicians to be silent.

"Jancy has been like a . . . ah . . . a sister to me," he began, his chin quivering a little, the corners of his mouth drooping. "One I liked."

The crowd roared its approval.

"Give that man a drink," someone shouted.

"Believe I will." Mallory staggered to the keg, placed his mouth beneath the spigot, and guzzled a healthy swallow, drawing another roar of approval. He rambled back to the podium to continue.

"This fellow Jancy is going to marry next Saturday night—a week from tomorrow, sweetie, unless you come to your senses or he comes to his." He paused.

I looked at him, giggled, and shook my head, denying such a possibility.

"Well," Mallory continued, "he's a good guy—good enough, anyway, for most women. Actually, too good for most of the women here."

He paused, a little taken aback by the high-pitched boos his statement precipitated. "We all know that's a fact," he defended. The boos and catcalls increased in number and volume.

"Get the hook," one woman yelled loudly above the booing.

Mallory twisted his face to express his chagrin.

"Anyway," he continued, shouting over the noise, "the only real thing I have against old Jim is that he wants Jancy all to himself."

This time men booed, interrupting the speaker.

"My sentiments exactly. Anyway, Ivy and I got the kid a token of our esteem and you all know me, I don't have that much esteem for people, generally speaking."

That statement drew a mixed chorus of boos.

"Cut that out, now. I bought the beer."

Cheers all around.

He nodded approval, then motioned for me to open the last remaining gift. I obeyed, blushing brightly as I fumbled with the wrapping. Finally, I lifted a red teddy from the tissue paper.

"Jancy, some of the guys only came here tonight because I told 'em you'd model that thing for us."

The men cheered and hooted, daring me. Mortified, I shook my head, scanning the room for a friendly face, then smiled as I found and tried to focus on Thad.

"Not a chance." I shook my head more emphatically and I guess it looked like I was talking to Thad. He returned my smile as I held the lingerie in front of my face. I could still see Thad and the other onlookers through the fabric. "There's not enough material."

Ivy's voice rang out. "They wear like iron, honey. It's actually only a neck warmer, for the most part."

The crowd roared its approval and I felt my blush brighten. I risked looking up only a couple of times, and both times my eyes met Thad's. Meanwhile, Ivy continued.

"The deal is, you usually don't have them on that long when you do wear them."

The onlookers applauded and roared again as the combo started its last set.

The punch ran out at midnight.

The combo quit at twelve-thirty.

The keg was sputtering by one.

As the crowd diminished, Thad walked over to talk to me for the first time all night. Laughing at nothing, he casually put his arm around me. Returning his smile, I allowed myself to be gathered closely and leaned against him. The roving photographer snapped our picture. I saw Ivy shoot Thad a warning look.

He saw the look but ignored it as he turned his full attention on me. I gave him a winsome smile just as the photog took another shot.

The last guests left the shower at two A.M.

Staggering, Mallory announced he would see me home. Thad and Ivy both objected at the same time.

"I'll take Jancy back to her hotel," Thad said casually, but his offer seemed to offend Ivy and Mallory, too, because they both objected loudly. I was getting sensitive to loud noises by then.

Thad insisted. "It's on my way and I can help her carry all this stuff up to her room."

"Mallory lives out my way," Ivy said, thinking out loud and acquiescing a little. "We can load gifts in both wire service cars and leave them in the parking lot. When Jancy and Mallory are in better shape—tomorrow—they can transport the rest."

"Sounds good to me." Thad immediately began gathering packages.

We carried the larger, more cumbersome gifts to the pressroom to store until later, then the four of us loaded all the presents we could manage into boxes and shopping bags with handles and made several trips to and from the parking lot.

Mallory complained about having "to do all this work" when he was so tired. I was in a stupor and moved obediently but dumbly on Ivy and Thad's commands.

Finally, when the trunks of all three cars, Thad's and the two wire service vehicles, were loaded, Thad gently guided me outside and put me into his tiny sports car. His face was set with uncharacteristic determination as he closed the passenger door.

But before the young detective could get around the car to the driver's side, Mallory appeared, reopened my door, shoved me forward, and clambered into the car's token back seat. Ivy Work scurried out the basement door of the building scanning the parking lot for her errant charge. Wedged inside, Mallory refused to get out of Thad's car, despite Ivy's urging.

Bias appeased them both finally. "I can run Mallory out to his place and deliver Jancy too. I don't mind. Really."

When Ivy's eyes met Mallory's through the car window, she smiled knowingly and nodded her agreement.

Thad pulled onto the street and turned toward the freeway to Mallory's place.

"I'm not going home," Mallory declared loudly. "I'm staying at the Chestnut tonight."

I turned all the way around to glare at him.

"Not with you. They know me. They'll find me a bed . . . charge it to the wire service. It's a hell of a lot closer."

I shrugged and nodded. The tires squealed as Thad spun the car into a U-turn. Staring straight ahead, he was silent as he drove to the hotel.

At the Chestnut, Mallory balked again.

"I don't want to carry all this crap upstairs tonight. We can get a bellhop to do it in the morning."

"Just one load," I coaxed. "You're going up anyway. You might as well carry a couple of things. Thad doesn't want to drive around all night with all this stuff in his car."

Sulking, Mallory planted his feet and allowed me to loop the handles of shopping bags full of gifts over both his arms. I gave him a firm shove in the right direction, then I scooped up all I could carry, but I wasn't very steady on my feet either.

More willing than Mallory, and insistent, over my token objections, Thad stacked several boxes and juggled several sacks as he trailed Mallory and me inside.

The desk clerk said he had a room available on nine, two doors down the hall from mine. Mallory said he'd take it.

On the elevator Mallory complained that his stomach was uneasy.

We stopped first at my room to unload the things we were carrying.

Free from the confines of the elevator and the burden of the packages, Mallory lurched and ran to my bathroom. He began vomiting before he reached the toilet.

Trying to ignore the sounds coming from the bathroom, I helped relieve Thad of his armload of boxes and bags. I was feeling a little queasy myself.

When I put the last stack of packages on the dresser, I turned around to find Thad standing at my elbow.

"How about if I hang around a while?" he said, all wide-eyed innocence.

"You'd probably better not."

"Why not? I can help you get Duke to his room. Jancy, this may be our last night together. Let's make it count."

My eyes didn't focus. "Thad, I'm taken. There are lots of other fish in the sea."

He stared into my face. "But I want you. And you want me too. You just won't admit it."

Wavering slightly, I looked at the floor to give myself a moment.

"I do like you," I admitted finally, without looking up. "You're a wonderful friend. I would have been lost without you the last couple of months."

Thad winced. "You have that bunch of old people in the pressroom for 'friends.' " His voice had a hard edge to it. "I thought I was more than that. I saw the way you looked for me tonight, the way you looked when you found me."

I again tried to focus. I felt dizzy. I thought hard for a moment and then spoke quietly, soothingly. "No. You're my friend, just like the people in the pressroom. No more and no less."

His expression deteriorated as he grabbed my upper arms.

He held me tightly then slowly stepped forward and pressed our bodies together. His face reflected cold determination as he lowered his mouth. I turned my head just before he made contact. His lips felt hot and determined against my cheek.

Thad recovered quickly enough to kiss my face. He moved his lips over my jaw line to my neck, which is especially sensitive. I didn't intend to cooperate but his lips were there, searching . . . wanting. His passion flattered and, I have to admit, aroused me. Warming to him, I rose onto my tiptoes.

Then his arms wrapped around me, those long snaky arms, snaring and entangling. He reminded me of a spider spinning a web. Suddenly panicking, I pushed him away and struggled to put some space between us. Thad released me but his face was an odd combination of anger, confusion, and apology.

Confronted with what must have looked like revulsion, he said, "All right. If that's the way you want it." He dropped his arms to his sides. "I know you don't hate me. You can't hate me." He looked genuinely concerned.

Shamefacedly, I shook my head, but I didn't dare try to explain. I just wasn't up to it. "Thanks for the lift."

I mumbled more, a mix of appreciation and apology, as I walked toward the door to the hallway, which had been left ajar.

Bias followed, looking sad. I thrust the door open wide. He stepped through and into the hall. He turned around and started to say something, but I was too tired to hear it, so I pushed the door. It swung quietly closed in his face.

Mallory hung over the side of the toilet, reduced to dry heaves. I helped him up and guided him to the bed. I propped all four pillows behind him, put a cool towel on his head, and grabbed my nightgown and toothbrush.

I took both keys, slipped out of the room, and snapped off

the light as I headed down the hall to the room assigned to Mallory for the night.

After the sleep interruptions of the preceding night, the booze, Thad's peculiar behavior, and the lateness of the hour—it was after three A.M.—I took a hot bath, then dropped into bed and slept soundly. The room was different, but the bed was familiar, as were the hotel's sounds and smells.

Mallory called and woke me up at ten. My head throbbed. It was worse when I opened my eyes and worse yet when I moved.

He apologized for the mess in my bathroom. He had called housekeeping. Would I like to meet him in the coffee shop for breakfast?

I said, "Sure."

I dressed in my clothes from the day before, stuffed my nightie and toothbrush in my purse, and went downstairs.

Mallory stoically accepted his anticipated headache but complained loudly about the several late-night phone calls he was forced to ignore. He refused to answer my telephone and finally stuffed it under a pillow in the night table drawer. He insisted it rang all night long.

Driving from the Chestnut to the office on Monday before I was scheduled to leave on Tuesday, I watched in horror as the elusive Charlie Denim peered down from the window of a city bus that lumbered through an intersection right in front of me.

I craned my neck and rolled down my window, desperately signaling to change lanes, but traffic was heavy and cars behind me honked when I attempted to wait for oncoming traffic in the next lane to clear. I made a U-turn in the next block and gunned the car to the next thoroughfare where a dozen city buses vied for position in the rush hour confusion.

Mallory was at the office, standing at his desk, when I arrived, his presence at eight-thirty in the morning a precedent in itself.

"What are you doing out so early?" I felt washed with relief as I approached our workstation, eager to tell him about catching another glimpse of Candlesticks. I held out my car keys—the ones to the wire service courtesy car—and started to speak, but the look on his face silenced me.

"Don't tell me you're going to miss me," I said.

Mallory looked old and craggy. "Paula Hudson was found dead in her apartment this morning."

"Oh." My stomach plummeted and I had to remind myself to exhale. I stared at the surface of my aged desk, remembering gentle little Mrs. Hudson. Mallory waited, as if allowing me time to digest the information. In a minute, I glanced up, giving him mute permission to relate more.

"She was locked in her apartment," he offered. "A neighbor got concerned that he hadn't seen her in a couple of days. Alerted the manager. They couldn't rouse her pounding on the door and she didn't answer the phone. They went in. She was in bed, in her nightgown. Everything looked kosher. She'd been dead quite a while. They called an ambulance.

"Everyone assumed it was natural, but I called O'Brien and turned the screws. He's ordered an autopsy. It's probably just housekeeping, but I have a weird feeling. They're supposed to run an autopsy anyway when there's an unattended death like that—no medical people around."

He started to say more, then apparently changed his mind. He studied me for another moment, then dropped heavily into his chair and swiveled to his desk.

I swung my purse into its usual spot on the floor beside my desk and eased into my chair.

Chapter Thirteen

Jim was in the terminal with my family when my plane landed in Dominion early Tuesday afternoon. He looked wonderful in jeans, a sport shirt, blazer, loafers, and an overcoat.

Mom and Dad stepped up and hugged me tightly, not surprising as I had been away from them for a record two months, before they deferred to Jim and stood back to watch as he gathered me, giggling, into his arms. My brothers both patted my shoulder and the top of my head, which I appreciated, knowing how self-conscious they felt about showing affection to their big sister in public.

There was a carnival atmosphere as the six of us collected suitcases and ambled through the building. Mother and I exchanged and reiterated wedding updates. Jim and Dad juggled the large pieces of luggage and joked about how they were going to fit it all into only two vehicles.

I was nearly driven backward as I stepped up to push open the outside door.

I had left California in a calm, sixty-two-degree overcast. Outside the glass door I was seared by the nearly forgotten bite of an Oklahoma trademark: winter's relentless north wind. Catching my breath, I clutched my sweater, trying to wrap it more tightly. I held the door as the party passed through, then danced little jigs for warmth as I trailed them to the cars. There, Jim noticed my lack of appropriate clothing. Gallantly, he removed his overcoat and draped it around my shoulders, snugging it at my throat.

At Mom's insistence, I rode with Jim the twenty-seven miles to his condo in Bishop. I had shipped four cartons of belongings and wedding gifts to his place from California, plus, I was eager to see which of my things Jim and my parents had already brought from Carson's Summit and how they fit into Jim's motif.

Shivering involuntarily, I nestled close to Jim's warmth and chattered. His arm around me, he listened, tossing out an occasional question, probably assurance he was paying attention.

I relished telling him every unusual detail of the night of my "bachelorette party" and shower. He laughed in all the right places.

Before describing Doctor Dick, I patted Jim's very solid biceps, their prominence obvious even beneath the blazer. I passed along Bruce Edison's observation, then proceeded to describe to Jim the self-proclaimed medic.

Studying Jim's profile, my conversation gradually ebbed until I finally became silent. I just sat there admiring the shape of his head, his dark watchful eyes, his straight nose, his thick neck well seated between powerful shoulders, his arms, the thickness of his hands, the chest hair taunting above the open neck of his shirt.

He glanced at me and smiled, his teeth even and very white. I smiled back.

"Don't look at me," I whispered. "I can hardly keep my hands off of you as it is."

"Why fight it? Go ahead. Touch me. Anytime. Anywhere."

I slid one arm around his shoulders and let my other hand trace up and down the placket of his shirt. We were in congested traffic, stopping and starting at the whim of the traffic lights.

Stopped for the moment, Jim caught my wandering hand, rubbed it slowly, sensuously over his chest, then guided it down across his stomach and stopped at his belt buckle where he allowed a pregnant pause. His hand remained atop mine as I began easing mine downward again. He caught my hand firmly and held. I looked at his face. He was studying me somberly.

"Be careful what you ask for," he cautioned as if he were speaking to a naughty child.

The traffic light changed and the cars in front of us moved. Jim drove but his dark eyes remained on me. I attempted to continue my exploration, but Jim's hand, still locked around mine, prevented it.

"You said anywhere." I felt a sulk coming on.

"Your mom and dad are right behind us."

"They can't see anything." I pressed my nose to his shoulder. He released my hand as I released my seat belt and shifted onto my knees to kiss his cheek and neck.

When we stopped for the next light, he grabbed my upper arms and pulled, trapping me between his body and the steering wheel. The overcoat slipped off my shoulders. He kissed me voraciously, his tongue exploring the hollows of my mouth as his hands just as eagerly swept over my back, under the coat, slowing as they outlined the curve of my hips.

Smushed so tightly I could scarcely breathe, I couldn't tell if my lightheadedness stemmed from the close accommodations or the passion he so easily generated.

The light changed. The car behind us honked three times in rapid succession.

I pulled back, settling into the seat beside Jim. He looked in the rearview mirror, then grinned and waved. I turned to see the laughing faces of my mom and dad through the windshield of the car behind us. They were the impatient motorists.

"Very funny," I muttered, but my face felt flushed and my heartbeat and breathing were rapid.

"Jim?" I pressed my face against his shoulder. "I don't think I can wait."

He grinned straight ahead. "Good."

"It's only four more days."

"Three more nights."

"We've waited this long."

"Okay." He slanted me a sly look. "We wait."

"Can you wait three more nights?" I regarded him seriously.

Again gazing straight ahead, he smiled a long moment before he began nodding, slowly. "I can, but we need to be careful not to put ourselves in any compromising situations. According to you, the thought is mother to the deed, and I think about it all the time."

"It? Sex? With me?"

"Yes." He spoke the single word emphatically.

"All the time?"

"Yes."

"What should we do?"

"We probably ought to get married. Don't invite anyone on the honeymoon." He flashed me a serious look before we both began laughing.

"I'll be careful not to. Where are we going?"

"Not far."

"Will we be back for Christmas?"

"Yes, but then we'll have another week away by ourselves after. We'll have the twenty-second and twenty-third alone, then go to Carson's Summit to your folks' house on Christmas Eve, in time for mass. We'll spend the night there. After we open presents and have a leisurely breakfast Christmas morning, we'll drive to Dominion to see my family, then on to Bishop. My plan is to spend Christmas night at our place, alone."

I smiled at the prospect. "Our place" had a nice ring to it.

"Tuesday morning we catch a flight for Colorado," he said,

continuing to spell out our itinerary.

"Our place," I repeated. He smiled but kept his eyes straight ahead.

"We'll have to get used to sharing things," he said quietly.

Concern flitted through my mind before I realized what he'd said earlier. "Colorado?" I sat straighter, filled with a burst of new exuberance. "Are we going skiing?"

He grinned. "Among other things."

"YES!"

He tapped an index finger on his lips. "But it's a secret. A lot of people might want to come along if they knew. We don't want a crowd." He gave me a meaningful look and shook his head, his eyes wide.

I threw myself against him, hugging his neck, almost choking him, making him veer right. "Jim, keep your eyes on the road."

"Are you going to start nagging already? We're not even married yet."

"Practice makes perfect, my dear."

"Whoa. What am I getting myself into?"

"I'm afraid it's too late, big boy. You are hooked."

"Yes I am," he said and the tone of his voice reminded me oddly of Thad Bias. The fleeting thought of Thad seemed sinister, unwelcome, and made me shiver.

Fierce activities occupied the balance of my first day back.

We unloaded and put away gifts, discussing possible changes—like moving some of his furniture to make room for some of mine—and politely welcoming and considering input from my parents. Neither of my brothers had much to say except to pronounce Jim's pad "cool."

"I can't wait to live here," I whispered into Jim's ear as he pointed out all the available shelving in kitchen cabinets, space this bachelor had never needed. I put in shelf paper he had purchased but never installed, and mentally designated areas for various dishes and glassware.

Late in the evening, Jim and I said good-bye. I hated leaving him . . . again.

Since I no longer owned a car of my own and the wedding was only three days away, I was to ride with my family to Carson's Summit. Once there, however, my old room no longer felt like home, which was ridiculous. I'd grown up in that house . . . in that bedroom.

Even before I was out of bed Wednesday morning, I felt restless being there. The wedding was planned and everything efficiently arranged. Mom, of course, still had last-minute errands, but I was afraid to go along, thinking I might put in an unwelcome opinion and ruin things.

Greg and Tim were still in classes at the university for another two days. Dad went down to the insurance agency, as usual. Wedding guests would not begin arriving until Thursday. Over and over again I wished I'd stayed in Bishop. At least there I could have seen Jim some and spent my free time puttering around the condo. In Carson's Summit, I felt completely useless.

Christmas decorations and most of the holiday cooking had been done well ahead to free the household for the wedding. I decided to make a batch of divinity, then grew impatient beating it, gave up, and dumped the whole bowl. I would've liked to hang on the telephone with Jim, but I didn't want to pester him, knowing he was trying to finish up at the office before his extended leave.

Mom came in with wedding gifts she'd picked up at the jewelry store where we were registered. I opened those, then developed a bad case of the nervous fidgets trying to arrange and rearrange gift display tables set up in the living room.

Delivery people and family friends made quick calls, but

most of them had last-minute Christmas preparations and no time for prolonged visits.

The fabric tulips for the rice, the ring bearer's pillow, and the flower girl's basket had been worked and reworked. As far as I could tell, everything was ready. It was just a matter of breathing in and out until the appointed time.

Rosie Clemente and Liz Pinello, friends and former housemates promoted to maid of honor and bridesmaid, would arrive Thursday, in time for the rehearsal. Keeping to his work schedule, Jim would arrive late Thursday as well.

I wrote thank-you notes for gifts received and tried to get interested in something on TV, but couldn't. As a last resort, I paced and fretted.

Therefore, when Paul Wills, Jim's older brother and best man, called from Dominion and offered to drive up and take me to lunch, I accepted eagerly. Mom was at the church helping with the children's pageant, something she'd done since her own children were small enough to participate.

Paul arrived early, at eleven-fifteen. I answered the doorbell with a hot curling iron in my hand and curls bouncing around my head.

"You're early, you bum." I laughed as I pushed open the storm door to let him in. "I'll just be another minute or maybe ten. You can mill around. Admire the wedding presents in the living room or go in the den and turn on the tube, if you want to."

He just stood there like a lump. I looked him up and down, wondering what he was thinking. I was always surprised by how much Paul resembled Jim. People, even people who had known them a long time, often called one by the other's name.

Paul was as tall as Jim with the same dark hair and eyes and olive skin, but Paul was not nearly as muscular, his bone structure finer, more delicate. Personality-wise, I saw little similarity between them. Two years older than Jim, Paul had hustled me early on. I suspected it was a competitive thing, a fraternal desire to one-up his brother.

Paul was open about his alleged admiration, and eventually turned up in California on a business venture that kept him there several weeks. He had even lived in the Chestnut Hotel, his room two floors above mine. Missing Jim, I had enjoyed Paul's company but was careful to keep him at arm's length. Besides, I preferred hanging out with Thad.

Returning to the living room a few minutes later, I watched him examine the wedding gifts and couldn't help smiling. Paul's dark eyes were familiar as they regarded me from under equally familiar black brows. He wore his dark hair longer, combed back. Jim's was cut close, so short it barely laid down on top. Both Paul and Jim were just over six feet and sturdier than their younger brothers, Peter and Andrew, who were taller and fairer. Jim was much more muscular than his brothers. He said the bureau insisted agents stay in shape, but I noticed none of Jim's co-workers took the requirement as seriously as he did.

"I am glad you called," I said as Paul and I settled at a table in the restaurant and began scanning menus.

"I wanted to talk to you." Paul's tone and face were solemn.

"You sound serious." I studied his face, wondering what that stark stare was about.

"It is serious."

"What?"

"Let's order first."

Following my conscience, I ordered the chef's salad.

"You need more food than that."

"I'd like to fit in my trousseau."

Frowning at the waitress, he ordered chicken fried steak with cream gravy and fries, with ranch dressing on his salad.

"Best thing on the menu," I said, attempting to compliment

him as the waitress left. "Will you give me bites?"

"No. You should have ordered what you wanted, like I did."

I laughed a little derisively and nodded. "Okay, so what's this big, serious subject we're going to tackle?"

"I think your marrying Jim is a mistake."

I winced playfully. I thought he was joking, but he maintained his concerned expression.

"Well, I don't," I said firmly. I looked into his face for emphasis, but couldn't help fingering my silverware. "You're entitled to your opinion."

"What if you and I had met first?"

I tried to control my sudden vexation. "Paul, it's not like I was standing on a street corner waiting for someone to cruise by and whistle. I was not looking for romance. I was pursuing my dream career. I didn't want to fall in love and darn sure didn't want to get married. I still don't want to be married, not to anyone else, anyway. Not anyone." I hoped he'd get the point without my having to mention him specifically.

"So, what happened?" His voice sounded flat.

"I couldn't get happy—couldn't even be content, even out in sunny California—without him."

"But why him?"

I laughed, shaking my head. "I wish I knew. I've tried to analyze it. I didn't want to be caught. I squirmed and wriggled every which way to keep from being trapped. I went to California as a last-ditch effort, thinking I might be able to figure a way to manage without him."

I slumped back in my chair as the waitress served our food.

"I've told several people, my falling in love was like Br'er Rabbit and the Tar-Baby. The first time I saw him, all I meant to do was say howdy. Pretty soon I had my hands and my feets so stuck up, I couldn't get loose."

"Jancy," Paul's voice fell to a coaxing tone, "a lot of people think Jim and I look alike." He paused and waited for me to agree, or not.

"Yes, you and Jim do resemble each other physically."

"If you tried even a little, you might have those same 'can't get loose' feelings about me."

"That's the point. I didn't try with Jim. I even tried not to like him. I have this little trick. In the past when I've wanted not to like something—a dress I shouldn't buy, a friend I shouldn't hang with, anything—I would dwell on the negative things about them. I couldn't even find things to dislike about Jim. Everything about him suited me."

Paul regarded me with obvious disbelief. "Not everything."

"Physically, I can hardly keep my hands off him." I hesitated a minute to make sure the revelation didn't embarrass him. It didn't seem to. "He has huge integrity, which is the one single quality I admire most in people. He's energetic, generous, always truthful even when the truth is not flattering to him. He is selfless, tireless, modest, and devout."

"Bor-ing," Paul sang, interrupting. I didn't respond. "Besides, those adjectives all describe Jim and me both."

"They do not."

"What's that supposed to mean?"

"You're . . . ah . . . let's say lethargic."

"Lazy?" His eyes rounded at my nod. "Not about anything that matters."

"Not about anything that matters to you."

"Give me an example."

"At the cabin, when there were fish to clean or someone had to rescue Veronica from the snake or take Aunt Leta fishing, Jim was up and going."

"He likes doing that stuff."

"Probably not any more than you do."

Paul's eyes rimmed red as his anger festered. "I was there to rest. I had worked hard all week."

"So had he."

"And I'm sure as hell every bit as devout as he is. Growing up, I went to church every time he did, took my first communion earlier, took CCD, all the required stuff."

This was a ridiculous discussion but I didn't exactly know how to stop it, so I plunged ahead.

"Jim translates his faith from theory to practice. He lives it. You hang onto the theory as kind of a mental exercise, but your religion has nothing to do with your everyday life. It's something you trot out to use when it gives you an advantage."

"My religion is personal. I just don't flaunt it the way he does."

"Bullshit."

"What?"

"I don't know if you're able to fool yourself with this line of crap, Paul, but you darn sure aren't fooling me. I've got you pegged as a spoiled jerk who always puts himself first."

I almost regretted the verbal blow when he seemed so taken aback but I wanted to pound final nails in to make sure we had closure.

"Now to the finale. You are wrong, wrong about everything about me. I didn't want to love Jim. I tried not to. I've never loved you and it's been no effort at all. You're not my type. You've never been my type. You couldn't be. Don't compare yourself to Jim. You are not even in his league. You are lazy, self-ish, irresponsible, cowardly, stingy, and a braggart. I find all of those characteristics repugnant."

Paul's jaw locked and unlocked as he appeared to struggle for self-control or search for an appropriate retort. He propped his forearms on the edge of the table and lowered his eyes to stare at the plate in front of him.

We had skirmished over this same ground before, Paul

demeaning Jim, trying to tear his brother down in my eyes. The upshot had invariably led to my defending Jim by attacking Paul.

There was a long silence.

He looked injured. "All this because I wouldn't give you a bite of my chicken fried steak?"

I smiled, grimaced, then chuckled a little at my own tactlessness. "It's not you, Paul. Really. It's prenuptial jitters." Without any mental directive, my tone became kind. "Didn't you wonder why I was at the house today, a scant two days before my wedding, all by myself? It's because no one else can stand to be around me. I snap people's heads off or cry at the drop of a hat. I'm a basket case. You drove two hours, all the way down here, to get abused."

There was irony in his smile. "I knew you weren't the type to let a guy down easy."

I chuckled, laughing at myself. "I've been trying to let you down easy, to tell you subtly, for months. Today you caught me crouched and I sprang. I'm sorry to have unloaded on you like that."

"When you get right down to it," Paul said, nodding sagely, "you ain't all that great a catch."

I might have been able to maintain my solemn demeanor if it hadn't been for the look on his face. Obviously, he had intended the remark to sting and was watching my expression carefully to mark the injury. Instead, all my pent-up emotions exploded.

I rocked back and forth in that booth, laughing until tears filled my eyes and splashed down my cheeks. I gasped for breath. I crammed my napkin over my mouth, but the spewing giggles continued. I tried to muffle my loud guffaws and still catch a breath now and then.

Other patrons in the restaurant turned to look. Involuntarily, some even began laughing.

Embarrassed, Paul stood, patted me on the back, and quietly pleaded with me to stop. He suggested I try a sip of water.

His attempts to shush me only set off new rounds of laughter. He scanned the dining room sheepishly, resembling a cornered animal, frantically searching for a hole to hide in.

If I had, for any reason, tried to devise some diabolical punishment for Paul Wills, I could not intentionally have come up with a better plan. Mortified, he apparently dismissed the idea of escape and instead sat down to wait out the squall.

When I gradually quieted to only an occasional spurt of giggling, he took a last sip of his iced tea and stood. "Are you through embarrassing me?"

Wiping my eyes, I shook my head first, then nodded mutely and stood up without looking at him. I followed him to the cashier, then out the door.

He stalked off ahead of me several feet before he fired back. "You did that on purpose, to humiliate me in front of all those people, didn't you?"

I shook my head hopelessly. "You are a real trip, Wills, do you know that? You don't know any of those people and you'll probably never see most of them again. They're nothing to you. My senior English teacher and her brother were there. They probably thought I'd lost my mind. But you don't hear me whining around. Paul, you are the center of your own little universe, the star of your own little show. Your total self-centeredness absolutely irritates the fire out of me."

"Back to name-calling, are we?"

I didn't know what name he was referring to, so I didn't respond. I made myself not talk on the drive back to my parents' house, even when Paul made a wrong turn that took us two blocks out of our way.

"I'm sorry," I said as he pulled to the curb in front of the house. He didn't turn off the engine. I stepped out of the car, then turned back. "Would you like to come in for a while?"

The look he gave me was one of total incredulity. "No, ma'am." He looked like he was half kidding, half serious. "I think I've finally gotten a belly full of you, Dewhurst. This outing was better than a bucket of cold water in the face. I guess I should thank you."

I closed the car door as he accelerated and sped out of the neighborhood.

Chapter Fourteen

Action picked up late Thursday morning with the arrival of Rosie Clemente and Liz Pinello, maid of honor and bridesmaid, respectively. They honked as they pulled in front of the house and I ran out to help carry suitcases, hanging clothes, and boxes of gifts.

We all three talked at once as they fawned over the display of wedding gifts and helped me unwrap and place the new ones. Then they trailed me upstairs to Timothy's room. The younger of my two brothers had graciously agreed to take the sofa bed in the den, leaving the twin beds and trundles in his room to my bridesmaids.

My dad's parents were getting Gregory's room. Gregory wouldn't finish his finals until Friday, mere hours before the wedding. We'd cut that a little close.

Mom's family had booked rooms at the nearby Summit Bed and Breakfast. They insisted they didn't want to be in our way. Mom reminded me that they occasionally stayed at the inn even when there wasn't a wedding. They probably preferred the inn's quiet to the commotion—phones ringing, people in and out—of our household.

About midafternoon, a taxi pulled into the driveway and dropped Duke Mallory at our front door.

Running to greet him, I threw my arms around his neck and squeezed. "I didn't dream you'd come. I'm so glad you're here. Duke, you are the nicest present of all, but you'll . . . I guess you'll have to sleep in the den with my younger brother, Tim."

He just grinned and didn't try to get in a word, which he probably couldn't have anyway. Breathlessly, I introduced him to everyone.

Shortly after Mallory's arrival, Angela Fires and Theresa Graff, my last two former housemates, swept in, setting off new squeals. I couldn't stop smiling.

"I didn't know young females made so much racket," I overheard Mallory tell Tim. "I hope this is all of them."

"All the ones that're staying here, anyway."

"When do you people get your afternoon paper?"

"Should be pretty soon. It usually comes around three."

Looking at his watch, Mallory seemed consoled as he eased into the kitchen to help himself to the food trays strategically located by a pot of freshly brewed coffee. Trailing him, I could tell he was warming to this part of the celebration. He glanced at me and looked like he'd remembered something. Again I followed along as he got his bag out of the den closet and pulled out an unopened wedding gift.

"Jancy," he called, struggling through the gaggle of girls that had followed me into the living room, "we found this on your desk yesterday morning. Ivy had me bring it along."

Without acknowledging I had heard him, I finished listening to Liz as I reached for the gift. Mallory refused to give it up without some acknowledgment. Noting the stubborn cast to his face, I smiled and he released the package.

Sitting down, affording the gift only an occasional glimpse, I coaxed the ribbon off carefully without causing any lapse in the conversation with Liz about the quality of linens available in Bishop compared to the selection in Carson's Summit. I slit the tape with my fingernail, peeled back the paper, and opened the box. It was a highly polished, ornate sterling silver card tray.

"How nice," I said, tilting the silver to reflect the light. It looked familiar. I'd seen it before, maybe in a photograph. I felt my lighthearted mood deteriorate. "Oh, Mallory, no."

"They got your initials wrong," Theresa said. "PFH! You'll have to return it."

I turned my accusing eyes on Mallory.

"Who the heck is PFH?" He looked puzzled. "Who's it from?"

I pulled the card from the tissue. It was signed simply, "Denim."

"Denim." I breathed the name and shot another accusing glare at Mallory.

"Denim?" he repeated. "San Diego Denim? Charlie Denim? Our Charlie Denim? Nah."

I began nodding. I was at home, safe in Carson's Summit, far away from the little rat-faced criminal. San Diego was thirteen hundred miles away, yet suddenly I felt threatened.

Mom had come into the living room as I was opening the gift. She flashed a knowing look and sauntered to stand beside me. She didn't speak. She simply lifted the card and tray from my hands. I quickly snatched the tray back.

"PFH." I hissed, glowering up at Mallory. "Paula Faye Hudson." My throat burned. "The man gave me stolen property for a wedding gift." I began trembling as tears stung the backs of my eyelids. "And the actual little owner is dead."

Then, surprising everyone, including myself, I leaped up, walked directly to Duke Mallory, and threw my arms around his substantial frame, incidentally pinning his hands at his sides. Awkwardly, he freed his arms, wrapped them around me, and patted my back like someone might burp a baby.

The strain of the whole celebration probably was responsible for my crying jag, Mom said later, trying to explain my intemperate behavior. She didn't even know how I'd treated Paul the day before.

Mallory kept apologizing for bringing the present that had

set me off, but Mom was quick to absolve him, saying, "She's overwrought. A wedding is an emotional time for a woman."

Before I could get calmed down, I asked if anyone had heard from Jim. No one had, but everybody assured me he'd probably arrive any minute.

"You need to eat something, baby," Dad suggested when he got home to the commotion and house full of people. He apparently noticed I'd been crying. He pronounced the card tray "very nice," and the innocent remark earned him a noisy reprimand from my mother and dark looks all around.

I sat with an untouched plate of food, sulking in the den.

"If you're going to pout," Mom whispered finally, "take it upstairs. I'm tired of looking at that sour face. Things could hardly be better. We're ready for the wedding. You're surrounded by family and friends who love you. Some of them, like Mr. Mallory, have come a long way at considerable expense to celebrate the occasion with you. You need to straighten up. Think of someone besides yourself."

Mother's words carried a familiar sting. Obviously Paul Wills wasn't the only person who was the center of his own little universe.

"It takes one to know one," I muttered, thinking of how harshly I'd scolded Paul. "Get the log out of your own eye, Miss Perfect." I winced under my silent attack. I wished Jim were here.

"He'll be here, sweetheart," Mom said as if she'd read my mind. "The Wills are meeting us at the church at six. I imagine he plans to be there."

I looked at the sincerity in my mother's face and swallowed a little laugh. "I hope so. He's supposed to pay for supper. I'm sure not letting him out of that, or anything else."

Mom hugged me and we both laughed.

★　★　★　★　★

Jim and Father Gilstrap were standing together when we got to the church at six sharp. Seeing Jim, I suddenly felt completely benevolent and totally gracious. I smiled and said hellos all around, hugging Jim's three sisters, their spouses and children, with special attention to five-year-old Amanda, my first ally in the Wills clan.

I managed token hugs for all three of his brothers. And I made sweeping introductions, even calling all the names correctly.

I beamed at Jim's mother, Olivia, secretly rejoicing that we already were confidantes, and hugged William Wills, the hulking family patriarch of whom Jim appeared to be almost a clone.

As conversations ignited like small grass fires and blazed in groups around the room, I sidled over to Jim, where I smiled demurely and slipped my hand into his.

He looked puzzled. "I don't think I've seen you timid."

"I'm just glad to see you."

"Tell me it never occurred to you I wouldn't show." He leaned forward to look directly into my face as if he were trying to read an expression that was not familiar to him. I grimaced and shrugged, but couldn't meet his eyes. He stood straight again and squeezed my hand. "You're not usually clingy, except when you're scared." He gave me another searching look.

I stared straight ahead. "Where are you staying?"

"At the Timbers Inn."

"All of you?"

"Everyone's there for two nights, except me, of course." He ventured another look at my face. "We're still on for tomorrow night, right?"

I turned my best, most radiant smile on him. He smiled back, nodded, and took a deep breath.

I felt a pang of resentment during the rehearsal as Rosie

traversed the aisle in the bride's place, a time-honored good luck tradition, and stood beside Jim as Father Frank Gilstrap ran through the practice ceremony. From where I stood, off to the side, I tried to see Jim objectively.

He stood straight, silently absorbing the instructions, laughing at his brothers' occasional wisecracks. My eyes devoured him, sweeping from his strong chin, his full lips, his straight nose, to his forehead, past the dark hair on his perfectly shaped head, down his neck to his powerful shoulders and arms. His finely honed torso narrowed to his trim waist. I had always admired the way his slacks rode a little higher over his hips and lower in the front. His thighs shaped the front of his pant legs, his prominent calves the back.

He was a spectacular specimen. At that moment, when I was admiring him so blatantly, Jim turned his head and his gaze collided with mine. He frowned ever so slightly, more a look of puzzlement than anything else. "What?" He mouthed the word soundlessly. I smiled and shook my head, embarrassed to be caught studying him so intently.

As soon as the run-through was finished, he came directly to my side. "What were you thinking back there?" His face and his voice were serious.

"I think I may be a wanton woman, but I need to look up the word when I get home to be sure."

Again the slow smile crept over his face. "Yes, sir, I think this little arrangement we've made is going to work out just fine."

"And maybe just in the nick of time." I slanted him a sidelong look. We stood there, holding hands, grinning.

Moments later, my brother Gregory arrived and set off a whole new round of introductions and conversations. Jim turned to answer a question from his brother, Andrew, and easily recaptured my hand at the same time. Surprised that his touch was so comforting, I shivered and again eased closer to him.

Three long tables formed a "U" in the banquet room at the inn, allowing all the guests at the rehearsal dinner conversational access to one other. The two families melded noisily. Adding to the celebration were Jim's three sisters, two with husbands and children, and his three brothers. My grandparents from both sides also had joined us for dinner.

Duke and my four former housemates completed the mob. The girls of the wedding party glowed beneath the attentive glances of so many handsome, eligible men in one place. After dinner, the men offered toasts to the bride and groom, some salutes sentimental, others not. Finally Paul, as best man, rose to cap the evening's speeches.

"Jancy would be a handful, actually an armload, for any man," he said, regarding me with what looked like restored admiration. His dark eyes were so much like Jim's that the taunting arch of his eyebrows as he spoke prompted me to brace for whatever orneriness was coming. "I'm afraid Jim has need of our prayers if he is to withstand year after year of her wearying optimism and energy.

"As for Jancy," he raised his glass toward Jim, ignoring the warning look his mother aimed squarely at his face, "remember, brother, once a king, always a king, but once a (k)night is enough."

The diners caught his pun at different times and laughter sputtered like popcorn around the tables. Laughing, Paul drank from his glass, signaling others to do the same.

"Are you coming with us back to the motel?" Olivia Wills asked Jim as the dinner concluded.

"I'll be right behind you. I want to stop by the Dewhursts' for a few minutes. Jancy's riding with me. I won't get to see her again until church tomorrow night."

Olivia stalled and caught my eye. "I've been the only Mrs. Wills in this family for more than twenty years," she said as she and I looped arms, "since William's mother died. Tomorrow night there will be another one. I want you to know how tickled I am it's you."

Whether it was the wine or the words or the occasion, Olivia and I hugged each other tightly. Tears filled my eyes.

"I'm going to love being related to your mother, Jim," I said as he pried us apart.

Olivia smiled, swiping a tear of her own. "That goes double for me."

He raised his eyebrows. "She's sometimes opinionated, argumentative, and manipulative." She and I regarded each other blankly.

I gave up first. "Which one of us are you talking about?"

He looked from one pair of dark eyes to the other in the faces of two women he obviously loved, then he laughed. "Both of you." He ducked to dodge our bilateral attack.

Jim and I drove alone to Mom and Dad's in the comfortable stillness of the chill, wintry evening. I sat close beside him, my hand captive between his forearm and his body. I didn't feel a need for words. Being close to him soothed all the anxieties the week had presented.

"Did you pick up the rings?" I asked, finally.

He nodded. "Hmmm."

"Are you going to hide the car?"

"Andrew's doing it."

"Can you trust him?"

"Can't trust any of our brothers, yours or mine, but I doubt they'll do anything rank. We might get a little shivareeing, nothing damaging."

My parents had gone upstairs, but lights were still on in the den and the kitchen. Inside the front door, Jim took my coat, tossed it on a chair, and gathered me close. He took a deep breath and smiled, inhaling the scent of me, then put his nose against the side of my face. "I love you." He whispered.

"It's a good thing."

He pulled away and studied me a moment. "What was wrong this afternoon?"

"Nothing, really."

He waited for more.

"Duke brought us a wedding gift someone left on my old desk at the office."

"I was surprised to see him," Jim interjected. "Did you know he was coming?"

"No."

"Were you pleased?"

"Absolutely." I glanced at his face, looking for other meaning before I understood. "Oh, no, his coming was terrific. I was really happy to see him. It was the gift that threw me.

"I was talking to the girls and wasn't paying very good attention when I unwrapped it. It was a very nice sterling silver card tray. But it had the wrong initials on it. It had 'PFH' instead of 'JWW.' I thought it was a store mistake until I looked at the card. It was signed, 'Denim.' "

"Denim?" Jim repeated, momentarily at a loss before a look of incredulity replaced the confusion. "Charlie Denim? We got a wedding present from a fugitive? Who is 'PFH'?"

"I don't know for sure, but I think the initials probably stand for Paula Fay Hudson."

Jim's expression fell to an angry frown.

"That's right," Duke Mallory growled, appearing as if on cue from the kitchen. He carried a coffee cup and a handful of tiny cucumber sandwiches with no crusts. He took a swallow of coffee to clear his mouth. "I called O'Brien. I used my wire service credit card," he added quickly, as if to assure me he had not billed the long-distance charge to my family's telephone.

"He called back while we were partying, left a message on your machine. Your folks and I listened to it. The card tray with her initials was on Mrs. Hudson's list of stolen stuff."

"Do you think his sending a gift is a threat?" I looked from Jim to Mallory and back to Jim.

"No." Jim arched an eyebrow and flashed Mallory a warning glance. "Denim's a showboat. He's just being his usual obnoxious self, probably trying to get under O'Brien's skin."

"Or mine." I said. "You don't think he'll show up here, do you?"

"No, I don't," Jim answered firmly. "He likes to be the center of attention, but he's sharp enough to avoid a face-to-face. He probably thinks you and Mallory and I can identify him. We've seen snapshots of him when he was a kid. He doesn't know you can't tell dip from those pictures. But Jance, he also knows you've actually seen him, at the Town Tavern when he shoved you that night, in the reflections in the storefront, and on the bus. Maybe he doesn't want you to forget him."

"You practically had forgotten him," I said. "You didn't even recognize his name at first."

"Well, I wasn't thinking of him as someone who would send us a wedding present. No, if I had been at your desk or even in my office here, I would have recognized the name immediately. *And*, I will know his face."

"How could you tell anything from those early, fuzzy snapshots?"

Both Mallory and I regarded him oddly.

"I could pick him out of a room full of people right now, from your description."

Mallory was quick to agree, loudly.

"Shhhh," I cautioned. "You'll wake everyone up."

Jim and Mallory glanced at their watches at that same moment. Eleven-forty. Jim sighed and gave me an apologetic look. "I guess I need to get out of here." His eyes set almost wistfully on my face. He glanced at Mallory, then back at me, hinting.

Mallory shuffled his feet awkwardly. "I need to tell you one more thing." He seemed reluctant to share the information.

Both Jim and I looked at him expectantly.

"It might not be anything at all."

Neither of us spoke, encouraging him to move along.

"Do you remember Sean Smith's mother?"

"Who died on Thanksgiving?" I said. "Yes."

Mallory nodded solemnly. "It seems Mrs. Smith and Paula Hudson were sisters."

"What?" Jim and I breathed in unison.

"Why didn't Sean say anything?" I asked.

"He didn't know. It was just a fluke they found out at all. The beat cop who noticed the connection is now working for O'Brien. The captain's banking on this kid to make him a hero."

"Wait a minute," I interrupted. "Did O'Brien take Thad off the case?"

"Bias is gone. Quit right after you left. Got a new job somewhere up in the mountains.

"Anyway, the death certificates on both Hudson and Smith arrived at headquarters the same day. This kid was looking them over and noticed the two decedents had the same parents. He thought it was a mistake, checked back with the department of vital statistics. It was no mistake.

"Apparently they had been farmed out when they were tykes. Neither one of them had been legally adopted, so their original birth certificates stood. The information off those showed up on the death certificates.

"They were reared, married, and died all within a few miles

of each other. As far as we can tell, they never knew each other."

I shot Jim a questioning look. "It's awfully odd that they died within a couple of weeks of each other, too, isn't it?"

He shrugged.

I turned my attention back to Mallory. "Did they both die of natural causes?"

It was Mallory's turn to shrug. "Who knew to ask for an autopsy on Smith?"

"But you told O'Brien to do one on Paula Hudson." I had a niggling feeling he was trying to hold something back.

Mallory looked at Jim sheepishly, prompting me to turn a warning look on Jim. "Spill it, Mallory."

Jim picked up the explanation. "Paula Hudson was found in her bed and things looked kosher. But the autopsy revealed she was smothered. She struggled, got some skin under her fingernails. It's been categorized. When we get Candlesticks, we can run a DNA, see if he graduated from burglar to murderer that night."

"And Mrs. Smith?"

Mallory cleared his throat, studying his feet. "Like I said, who knew then to ask for an autopsy? She supposedly died of pneumonia and was buried. Her son sat with her most of the last couple of days, with only a few breaks. But Denim was, if nothing else, an opportunist. If and when we catch him, we'll ask if he did anything to help her along."

"Hudson and Smith were sisters," I repeated, wondering out loud, more to myself than to my two companions. "Mrs. Hudson's apartment and Mrs. Smith's son's place were burglarized by Candlesticks when both ladies were in the hospital. They're both dead. What in the world was going on? And is it over?"

Jim frowned at Mallory. "Do you know their family name, their maiden names?"

"Doctorman. But," he crossed his arms over his chest, "there's kind of an odd wrinkle there too. Their parents were Clint and Sarah Denim Doctorman."

My mouth dropped open. "What?"

Mallory nodded. " 'Denim' was the maiden name of the mother of Mrs. Smith and Mrs. Hudson."

I turned to Jim. " 'Denim' is not a common name." The statement was more of a question.

"It could be a coincidence."

"But you don't think so, do you?"

Lowering his gaze to the carpeting, Jim shook his head. His gloom was not very comforting.

I had convinced myself that Charlie "Candlesticks" Denim was no longer any of my business. Wherever he was, whatever he was doing, he was beyond me now, totally and completely out of my life.

Intellectually, I knew that to be true, but I had a peculiar feeling that neither Jim nor I was yet free from the influence of the elusive Charlie Denim.

CHAPTER FIFTEEN

Blustery wind growling outside my bedroom windows woke me on my wedding day. The sun struggled to show its pale face, but its efforts were thwarted by veils of thick, dark clouds that gathered and disbanded with meteorological ambivalence.

I had insisted my wedding gown be delivered to the house days before, rather than to the church on the big day. My nails were done and retouched. The females in the wedding party were "doing lunch" at eleven-thirty and the bridesmaids had insisted I schedule them exclusively until beauty shop appointments began at two-thirty.

I slipped out of bed into the airy coolness of my room, thinking of other special mornings: Christmas mornings when I'd leaped out of this same bed too excited to dress; mornings anticipating tennis tournaments, cheerleader tryouts, the state debate tournament, big dates, proms, graduation, and the morning I left for college. But I had never had quite this feeling of finality, of changes, which, once accomplished, could never be undone.

Walking to the window, I tugged the hem of my oversized T-shirt down to cover my thighs and shivered. I didn't know if it was actually cold in the room or excitement. The clock said seven-thirty.

What time will I be getting up tomorrow morning? I wondered idly. Was Jim an early riser or a late-night person when he was not on a schedule? I wasn't sure. Of course, he jogged early on work days. I knew a lot of things about him, but maybe not enough to be promising to join my life to his permanently. Forever was a very long time.

I could leave now, pack a bag, walk out the front door, and disappear. Of course, if I did, I would have to stay gone, not just from Jim, but from my family, and his family.

A mental picture of his mother drifted into my head. Olivia Wills was definitely an inducement in the deal. Then I thought of Amanda's freckled face, of the little girl's melodic giggle, of lying on the bed at the Wills' lake cottage, coloring together in the new coloring book, listening to the others talking in the darkness of the sitting porch, their voices wafting back on the warm south breeze.

I couldn't help smiling at the memory.

And I thought of Blue, the big black snake who had dangled so casually from the birdbath. Blue was gone now, of course. My thoughts drifted. Where had Blue spent the winter months when he was alive? Silly of me to worry about the hibernation habits of a dead snake. I hoped I'd remember to ask Jim.

My mind's eye conjured a vivid mental picture of Jim.

I had pegged him correctly from the first, a man's man, not a fawning lap dog. He had seemed frightening then, muscular, handsome, sure of himself; flashing dark, angry eyes, ordering me to stand clear of his investigation, only to admit later he had been smitten from that first intimidating encounter.

My mom and dad had taken to him immediately. My brothers, too. Their reactions were a sound endorsement.

I wondered what he'd be like as he grew older. Investigating murders might change him over time, make him hard. It might already have.

I had seen his anger unleashed, righteous fury facing down and subduing contract killers. I had even seen him kill a man with his bare hands. Jim's fury that night had raged and dissipated slowly. I'd had a glimpse of a darkness in him I would never have suspected. That view, brief as it was, had frightened me. Was it a forewarning of the depths to which he could descend?

I'd seen him angry other times too, even angry with me. Of course, our disagreements had not been life-threatening.

Staring at the bare, winter-stiffened branches of the oak outside my window, a different image pushed its way into my thoughts: the face of the elusive Charlie Denim, a face quickly replaced by a clear picture of Thad Bias, grinning, tall, angular, his hair the color of straw, his face sunny and his blue eyes flashing each time they met mine. Remembering his face always made me think of summertime and California.

"Thad is nothing to me," I whispered. "How can I think dreamily of Ichabod on the day I'm marrying Adonis?"

Frowning, I tried to banish Thad and Denim and Jim's dark side from my thoughts. To dismiss those thoughts, I had to replace them. I scanned for other, more pleasant images, but I couldn't seem to find one. The telephone rang.

"Jancy!" Gregory bellowed from downstairs. I picked up the extension in my room.

"I can feel you getting squeamish," Jim's voice grinned.

"Am not."

"Are too. My soul can feel yours quailing. Where are you?"

"In my room."

"You dressed yet?"

"No. Are you?"

"Been up for hours. Amanda and I went swimming in the dome at six A.M. I was stirring around trying not to wake my brothers when she tapped on the door. I wish you could have gone with us. An early morning swim certainly relieves the heebie-jeebies."

"You're having them too?"

He laughed. "Not really. I've been looking forward to this day for fifteen months. More accurately, to this night."

"It can't have been that long."

"I saw you the first time a year ago October fifth. Count it up yourself."

"But you didn't . . ." I couldn't reduce the thought to words.

"Want you," he whispered, finishing my question. "From that day to this, without a letup."

"Do you think you're obsessive?"

"Only about you."

"I don't understand."

He laughed again. "Neither do I, but I know this is the right move. Right for both of us."

"We're promising to stay together our whole lives."

"And we are going to have a ball, one adventure after another."

"I don't even own a car."

Jim chuckled again on the other end of the phone. "Where'd that come from? Do you think bringing a car into our marriage would be like your dowry or something?"

"No, but I don't really have a job right now, until and unless Riley reassigns me, which means I've got no income, in addition to no wheels. I'm not contributing anything. I don't even have a place to live except here with my folks."

"Sounds to me like you caught yourself a man just in the nick of time."

I groaned. "I'm serious."

Jim laughed heartily, obviously enjoying the conversation. "What kind of car do you want?"

"I don't know . . . and I certainly don't expect you to buy me one. I still have the insurance money they paid me for the Beretta. It seems like I've left a lot of loose ends out there."

"Tell you what I'll do. I'll go get a quit claim deed right now and put your name on my condo with mine. That way you and I will own it together, equally. Then you'll be a woman of means."

"Jim, prenuptial agreements are supposed to preserve the assets of the person who owns things. The idea is to protect the moneyed person's belongings from a gold-digging mate. What kind of lawyer are you, anyway?"

He ignored my interruption. "As soon as we get settled, you and I will go record the deed at the Bishop County Courthouse. I'll also change the title on the Civic to both our names. We'll put your name on my checking account. I have a couple of small investment accounts. We'll put you on those too."

I ran my bare foot under my unmade bed, feeling for my scuffs. I was freezing.

"Does that mean I have to put your name on my checking account and the savings where I have the insurance money?"

"No. Those can be yours. I'll buy you a car so you can keep the insurance money as your personal little nest egg. Your own private mad money. Now do you feel better?"

"No, I feel like a grasping, selfish brat. There was a time when I worried you might be stingy. Do you remember?"

"Yes."

"I take it back."

He laughed, then lowered his voice. "I like our whole wedding service but I particularly remember repeating the part, 'With all my worldly goods I thee endow.' I heard it loud and clear. I feel that way, honey. I want to share everything with you, everything I am or have or ever hope to be or have."

"What if I squander it?"

"Then I'll get more and give you that to squander, if squandering keeps you happy."

"Jim," I asked quietly after a lengthy pause, "do you think you might ever get mad enough to hit me?"

"No." His answer was quick and emphatic. "The Wills boys have never been allowed to hit girls. That's from Dad. And I can tell you, with three sisters, I've had plenty of provocation.

"Anyway, you know how my family feels about you. If I harmed a hair on your head, Dad would pulverize me. Paul's just waiting for the chance to be your hero. You don't seriously think I'd give him an opportunity like that, do you? Not to mention Peter and Andrew, who get blithery every time they're in a room with you.

"I think it's more likely you'll abuse me than that I will you. In fact," he added thoughtfully, "I think maybe you already have."

It was my turn to laugh.

"You are kidding, aren't you?" he prodded. "These are just wedding day jitters, right?"

I giggled again but didn't answer.

"You must be pretty hard up for something to worry about this morning, if you're grabbing at straws like those. Now pack your bag and put on some clothes. You've got company coming."

Suddenly alarmed, I said, "Who?"

"Didn't you say Theresa and Angela would be up and about early? I understand they're giving you an impromptu prenuptial courtesy at the Embers before lunch. I heard Veronica telling Mom and Amanda they were invited."

"Oh, Jim, I forgot. Kit and Kellan and the baby will be here this afternoon. Kit called Wednesday. I didn't think to tell you. We'll send them out to the motel as soon as they've said hello. What are you going to do all day?"

"Lift, shoot a little pool, swim, play ping-pong with the guys."

"Don't wear yourself out."

He cackled evilly. "You'd better hope I work off a little steam or you might not be ambulatory for a week."

My laugh sounded uncertain. "Have you got all your Christmas shopping done?"

"No. That's a good idea."

"You can go to the mall, but not out to Hopes or the shopping center east of there. It's bad luck for a bride and groom to see each other on their wedding day."

"I heard." He cleared his throat. "That's the line from my mom to Amanda and every woman whose age is between those two. I'm sure sorry to learn at this late date that you're superstitious."

"Yeah, bummer. I should have been more up front with you. I don't know whatever possessed me to keep that a secret."

"Are there any other little foibles I should know about?"

"Many, but you'll have to coax them out of me."

"I'll put that on my 'to do' list."

"Do you still have things on your list you haven't done yet?"

"Only the one."

"What one?"

Jim hesitated, allowing the suspense to build. "Dr. Linquist's little assignment."

"Oh." I sighed. "Well, I guess that's one you can't do ahead of time."

"No." Jim's tone was businesslike. "But rest assured, my dear, it will be accomplished in due . . . course."

The guests were seated, the priest in position, the organist playing and the groom and his men poised at the rail when my people crowded into the vestibule. We were concealed from the nave, the sanctuary itself, by broad double doors.

My brother Gregory, looking better than I'd ever seen him, slipped through the doors and took Mom's arm. She gave him a blinking smile as he escorted her into the sanctuary. If he followed orders, he would deposit her in her designated pew on the left side.

I gave the veil a final pat, then concentrated on the floor.

Moving on her musical cue, Rosie nudged Amanda and her basket of rose petals through the doors. I heard later that Jim's five-year-old niece performed a little more speedily than practiced, but her steps were in perfect double-time with the music.

Then Curtis and Maurice moved out, bearing the satin pillows on which rings—not the actual wedding rings, of course—were pinned, to insure no awkward spills or misplacement.

Liz stood motionless, peering through the door, awaiting Father Frank Gilstrap's nod. As people left, the vestibule got larger behind the swinging doors that separated it from the gathering beyond.

Duke Mallory came in from the outside just as Liz stepped through the swinging doors into the church. His arrival was accompanied by a gust of arctic air. He pulled the outside door closed, then grinned wordlessly at my dad and me, who had both turned to see who had come in late. We nodded but didn't say anything. My smile felt stiff. Dad looked determined.

It was Rosie's turn to traverse the aisle. When she had taken her place at the rail, the music swelled. My dad and I stood poised, arms linked, rigidly facing the doors. Neither of us moved. I don't think we even blinked.

The church full of family and friends rustled as the audience stood. Still, Dad and I stood in place. We both stared straight ahead at the closed doors that separated us from the celebrants inside. Gently, Duke Mallory placed a hand on each of our backs and pushed.

The doors opened and we stepped together, just like we'd practiced, right feet first, into the welcome warmth of the sanctuary. Dad's arm trembled and I felt a momentary spasm of panic. I turned my head to look at him. His face was level with mine. I'd forgotten that we always seemed the same height when I was in heels. I patted his arm reassuringly, then allowed my eyes to rove.

Mrs. Teeman, the SBI secretary, beamed at me from a pew on the groom's side. I returned the smile, drawing comfort from Mrs. Teeman's presence. My eyes wandered to the rail where, abruptly, they were captured.

Jim's smile highlighted an expression full of pleasure and anticipation and courage. I had felt pensive and uncertain until that moment, when my dark mood suddenly lifted, responding to his. His white teeth, dark alert eyes, and handsome features drew me. I took each step eagerly, suddenly achingly aware each brought me closer to our joining.

When Dad and I reached the rail, my father's profile interrupted my visual lock with Jim. Daddy was the only remaining obstacle between Jim and me as the three of us stood facing Father Gilstrap.

The congregation behind us rustled again, responding to the priest's signal to sit. I have no memory of his salutation and opening words as I stood there, knees locked rigidly, staring straight ahead.

Amanda reached out and patted my arm, breaking my trance. I smiled down at her, then looked beyond her to Rosie and Liz. They beamed back at me.

"Who gives this woman to be married to this man?" Father Frank's voice boomed.

"Her mother and I do," Dad said, then took my right hand and eased it toward Jim's large, thick familiar one. Jim didn't reach out, but held steady, waiting for me to put my hand in his.

As if I were an impartial observer, I saw my hand slide into Jim's and absorb its warmth. His calm, the solid feel of his hand compared to Daddy's cool, trembling one, comforted me as only Jim could.

Daddy eased from sight and I knew he was joining Mom in the first pew on the bride's side.

I looked into my groom's face with a sense of wonder.

Jim bore a look of imperturbable assurance. He seemed tall and straight and confident as he flashed me an easy smile. His steady gaze was heartening. My confidence building, I returned his smile, drew a deep breath, and straightened to my full height beside him. Even when I was in heels, he had two or three inches on me.

Father Frank droned the words I'd heard dozens of times before, in other weddings where I stood with friends or sat as a guest, but this time the words seemed more serious, certainly more binding.

I repeated the words I was supposed to say on cue and hesitated only a moment over "for richer or for poorer," glancing at Jim to make sure he agreed. At my questioning glance, his smile broadened.

Then we were on to the rings.

I had forgotten to move my engagement ring to my right hand for the service. Father Frank whispered that we could switch them later, but Jim shook his head and helped me remove the diamond. Paul, his best man, produced the plain gold band. Jim slipped it into its rightful place, then returned the diamond to nest protectively against the wedding band.

Rosie handed me the groom's ring, which slid snugly over his knuckle and into place.

Jim and I knelt and took communion before Father Frank said the final words, blessed us, and told Jim he could kiss his bride. Jim steadied me before he planted a warm kiss on my lips.

The congregation applauded as Father Frank introduced "Mr. and Mrs. James William Wills," and sent us scurrying up the aisle as the organist launched into the recessional.

"I want us to make a deal," Jim said quietly, as he opened the door to the vestibule.

"Okay. What?"

"We agree here and now never to remove our wedding bands, not for any reason. Agreed?" He looked serious.

"All right," I said just as the groomsmen and bridesmaids exploded through the swinging doors behind us.

Then we were engulfed in noise and commotion and chatter. The crowd of well-wishers swept through congratulating and hugging as they hurried away to the country club for the reception.

Jim and I, the wedding party, our families, and Father Gilstrap regrouped at the rail for pictures.

I drank champagne at the reception, circulating, laughing with friends I had not seen in months, even years, enjoying the four-piece combo and finger foods.

Paul asked me to dance first, but got intercepted as Jim swept me into his arms. We got only once around the floor before other partners descended on us, Dad and Father Frank leading the charge. I danced and mingled with our guests until my feet began to throb. Then Mom signaled.

"It's getting late, you need to change your clothes."

Rosie, Liz, Teresa, and Angela went with me to the ladies' dressing room, each of them carrying two goblets of champagne. I eyed the goblets suspiciously.

"Are we going to have a private little party in here?" Squirming, I unhooked my dress, which pooled on the floor so I could step out of it. Liz set two drinks on the dressing table.

"No, honey," Rosie cooed as Liz picked up the dress and shook it straight, "these are all for you. This, honey, is where the honeymoon really gets started."

They all laughed as I objected.

"I've already had three and I didn't have any supper."

"We'll help you." Liz giggled. As if on signal, each girl in turn tossed back a gulp, then presented the balance of their glasses to me. One at a time, as I changed into slacks and a sweater set, I drained the offered stems.

In slacks and a blazer, Jim was waiting outside the ladies' lounge when we emerged.

"Ready to run the gauntlet?" He grinned. Feeling dizzy but willing, I nodded. He helped me into my coat, then took my icy hand in his warm one and tugged me toward the waiting well-wishers armed with the traditional rice.

As we made our escape, one large hand reached into the back of my sweater and released a fistful of rice. I squirmed as it sifted down my back, but I kept moving in step with Jim.

He pulled me toward a dark blue four-door sedan I hadn't seen before, rather than to his aged Civic, which had been gaudily shoe-polished and canned for the occasion. He put me inside the blue car, climbed into the driver's side, and hit the electric door locks just as Andrew grabbed a handle. Laughing at his brothers' foiled antics, Jim started the engine and swept down the driveway.

"Where'd you get the car?" I asked as we drove.

"At the car-getting place. Do you like it?" He called my attention to the off-white interior, the moon roof and other amenities, and described a CD player located in the trunk. "Do you like it?"

"It's got a lot of bells and whistles," I said. "I love the color. And I've always preferred four doors, if it doesn't make the car look stodgy. Yes, I do like it. What is it?"

"A Mercury."

"Whose is it?"

"Title says it's yours."

"Oh, yeah?" I beamed. "Are you trying to butter me up?"

He smiled suggestively. "Could be. Is it working?"

"Yes, it is. It's going to get you anything you want."

"In that case, I should've bought you a car a long time ago. We could've skipped the ceremony."

I glowered playfully. "You could have had me anytime from October first on," I muttered. "You could've skipped getting married altogether."

"But having your body wasn't enough." His teasing look was gone. "I wanted your mind," he continued, speaking slowly, deliberately, "your spirit . . . your soul. To get the package I had to make you swear solemn oaths in front of everyone you respect most in the world."

I looked down at the rings on my left hand. It was still a hard concept to grasp. I was married, yet I felt released, as if I'd suddenly broken free from every binding. Marriage, at least marriage to Jim, might not be all that confining.

It didn't matter. For better or worse, our life together had begun.

CHAPTER SIXTEEN

I tried not to move, not to breathe, but rice spattered the slate floor as I stood waiting for Jim to check us into the hotel. Women passersby looked at me, smiled, quickly averted their gazes, and hurried on. Men looked at me, then at Jim, then smiled and arched their eyebrows. I would have sworn the guys stared until they were prodded by their ladies, but it could have been my imagination.

Then Jim caught my elbow and turned me toward the elevator. He didn't say a word, just flipped the key card ominously with his thumbnail. The bellhop trailed us, wheeling our luggage until he turned toward the freight elevators. I glanced at Jim. He gave me a kindly, reassuring smile and winked, which didn't help my nerves one bit. Neither of us spoke.

The door to the suite was open when we got there. Jim pocketed the key card, then put a staying hand on my arm before I could step into the room. He shook his head. I giggled when he scooped me up and carried me over the threshold.

"A little superstitious yourself, I see," I said quietly as he set my feet on the floor. He grinned.

"It's traditional and we want to do this thing right, right?"

"Right."

The suite had a bar/sitting area. To the right were a love seat, a writing desk, and an entertainment center. Straight ahead, beyond the coffee table, sofa, and a small table flanked by two occasional chairs, was a sliding door to the terrace complete with a hot tub, bubbling uncovered, defying the frosty night air. The bellhop had thought of everything.

Through a door to our left, light from the sleeping area was mellow. In that dim light loomed what appeared to be an enormous bed. I glanced at it then quickly away, reluctant to look at Jim, who was watching me closely. I wasn't quite ready for the bed yet.

Jim pulled out money to tip the bellhop. The uniformed man eyed the currency, smiled his approval, and said, "If you need anything, ask for Bert," then hurried out, closing the door behind him.

Jim gave me a teasing look. "What would you like to do now?"

When I looked at him, maybe a little startled, he grinned. I giggled nervously. "How about a hand of gin rummy?"

"I didn't bring any cards." His grin continued. "Did you?"

I bit my lips and shook my head. "We could call Bert."

"Bert's busy. Think of something else."

"How about a hot bath?"

He looked surprised, then glanced toward the terrace. "As in hot tub for two?"

"I'm a little nervous and freezing. I was thinking more of a regular bath . . . alone."

His taunting grin waned. "Not exactly what I had in mind, but if you want to take a bath, it's okay with me."

He went through the bedroom area to the dressing room, checked to see that my suitcases were on the caddy, then stepped into the bathroom and turned on both faucets. "Bubbles?"

"Yes, please."

"Thought so," he muttered.

"I'll change clothes while you're in the tub." He waited for a response. I couldn't look at him.

Still mute, I went into the dressing room and closed the door.

I stripped, folding my clothes a little haphazardly, hurried into the bathroom, and closed and locked the door. I heard Jim say, "Don't worry about me. I'm fine. No hurry here."

A moment later, I heard him talking to someone, apparently on the telephone. Later, there was a knock on the outside door and more conversation, then the visitor was gone. Jim rustled in the dressing room, evidently changing clothes.

He walked to the dressing room where he changed his clothes, then removed the case from a spare pillow. Smoothing it, he placed it between the sheets in the center of the bed and arranged the covers over it. Then he settled on the small sofa in the sitting area.

He didn't want to turn on the television, didn't want any noisy distractions.

"A little music?" he asked the room at large. He turned on the radio, found a mellow sound, and turned off the alarm, which had been set by a previous tenant for six-thirty.

Hearing the bathtub draining, he positioned himself on the sofa, where he broke open the new deck of cards, removed the jokers, and shuffled. He had just dealt two hands face down on the love seat when his bride emerged.

She wore a long white nightgown that draped delicately from two tiny white straps and outlined her body all the way to her bare feet. What was showing of her flawless skin was pink from the heat of the bath and her straight, dark, blunt-cut hair shone. She kept her eyes focused on the floor.

Jim's breath caught and he scarcely realized that he had stood at the sight of her. As she raised her eyes to meet his, she smiled self-consciously, scrutinizing his face.

"No matter how long I live," he said softly, "I will never forget this moment."

★ ★ ★ ★ ★

I got out of the tub, finally warm, and put on the silk gown and robe the bridesmaids had given me at our luncheon earlier in the day. While my clothes were still in the chair, Jim's had been neatly hung in the closet.

I emerged from the dressing area to find Jim sitting benignly on the love seat, dealing cards. He looked perfectly normal, except he was wearing midnight blue boxer shorts and a matching shirt, which he had left unbuttoned. Wow.

He stood and my eyes teared just looking at him. He was just about the most beautiful human being I had ever seen. He crooned lovely words indicating he was entertaining similar thoughts about me. It was a moment to last a lifetime, which is exactly how he summed it up too, later.

"I thought you didn't bring any playing cards."

He didn't answer for a minute, just continued the devouring look. Finally, he smiled and licked his lips. Although I was terribly self-conscious, I found myself staring back. He had to be absolutely the sexiest man I had ever seen.

"As you suggested, I called room service," he said, interrupting the lascivious looks between us. "In ten minutes, our friend Bert delivered a deck of cards, two ham sandwiches, two milks, and a piece of cherry pie, with two forks. While he was here, he also turned down the bed and left a red rose and a piece of chocolate on your pillow. I sure as hell hope he's not hustling you."

"If he is, he's coming with too little too late." Once again, I couldn't take my eyes off of Jim. His natural tan was emphasized by the midnight blue boxers and the matching shirt exposing his magnificent chest and stomach. "Where'd you get the outfit?"

"My sisters gave it to me at the motel this morning. They said you weren't the only one getting married, that this was my trousseau. They made me promise to wear it tonight. I told them I hadn't planned to wear quite so much. They twittered and suggested I start out in it, anyway."

"You look really . . . sexy."

"I think that was the idea. Be careful about admiring me too much. My plan for our activities tonight is to take things slow and easy, to give you plenty of time, plenty of space, but I didn't count on having to keep such a tight rein on my libido."

I glanced from his face to the two hands of cards on the sofa behind him, to the food tray on the coffee table, and back to his face. My quivery little smile became genuine.

He opened his arms and I walked into them with no other inducement.

We began to sway to the music lilting from speakers strategically placed about the room. A moment later, we were kissing and touching and warming. I moved easily in his arms, following his usual smooth lead.

As he guided me slowly about the sitting room, he kissed my throat. I kissed him back, scarcely noticing as he maneuvered us into the bedroom. As our feet moved, our hands glided, surveying one another. Smoothly, Jim snapped off lights, one by one, until the dim glow from one bedside lamp was all that remained.

"Which side of the bed do you want?" he whispered.

I shivered, not wanting to abandon the heat his arms and body generated. "The warm one."

"Wherever you are will be the warm one tonight, sweetheart, I promise."

Having glided to a standstill beside the bed, we kissed and caressed each other, rather meaninglessly at first, then with increasing heat. It was harder and harder to catch my breath. I didn't object as Jim coaxed the gown's straps off my shoulders and the silky garment slipped to my waist. It held there for one breathless moment, then slid over my hips and pooled in a soft heap at my feet. Jim held me close as if he didn't want me to realize or be self-conscious. With little encouragement, his upper body came free as I pushed his silk shirt off to drop on top of my gown on the floor.

He continued kissing, fondling, and caressing, his attentions more intense, his breath coming hotter and faster. I slipped my hands under the waistband of his boxers and pushed. It didn't take much. Then we were completely naked together, for the first time. His mouth consumed mine and my body responded, his heat drawing me closer, pressing my thighs tightly to his.

My fingers crept nimbly up his arms and over his shoulders as his huge, hot hands fondled the parts of me I loved him to touch. Then, slowly, feverishly, he sent his hands lower, to survey the hollows and crevasses where those hands had not been before. I moaned, the sound muffled by his mouth covering mine.

As I grew more frantic, Jim continued moving slowly, deliberately, as if he were in no hurry. I might have felt frustrated by his pace, except his breathing quickened as his body warmed and became tense. I panted, trying to control myself, my desire accelerated by the heat emanating from his body like a fever.

His hands flattened at my waist and roved to the small of my back where he pressed me firmly, aligning, introducing the most intimate parts of our bodies to one another. He swayed and suddenly his legs were between mine. He sat me on the side of the bed, then eased me back to lie there primed, aching with need. He reached back then to snap off the lone, dim light.

Murmuring sweet words, he lifted my legs, stretching me lengthwise on the bed, kissing and caressing them as I groaned with animal pleasure. As he moved up over me, I tried to lie very still, but I couldn't control the trembling. Jim hesitated and my eyes popped wide open.

The only light filtered through the sheer draperies covering the sliding glass door to our small, private terrace. The muted light outlined his perfect profile, his marvelous shoulders and biceps. Looking at him in silhouette, I could scarcely breathe.

"You all right?" he asked quietly.

"Yes." I sounded uncertain. "You do know what you're doing, right?"

"Yes, I do." He put his lips to my ear, which made me gasp. "Can I . . . help?"

"No. Think of something else. Just ignore me."

I put staying hands on his shoulders. "Will I hurt you if I do something wrong?"

"No. Relax. I love you. I love you more than anything else in the world." He nuzzled my throat.

I rocked my head to one side to allow him better access. "Relax," I whispered. "That's what the dentist says."

"You're ruining the mood."

I couldn't see him, but I could hear him grinning. "You mean if I talk too much, you won't want to do this?"

He lifted himself, separating his body from me. "This was on my 'to do' list, remember? You assigned me the task, now hush and let me do it."

"It's a dirty job but . . ."

"Somebody's got to do it," we finished together.

He continued touching and kissing me in the most intimate places imaginable until I writhed with need. Mesmerized, I couldn't think. I wanted only to feel the building excitement generated by his searching hands and mouth. Then he spoke again.

"And since we think you're probably not going to enjoy this little exercise the first time anyway . . ."

"Huh?" It took me a minute to understand. "Oh, yeah, we might as well . . . get the first time . . . over with." Oh, Lord, I wanted him too much to hold a thought, much less talk.

"Let me . . ." he whispered as he coaxed my knees further apart. I groaned with pleasure as he settled the heat of his hips between my thighs, then whimpered as his fingers brushed the sensitized vortex. As he increased his fingers' pressure, I moaned and twisted, writhing, first to escape his hand invading the down, then to encourage it.

He hesitated as if collecting himself. My breath came in short, quick gasps. Then I opened wider for him, arching, pushing my mound against his hand.

Throbbing, pulsing, a low whine issued from my throat and seared between clenched teeth. I thought nothing could ever be more exhilarating than the sensations he produced at that moment, but just as I thought that, the excitement climbed again.

His fingers and hands tantalized and titillated until my soft moans became noisy pleas. I opened my legs wider and bent my knees to cradle and encourage him. I arched my back to push my hot, hardened nipples against his chest. Below, he continued fingering me. I felt the moisture as I creamed, some instinct driving me toward an elusive crescendo. I bit my lips to muffle my more and more frequent cries of pleasure.

I splayed my hands on his shoulders, explored his chest, the hardness of his stomach and down to spread my hands over the taut muscles in his hips.

He braced himself on his arms and his penis replaced his fingers down there, arousing, bewitching as he located and followed the prepared path. His every move was slow and deliberate. He'd said we had plenty of time—a whole night, a lifetime. But my want was desperate. I needed him and that need was becoming urgent.

I clawed at his arms and shoulders and strove beneath him. His own breathing had become a pant, electrifying, rousing me to a higher level.

Quickening, I dug my fingernails into his biceps, rolled my

head back, and arched, pushing against the bed with my elbows to elevate my torso to seal my heat-moistened body with his. I whimpered, ready to cry with frustration. "Please. Jim, please."

He must have heard my desperation because at that moment he slid inside me.

He pumped slowly, gliding in a little . . . out . . . in a little further, patiently. He stopped when he met the natural barrier inside me. He lowered himself, smashing my body flat. He kissed me ravenously, then he was back on his knees pumping harder and deeper with more power, as if he could no longer control the urgency.

He plowed into me hard once, then twice. I held my position. With his third push, the barrier gave. With the fourth, it broke.

The cry that escaped in spite of my best efforts to hold it in was caught in his cavernous mouth sealed tightly over mine. Involuntarily, I stiffened, uncertain if the discomfort at the breach might continue or worsen, but I was determined not to resist. When I didn't struggle, he thrust once more, this time reaching unhampered into my depths.

Most women know what I knew at that moment. In an instant, I was caught, his forever. What happened between us in that second was as old as mankind. It was the claiming of a man and his mate.

He pumped again slowly, then again. I had just begun to follow the rhythm, to join in the dance when I felt his release. With his surge, I felt power abandon his body, penetrate and find its home in me—his woman, his wife.

The rush of sensations one right after another continued as he spasmed. The paroxysm lasted several seconds, then it was over and he was finished.

I felt his passion ebb, but he remained inside me, holding himself braced, poised over me. I pulled on his shoulders. I wanted to feel his weight, to have him lie on top of me, but he wouldn't.

Gradually he began again to breathe, panting at first, as if to restore depleted oxygen. We both held very still, a statue of lovers frozen in the throes of passion.

As if waiting for me, he remained silent. I lay quietly beneath him, scarcely breathing, feeling strangely fulfilled, though I knew I had not climaxed. In those hushed moments, I knew an ecstasy and a terrible uncertainty I had never experienced before.

"I love you," he whispered at last. "Did I hurt you?"

"No, my darling husband, you didn't."

"I want to thank you," he wheezed. "To honor you. I've always loved you, Jancy, from the first day. As impossible as it seems, I love you more for this, for tonight; for the virgin's barrier; for your never having known another man. It makes our union all the more sacred."

As his strength returned, joy surged into the man who was truly now my husband. I don't think it was only the physical satisfaction, which I knew he had known before, but it was a soul-consuming peace. He didn't make any effort to come out of me and I didn't know whether we were finished or not.

Scarcely breathing, he bent his elbows to lower himself. He kissed me once, a tender, lingering kiss, then he kissed me again . . . and again.

"Do you need time, you know, to recover?" he asked.

"No. Why? Are you not finished with me yet?"

He chuckled in the dark but remained firmly inside me.

"No, I'm not finished with you yet. I doubt I ever will be."

"Want to do it again?" I squirmed just a little, shifting my hips to get more comfortable. He lifted himself enough to allow me wiggle room.

"I love you," I whispered. Although I couldn't see his face

clearly, he appeared surprised by the uncertainty in my voice.

"What?"

"I . . ." I stammered and my voice broke. I could feel tears gathering in the corners of my eyes.

"Did it hurt that badly?" His voice was full of concern.

"No."

"You can't be sad, not when you've given someone the pleasure you have just given me." Holding himself on one arm, he dabbed at my tears with his thumb.

"Are you sure you still . . . love me?" My voice quaked.

He shook his head in disbelief. "There has to be another word, a bigger, more important word for it. What I feel for you, Jancy, goes way beyond love. It's more worship. Adoration. It is marvelous. Magnificent. The love I feel for you may be blasphemous." He forced himself to withdraw from inside me and shifted over, putting his head on the other pillow.

"I thought I loved you before," he said. "I didn't know I could feel . . . like this."

I sniffled. Quickly he was on his knees, startling me and grop- ing down my leg to my foot. Locating my little toe, he lifted it to his mouth to suck and caress it with his tongue.

"Quit!" I yelped, giggling and squirming to get away.

"Is there any part of your body that you consider less significant than this little toe?" He clasped my ankle firmly.

I continued laughing and trying to reclaim the foot. "No."

"The way I love the least significant thing about you is vast compared to the way anyone has ever loved anyone else in the history of the world."

"Because I let you screw me?"

He stopped still, then sputtered before a yowl broke loose without any warning. He rolled onto his back laughing and coughing.

"I don't think I understand," I said quietly to the darkness.

My confusion only seemed to refuel his raucous laughter. His joy subsided slowly.

When he had it under control, I whispered, "Would you like to do it again?"

As if eager to accommodate my request, Jim rolled onto his knees. Immediately he began stroking my arms, caressing his way over my body, and eventually again coaxing my legs apart. He bent and skewered his tongue into my belly button before his warm mouth planted kisses from my tummy up, between my breasts, nuzzling my throat, over my chin, and settled, hotly, at my mouth. As his fingers fondled, my mind slipped again, giving way to the pleasures of the flesh. Soon he was reopening, encouraging, again preparing the channel and I was boneless.

I writhed, halfheartedly attempting to stay his mouth or his hands, then groaned if his movements slowed or even faltered.

Then he was on top of me again, inciting me. The hot, eager probe located its path, this time with less urgency. He entered easily. The passage was well lubricated and I, eager.

Aware of him for only a moment, I lifted to soar, like an eagle in an updraft, climbing higher . . . higher . . . so high the air was too thin to sustain thought and I floated lazily beyond all caring . . . with Jim, who took me there.

After the pinnacle came the descent. Oh, how I hated that return. I wanted to stay in that ethereal place, beyond time and need and earthly concerns.

As our breathing returned to normal, we lay side-by-side in the dark. Dozing, I was afraid to review our activity too closely.

When I finally came fully awake, he was breathing evenly. I thought I might slip out of the bed but he roused when I stirred and he wanted me again.

After the third time, I sat up on the side of the bed. "I feel messy. Can I please go clean up?"

He rolled over and turned on the bedside lamp. I yanked the

sheet to my neck, covering my entire body.

Deferring to my sudden modesty, Jim draped the other corner of the sheet over his lower body. My eyes followed his as he glanced down at the bloody show on the pillowcase that he had so wisely spread beneath us. He folded the case. I watched without asking. He smiled at me and I smiled back, maybe a little uncertainly.

"How about a dip in the hot tub?" he said.

I felt too embarrassed to look at him. "Please, could we turn the light off?"

He snapped off the lamp.

"Thanks. Don't you think it's too late for the hot tub?"

"We're not on any schedule."

"Or too cold?"

"It'll probably help us sleep better."

"I didn't bring a bathing suit."

"We're on the eighteenth floor. No one can see you on our little balcony but me. We'll wrap up in a couple of those big towels, leave them on a chair right beside the tub, in easy reach."

Not wanting to be a spoilsport—a wet blanket, so to speak—I nodded uncertainly.

Jim leaped from the bed and hurried into the bathroom.

Embarrassed but curious, I strained against the darkness to see him, surprised to be so curious and startled that his naked silhouette, or what my eyes could make out, gave me such a wicked rush. I was amazed that his man's body could carry me to such an outrageous level of exhilaration or pleasure or whatever it was I experienced in his arms once and then, quite surprisingly, again and again.

He turned on the bathroom light and pushed the door nearly closed, then left it on when he peeked out at me.

I bit both lips to contain the pride I felt at having pleased him, that he seemed to take such genuine satisfaction in me.

As he turned to smile back, I continued my secret little survey. His broad shoulders had always appealed to me, as did the narrowing of his frame to the trim waist and down, sweeping to those surprisingly muscular hips. I admired the brawn of his marvelous thighs and calves limned by the light behind him. Clearly a magnificent specimen. And he was mine . . . because he loved me, slob that I was. I trembled and leaned backward, nestling into the pillows he had propped at my back.

He was in the bathroom a couple of minutes, then returned wrapped in a towel, covered from waist to knees, and carrying one of the large bath sheets.

"Let me help you," he said, coaxing me up by holding the bath sheet and indicating he would wrap it around me when I rose naked from the bed. But when I wiggled free of the sheets, he took a step back and looked me up and down, from head to toe. He studied me a long moment in the semidarkness before our gazes met.

"I've never seen you altogether." His voice was quiet, nearly hollow in the still silence of the late hour. "Even in a bathing suit, I didn't realize you were so perfectly proportioned."

I took a step forward and he wrapped the towel around me, his hands stroking casually, then gathered me in his arms and guided me to the sliding glass door.

Dreamily, I fairly floated at his side until he opened the door. The blast of arctic air caught me full in the face. I tried to retreat, but Jim blocked the way back.

Without giving me time to argue, he shoved me through the open door and onto the frigid terrace. He delayed just long enough to slide the door closed behind us, removing any option. With a squeal, I dropped the bath sheet and scurried into the tub. It was the most immediate sanctuary.

In spite of the icy temperature, Jim dropped his towel and hung back, uninhibited by his own nakedness, allowing his eyes to feast upon me. I kept my gaze on my hands waving back and forth under the water. The tub smelled of cleansers and chemicals.

"I have ugly legs," I said quietly as Jim eased into the water beside me. The water level rose as his shoulders submerged. I felt terribly self-conscious being nude and out in the open like that, especially as he persisted in looking at me. Finally, I returned his stare. I loved the dreamlike quality of the refracted shape of his body beneath the water. With what appeared to be heroic effort, he finally averted his gaze, pretending an interest in adjusting the jets.

"No, your legs are beautiful. You've got straight, sleek, gorgeous gams." He smiled. "A man could make a permanent home between those legs."

"I like dancers' legs, with muscular calves and bony ankles."

"You have trim, well-turned ankles, more like a girl than a guy." He ran a flattened hand over my thigh. "And feminine calves. Looking at you, I keep forgetting to breathe." He grinned and, seeing the ornery look, I braced for whatever was coming. "Of course, I've always been a boob man myself." The roving hand brushed over my breasts. "And you, woman, have got the greatest set of knockers I have ever seen. The first time I saw them—when we petted that first time, there in my kitchen—I nearly lost it. You were almost in serious trouble that night."

"What stopped you?" I splashed warm water on my face and tried to ignore our nakedness.

"I had a feeling then that tonight was coming and I had a little premonition; if I pushed too hard that night, we might not make it to this one."

I rocked my head back to look up at the clear, cold, star-studded sky. "I think I'm going to like being married."

"Oh, yeah? Why is that?"

"I think it might turn out to be an adventure." I shot him a timid look. "With new experiences . . . and sensations." I giggled and couldn't look at him again.

We were quiet a long time before my hand floated over to his. He squared himself, placed his hands on my hipbones and lifted. I floated easily, not interested in resisting. He set me astride his lap, facing him.

Although in that position my shoulders were out of the water, exposed to the cold air, I stayed, scarcely breathing, eager to see what came next. So far this night, he had come up with some seriously erotic activities.

We both watched his hands as they caressed and fondled my legs before he pleasured me in ways I had never imagined. I squirmed a little as he entered me, then I took a deep breath and looked to the heavens. Rakishly he toyed with me. I tried not to cry out, but I'd never known the kind of pleasure he generated as we made love again, while the water burbled around us and the heavens looked on.

Sometime in the early morning hours, we made our way back into our bed and slept—a deep, dreamless sleep—clothed, not in the expensive trappings of our separate, carefully selected trousseaus, but bundled together in a dry hotel bath sheet in our marriage bed.

CHAPTER SEVENTEEN

I opened my eyes in the early morning darkness uncertain for a moment where I was and decidedly concerned by the many unusual muscular aches, specifically between my legs. It wasn't until I heard breathing behind me that I remembered.

I moved cautiously. The insides of my thighs were tender, as if I'd been horseback riding after a long time away. Whisker burns around my mouth and face and neck, even between my legs, triggered other embarrassing reminders. My skin felt dry and itchy and I had a headache behind my eyes.

I eased the covers back but found I was wrapped in a large bath towel, the other end of which was anchored beneath the form sleeping behind me.

Carefully removing the towel, I inched out of the bed, not wanting to disturb my slumbering partner. Free of the towel, naked, I scurried to the dressing room.

In the darkness, I fumbled through the clothes on the hanging bar, hoping by touch to find the comfortable terry cloth robe my mother had strongly suggested I not take along on my honeymoon. But it was there, much to my relief. I needed not only its warmth, but its familiar smell and feel.

I hobbled on into the bathroom and stealthily closed and locked the door before I turned on the light.

My reflection in the glaring fluorescents was shocking.

The heavy makeup I had worn for the big occasion was gone, washed away, probably in the hot tub. My hair was spiked and sticky from the excess hairspray and, I supposed, the moisture from baths and perspiration.

Studying my reflection, my confidence tanked, but only for a minute, before I took hold. No use crying over damage done. My condition demanded attention and repair. I soaped a washcloth and scrubbed my face, rinsed it well, then scrubbed again.

I double-checked the mirror image and wondered if reparation were possible. I stared at that hideous reflection and shook my head covered with that wild hair. How could I be such a total disaster?

And there was more. How had I gotten myself into this? I felt like an animal caught in the iron teeth of a claw trap. Was escape possible? Was I willing to try? No, I was only fooling myself. My fate was sealed. My future appeared too ghastly to contemplate at that moment, a life of drudgery and servitude, absent the glamour and exotic people and places I had planned and worked toward.

I began scrubbing my throat and shoulders. Then I dropped the bathrobe and frantically went over my whole body with that cloth. Shivering, I again covered my splotchy body with the trusty bathrobe and snapped off the light before opening the door.

There were no sounds, nor any movement. The mound of bedclothes concealing my companion didn't appear to have moved, so I ventured out.

I eased beyond the bedroom and into the sitting area. Cold, I wrapped the robe more tightly and stepped around to lean against the back of the sofa. I folded my arms across my chest, and gazed out the sliding glass door—beyond the hot tub—at the city below. Smog hovered above the streetlights, which seemed to take turns closing their sleepless eyes for brief respites.

I took little comfort in the fact that I had been right about one thing. I could not have had sex before and walked away unscathed. I doubted if, from this point forward, I could ever recover my old individuality, my individual identity or joy or optimism.

It was my own darn fault. I hadn't been coerced. I had repeated the words before God and, as Jim pointed out, all the people who mattered most to me in the world, that I was giving myself to him, and for keeps. Several times—four, precisely—through last night, I had honored that promise by yielding my physical body. I felt like I had sacrificed my autonomy, renounced myself, even my own name. Quietly, I lowered my head and groaned in despair.

"Hey." Jim's voice was a little husky in the early morning quiet. I turned my head and my eyes—which hurt—to peer at him. He was lying there, exactly where I had left him. Had he seen me grieving, mourning all I had lost?

He lay on his side, one arm bent back, propping his head. When he had my attention, he folded back the covers. I could barely see his facial features in the half-light, but what I could see looked fresh and innocent. Exposed, his marvelous chest and stomach beckoned me. His voice less confident than his pose, he whispered, "Get back in here where you belong."

The bed looked warm, his body inviting. I was shivering in the chill of the room and in anguish over the drastic step I'd taken. He probably wanted to do the pleasure thing again. "Sex" was not an adequate word for what I had experienced through the night in his arms.

I might as well, my wiser self urged. It's too late to undo your commitment now anyway. You have, girlfriend, made your bed. Now you must lie in it.

I shuffled back to the bed, crawled in, and lay down, my back to him. He pulled the covers up and tugged me close, spooning my backside against the front of him, immediately warming me from tip to toe.

His hand stroked me gently. Instead of tensing, I relaxed. He handled me so carefully, he made me trust him. Slowly, he untied the terry cloth sash, opened my robe and splayed his warm hand over my midriff. Eventually that roving hand cradled and warmed my breasts. Then he became completely still. I hadn't intended to go back to sleep, but the bed and Jim's body were warm and welcoming, his breathing deep and steady, and . . . I did.

There was a cycle to that first day. We made love, slept, bathed, and ate, ordering breakfast and lunch in the room. That evening Jim suggested we dress and go out for dinner. I warned him it would take me a while to become presentable. After another round in the bed and a brief nap, he told me to get ready quick before the urge struck again.

It was December twenty-third, stores were open late and shoppers moved briskly. Catching the holiday spirit, we talked about doing a little additional Christmas shopping. After a leisurely dinner, however, as ridiculous as it sounds, I couldn't get back to our hotel room fast enough and remove the clothes that suddenly stood as annoying barriers between us.

Jim chuckled out loud at my feverish efforts to strip, but I didn't have to ask twice.

CHAPTER EIGHTEEN

In the bathroom loading toiletries into his kit, Jim said, "Jancy, call the front desk, will you, and ask them to send Bert for our bags."

I stalled, wandering around the room, touching things and glancing occasionally at the covered hot tub beyond the sliding glass door. I wasn't ready to leave.

It was mid-afternoon, Christmas Eve. Jim had promised my parents we would be back in Carson's Summit in time for mass. Initially, I was pleased with his thoughtfulness, but the more I thought about it, the more annoyed I got. I didn't want to mingle with a mob of other people, even family. I liked having Jim all to myself. Was that selfish of me? Sure it was, but I didn't care.

"Check-out time was noon," Jim reminded. I had dawdled all morning, between sessions of mindless, breathless lovemaking. As I stood staring out the sliding glass door, Jim slipped his arms around me. "We can come back," he whispered.

"It won't be the same."

"No, but maybe next time we'll look forward to it with less angst."

Probably true, but the changes that had occurred in me during our time together there could never be reversed. I could never reclaim my innocence, not that I would want to.

I pivoted in Jim's arms, the scent of him arousing me, inciting the tingling that had become so familiar in the last forty hours.

"What?" he asked.

"I'm just like Pavlov's dogs. They responded to the stimulus of a bell. I respond to you. As soon as I smell you or hear you or feel your arms around me, I start salivating." I gave him a grin. "So to speak."

Jim flashed his own Machiavellian smile. "I know what you mean. My biggest concern right now is when we'll be naked and alone again."

"You sound like an addict." I stroked his face.

He arched his eyebrows. "And you're my supplier."

Bert rapped lightly as he came through the open door wheeling a luggage carrier. Apparently Jim had summoned him. I sure hadn't.

"Do you want to hear another old wives' tale?" I asked as we made the two-hour drive to Carson's Summit.

"Sure." He smiled at the highway rolling out in front of us. "Are those things—those tidbits of wisdom from the old wives— are those written down anyplace?"

"I don't think so. If they were written down, some man would have analyzed them to pieces and destroyed the mystique."

"I see," Jim said, nodding with mock seriousness. "These truths are valid but cannot withstand the scrutiny of men, is that it?"

"This one came from Ivy Work." I pressed on, ignoring his comment. "She said there's an old theory that if a bride puts a bean in a jar every time she and her husband make love the first year and then takes a bean out of the jar every time they make love after the first year, that she'll never remove all the beans from the jar."

Jim's grin broadened. "Because they'll make love more times

in their first year than they will all the rest of their married lives?"

"Right."

"Has that been researched?"

"See!" I growled, "that's just like a man, questioning a perfectly reliable truism."

Jim flashed a skeptical look and we both laughed.

When we drove into my mom and dad's driveway, Jim commented on the many Christmas decorations adorning my family's two-story home.

"The outside of the house was completely decorated before the wedding," I reminded.

"I guess I had other things on my mind then and didn't notice."

"I guess." Gazing at the house, I felt suddenly embarrassed and flustered.

My grandparents' cars were there. All four of them were in the house. I had grown up in that house. Mom and Dad and my grandparents and brothers had witnessed my successes and failures. They had congratulated and teased me about my achievements, and consoled me when I miscued.

But this was different.

How strange it would seem to take Jim into my bedroom, to shut the door for the night with him inside. Of course, we couldn't make love, not there in my parents' house, practically in the lap of my entire family.

I hadn't anticipated all this emotional turmoil and, if it was that bad sitting in the driveway thinking about it, what would it be like inside, particularly as bedtime approached?

Jim nudged my arm. He grinned, a taunting, annoying expression at that moment.

"What?"

"They know we did it, Jance."

"I know."

"All of them know."

"Don't be a jerk. I know they all know."

His tone and his face became serious. "We can leave, if you want to. We can avoid them for the next year or so, until the bean jar's full. Maybe they'll forget about it. What do you think?"

"Hell's bells, Jim!" I could barely breathe.

"What?"

"Leave me alone." I stepped out of the car into the rosy twilight, which belied the twenty-five-degree chill. "Open the trunk."

Jim's eyes narrowed and I adjusted my tone and my attitude. "Please."

He pressed the trunk release on the driver's-side door and the lid popped up.

Juggling my purse, I picked up my weekender and the bag of hanging clothes and stalked toward the house without looking back, leaving Jim to manage the rest.

I was struggling to open the front door as he caught up. I turned my head to look at him. He eyed my shoulders. His gaze followed the curve of my back downward.

"Clothes no longer conceal the long, smooth arc of your back," he whispered. "Your curves are burned into my memory. I know how the graceful sweep of your spine curves to your lush, rounded hips and how those hips fill my hands. My body knows the feel of those long, shapely legs, open and warm and welcoming."

He was being ornery, kidding and serious and turning me on. I pivoted all the way around to brace him. He looked away but not before I registered the expression on his face.

He stepped close, put one suitcase down and reached around to open the door.

"Please don't look at me that way while we're here," I said, annoyed by the pleading in my voice.

"I'll try not to."

"And don't think about sex, okay?"

"Jance, I'm a newly married, duly enfranchised, male human being." He mouthed the words near my ear. "That's mostly what we think about. Besides, I can't help thinking about sex when I look at you, or smell you or hear you or . . . talk about Pavlov's dog.

"And, it's your own damn fault," he continued, barely taking a breath. "I can practically feel you touching me right now, a little timid, very curious. It doesn't take much to remember you purring in my arms, to recall how it feels when you nuzzle against my chest, or how you moan your objection every time I come out of you."

"Don't say things like that."

The door opened abruptly and my twenty-one-year-old brother Gregory suddenly loomed in front of us. The sweet smells of Christmas wafted from inside the house: yeast rolls, roasting meat, coffee.

"Say things like what?" Gregory said defensively, obviously puzzled. "I didn't say anything."

"I didn't mean you, goofus," I said, the spell Jim had cast broken. "Here, make yourself useful." I jammed my weekender and the hanging bag into Gregory's arms. "Take these up for me, will you?"

"Right," he said, eyeing Jim, "I see marriage hasn't taken any of the edge off her bossiness."

"Not yet," Jim said, setting his suitcases beside the stairway, "but we're working on it."

"Whose wheels?"

"Mine." I didn't try to hide my pleasure. "A wedding gift from my very own, practically perfect husband." I flashed a superior, Cheshire cat grin at Gregory, silencing further inquiry, and moved inside to peek into the living room.

The tables and wedding gifts were gone. The porcelain crèche occupied its usual holiday place on the coffee table. Jim trailed along as we proceeded to the den where the Christmas tree was barely visible above the mounds of wrapped and ribboned gifts. Coals from an earlier fire still glowed in the fireplace. The five stockings hanging above the hearth had become six, with "Jim" emblazoned in hand-sewn, multicolored sequins on the new addition. I walked directly there and fingered it, smiling warmly. "Grandma did it for you. She's done all of them."

Jim smiled.

Voices in quiet conversation came from the direction of the kitchen. I took Jim's hand and a deep breath and led him toward the voices.

Duke Mallory leaned against a cabinet, a cup of coffee in one hand, a cinnamon roll in the other, talking quietly with my mother as she stirred brown gravy in a skillet on the stove. Mom's mother sat at the breakfast table scowling over a crossword puzzle in the newspaper.

"Hello, there," Mallory said as we stepped into the room. Mom's face brightened. She put the spoon down and, looking intently into my eyes, opened her arms. After a big hug, she stepped back to look me up and down.

"She's none the worse for wear," Jim assured them from the doorway.

Mallory's expression, which had turned grim as he looked at Jim, suddenly broke into a broad smile. He put his roll on his cup to free a hand, and shook my husband's.

"She's even prettier," Mallory said. "It looks like marriage agrees with both of you."

Unable or maybe unwilling to extricate myself from my mother's embrace, I smiled over her shoulder and mouthed

"Hi" to my grandmother, who remained at the table. Then I focused on Duke. "What are you doing here?"

"I'm family now, hadn't you heard? Gregory and Tim call me 'Uncle Duke' or 'the Dukester.' Your Grandma will probably make a stocking for me next year."

"You scammed my Midwestern, gullible-type family into adopting you? You old con artist, you."

Mallory's roar of approval muffled laughter from Mom, my grandmother, and Jim, who remained a silent audience for the repartee. Without another thought I stepped around my mother and leaped into Mallory's arms. His hands again occupied with cup and roll, he let me hug him without returning the favor.

"I don't remember your being this affectionate before." Mallory's observation triggered a round of twittering laughter.

"Before what?" I asked, arching my eyebrows and pretending innocence. There was a loud guffaw from the bystanders, the loudest from Gregory and Jim. Mallory grinned sheepishly. It was the closest I had ever seen him to embarrassed.

"This may not be as tough as I thought," I said in a stage whisper to Jim as I slipped over to loop my arm through his.

Mallory pretended to be fascinated by the half-eaten cinnamon roll and Jim smiled, acknowledging my little victory just as my dad, granddad, and younger brother Tim exploded through the garage door, loaded with grocery sacks. Granddad hugged me first then said a more formal hello and offered Jim his hand.

Daddy beamed. Relieved of his sacks, he threw his arms around me and squeezed. "My little girl's back."

"Afraid not," Jim corrected, his voice quiet with authority. "She's mine now." Dad frowned at Jim before he gave up a crooked smile, and the two most important men in my life shook hands.

Mom wrapped a protective arm around Jim's waist, the other

around Daddy's. "Now, boys," she warned, "you know if you're going to fight over her, you'll have to take it outside."

Daddy stared at her. "It's freezing out there, woman. I think we can get along." He smiled at Jim. "Can't we, son?"

Jim returned the smile. "Yes, sir."

Mom wanted to know where we'd been, what we'd done, "for entertainment," she added lamely, then quit trying to clarify her question amid sporadic, self-conscious twitters of laughter.

"I'll tell you all about it later," I said, winking. Jim raised his eyebrows, half pretending to caution me as I laughed.

"Things sure smell good," I said, ignoring Jim's eyebrows and locating napkins and silverware to begin setting the table for Christmas Eve dinner. "How many?"

"Twelve," Mom said.

"Who else is coming?" Dad asked.

"Gregory invited Rachel for dinner and mass." She shrugged off my dad's unasked follow-up questions.

The conversation had turned to Jim and my upcoming, continuing honeymoon trip to the slopes, when Jim suddenly remembered an errand and pulled the car keys out of his pocket.

"What do you hear from San Diego?" I asked Mallory as I set the table and he filled water glasses with ice. I didn't want to appear too curious about Jim's sudden, mysterious errand.

"Not much. Thad Bias left. I already told you that."

"Where'd he go?"

"East. Ivy said he's turned into a cowboy now, someplace rural. He moped around a couple of days, mooning over you I expect, then he took off. He gave O'Brien two weeks' notice, but the captain kept it quiet. You know O'Brien, likes startling us with late-breaking news; makes him feel important, being privy to someone's secrets."

I don't know why I felt disappointed. Ichabod had returned to Sleepy Hollow. So what? Still, not knowing where Thad was made me oddly uneasy.

"Have there been any more candlestick burglaries?" I asked casually, not wanting my concern to show.

Mallory puckered and shook his head.

I didn't mention Thad's departure to Jim, but then I was distracted when he returned carrying a large gift-wrapped package, which, on questioning, he declined to explain.

Jim had never been upstairs in my family home. Before dinner, I suggested we move our luggage up to my room and I gave him a quick tour.

"Do you like it?" I asked, referring to my bedroom.

"Very nice. I've never slept anyplace this pink and flowery before."

I reevaluated the room with new eyes. "I guess not." I giggled self-consciously, particularly as my eyes followed his to the bed. "Do you think we'll be too crowded? It's only a double."

"It's cooling down outside. Do your folks keep the heat up at night?"

"No."

"We'll probably need to snuggle . . . for warmth."

"And that's the only reason?"

"Maybe."

"Jim, this is my room."

He arched his eyebrows and lowered his voice. "My plan is to initiate every room we sleep in exactly the same way." He added quickly, "And if you don't want to hear the next, obvious answer, you'd better not ask the next, obvious question."

Sometimes having a transparent face can be an advantage. At that moment, I'm pretty sure mine reflected a tiny bit of trepidation along with a bunch of excited anticipation.

Dinner was delicious, the air laced with noisy conversation, our usual family enhanced by the presence of both sets of my grandparents, Rachel Rodriguez, Gregory's girlfriend—with her dark skin and her startling gray eyes—and Duke Mallory.

At ten-fifteen we bundled up, dashed out into the seventeen-degree night with a wind chill factor that dropped the temperature to minus four, loaded into three vehicles, and motored off to Christmas Eve Mass as my family had done every year for as long as I could remember. Tim, Gregory, and Rachel opted to ride with Jim and me.

Most members of the small Episcopal church in Carson's Summit had met Jim. Only a few knew Rachel Rodriguez, who was a relative newcomer to the community and a Roman Catholic besides, or Duke Mallory. Our guests were greeted warmly and escorted into the church to find a place in the same general proximity despite the usual crush.

Nestled under Jim's arm, after the caroling I tried to stifle recurring yawns. The big supper, the lateness of the hour, and the activity of the last few days, combined with the familiar comforts of home, had taken a toll. When I raised my face to admire my handsome husband, Jim returned the look. I smiled. He turned his eyes to the front and I sat up straighter, straining to put my nose against the side of his cheek, near his ear, to smell the mingled fragrances that were him. My breath caught as I inhaled his scent. He turned his face toward me and smiled again.

"Just Pavlov's mutt sniffing around," I whispered. He continued his knowing smile.

I was thankful Father Frank didn't use incense, which always made me sleepier, but time seemed to drag. I was eager to get home to a hot bath and warm bed. I had almost reconciled myself to the idea of sharing—the latter, not the former. The sermon over, we processed through communion, sang final carols, and adjourned.

It was only twelve-thirty but seemed much later. The wind blasted ice flecks in our faces as we made a run to the cars and hurried home, via Rachel's. Avoiding the side trip, Tim rode with Mom and Dad.

I don't exactly know why I was surprised to see Gregory kiss Rachel good-night. He did it casually, as if that kiss at her door were not their first.

"I hadn't realized . . ." I said, turning to Jim. "I mean, he's my little brother. I never think of him . . ."

"It's better not to get involved in your siblings' romances," he said. "You've got your own fires to tend." With that, he planted a firm kiss and, surprisingly, snaked a cool hand under my skirt and up the inside of my thigh.

"Jim, don't be naughty when we're around other people."

"Okay." He laughed, but kept the hand under my skirt. "I'll wait until we get home."

"You don't mean Mom and Dad's."

"Damn straight. I haven't had a fix since this morning. I'm not waiting past bedtime."

"But Jim, what about my mom and dad and my grandparents and the boys . . . and Mallory?"

"They're not invited."

"No, I mean, they'll hear us. They'll know."

"They may suspect, but they'll suspect whether we do or we don't. All you have to decide is if you want your bath before or after." He paused a minute. "Maybe we'll make it both.

Jim withdrew his hand from under my skirt and I slumped back against the seat as Gregory opened the back door and got into the car.

"Cute girl," Jim observed as he pulled the car away from the curb.

Gregory frowned. "Yeah. Too bad."

Neither Jim nor I asked what he meant.

"Honey, run on up and take your bath so you won't keep us all up," Mom said to me as soon as we walked in the house.

I flashed Jim a warning glance before I took his hand and led him through the hallway and up the stairs.

"Jim," Mom called, "you can stay and have a piece of cake with us while Jancy bathes, if you like."

"No thanks," he called back, then whispered words I hoped only I heard, "I'll have my piece upstairs, thanks."

I squeezed his hand to shush him, an admonition that turned to muted giggling as I locked my bedroom door behind us.

I grabbed my toothbrush as Jim peeled down to his shorts. Hesitating then, I watched as he meticulously hung up his clothes and pulled back the bed covers before he turned those black, fathomless eyes on me. I had stepped out of my skirt and removed my sweater and pantyhose and, in my half slip and bra, searched through my suitcase for a nightgown sexy enough for a bride and stodgy enough to be seen by my family as I shuffled to and from the bathroom.

Coming up behind me, Jim wrapped one arm around my shoulders, one around my waist and buried his face in my neck. In the next heartbeat, he lifted and carried me to the bed. Kissing me, he positioned me carefully and turned off the bedside lamp.

It had been nearly twelve hours since we had made love. The foreplay was abbreviated and I wasn't quite ready when he entered. He finished quickly and lay back, tucking the covers around me. A moment later, a little disappointed, I got up, collected my gown and robe, and started toward the bathroom. Jim leaned up on one elbow.

"That's our last quickie, I promise. That one was kind of an emergency. From now on we'll take our time and let everybody enjoy the ride."

I tried a game smile. "It didn't bother me that much."

"Well, little girl, I want it to bother you. I want it to bother you a whole lot, every single time. Come back here." He folded the covers back. "We'll give it another run."

Giggling, I tossed my clothes onto a chair and jittered on tippy-toe back into bed.

CHAPTER NINETEEN

Despite all the wedding gifts strategically stashed throughout the house, Jim and I opened another dozen Christmas presents found under the tree on Christmas morning. Among them was the mysterious box Jim had purchased when he ran his secret errand after we arrived in Carson's Summit. The tag said: "To Jancy, from Jim."

Inside were bags of colored gumballs and a wide-mouthed glass jug with an oversized cork stopper lid. I examined the contents curiously, then looked to Jim for an explanation.

He leaned close. "It's this century's version of a 'bean jar.' "

I gasped, then laughed quietly, trying not to provoke any interest from other people all around us tearing into gifts of their own.

Later in the morning, after breakfast, as the family drank coffee at the dining table, avoiding the den and its prolific aftermath, Mom asked what was in the box from Jim. I didn't risk a look at him and dodged the question by asking one of my grandmother. But Gregory's curiosity was aroused and he came back to it like a bulldog.

"Jance, what's the story on the gumballs and the jug?"

"You wouldn't get it," I said, trying to dismiss him with superiority, which had usually worked when we were growing up. He persisted. I looked to Mom for help, but she only shrugged.

"If you must know, it's an updated version of a bride's bean jar," I said finally, quietly, speaking more to my mother than to Gregory.

Mom's eyes widened and darted to Gregory. "I'll tell you later," she said in a stage whisper.

"I want to know now."

Seated at the table studying an instruction sheet, seemingly oblivious to our conversation, Daddy cleared his throat. "Drop it, Gregory. I'll tell you later."

Grinning down at his coffee cup, Jim pretended to ignore the exchange. I could have clobbered him.

We took our time loading my new car to the gunnels with all the Christmas and wedding gifts we could cram inside, leaving barely enough room for us. Gregory and Tim would ferry Mallory to the airport in Dominion on Tuesday for his return to California, but he wouldn't be seeing us again. We promised to keep in touch, but I think Mallory and I both knew that was unlikely. We were headed separate ways.

A little before noon, with a noisy flurry of good-byes, we squeezed into the midnight blue Mercury and drove away.

We drove directly to the Wills' home in Dominion for an afternoon of too much food, football on television, and a brisk family walk to shake off the drowsies. Self-conscious at first, I was soon comfortable again with Jim's family. I was delighted, of course, to be with Olivia and William, Jim's mother and dad.

The crowd included the four members of the Peck family: Paul, who scrutinized us closely all afternoon; the four Colettes; Jim's younger, taller, fairer brothers Peter and Andrew; and Eve, the baby of the family.

It was late afternoon when the guys chose up sides for a little tag football in the backyard. I didn't know why five-year-old Amanda and I were the only females willing to play.

At first the men gave us the ball some, but as the intensity of the game increased, so did the tags. When Paul rudely knocked me on my keister short of the goal line with a bone-crunching tackle, it knocked the wind out of me.

"Paul, take it easy," Jim yelled as he knelt beside me. I was scared to death, felt like I'd never take in air again, but Jim provided soft reassuring words and touching.

"Relax," he crooned. "You'll be able to breathe in a minute. Easy now. Don't fight it."

Paul was full of bluster. "A visitor's got no business playing with our family anyway. If she can't stand the heat . . . keep her off the field."

"Like you were ever tough enough to take it," Jim taunted, without looking up. "Beating up on girls is about your speed. I'm surprised you haven't decked Amanda too, a big stud like you."

Sputtering, I was just beginning to breathe when Paul suddenly flew over my prone body and rammed Jim, flattening him against the ground. Paul scrambled to wind up on top. Not sure what was happening, I watched, horrified, as Paul landed a fist to Jim's stomach. It was the only punch thrown.

In a blink, Jim rolled from bottom to top, pinned Paul's arms at his sides, then stared down into his older brother's face. They remained that way for a minute before Paul began yelling for Jim to stop.

Leaning up on an elbow, I tried to see what was happening. Whatever Jim was doing obviously was excruciating but I couldn't tell what was causing Paul's alarm. Amanda came over as I sat up and draped her little arm protectively around my shoulders as we watched her two grown uncles.

"What's Jim doing?" I asked. "Why is Paul having such a fit?"

"It's the spit."

I looked more closely. A loogie oozed from Jim's lips and

hung precariously above Paul's very vulnerable face. Paul rocked his head from side to side, bucked and kicked and struggled but Jim kept him firmly pinned to the ground. Jim spat the loogie off to the side. "Apologize."

"I'm sorry I tackled your woman."

"Not to me, pea brain, to her."

Paul turned his face toward me. "I apologize, Jancy, now call him off."

A new bubble of spittle appeared. Amanda and I looked at each other, cringed, and began giggling. "Jim, that is so gross," I said. "Quit."

He didn't move.

I rolled onto my knees, crawled over to him, picked a blade of dry grass, and tickled his ear.

Jim spat on the ground close beside Paul's head, then turned his attention to me and smiled menacingly. "You're next."

I put both hands on his shoulders and shoved him off of Paul onto the grass. Free, Paul leaped to his feet and scampered sideways to get out of Jim's reach, but Jim obviously had fresh prey.

Wrapping his arms around me, he carefully rolled us over and over on the dry grass. I sputtered and giggled. Running along beside us, Amanda suddenly threw her small body on top of us and yelled, "Dog pile."

Alerted, the other players from both teams ran toward us.

Curly and Moe leaped on Jim's back, carefully avoiding Amanda. With a whoop, Peter and Andrew hurled themselves into the fracas.

Using his body as a tent over me, Jim said, "Scoot out of here."

I shimmied out from the bottom of the human heap just as Peter and Andrew landed.

The combatants rolled over and over in the grass, laughing

and trading insults. Just clear of the pile, I sat leaning back on my arms, enjoying their antics and the fading sunshine and the sight of my brand new, beautiful husband roughhousing.

Even with the pleasant prospect of the first night in our own home, I was reluctant to leave the Wills and their house full of excitement that never seemed to ebb. Beth put Baby Jim to bed and Amanda was glassy-eyed by the time Jim coaxed me out of there. We would be back after our Colorado trip to collect the odds and ends that would not fit into our already overloaded vehicle.

In the darkened car en route the seventeen miles to Bishop and Jim's condo, I leaned back and drew a deep breath. "How many children would you like to have?"

"A dozen."

Only mildly alarmed, I looked at him.

He grinned. "I think the more practical question is how many do we want to raise?"

I tried to fathom the look on his face in the partial light of the darkened car. "Do you mean how many we can afford?"

"No. I guess we probably need to consider that, too. My folks never had a lot of money and we all got grown. We all had as much or as little college as we wanted. No, I'm talking about time.

"There are a lot of things to take people's attention these days. Many of them are legitimate, worthwhile projects. Women today work outside the home to make money or pursue fame or something. They seem to need the stimulation of having paying jobs."

Oncoming lights illuminated his face and I could see he was serious.

He continued. "Most men don't mind if wives get up and leave the house with them in the morning and bring home a paycheck, too. But it means stashing the kids someplace, letting them grow up learning their morals and attitudes and behavior from caretakers. It looks to me like a lot of day care employees are people who aren't qualified to do anything else. That means we leave our most valuable possessions in the care of our least capable caregivers. I don't want that for our kids.

"I don't necessarily want a pack of little clones, but I want us to influence them—their thinking and standards.

"So, actually, how many kids I want depends on you—not on how many you're willing to bear but how much of yourself you're willing to give to them and me."

I felt the familiar burn in my throat and behind my eyes. "Listen, you," I said, swallowing and blinking, "I'm not going to be the heavy in this deal."

"Okay." He let up a little on the accelerator. "Let's say America sends a peacekeeping force to Syria and Riley Wedge wants you to go. Will you pack a duffel and kiss me and the kids goodbye?"

"You said I was free to pursue my career."

"Right, which is exactly why I'm hedging about kids. Children are important. It's not enough to tell them they are. They have to see they're important. Kids are astute and they have their own peculiar priorities. Was your mom a homeroom mother?"

"Yeah."

"Do you remember when you were in grade school and she brought the cookies or the punch or whatever for a party?"

"Sure."

"I can see the pride in the look on your face right now. Your mother didn't ever bring 'store-bought cookies,' did she?"

I was surprised at the suggestion. "No. Sometimes they were even still warm from the oven."

"And did the other kids tell you how pretty she was?"

I couldn't stop the laugh rolling up from deep in my throat.

"And I wanted to be just like her."

"Which do you think is more important, running from rock to rock imbedded with American troops, or baking peanut butter cookies for the second grade?"

"Well . . ." I was hard-pressed. "You tell me, which one is more important? What's the right answer?"

"Whichever you decide is the right one, so long as you don't entertain some goofy idea you can do both. You can't. Even you, Jancy Dewhurst Wills, super woman, can't do it all."

"A lot of women today juggle careers and homes."

" 'Juggle' is a good term for it too. And they are frustrated and frazzled and go around feeling inadequate. They cope with other people all day and get home tired. They need to ease up, pamper themselves or be pampered a little. Instead they hurl headlong into shuttling kids to gymnastics or piano lessons, fixing meals, giving baths, doing laundry, looking at homework, coping with a whole new bunch of problems to solve.

"They're tired. It's no wonder they get resentful. They only get the same twenty-four hours a day the rest of us get. No matter how hard they try, they can't spread themselves thin enough to cover all the bases in only twenty-four.

"Pretty soon an overworked, overtired wife/mother/career woman gets to feeling rundown and inadequate. She takes pills and alcohol or drinks too much caffeine to boost her energy, but it's not enough. She is then ripe for what I call 'a friendly takeover.' Some guy at work who's not getting sufficient attention from his own wife/career woman picks up on our gal's signals. He says something nice. She likes it. They slip off for a drink or a quiet dinner. They unload their woes on each other's sympathetic ears. Before long they're looking for a more private place to talk, a place that's serene—not like home—a place where they can get and give a little undivided attention, a little of that pampering we mentioned. They mistake the quiet for new love.

"The next thing you know there's domestic violence, divorce, custody battles, battered kids, and even killings, and society acts surprised.

"You know I'll be there, too, but a mom's attention is important. Doing school stuff for her kids says 'I love you.' That's a message kids can see. You can't mail that one on postcards from exotic places, or even fax it from an office downtown."

He'd made some good points, but I wasn't ready to yield the argument. "Most families have to have two paychecks."

"Only if they have to have two cars, and a house with a pool, and uptown wardrobes for both adults, and child care, and eat most of their meals out."

"Jim, I'm a good reporter. No one goes into journalism for the money. I might not be a good wife or mother. I'm an unknown quantity in those areas, but I've proven myself at reporting."

Jim took a breath like he was going to argue, but he hesitated, obviously changing his tack. "How did you know you would be a good newspaper person?"

"I just had a feeling I might be."

"Do you have a feeling you'll make a good wife?"

I brightened. "Haven't had any complaints."

He grinned. "Yeah, you seem to have a flair for it." He set his eyes back on the highway.

I thought about what he'd said. "Being a wife and mother doesn't pay much."

"Food, shelter, clothing, and security for as long as we live. I promised."

"Jim, be serious. I'm a good financial resource. I probably won't make a lot of money, but I can contribute."

"Honey, neither one of us is 'thing happy.' I make enough money to support us and I can make more, if we need me to. I can provide everything we need and most of what we want. You don't have to work. But you like the work you do. You might not be happy lying on the sofa watching soaps and eating bonbons."

I laughed. "Then again . . ." I didn't finish the sentence.

He laughed with me and pushed the accelerator, speeding up. "We don't have to decide anything tonight. We can discuss it, make up our minds when we're ready."

I nodded in the darkness but I suddenly had a whole new subject to ponder. Was a career as full-time wife and mother important enough for an ambitious woman to dedicate herself to that alone?

CHAPTER TWENTY

The weather was raw and blustery. Except for one trip to the grocery store, Mr. and Mrs. Jim Wills hibernated the next thirty-six hours, even let the answering machine field our calls.

We rose in the chill half-light of morning on December twenty-seventh, shared a hot shower, dressed, loaded our suitcases, and drove to the Dominion airport, where we boarded a plane and flew to Colorado Springs, gaining one hour as we traveled west into the Rocky Mountains.

A native flatlander, I had never seen real mountains except from an airplane window at thirty thousand feet, nor had I imagined the splendor of the great looming peaks clothed in their winter whites, mute sentries separating the eastern United States from the west.

The air was frigid when we deplaned, but there was no wind and the sun seemed unusually bright. I stood quietly gazing at the peaks while Jim rented a car.

We spoke only occasionally as we drove north on Interstate 25 to Denver, the great hulk of mountainous earth maintaining, even increasing, its mass as we traveled. We made one detour, to see the Air Force Academy reclining comfortably in the abundant lap of the Rockies north of Colorado Springs. Although Jim watched me, he didn't press for conversation.

From Denver, we turned west toward the Great Divide, the mountains again intimidating me to silence.

"Do you like them?" Jim asked finally.

"They are massive, marvelous monuments to God," I said reverently. Jim's eyes followed mine to our left where lofty peaks swallowed the early afternoon sun, leaving only blazing shades of orange streaking the sky in its wake. The streaks reflected off ominous gathering clouds.

We had a late lunch in Boulder and toured the university campus quickly, hurrying to beat the snow, which, without fanfare, began falling in great, lacy flakes.

"It looks like duck down," Jim characterized when I mentioned the size of the flakes.

The southwest motif of the university's buildings was lost on me. I couldn't take my eyes off the mountains, while my hand just as constantly held tightly to Jim's.

"The mountains are awesome," I breathed quickly, inhaling again and again. I could not seem to get enough air. "I never imagined anything like them."

Back in the car, we wound our way to Estes Park, creeping the last twenty-two miles as the snowfall became heavy. We drove steadily, however, trailing a snowplow that was clearing drifts before they could gather to thwart weary travelers.

As we drove through the pass that opened upon Estes Park nestling against the breast of the Rockies, I drew another deep, deep breath and shivered a little.

"Are you cold?"

"Not exactly, but Jim, when you look at them, do you hear something, a kind of humming in your chest?"

"No, I don't believe I do."

"Every time I see a different peak looming in the distance, I feel this low sound vibrating inside me. It goes, 'Mmmmm.' " I made a low, groaning sound that vibrated my chest. "It's actually more like a pulse than a tone. It may be the mountains singing, but it's so low I can't actually hear it, but when I listen, I can feel it. Are you feeling anything?"

He nodded slowly. "I guess. Maybe. I may have felt it when I was here before, but it never got into my conscious mind. I've never heard anyone describe it. Yes, I guess maybe I do feel a hum."

I squeezed his hand, but kept my eyes on the expanses, afraid the phenomenon would vanish.

The hotel room was warm, with a king-size bed and dark, luxurious furnishings. The bellman apologized that the television reception was poor and that their cable was on the fritz. Jim and I glanced at each other and laughed.

"They have a famous restaurant here," Jim said when the bellman was gone. "Are you hungry?"

"No." I gazed at the breathtaking view from our window. The snow had stopped.

"I think they have night skiing, but beginners probably should wait until tomorrow and get started in the daylight."

I looked at him, curious about what he meant.

Taking my hand, he tugged me toward the bed. "Come on, let's take a little nap."

I stepped out of my shoes and folded the quilted bedspread back as Jim took off his shoes. We lay down fully clothed, side-by-side, holding hands.

Too keyed-up to sleep, I rolled toward him and ran a hand up his arm. He flexed and grinned, as if he were glad to have finally gotten my attention.

I loved touching the muscles in his arms, feeling the strength in his shoulders. When my wandering hands reached his neck, I pushed his head the other way and squirmed to kiss his jaw.

"I hope you brought your bean jar," he said softly.

"What's it to you?"

"Nothing." Methodically, he began coaxing me out of my clothes, fondling, whispering, persuading, taking me to what he called "the thin air," excursions in which I participated more eagerly each time.

Later, he covered our warm, naked bodies with the quilt, draped his arm over me, and closed his eyes.

I yawned. "Just a short nap, then we have to get going, see things, listen to these people talk. The way they clip their words, they make us sound lazy."

Jim mumbled agreement. The steady rhythm of his breathing lulled me until I, too, slept.

Housekeepers rattling their carts down the hallway woke me up at nine A.M. Still naked beneath the cover, I felt refreshed and hungry after our thirteen-hour hibernation, and warm despite the cool room. I lay with my back spooned against his chest. His arm over me, his hand cupped one of my breasts.

I stirred, rousing him, and stretched. "What happened?" I tried to think what might have tranquilized us. We hadn't eaten or drunk anything.

Jim curled his warm hand around my waist. "I guess the mountains hummed us to sleep."

"Really?" I rolled over to face him.

"No." He nuzzled my neck. "It's the altitude. It'll wear us out for the first couple of days. Even in this valley, we're at twenty-seven hundred feet. The air's a little thin up here for folks who are two thousand feet above their usual."

"Is that what you mean when you talk about 'the thin air?' " I smiled without opening my eyes.

"No. Come here and let me jog your memory."

We made love slowly, using all of the king-size bed, touching, kissing, teasing in our increasingly comfortable ritual.

Afterward, Jim shaved, then we showered together, laughing, even singing occasionally, seldom out of each other's reach.

Dressed, we went to the restaurant for breakfast. Jim asked about skiing lessons for beginners. The hostess said the man who owned the gift shop in the colonnade in the hotel basement occasionally helped novices, when he was available.

Ed Ramsey was probably fifty years old, robust, jovial, and pleased to be asked. The hand he offered during introductions was thick and calloused, making him seem capable.

Lessons from a certified instructor usually ran forty dollars a person, Ramsey said. He could give us enough information to master the beginner's slope. After that, "you'll know how deep you want to get into this skiing business."

We could rent equipment in the ski shop just down from the hotel. He would meet us there in twenty minutes.

The young man running the ski shop recommended a lot of equipment. Neither Jim nor I were certain how much of it was necessary for our limited skills.

Then Mr. Ramsey blustered into the shop, swept through, snatching items here and there, rejecting some for others that appeared to me to be identical. Ramsey acknowledged but generally ignored the persistent advice of the young clerk.

When he had finished gathering gear, he plopped it on the counter and motioned to Jim to pay up. Jim waited for the clerk and Mr. Ramsey to thrash out the necessity of several other items as I, loaded down with gear both advisors deemed necessary, got to the exit. Someone pushed the door open from the other side. When I looked up, there, holding the door, poised squarely in front of me, stood Thad Bias.

CHAPTER TWENTY-ONE

Thad and I stood face-to-face, practically toe-to-toe, speechless for one breathless moment before we found our voices and said, almost in unison, "What are you doing here?" Then we both laughed.

Thad glanced quickly up and around, confirming that Jim was there, then turned a less pleased expression again on me. "You're honeymooning here?"

Smiling broadly, I gave several staccato nods. "Mallory told me you'd left, but he didn't know where you'd gone. Are you working here in Estes Park?"

"I'm police chief in a little town about thirty miles over in the mountains."

"Is that a promotion?"

Thad shrugged. "It is if you can live on the money. It's easy and a big improvement over having a guy like Murray O'Brien riding your back, then taking credit for anything you accomplish."

Jim, also loaded with ski equipment, stepped up beside me. He didn't look particularly happy to see Thad, or even say hello. In fact, he smiled vacantly. At that same moment the hotel photographer popped in front of us and snapped several pictures. Thad threw his hand up to cover his face, then grinned sheepishly.

"An old habit. I used to work undercover on drug cases. I'm still a little skittish about having my picture taken."

"Jim," I said, concerned about why he looked so blank, "you remember Thad Bias, don't you?"

Jim flashed Thad a polite smile, and shook his head. "No, I don't believe so." He juggled equipment to free his right hand and offered it. Thad studied Jim a long moment before he took the offered hand.

I had always thought Thad unusually tall. I was surprised he and Jim were the same height. Thad looked thin and very pale—fragile, even—as he stood there staring at my husband.

"I . . . ah . . ." Thad stammered, looking from Jim to me and back, "I guess we missed one another in San Diego."

Jim appeared puzzled by Thad's obvious effort not to look directly at either of us. "I guess so. Are you a newsman?"

Thad shot me an accusing glare. "No, I'm law enforcement, like you." His eyes swept the ski shop. "Are you staying here at the hotel?"

Both Jim and I answered affirmatively.

Thad's restless eyes again settled on my face. "It's good to see you again, Jancy. How long will you be around?"

I looked to Jim. He hadn't told me our plans, just that we would be back in Bishop for New Year's Eve.

"Until Saturday," Jim said, but he didn't make any overtures or try to ease Thad's obvious awkwardness.

"So you're a skier?" I said, speaking to Thad, filling the gaping silence.

"Nah, mostly I just come up here to scope out the snow bunnies, you know, the dollies who lounge around the bars at the bottom of the run. They wear the togs but don't ski. They don't want to risk breaking a nail, much less a leg."

Jim and I laughed politely.

"A little variation on the term 'hot pursuit,' " Jim said, nodding sagely.

It was Thad's turn to chuckle. "Yeah." He cast an odd, lingering look at me. Embarrassed, I lowered my eyes, but not before Jim noticed.

"Well, I'd better get going," Thad said. "The bunnies await."

Jim nodded, glancing from Thad to me and back.

"See you kids later." Thad again looked inquiringly at me. I glanced up, but the smile I gave him was my polite, impersonal do.

Thad mumbled something about being glad finally to have had the opportunity to meet Jim, turned on his heel, and abruptly strode back out the door, apparently forgetting or dismissing whatever had brought him into the ski shop in the first place.

I stole a quick look at Jim.

"I'm not the jealous type." His dark eyes were playful. "But I'm sure glad that guy didn't have any more time alone with you in San Diego."

When I didn't rise to the bait, he dropped the subject . . . for the moment.

Jim looked back to scan the parking lot as we left the shop, and my eyes followed his to see Thad fold his long limbs into a small, blue Geo. He did not immediately start the engine.

"You said he's a cop?" Jim asked.

"Yes. Why?"

"I don't know. There's something a little sinister about him, a look in his eyes. If I were guessing, I'd say he's done time."

"Jim, how can you even say such a thing? Thad Bias is one of the kindest people I've ever met. He's got those sincere blue eyes and that sweet, sweet smile. Why, he's almost angelic."

Jim looked incredulous. "Angelic?"

"Okay, that may be a bit much." I thought about what he'd said. "Maybe hanging out on the opposite side of the bars can taint a man."

"Maybe. It sounds to me like you escaped his clutches just in the nick of time. He gave me some seriously bad vibes." Nudging us on toward the slope, Jim glanced back a time or two.

"What are you looking for?" I asked.

"Just wondering why Bias left the ski shop without whatever he went in there to get, why he's still sitting in his car, and what made him change his mind about hustling the snow bunnies in the bar."

"Oh," I said, and I began wondering about those same things myself.

Mr. Ramsey spent nearly an hour giving us the basics. Jim had skied before but insisted he needed the review. I was, as usual, a quick study physically but was plagued by conscience late in the session when I realized we had taken so much of our tutor's time.

"Mr. Ramsey, we have to pay you for this," I insisted when he turned us loose to tackle the beginners' runs on our own.

Ramsey was firm, insisting instead that we provide him progress reports of our future success on the slopes. He snickered. "If there's any to report." He laughed boisterously at my grimace.

"What? You think I'm not going to be able to do this?"

He guffawed again. "Nah, you'll do fine," he assured, but continued to enjoy his little joke a little too much.

We made a couple of runs off the short trails, but I quailed when Jim suggested we buy tickets for the lift.

"I need a break," I said. "Let's wait until this afternoon to go up higher."

Since we had rented the gear for the day, we didn't return to the ski shop but made our way back through the parking lot and the hotel lobby. We both noticed that the small blue Geo was gone, at least from its earlier parking place, but neither of us mentioned it until much, much later.

In the room both of us peeled down to our long handles and fell across the bed. Lying on our sides facing each other, heads propped on our hands, we discussed and then decided to order lunch in the room. Reaching over me for the phone, Jim called to order club sandwiches, soft drinks, and, as an afterthought, a newspaper.

"Yes," he said, "The *Denver Post* will be fine." He hung up, but his hand lingered at my waist as he returned to his position stretched on his side facing me. "Was Thad Bias in love?" His hand followed the line of my hip.

I smiled, but didn't look at his face. "Probably not."

"Oh, yeah, I'm afraid probably so." He arched his eyebrows and gave me a steady look. "So what's the story on you two?"

"You." I lunged, shoving him down hard on his back. "You fouled up one honkin' great love story." Jim yielded easily and I wound up propped on top of him. I bestowed a casual, sisterly kiss. Suddenly we were revitalized, kissing and rolling, and I began frantically unbuttoning my underwear.

"We probably ought to wait 'til the bellman brings the food," Jim said, but the idea was too late. I kissed him feverishly as I squirmed out of my union suit.

"I think I've created a monster," Jim muttered, pretending to be shocked.

I touched his warm stomach and chill bumps peppered my arms. I shivered and Jim rolled up over me like he planned to protect me and keep me warm with his body heat and . . .

I watched as he lay sleeping, recovering. For me, the sex just kept getting better and better.

Methodical by nature, Jim made love slowly, playfully igniting my passion and then lifting, enhancing it to an ethereal place where idle thoughts chased each other dreamily through my mind but defied capture.

225

Trying to analyze it, I was baffled. Sex was physical pleasure, certainly, but the act itself went far beyond that. "Having sex" was too shallow a term for the passion I experienced in those moments when our bodies were linked and my mind surrendered its domination, when my flesh yielded to the pleasure Jim produced, when my soul flew, exquisitely, blissfully beyond the here and now. Making love with Jim was life's purest form of escape.

Before we married, I thought I would merely endure intercourse until I grew to appreciate it, no matter how offensive it was, as women historically had endured it—courageously, with a martyr-like mindset—for centuries. I expected to be acclimated to it by the time we had been married six months or so; therefore, I figured I was precocious, sexually speaking, since after so short a time I anticipated intimacy excitedly. I thought of lovemaking at inappropriate times and in inappropriate places, thoughts triggered by the scent of him standing beside me in an elevator, by his touch as he guided me through a department store, by simply looking at his profile as he drove.

Rationalizing, I forgave my wickedness. After all, having sex with my husband was my duty. I shouldn't feel guilty that I enjoyed fulfilling my duty—craved it, even.

As most women did, I enjoyed the foreplay, the long, penetrating kisses, his warm hands. Jim was expert at raising the level of my passion before venturing to the next level.

As I became less apprehensive, more yielding, I thrilled to the entry, the joining of our two bodies, those moments when I had him completely in my control. I'd never felt such power.

Finally, I relished the culmination of the act itself, the time when I could not hold a thought; when I realized Jim, whose mind and judgment I admired so much, was, in those moments, beyond rational thought, too. From that I progressed one step further.

When I either initiated sex or simply indicated I was interested, his response was predictable. When desire took control, Jim became like a zombie with no will of his own.

Looking at him, I was almost ashamed that I felt such triumph in reducing this sleeping paragon of manhood to my will. Enchanting a less manly specimen would not have afforded me the satisfaction I gained from the spell I innocently cast over him, when his strength, his will, his whole being yielded to mine.

In those moments, I held the scepter. He was physically stronger, occasionally smarter, certainly wiser, more courageous and daring than I was, but he was weakened by his need for me, Samson to my Delilah. During lovemaking, he was my slave.

And I noticed something else. After we made love, Jim needed to sleep, to recuperate. I, on the other hand, came away energized. It seemed almost as if he transferred his vitality to me during sex.

Narrowing my conclusion to personal victory, I giggled at my feeling of superiority.

Often disheveled, sometimes tactless, always nosy, I had considered myself attractive, but had never considered myself desirable, not until I began seeing myself through Jim's eyes.

Obviously love distorted his clear view of me. Ridiculous, I thought, as I sat gazing at his sleeping form. What about me could possibly have captured him? That question baffled me and I was reviewing it yet again when the bellman delivered our order, including the day's newspaper.

Covering Jim, whispering assurance, I jumped up and slipped into the terry cloth robe. Opening the door, I signed the ticket and exchanged three one-dollar bills—a tip—from Jim's billfold for the tray.

Not wanting to disturb my sleeping spouse, I put the tray on the desk, took a bag of chips and the newspaper, and curled onto the love seat. I opened the paper, skimmed the headlines, then settled into the lead story, an end-of-the-year national financial wrap-up.

Following another story to the jump page, I skimmed and then skipped most of the local stuff, except one article about a female bear and her two cubs shot out of a tree by a man called to a neighbor's house when the mother bear attempted to forage into the neighbor's kitchen through a sliding glass door. All three bears had died either of gunshot wounds or the fall from the tree. There apparently was a public outcry. People wanted criminal charges brought against the Samaritan who had come to his neighbor's rescue.

"Colorado is a weird place," I muttered. Jim roused and sat up on the side of the bed, his back to me. I admired the outline of his dark hair against his brown neck, the way that neck sat on his muscular shoulders, the way those shoulders narrowed to trim waist and on down to firm haunches. He got up and, without any attempt to cover his nakedness, he walked into the bathroom. I thought he'd forgotten there was a female in the room until he flapped me a wave just as he went through the bathroom door.

A little disappointed for him to be out of sight, I turned my attention back to the newspaper, scanning ads and the sports pages. I heard the shower. Several minutes later, Jim emerged in boxer shorts, a towel around his shoulders, obviously refreshed.

"What's been going on in the world while we've been holed up?"

"Tell you later," I said. Not daring to look at him, I began reading another item of interest, one from the police blotter. I read the first paragraph of the story languidly, then narrowed my eyes and reread the same lines.

"Jim."

He had settled at the desk over a sandwich.

"Listen to this. 'Fourth Home Burglarized In Sequoia District. Police continued their search today for leads in the recent outbreak of burglaries in the posh Sequoia residential district . . .' "

"Okay," Jim said, taking a sip of his pop. "Did you think Colorado was crime free?"

"It says the homes were burglarized between two and four A.M. when residents were away, all of their absences unscheduled. Now, what do you think?"

"I think you're seeing ghosts."

"But you see them too, don't you?"

Jim nodded grudgingly and put his sandwich back on the plate.

"Could we at least call?"

"And ask what?" He sounded impatient.

I thought a minute, eyeing him. "Ask if candlesticks are on the lists of missing items."

"Will knowing that satisfy you?"

"If there aren't any candlesticks, I'll let the locals handle it and I won't even try to get involved."

"And if there are candlesticks missing?"

I gave him what I hoped was a placating smile. "If that's the case, you and I probably will need to discuss it further."

He studied me a long moment before shaking his head, surrendering. "Go ahead and call, if you want to."

I hopped up, pulled the city telephone directory from the drawer in the bedside table, looked up a number, and dialed.

"I'm a news reporter visiting Estes Park and I happened to read about the burglaries going on in the Sequoia area." I paused to take a breath. "Several weeks ago, I covered a series of burglaries in San Diego that sounded remarkably similar to what's going on here. I know burglaries are common, but that's why I'm calling. The thief in San Diego got away. He had kind of a peculiar signature. No matter what other stuff he stole, he always took candlesticks."

I gave my name, address, and temporary phone number and said they could contact me here for the next few days.

I held the receiver away from my face. "He put me on hold. Said I should talk to the detective in charge. Lieutenant Udouj, who is a she."

When Lt. Ernestine Udouj was on the phone, I repeated what I'd told the sergeant. "I was out there on temporary assignment with the wire service," I explained. "I'm about to resettle in Oklahoma. I'm here in Colorado on my honeymoon.

"Yes, thank you. We're getting along fine. What? No, I'm not bored, it's just that I wondered about the story in today's newspaper and wanted to call in case it's the same guy."

Udouj's questions sounded skeptical, but she reviewed my contact information.

"We're at the Regency. Yes, my husband knows. He's in law enforcement himself, but calling definitely was my idea." I smiled at Jim. "He's not as nosy as I am.

"You can get rid of me by answering one simple question. Did the burglar take any candlesticks, or didn't he? If he didn't, I'll forget it. If he did, we might be able to help.

"Okay. Thanks very much. I was just being a good citizen. Sorry I butted in. Yes, the Regency. Until Saturday. Thank you."

As I cradled the phone, I gave Jim a sheepish, apologetic smile.

"They didn't have an itemized list, right?" he guessed. I nodded. Jim returned my smile. "You may have caught her with her pants down. When investigators get questions we don't have answers for, we get a little curt. Offense is a good defense, you know. A firm put-down keeps you nosy news types in your places. We don't want you getting more uppity than you already are."

He stood and walked over to slip an arm around me. "You're a good citizen, wife of mine. You did your part and I'm proud of you. If Lieutenant Udouj doesn't appreciate it, that's her loss.

"Now, back to the honeymoon. Let's eat and get dressed. We are about to conquer a ski lift and maybe even a moderate slope."

CHAPTER TWENTY-TWO

Standing at the top of the intermediate run, I looked at the snowy course before us, set my teeth, and crouched. I probably looked like I knew what I was doing, was an accomplished skier, tall and well turned out in my lavender snowsuit and gloves. A white headband covered my ears and kept my hair from obscuring my vision.

"Nothing to it," Jim said.

I cast a pleading look his way.

"Remember Harold's Hill last winter?" he reminded. "You were cautious at first, then you wanted to sled farther and faster. And we did. You were exhilarated, exuberant, and excited. Remember?"

I nodded, still feeling uncertain. "But this is different." I looked at the downhill run, which had not appeared nearly that forbidding from below.

There had been more skiers on the two beginner slopes. Mr. Ramsey had assured us the intermediate course would be less crowded. I was relieved that there would be no congestion in my traffic lane; still, I didn't exactly rush into it.

Jim's grin exuded confidence. "This is snow. Push off. Watch me. Watch where you're going. Go as fast or as slow as you want. We'll go together on three." He gave me a steady, reassuring look. "Easy does it. One. Two. Three."

Moving in slow motion, Jim shoved his poles into the powder, lifted his skis a little, and pushed.

Mimicking him, I began sliding forward, but at first mine was a slow, tedious descent. As my confidence grew, however, I pushed harder on the poles, picking up speed, and finally laughed out loud at nothing in particular. In front of me and off to one side, Jim grinned back over his shoulder and stayed well ahead of me.

Once begun, of course, I didn't want to stop, although I did decline his offer to try one of the expert tracks. I preferred to stay on the now familiar intermediate slope. Jim didn't insist. After a second go, then a third, the exertion and the altitude took its toll.

The sun was down but it was not yet dark when I relented and agreed to break for supper. He appeased me by saying we could try night skiing if I wanted to later.

"Let's dress up and go to The Livery," Jim said as we got on the elevator. The Livery was the hotel's nationally acclaimed restaurant, which offered excellent service at exorbitant prices, but we both were in a mood to splurge.

Inside the hotel room, locked in a tight embrace, Jim pointed to the message light on the telephone. It was blinking.

A woman visitor had asked for us, the clerk said. She hadn't left a name. She was waiting in the coffee shop. Jim asked for a description of the woman and relayed the message. I whipped a brush through my hair and hurried to catch up as Jim started toward the door.

"This is an odd honeymoon, don't you think?" I asked as we rode the elevator down.

Jim shrugged. "It's the only one I've ever been on, so I can't say for sure, but I didn't think there were supposed to be quite so many people participating."

I nodded, pretending uncertain agreement, but when I rolled my eyes to his, we both laughed.

Lt. Ernestine Udouj stood as we walked into the coffee shop.

She smiled a stern little smile, introduced herself, shook our hands, and invited us to sit.

The lieutenant was thirtyish, short—almost dumpy—with a pleasant face except for the lines that pulled the corners of her mouth down and gave her a dour look even when she smiled. She studied us without saying anything for a long moment.

"Do you have any identification?" she asked finally.

Still in ski togs, I had no pockets and hadn't brought my purse. From an inside pocket, Jim produced his badge case with picture ID and his driver's license. Udouj took and stared at both items; then, apparently satisfied, returned them.

"You hit the nail on the head, Mrs. Wills," she said.

I couldn't help smiling and I guess she thought that peculiar.

"What's funny?" Udouj looked concerned.

"We just got married. I'm not quite used to my new name."

"Okay." Udouj's mouth pursed with what looked like disapproval and I fell silent. "There were candlesticks missing." Udouj paused.

"In every burglary?" I prodded.

Udouj nodded, narrowing her eyes as if trying to see inside my head, searching for the truth. I ignored the scrutiny.

"I'll tell you who I think you need to look for and Jim can correct me if I get off." I looked to Udouj, then to Jim for nods.

"Your subject is male, thirty to thirty-two years old. He's a little over average height, slim, has a prominent nose and beady little eyes set close together. In San Diego he worked graveyard at a hospital as a male R.N. When they finally got around to checking, his credentials were bogus. The professional staff there at St. Simeon's praised his work. His patients adored him. He gave them thoughtful trinkets and, occasionally, expensive gifts. It turned out the presents were contraband—things he had stolen.

"His victims were all either patients in the hospital or family staying with patients. He had their addresses from hospital records and knew when they weren't home. When he got off work early in the mornings, he did the burglaries on his way home, like you might stop off for a loaf of bread or a quart of milk."

"How," Udouj interrupted, "did he get the addresses of family members, people who were only visiting patients?"

Puzzled, I looked to Jim. I didn't know how he knew.

Jim stretched his legs, crossing them at the ankles. "All the ones whose homes were burglarized were careful to let hospital personnel know where they would be at what times so they could be reached in case of emergency. They provided detailed itineraries. When a promising subject didn't volunteer the information, our guy just asked for it."

Lt. Udouj looked surprised. I shook my head, marveling all over again at the gall of the man.

"We don't know his real name," I said, picking up the story, "but out there he used aliases with the initials 'C. D.' "

"We believe his real name is Chester Doyle," Jim added. "He's used aliases Carl Donnan, Clarence Denver, and Charles Denim. There may be others."

I interrupted. "He had a newly issued Social Security number, no driver's license, and no car to trace."

Lt. Udouj wrote quick notes on a tablet she had propped on the table. "Did the police have a mug shot from earlier arrests?" She looked at me.

"Call Captain Murray O'Brien with the San Diego police. He'll be able to tell you if they have a picture, maybe even fax it to you.

"You know what?" I said, suddenly brightening with a new idea. "There's a young guy, a cop who worked that case who is now right here in Colorado. His name is Bias. Thad Bias. He's police chief in some small town thirty miles or so west of here.

We ran into him this morning. He might be able to help you, Lieutenant."

Udouj looked up from her notebook. "Call me Ernie." She glanced from me to Jim, then back at the tablet of notes.

When we'd provided all the information we could recall, the lieutenant stood. She shook our hands. "If you think of anything else, call me. If I'm not available, talk to John V. or leave a message. How long will you be around?"

"Until Saturday," I said, but the lieutenant was looking at Jim, who was frowning.

"Something else?" she asked.

Jim hesitated. "Has there been a death?" He framed the question cautiously. "Has anyone even remotely connected to these burglaries died?"

I stared at him.

Thoughtful for a moment, Udouj shook her head.

"When you locate the connection linking these thefts," Jim said, "and I think you will, check thoroughly. If there has been a death, even one that appears to be from natural causes, I would urge you to order an autopsy."

Udouj's eyes widened as she cocked her head in birdlike fashion. "You are saying what?"

Jim shook his head uncertainly. "Two older women connected to the San Diego incidents died, possibly of natural causes, but maybe not. Peculiarly, the police later learned that they had been sisters, separated as small children, taken by different families. No one knew they were related until a clerk cop working records stumbled onto it. I just have a weird feeling about it, that's all."

Udouj scribbled another note.

After she had jotted down our home address and telephone number, the lieutenant put the lid on her pen. We walked her to the lobby.

"I thought Charlie Denim was a part of our colorful past," I said as Jim and I climbed the picturesque spiral stairway to the mezzanine before catching the elevator. Jim grunted acknowledgment without offering additional comment.

Secure in our suite, Jim called room service. He ordered a bloody Mary for me and a bourbon and water for himself.

Struggling with a stubborn zipper on my pillowed jacket, I finally gave up and squirmed out of it, along with the rest of my ski clothes, which had been much too warm in the confines of the coffee shop and were even worse in our room.

"Here, let me help." Jim stepped in front of me as I fumbled with the buttons on my long johns. He was still fully clothed.

"Where were you when my jacket zipper was caught?"

He grinned and arched his eyebrows. "Anticipating."

"Okay, you can help." I spoke in a playfully threatening tone. Unbuttoned, I quickly peeled down to my panties and bra. Jim grabbed me and laughed loudly when I shrieked, objecting to his icy hands on my bare torso.

I offered only token resistance as he unhooked and discarded my bra and ran cold fingers under my panties and down over my hips.

Laughing back, I wriggled, dancing out of my panties, then caught a breath and came to full attention in front of him, unabashedly nude.

His grin became a frown. His eyes swept from my smile down as he began fumbling in earnest with the obstinate zipper on his own ski jacket. His breathing became labored and sweat prickled his upper lip.

Enjoying his dilemma, I leaped into his arms. My momentum carried us onto the bed, Jim fully clothed on his back, helpless, with me on top. I writhed, loving the feel of the cool parachute cloth of his jacket slithering over my naked body. Squirming, I pushed a naked breast to his mouth.

Still grappling with the zipper on his jacket, his mouth welcomed the offered breast. His warming hands flew over my heated, bare skin.

When he had nuzzled one breast, I offered the other one, wiggling, giggling, taunting him. Jim attempted to sit up, but I shifted to put my full weight on his chest.

"Woman, you are asking for trouble with this little game." His words sounded threatening, but he couldn't keep from laughing at his untenable predicament.

His face grew flushed as he struggled to sit despite my determined effort to keep him down, levering my full weight from his chest to his stomach, refusing to let him up.

Suddenly he fell back. "Okay. You asked for it. Now, you're going to get it."

Placing both hands firmly on my hips, he lifted and shifted until he had my stomach positioned over his face, his mouth on my abdomen, my legs straddling his chest. He blew on my tummy, producing rude noises—zerberts.

I squealed and wriggled, but he held me firmly. Slowly, he guided my torso across his face, blowing, shifting, and blowing again until his tormenting mouth posed a strange new threat. My shrieks got louder, broken by involuntary giggles when I realized the ridiculous predicament.

Then he went completely still and I got quiet. Motionless for a moment, his palms firmly holding my hip bones, he lifted.

"Unzip my jacket." His deep voice sounded serious. Placing my knee on the bed to one side of him, I tried to lift myself away, but he held me fast, allowing only breathing space between us. Obediently, I unzipped his jacket and pushed the sides apart.

"Now my pants." There was a threat in his softened tone. His flushed face looked strangely serious.

Again I complied, laying open the pants to reveal the familiar arousal scarcely concealed beneath his shorts. "Open the fly," he ordered.

Again I complied.

"Now sit on it and rotate," he said somberly, quoting an old put-down.

I thought he must be kidding. "What?"

"Do it."

I looked at his face. His expression was set, his eyes narrowed to slits. His hands positioned me; then slowly, cautiously, I eased myself onto him.

When his stiffened phallus entered from that position, it extended too far. I tried to retreat. His hands moved to my waist and held. His thumbs were firmly set just beneath my ribs. The chill was completely gone from his hands, which felt hot.

I looked to his face for reassurance but his expression remained set and menacing. "Jim, you're hurting me."

"Hmm," he said, but he made no attempt to alter our positions.

"Jim, I don't like it here. I don't want to sit up here . . . exposed . . . like this." There was no word, no movement for a long moment; then, slowly, his hands guided my naked body gently as he rolled, maintaining the erection linking us.

On top, he began stripping his abundance of clothing, pausing to touch and kiss me, all the while maintaining his ominous silence and the stoic expression.

He had to pull out of me to remove his ski pants and shorts, but he maintained intimate contact, his mouth on a breast, his hand on the mound between my legs, his fingers toying inside me.

On my back, excited at the sight of his provocative strip tease, I pushed against him, striving to maintain our erotic contact.

"Please," I begged finally, trying to hurry him. "Do it with your clothes on."

He smiled for the first time and shook his head. "I don't want anything—not even the sheerest fabric—between us." His voice had become husky. "Not now." He pulled off his shirt. "I like to feel every bit of you feeling every bit of me."

I lay back and groaned, watching and waiting.

Nude, on his hands and knees, he crept up over me, licking unfamiliar places as I undulated, arching, needing him, willing to do anything if he would just . . . do it.

The dining room was no longer crowded when we went down at nine-thirty. Jim put his hand on the back of my neck when the maitre d' turned to escort us to a table. As we walked, Jim's hand casually slid over my shoulder and arm, by my waist and down until it rested on my hip. I exaggerated the sway as his hand rode my silk skirt, which swished as we moved.

"Why do you touch me that way?" I asked after we were seated and browsing the menus.

Jim glanced at me, his gaze dark. I tingled, remembering what we'd been doing less than an hour before.

"Touch you like what?" he asked.

I tried to dismiss those lecherous mental images and the wanton tingles they precipitated. "Ah . . . your hands. When we're in public. They . . . well, you kind of grope . . . subtly, of course, but kind of intimately."

"I guess I didn't realize I did. Does it bother you?"

"It gives me a perverse sense of pleasure." I flushed. "It feels like you're showing everyone in the room that you own me, that you have the right to take liberties with my body."

A slow smile indicated he was recalling the same mental images I had just dismissed.

"Maybe it's an animal thing, a subconscious warning to other males to stand clear: this is my woman." He smiled at the menu.

"Like I'm a possession?" I was getting angry.

Jim looked into my face. "It could be. But I think it's more likely that I just enjoy touching you."

"My hips?" I asked in disbelief.

He looked surprised as he leaned closer. "Yes, your hips." His eyes dropped from my eyes to my mouth. "And I'll tell you something else. You can deny it, but you're putting out little asking-for-it signals all the time. If you didn't want me touching you, you could walk a little faster, move out of my reach, but you don't. You do the same thing in our room and in bed."

I felt the anger swell. "What's that supposed to mean?"

"You are hot."

"What?" I gasped, trying to remember to keep my voice low. "I don't even know what I'm doing when we make love. How can you say that?"

The familiar throaty chortle rumbled from inside him. "You are an exceptionally responsive woman. I don't know if it's because those buttons haven't been pushed before or what, but you, baby, are awesome between the sheets."

I tried to frown, fighting a smile at this wild conversation, which was taking a decidedly flattering turn. "It's probably you. You're the one who makes things happen in our bed."

"Not so. Anyway, we need to quit talking about this."

I glanced around concerned. "Why? Is somebody listening?"

"No, because I'm getting turned on. If you hope to have supper here in this upscale restaurant tonight, we'd better change the subject. Temporarily, of course. Put it on hold until we're back in the room."

We had a long, leisurely dinner but over coffee, I noticed Jim looking more and more often at the neckline of my dress.

"Don't tell me I spilled something."

He laughed at my quick survey. "No. I was just admiring you.

You've got absolutely the greatest pair of knockers I've ever seen."

There it was again: sex talk. "Have you ever noticed how many synonyms we use for that particular body part," I asked, a little miffed.

"Yeah, it's an important part of a guy's vocabulary. We call them breasts, bosoms, boobs, ta-tas, jugs, hoo-haas . . ."

My fomenting anger must have become obvious, because one look at my face and he stopped.

"Of course," he said, as if he were attempting to pacify me, "there are a lot of names for a penis too. It is otherwise known as a phallus, a Johnson, a rod, a dick, a joy stick, pecker, and, of course, the ever popular 'wiener.'" He paused, focused again on my face. "You don't suppose anyone in here reads lips, do you?" He rolled his eyes.

I pretended to cringe and eyeballed the other diners.

He leaned closer. "Do you want dessert?"

"No, thank you. Why?"

"I thought we might continue this conversation upstairs. We can take off our clothes and have some visual aids to work with."

I nodded and Jim signaled for the check.

As he followed me out of the elevator on our floor, Jim very purposefully placed both hands on my hips, which I rolled, giving him a little bump and grind. Outside our room, he fumbled with the key card, slipping it in three tries before he could get the door open. He hung the "Do Not Disturb" sign on the outside knob.

Inside, he snatched at my clothing, grabbing handfuls of skirt and lifting it as he pulled me snugly against him, sliding his hands into the back of my panties and splaying them on my hips. I retaliated wordlessly, smothering his neck with kisses and wantonly unbuttoning and unfastening and running my hands inside his clothing.

Neither of us spoke until much, much later. There was no further mention of night skiing.

CHAPTER TWENTY-THREE

The telephone's ring shattered the predawn stillness of our room long before we were ready to rise. Answering in a gravelly voice, Jim was unconvincing as he tried to assure Duke Mallory that his call hadn't awakened us.

I stretched luxuriously, my eyes squinty as I tried to study Jim's features, which were dimly visible in the light filtering into the room through seams in the heavy draperies.

I looked at the digital clock on the bedside table. Nine-fifty. Later than I thought. Jim looked at me as he responded to Mallory, who was obviously asking about our trip.

"How did you find us?" Jim asked, then glowered at the response on the other end. Covering the mouthpiece, he said, "I didn't know you'd called your parents." I nodded. After a couple of minutes exchanging war stories about highway travel in Colorado in winter, Mallory said that although there had been no new information on Candlesticks, he had some news we might find interesting.

"Candlesticks may be here in Colorado," Jim volunteered, interrupting, "not where we are, but maybe working a Denver suburb."

Hearing Mallory's noisy objections emitting from the receiver but unable to decipher his words, I scrambled out of bed, grabbed my nightgown—which had landed on a bedside table during one of our nighttime romps—and danced across the chilly room to the extension telephone on the desk. Instead of putting my gown on the regular way, I hurriedly wrapped it around me. I was super eager to hear both sides of this conversation.

"We contacted the police," Jim was saying, his eyes following me. "A lieutenant came out to talk to us."

"The hell you say," Mallory answered. "What made you think it was Candlesticks?"

"He's in his same routine, hitting homes in an upper-middle-class residential area, ones where the residents had unscheduled absences but haven't left town on trips or anything. We suggested they check the lists of stolen items."

"And they came up with candlesticks? That sure prickles my nose hairs."

"As I recall, it doesn't take much to stimulate your nose," I said, chiming in.

I could hear the laughter in Duke's voice. "Hey, honey, how's it going? Are you getting your husband trained?"

I shot Jim a glance and lowered the edge of the nightgown, flashing one breast before I covered up again. Jim squinted and arched one brow, a thinly veiled warning.

Duke let the question die as he followed with another. "Did you tell him about the hospital connection?"

"Him who?" I asked.

"The police lieutenant."

"He's a she, Mallory."

"The officer in charge of the case is a woman?"

I made my voice intentionally cool. "Yes," then I paused to allow Mallory to digest that, before I followed with a question. "Duke, how long have you known Thad Bias?"

"I don't know. Three or four months, I guess, why?"

"I thought you went back a long way. He talked like you were old friends."

"Nah, he wasn't around when I left Dago three years ago. I

met him after I got back last fall. Why?"

"We ran into him at a ski equipment shop. He's a police chief around here someplace. He didn't name the town. I mentioned Thad to this lieutenant. Told her he had worked on the case in California and thought he might be able to assist their investigation, but we don't know how to contact him. I thought maybe you could turn up his new address or phone number."

"I might be able to do that. Then I might come see you. How long will you be there?"

Jim's voice was a growl. "We're honeymooning here, Mallory. We don't need visitors."

"You should have mentioned that to Candlesticks," the older man said. "Okay, I'm not needed, is that what you're trying to say?"

"As tactfully as I can." Jim laughed.

"How long will you be there?"

"We're on a flight home tomorrow night. I promised people we'd be back in Bishop for New Year's."

"I want to get this information to you. I think it might be important, maybe even more so now. I'll send it to the hotel's fax machine."

"What kind of information?" Jim's interest in the conversation appeared to be waning as he flashed me scurrilous looks.

"It's about the family of Clint and Sarah Denim Doctorman."

Jim blinked, turning rapt attention to the telephone. "Denim Doctorman?" Jim repeated. I nodded confirmation of that tidbit Mallory had shared with me before, one I just hadn't thought to mention to Jim.

"Right, I'll get to that in a minute," Mallory continued. "They were twentieth-century pioneer types. They started out in Oklahoma in the Dust Bowl days, in the twenties and thirties. Had seven kids . . ."

"And Mrs. Hudson and Mrs. Smith were two of those children?" Jim asked, his curiosity racing ahead of the story.

"Right again. The Doctormans couldn't take care of their brood, so they farmed them out to relatives, friends, anyone who could feed them." Mallory droned on, providing a lot of unnecessary details of how Hudson and Smith both wound up in Southern California.

"Can't I just read all this in the fax later?" Jim pleaded finally, interrupting the recitation, again slanting looks at me. I rolled a shoulder and slipped the gown down for another peep.

"No." Mallory's shout made me jerk the fabric back up and frown curiously at Jim, who was also frowning. "It gets urgent here.

"I sent a query to all the member newspapers asking for information about burglaries, any series where the victims were away on unscheduled errands when their homes were broken into and where the list of stolen items included candlesticks. I also asked for details about any natural deaths that occurred incidental to the crimes. It was a little thin, but something." He paused.

"Go on," Jim said. Mallory again had his full attention.

"I had to have a swig of coffee." Mallory swallowed audibly. "I've been getting calls all week, but they boiled down to two probables.

"There was a rash of those kinds of deals last February and March south of Kansas City, a bedroom town on the Missouri/Kansas border. Someone just happened to make a notation that candlesticks were taken every time. The local news hound had called it to the investigating team's attention. Did you hear that, Jance? I figured you'd appreciate that there were other bulldog types in this business besides just you."

Jim grunted, not wanting Mallory to interrupt his story.

"An elderly widow lady died the same night her house got

ripped off," Duke continued. "She'd been sick with pneumonia but was improving. They didn't order an autopsy. She was cremated, authorized by a nephew who showed up right after she died. He claimed to be her next of kin, told people she'd had a child but the kid had died a long time ago.

"The woman, Cora Dibble, had been living in a nursing home. Her bills were paid by Social Security as far as it went, then by the local welfare. This nephew offered to pay for the cremation. After he offered to foot the bill, no one questioned his interest or asked for any ID.

"The reporter, the one who contacted me, was pretty interested. He's on a weekly paper, actually more of a shopper. He doesn't see much action. He wanted to track down the nephew for a story. Human interest stuff. He never could make contact.

"Also it seems the nephew got off with all the copies of the death certificate. This reporter, being kind of a nosy cuss, hustled around and made himself a copy of a copy the funeral home had. Guess what?"

Jim cleared his throat. "I figure you wouldn't be telling us all this unless she was originally a Doctorman, right?"

"Right."

Jim sat up and pivoted to perch on the side of the bed, covering himself with the corner of the sheet. My heart was beating faster, alerted by Mallory's words. There was no trace of my earlier drowsiness.

"Was there a description?" Jim asked.

"The reporter didn't actually see the nephew, but the people who did said the guy was tallish, slim, fair, and—this struck me as odd—they said he was clean-cut."

I couldn't help shivering as I remembered Denim's narrow, rat face. Maybe the witness was trying to be kind. Anyway, beauty is in the eye of the beholder. Still, I was puzzled by what seemed an exceptionally generous description.

"Anything else?" Jim prodded.

"Yep. Almost the same story down at Bocco, Texas, this time a man, not quite as old but in the same generation. His name was A.J. Doctorman. He taught high school math.

"This Doctorman was married twice, divorced both times. No kids. No other family except a nephew who turned up about two days before the old man died. No one remembered having seen or heard of him before. It was the same story. This time the newspaper editor, who is also the only reporter, trying to get info for an obituary, could never even get the nephew on the phone. The nephew got off with all the death certificates, again. The newspaper was out ten bucks to get a copy from the state. The gal I talked to was still steamed about that."

Jim laughed incredulously. "I'll reimburse her."

"I already did."

"I don't suppose anyone bothered to get a description of the nephew?"

"Nope. I asked. Referred me to a couple of people at the funeral home. One of them can probably tell us."

Jim sat scowling at the carpet. "So now we can account for four of seven original Doctorman offspring, is that right?"

"Right."

"Is there any way to track these people except through their death certificates? It would sure be nice to talk to one of them while he was still breathing."

"I've got people on it," Mallory said, "which brings us to the reason for this call."

"You already knew about the burglaries in the Sequoia area."

"How'd you know?"

"It's a pretty obvious conclusion."

Mallory growled as if it had not seemed that obvious to him. "There were five Doctorman girls and two boys. It took some digging but the fifth sister lives there in Colorado, near Denver, not actually in the Sequoia area, but close.

"She's seventy-three years old and lives alone. Her husband died several years ago. They had two kids, boys, both died as infants. Her name's Berry. Hazel Doctorman Berry. I think maybe you two had better find her."

"Yeah." Jim looked at me. I was nodding like crazy.

"Lieutenant Udouj will probably help," I said.

Jim agreed and said, to include Mallory, "Udouj seems sharp and the case has definitely piqued her interest."

Mallory backtracked. "Sounds like you've seen plenty of people, running into Bias like that, and getting acquainted with the police woman. You sure you don't want me to come? I could run interference, entertain some of your company."

Jim laughed derisively and looked at me in the half-light of the room as Mallory began theorizing. Leaning on one elbow, Jim reached for the lamp switch, then changed his mind, sat up again, and beckoned me to come to him.

Shivering, I silently hung up the extension phone, as Mallory's voice droned on. I slipped the nightgown on over my head, wiggling to help it settle over my body, and darted back across the room.

Jim smiled, squinting appreciatively as he continued listening to Mallory.

I sat down, squeezed close beside him, and began nibbling on his shoulder. A moment later, I lay back and inhaled provocatively. Jim's eyes narrowed and he ran a warm hand over my abdomen as he leaned on the other elbow.

"No more company," Jim said quietly, speaking both to Mallory on the telephone and to me stretched beside him on the bed. Pushing his shoulder, I managed to nudge Jim back to a sitting position. I sat up beside him and he reached over my legs to pull me closer. I wrapped both arms around his biceps and propped my cheek on his shoulder. He gazed down the front of the nightgown, which gapped, allowing him full view of my breasts, the tips of which had gone on alert. He took a deep breath and interrupted Mallory's monologue.

"Let's talk about this later, Duke. We'll call you back in a little while. Are you at the office?"

"Yeah, or we can just go ahead and thrash it out now, on the company's dime."

Jim shook his head, his unwavering eyes still on my breasts as I emphasized their size by inhaling and writhing a little.

"No, we'll call you back," Jim repeated, then unceremoniously hung up. He rolled up over me as I again lay back on the bed, bare feet still on the floor.

"I haven't brushed my teeth," I whispered, but as I warned him, he eased the straps off my shoulders, kissing my neck and newly naked breasts. "You're going to think I'm sleazy easy," I moaned.

"Yeah," he drawled, setting me free from the rest of the gown. He rearranged me, stretching me lengthwise on the bed. As he positioned himself over me, I laced my fingers in his hair. Denim-Doctorman would have to take a number and wait.

CHAPTER TWENTY-FOUR

"Do you have brothers or sisters?" I asked two hours later when Jim and I were seated in the dated, comfortable home of Hazel Doctorman Berry.

Having devised a tentative plan, we had called Mallory back to get his input. Then I called Mrs. Berry for an appointment, saying we were doing historical research, gathering information about her family. Mrs. Berry naturally assumed our inquiry was for a genealogy and I didn't correct her.

The elderly woman was receptive to a couple of strangers, even over the telephone. She would be delighted to see us, could allow all the time we needed.

Although my curiosity was stimulated by the Doctorman matter, I complained and gazed back longingly at the ski trails as we drove toward town.

"We'll ski later this afternoon," Jim said.

Yeah, right. I knew how a criminal investigation could devour a day.

Mrs. Berry was petite and I was surprised that her alert, bright blue eyes were so eerily like Paula Faye Hudson's. Mrs. Berry walked with a cane, even in the confines of her home.

After introductions, our hostess led us back beyond the broad entryway with its authentic Persian rugs and lavish appointments, past a dining room on our right filled with massive mahogany furnishings, and a formal living room on the left, the center focus of which were a concert grand piano and an immense fireplace.

I did a double take. "What a beautiful piano. Do you play?"

Mrs. Berry's shuffled footfalls stopped as she turned stiffly, shaking her head. "I'm not able to sit on the bench as long as I once could. My husband was the true musician. He played beautifully." Her movements were frozen in reverie and Jim and I waited until Mrs. Berry recovered sufficiently to continue our trek.

Eventually we reached a small sitting room off the kitchen, a cozy little nook that obviously served as both den and breakfast room. The morning newspaper lay open on the dining table, a cup of mocha liquid and a tray of butter cookies nearby.

"I made coffee and hot tea both," Mrs. Berry said, motioning us into chairs at the table. "Which will you have?"

I helped our hostess put the filled cups on the table. Duties completed, Mrs. Berry hung her cane on the corner of the table and slowly positioned herself in her chair as I asked about her siblings.

Yes, she had had a brother and a sister. Unlike her, they had actually been adopted by the Tennysons. Adoption had been difficult in those days and, because she was older and accustomed to her family name of Doctorman, the Tennysons had decided not to go through the adoption process with Mrs. Berry.

"These were not natural siblings, then? Not Doctorman children?"

"No, but dear, it made no difference at all," she said. "I was treated every bit as well as the younger two; probably better, because I was the first. Our mama, Mrs. Tennyson, was barren, you see.

"They were people who enjoyed having children around. They provided a good home, college, and a fine wedding when I married."

With some tactful prodding, she explained that the Tennysons had divided their estate equally, bequeathing one-third to each of their children when they passed.

Although well provided for, Mrs. Berry said she had occasionally wondered about her birth parents over the years, curious about whether she had natural brothers and sisters.

Jim gave her a kindly smile and put his cup down. "There apparently were seven Doctorman children originally. You had four sisters and two brothers. Two of those sisters and a brother have died in the last month."

"What is it exactly that you do?" Mrs. Berry asked, the bright blue eyes suddenly piercing.

"I am a news reporter with the American Wire Service," I said.

Mrs. Berry nodded, turned her no-nonsense expression on Jim, and waited for him to own up.

"I work for the Oklahoma State Bureau of Investigation." As he met her look, Mrs. Berry frowned. "But I'm here as a new husband on his honeymoon, not as a cop."

"It sounds like there's been an epidemic of some kind among Doctormans," Mrs. Berry allowed. "Had I better watch my step?"

I risked a look at Jim, who kept his eyes trained on Mrs. Berry. Obviously he was debating how much he should tell her, but Mrs. Berry seemed able to read his musings.

"Is that the real reason you're here?"

Jim nodded, gazing frankly into her face. "It is why we dropped by to see you. Yes, ma'am." He smiled into those inquisitive blue eyes. "The epidemic brought us."

Her expression grew solemn, the polite smile gone. "And are you really husband and wife?"

Jim smiled. "Yes, we are. We're actually on our honeymoon."

Rallying, Mrs. Berry smiled back at him. "A working honeymoon? Whose idea was that?"

"Not mine," Jim and I said, practically in unison.

Mrs. Berry lost her kindly old lady look and adopted one that resembled more closely an angry blue jay. "Okay," she said, "let's get down to brass tacks. What's going on?"

Together we recounted the story of Charlie Denim and the Doctormans, sticking to solid information, including only conjecture that had been verified. Mrs. Berry listened intently, asking an occasional pertinent question.

"The bottom line is this," Jim said, concluding our narrative. "There appears to be some connection between the Doctorman clan and Charlie Denim. It looks like he's part of the family."

Looking at Jim, I brightened. "Jim, Charles Denim is now one of only three or four surviving members of that family."

"We haven't yet found his parents in this mix, have we?" Jim said, picking up my line of thought.

I felt the old butterflies in my tummy break loose. "There has to be money involved somewhere."

"A lot of money, probably."

Both of us ignored our hostess for a moment, until she spoke. "There is. A lot of money. The Tennysons left a nice estate. I received a one-third share, one-third of fifteen million dollars. But, you see, my husband had already built two franchise fast-food businesses. He used some of my inheritance to build others. He was very astute and really quite successful, financially. He left a large estate, all of which came to me."

She suddenly had our full, astonished attention. I recovered first. "Larger than five million?" Realizing how rude the question sounded out loud, I shrank back, frowning, but Jim regarded Mrs. Berry intently.

"Who inherits from you?" he asked

Mrs. Berry returned his frank gaze. "As I said, our children didn't live. We wanted children very badly." She hesitated a moment as if contemplating something. "I've made bequests to our church and to a number of charities, also college scholarship funds for underprivileged children who cannot afford to continue their schooling."

Something about her measuring her words so carefully gave me a feeling of urgency. "What about your two Tennyson siblings?"

Jim flashed me a quick frown that melted as he read the anxiety in my manner.

Mrs. Berry smiled at both of us, apparently forgiving our individual fervor. "They already have more than they will ever be able to spend. They both have families, children and grandchildren. They're all intelligent people who know about hard work and the importance of education. They will all prosper without any handouts from me.

"Hershel and I decided to leave the bulk of our money to people we had reason to believe came from poverty and probably stayed poor, that is, my birth family. We even hired a detective once—probably twenty years ago, now—to locate those people, thinking to set up some kind of trust to provide for them, if they were in need.

"I was nearly five years old when I went to live with the Tennysons. Growing up I had only faint, unpleasant memories of my early life, of California, of hot sand. I've always had a terrible fear of being without water and I have vague memories of spending time with a whole tribe of noisy, unkempt children and being thirsty and often hungry.

"We asked the detective to try locating people named Doctorman in the desert areas of Southern California. He followed every kind of lead to dead ends. He spent two or three months and we, upwards of twenty thousand dollars before we all gave up.

"Some of his feelers did pay off sometime later, however. We received a collect call from a Jeremiah Doyle. He was in prison in Texas. He said he was my brother-in-law, married to my sister Cletis. He said he was an innocent man, serving time for a crime he did not commit. All he wanted was to be exonerated and returned to his wife and children.

"I was very excited. I thought I remembered a baby called Cletis.

"Mr. Doyle refused to give us information as to the whereabouts of his family until we showed our good faith by providing funds to help him.

"Hershel asked for details of his situation. Mr. Doyle did not want to talk about the allegations over the telephone. He asked us to send money for a lawyer. He said his own lawyer had 'sold him out.'

"Hershel contacted the prison warden and found out where this Jeremiah Doyle had come from, then contacted the court clerk in the county where Mr. Doyle was convicted. We obtained a copy of Mr. Doyle's police record. It was lengthy. He had been charged with numerous crimes but was convicted only four times. He was what my husband termed, 'a pretty bad egg.'

"This Jeremiah Doyle began calling several times a week, always collect, always asking for money. He was a very persistent man.

"He wanted us to sponsor him for parole, to promise to provide him a job and a place to live. The prison officials informed us that Mr. Doyle had no visitors, neither family members nor anyone else, and very little mail.

"I wanted so desperately to locate my own brothers and sisters that we had about talked ourselves into helping him when Mr. Doyle's requests became more insistent, more like demands accompanied by some onerous threats.

"At last, we decided we weren't interested in helping a man like that get back into society. That's actually when we gave up on ever locating members of my birth family.

"But I must say my curiosity was piqued by your call today. You see, last Sunday a man called here asking if my maiden name was Doctorman. My name has been Berry for the last fifty-two years, so it came as something of a surprise, but not altogether an unpleasant one. He said his name was Clovis Davisson." She spelled the last name.

"Clovis Davisson?" I repeated and looked sharply at my husband. "Initials C.D."

He nodded.

"Like you," Mrs. Berry said, after a brief pause, "he said he was doing research. Naturally I was curious.

"He travels for a living. He is to call back when his business brings him closer to Denver. I thought you might be associates of his when you called, Mrs. Wills. I thought it peculiar that someone else would be conducting a genealogy search regarding the Doctormans. I was at once curious and delighted."

Jim and I looked to each other as if wondering what our next move should be.

Without a spoken agreement, I began to tell Mrs. Berry about Paula Faye Hudson, a petite woman with piercing blue eyes, a woman I had met and liked. I described Mrs. Hudson's features, her modest demeanor, and detailed her mannerisms. Mrs. Berry listened intently, occasionally nodding when something seemed to have a familiar ring.

"I am seventy-three," she inserted at one point. "I faintly recall an older girl whose name I remember as 'Polly-fee.' She had delicate hands and long fingers. She seemed very bossy to me then. Isn't that strange? Did Paula Faye Hudson have children?"

"No."

"Perhaps they died at birth, as mine did." The older woman frowned thoughtfully. "May I have her address?"

"Mrs. Hudson died shortly after we met," I said, dreading

the disappointment that marred her face. "Actually, she died the Sunday before Jim and I married, December seventeenth. She had health problems."

"What kinds of health problems?"

I looked to Jim, who nodded encouragement. "She suffered severe migraine headaches."

"I know something about those," Mrs. Berry muttered. "For me the problem turned out to be caffeine. How old a woman was she?"

I again looked to Jim, who said, "Seventy-seven, according to her death certificate."

"And she said her maiden name was Doctorman?"

Jim shook his head. "No, she listed it on hospital records as Dillon. After her death, however, the bureau of vital statistics' records revealed that her birth name actually was Doctorman. Like you, she had been reared by another family but had never been legally adopted."

"And the others?" Mrs. Berry prodded, obviously eager for more information.

"Constance Smith," Jim said quietly, again nodding me a look of encouragement.

"Connie, of course." Mrs. Berry looked wistful, obviously again remembering folks who peopled those arid days in California. "She was the little copper-colored one with the curly yellow hair who liked to hug. Have you met her?"

I shook my head and gazed at the floor. "She died on Thanksgiving Day, less than a month before Mrs. Hudson's death. They had lived most of their lives in the same part of San Diego—may even have known, or at least have seen, each other—and apparently never realized they were related."

Mrs. Berry's shoulders slumped. "A shame to have had true sisters, blood of my blood, and never to have known them. Did Mrs. Smith have children?"

"Yes." Remembering Sean Smith, I perked up. "His name is Sean. He's a big, all-American type guy, fair, nice looking, thirty-five or so. Single. He seemed very devoted to his mother."

"Was he with her when she died?" Mrs. Berry frowned.

"No. He'd gone home to clean up. He found his apartment ransacked. He didn't get back to the hospital until after his mother passed away."

Mrs. Berry again succumbed to gloom. "What a shame."

"Mrs. Berry," I said, taking a deep breath and avoiding Jim's eyes, "can I ask you a very personal question?"

"I suppose so."

"I mean a very private question?"

Mrs. Berry regarded me steadily. "Well, certainly I won't answer if I prefer not to."

"You hedged a while ago when we asked who was beneficiary of your will. You mentioned bequests to the church and the charities, but you didn't say who inherits the bulk of your estate now that you've discounted your adopted relatives."

Mrs. Berry nodded, acknowledging the statement, but she remained silent.

"Would you rather not say?" I added lamely.

There was another lengthy silence before Mrs. Berry began nodding assent. "My will provides that the residue of my estate, the remainder after the individual bequests, goes to my natural brothers and sisters who survive me, in equal shares. I've made a generous provision for the search for those siblings, since that task proved to be so difficult when we attempted it before. I thought I would have the search begin again after my death; however, I changed my mind. It's being done now, through my attorney. He has had an investigator assigned to the task for over a year. The man has had some success. He has even provided smatterings of the same information you brought me today.

"Early in his search, he came across a young man named Chester Doyle."

I sat up very straight and stared at Mrs. Berry in disbelief. "Wait." My mind raced. Turning, I glared at Jim, whose eyes moved from one tile floor pattern to another. I thought the wheels whirring in his brain were almost audible. "This isn't the guy who was serving time in prison?"

"No." Mrs. Berry sounded as if she were trying to calm me. "This was that man's—that Jeremiah Doyle's—son."

"Did the investigator give you a description of Chester Doyle?" Jim's full attention was on our hostess.

"Yes, simply because I wondered if there were a family resemblance. I asked him to take pictures from then on of all the Doctormans and their offspring. He has complied with that wish since then, but he didn't retrace his steps to obtain a photograph of Mr. Doyle.

"He said my nephew was about thirty years old, had sandy hair and shockingly blue eyes, was tall and slim and had rather a prominent nose. When pressed, he insisted that Mr. Doyle was not unattractive, but of course, he knew that was what I wanted to hear."

Again recalling Doyle's rat face—the small, gleaming eyes and the long, narrow nose—I decided that even in my most generous mood, I would never have described him as either "tall" or "not unattractive." Of course, Mrs. Berry was no doubt paying the investigator a lot of money to find her relatives. I suppose the investigator was giving his report the best spin possible.

When I looked to Jim, I knew he saw my confusion. He allowed a smile and shook his head ever so slightly.

"Where did he see Mr. Doyle?" Jim asked.

"It was a small town in Texas somewhere."

Jim nodded and made a note. "When was that?"

"Late last spring."

"Has your investigator turned up any other relatives since then?"

Mrs. Berry closed her eyes for a moment before answering. "None he could speak with. He had a lead on a Cora Dibble in Kansas, but was unable to locate her. He had information on two others in California, the two you mentioned, Mrs. Hudson and Mrs. Smith. He was able to locate them, but they were both deceased by the time he got there."

CHAPTER TWENTY-FIVE

"So now we've accounted for five of the seven Doctormans," I said as we drove back to the hotel. "But I still don't understand."

Jim smiled a little sadly at the winding mountain road. "What possible motive could there be?"

I knew he was baiting me. "The money, of course."

"What money?"

"The residue of Mrs. Berry's estate. But it sounds like there's plenty. Why kill off her siblings?"

"What does her will say?"

"That it all goes to her siblings, in equal shares."

"That's not exactly what she said. She said it goes to her siblings who survive her, in equal shares."

"Whoa!" I gasped. "That does make a difference. So what does that tell us, exactly?"

"People who don't have lineal heirs—kids or grandkids or parents—often leave their estates to their siblings. If a brother or sister is deceased, the share that would have gone to that deceased person can go to his or her heirs. But Mrs. Berry's will does it differently. If one of her siblings predeceases her, his or her share goes to those of her natural brothers and sisters who survive her."

"So?"

"For one thing, it tells us that Doyle/Donnan/Denim's mother—who, it appears, may be Mrs. Berry's sister—is still alive, at least for the time being, making her eligible for the jackpot."

"Okay. Sure. That's obvious. So, how many heirs are left?"

"Assuming Mr. and Mrs. Doctorman are deceased."

"If they weren't, they'd be well over one hundred years old by now."

"Right. Anyway, assuming neither one of the parents is a consideration, there were seven Doctorman children originally. Can you name them?"

"I don't think so." I glowered at him.

"Try. You may be surprised."

I fished an old envelope and a pen from my purse, and tore the envelope open to use as a scratch pad.

"I understand things more clearly if I see them written down," I said. "Okay, I know about Paula Faye Hudson." I wrote the name.

"How old was she?"

"Seventy-seven," I said with some amazement at having remembered that detail.

"Was she married? Did she have children?"

"She was a widow. She had had two sons, both deceased."

"Who else do you know about?"

"Sean Smith's mother Connie," I said and scribbled her name.

"Age?"

"Seventy-six."

"Marital status? Children?"

"Widowed. One son, Sean. Alive and well."

"And likely to remain so. He's not a player."

I looked at Jim a long moment, realizing that when his mother died, Sean's claim to the fortune was severed.

"Who else?" Jim prodded.

"Mrs. Berry, I suppose."

"Let's put her down last."

"How about this guy Clovis Davisson who contacted her?"

"Interesting initials, don't you think?"

My anger burned. "Sure. He's Denim, isn't he?" I hesitated, watching him. "But he's next generation. Okay, who else?"

"You tell me."

I shrugged so he gave me a hint. "Kansas-Missouri border?"

"Oh, yeah, one of the ones Mallory told us about. I don't think I know her name."

"Yes, you do," Jim prodded. "Mrs. Berry provided it."

Again I was amazed to be able to recall the name. "Cora Dibble?" I wrote furiously, hesitated, and looked up from the paper. "Odd," I mused, "her initials being C.D. Do you think that's just a coincidence?"

Jim rolled his shoulders and continued gazing straight ahead at the roadway. "And her age?"

"I think Duke said she was seventy-four." I absently turned back to my list.

"Who else?"

"The retired teacher in Texas. A.J. Doctorman."

"Age?" Jim asked.

"Sixty-eight."

"We know there were how many boys?"

I felt triumphant. I love coming up with right answers. "Two."

"How many have we accounted for?"

"A.J.'s the only boy so far."

Jim shot me a look of open admiration.

"And we've got Mrs. Berry." I felt like dancing.

Jim nodded. "How many does that leave?"

"One boy and one girl that we don't know about."

"Were any of the people we do know about adopted?"

"No." My answer came almost reverently.

"Then the boy most likely still carries the name Doctorman.

Is he Doyle/Donnan/Denim's parent?"

"No." I whispered. "You were right. The one remaining sister has to be Denim's mother."

"Now, is she likely to be forty-five or fifty years old?"

"Not likely. The Doctorman kids are stair steps." I glanced at my list. "The ages range from Mrs. Hudson, who appears to have been the eldest, seventy-seven, down to A.J., who was sixty-eight." I stared at the envelope. "Jim," I gasped, "they died in chronological order."

Jim pulled the car off the road into a truck stop parking lot, cut the engine, and stared at me.

"I hadn't realized that." He sat studying my face a minute as if he would find solutions written there.

"Is it important?" I asked.

"I don't know. What I do know is that we have verified the deaths of four of the seven and can account for the sparing so far of Mrs. Berry and the one we assume is Denim's mother. We need to know the name of the lone surviving brother, Denim's uncle—because, Jancy, he is likely the killer's next candidate."

Of course. It was a logical progression.

"Maybe Mrs. Berry's detective has some information that'll help," I suggested, trying to come up with an idea that might save a man's life.

"Maybe he could make better headway if he knew to concentrate on finding only that particular one of Mrs. Berry's siblings." Jim's voice was low. "Maybe you and I can contribute information that will save this last brother." Frowning, he bit the inside of his lower lip, a mannerism I had come to associate with his thinking process. Without another word, he started the car and turned it back the way we had come. Forty minutes later, we again pulled into the circle drive in front of the Berry home.

Mrs. Berry opened the front door before we rang the doorbell.

"I just called to leave a message for you at the hotel. First, Mr. Grimm, the private detective I hired, called. He's on his way over now with another bit of news.

"Also, Mr. Davisson called not ten minutes after you left. He asked if he could come to see me about five o'clock."

"Today?" I stared at the woman's face, then twisted trying to read Jim's watch. I was frightened, but excited, too, at the prospect of actually coming face to face with a murderer, a serial killer, the rat-faced man with the beady little vivid blue eyes from San Diego. Would I be able to stand calmly confronting him face to face?

I didn't know, but Mrs. Berry saved me, at least from that immediate dread.

"No, dear, tomorrow. He'll be here tomorrow afternoon at five. Only Mr. Grimm, my private detective, is coming today."

Chapter Twenty-Six

Detective Dale Grimm had been too late . . . again.

Neil Doctorman, sixty-six, was dead on arrival at St. Mary's Hospital in Tinkerstone, a small town in the Texas panhandle, the day after Christmas.

Grimm gave his report in even tones, seated in the formal living room in the Berry home. His audience included Jim and me, Mrs. Berry, and Lt. Ernie Udouj, whom I had called, thinking she needed to hear Grimm's report. Udouj thought so, too.

Only Grimm and Mrs. Berry sat. Jim leaned on the doorjamb between the living room and the entry hall. Udouj, who also preferred to remain on her feet, stood gazing out a front window. I felt more comfortable away from the group, standing beside the highly polished grand piano. I was careful not to touch that glorious instrument for fear of marring its sheen.

Fire danced around artificial logs on the aged hearth, but the heat coming from them was negligible. The old house felt drafty and those present retained our layers of clothing. Of course, it was not nearly as cold inside as it was out.

Before the others arrived, Mrs. Berry said she preferred we meet in the formal living room in the front of the house. She didn't like taking business acquaintances like Dale Grimm and Lieutenant Udouj to the intimacy of her breakfast room. I took that as a compliment. Jim and I had been invited back to the breakfast room at our first visit.

Evidence, the investigator said, indicated Neil Doctorman

had drowned while ice fishing. There was no other plausible explanation for the circumstances of his death.

His wife called neighbors late in the evening to help her search when he didn't return from his Christmas afternoon outing. They found his body shortly after dawn the next morning, visible under the ice, floating just beyond a hole in the small pond he often fished in winter. He had drowned in a scant seven feet of water.

There was speculation at the scene that Doctorman had had a stroke or a heart attack, fallen into the hole he cut for fishing, struggled but was unable to escape before hypothermia or the medical incident or a combination of the two took his life.

I stared at Grimm, dumbfounded, as we listened to the account he read from a small notebook.

"This makes me furious . . . and frightened," I rasped, speaking to the design in the Persian rug that spanned the huge room. Jim walked over closer to me but kept an eye on Mrs. Berry, who stared straight ahead. When Jim's gaze fell on Udouj, she met it and shook her head.

"And then there were two," Jim said. The comment gave no comfort.

I looked at him. "Two?"

"Mrs. Berry and her sole surviving sister, Denim's mother. I was afraid the other brother might be dead when Clovis Davisson asked to come see her." Jim looked at me rather indifferently, his thoughts elsewhere. No one spoke for several heartbeats.

"Do you think he has contact with his mother?" I asked finally. Jim nodded.

"I wonder if she has any idea how treacherous he is." I shifted my weight from one foot to the other. I wanted out of there. I wished I didn't know about this, not any of it. Jim nodded, agreeing with my assessment of our opponent, but again his eyes locked on Mrs. Berry's stricken face.

"I hate being able to see this coming," I continued, rattling, I guess, to fill the ominous silence. "How do we defend against something that looks so inevitable? Does he get away with murdering Neil Doctorman too?"

Forcing his eyes from Mrs. Berry, Jim looked directly into my face and shook his head almost imperceptibly. He seemed to be trying to shut me up. Relieved to be absolved of the responsibility of filling the oppressive quiet, I quit talking.

"We can alert the Texas authorities, tell them the story," Udouj said eventually. There was a dejected tone in her voice. "See if they can find his mother, a needle in a haystack, I'm afraid."

"Why Texas authorities?" I asked.

"She was married to Jeremiah Doyle. We know he was in prison in Texas twenty years ago. We can follow that lead, find out what happened to Mr. Doyle and see if we can track Mrs. Doyle through him."

"If Jeremiah Doyle's still around." I turned to Jim. "Is he important?"

"If they're divorced or he's deceased," Jim speculated, returning my look, "he's inconsequential, at least to Denim. But . . ."

"What?" I felt the urgency welling up inside again, almost like vomit.

"Texas and California are community property states. Unless it's spelled out differently, half of whatever she inherits is his."

"So Denim wouldn't inherit from his mother if his dad were still in the picture?"

"Not nearly as much, anyway. He seems to be pretty well intent on getting the whole shebang."

"So, we definitely need to find out if the dad's still alive and find him."

"Yes, we do."

"Use my telephone," Mrs. Berry offered. She apparently had been following the conversation and sounded decisive about what needed to be done. We turned puzzled expressions on her. "To contact the Texas prison people about Mr. Doyle," she expanded.

Jim turned on his heel and aimed toward a telephone, the one in the kitchen.

"Are we staying?" I asked as we drove back to the hotel.

"It looks like Denim's coming to call tomorrow afternoon," Jim said incredulously, turning his attention from the winding highway to look at me. "Could you leave now?"

I shook my head as he shifted his eyes back to the road. When he spoke again, the tone of his voice was kind, solicitous. "Do you want to leave?"

In lieu of an answer, I released my seat belt, slid over next to him, and looped my arm through his. "My only priority is being with you, wherever you are."

We were back in the hotel room before what I considered our burden began to lift.

"I could call Mallory," I said as I sat on the side of the bed watching Jim pace. "Have him notify the media everywhere. A little high-profile pressure from the press wouldn't hurt, do you think? Maybe we could even turn up a picture of the Doyles to run."

"Good idea." Jim paused in the center of the room. "You obnoxious news types may serve some useful purpose after all."

Not at all offended, I picked up the phone and began punching in credit card and phone numbers, started to say something, but hesitated. Jim gave me a curious look.

"What is it?"

"Speaking of earning my keep . . ." I began, then hesitated again, concentrating on the phone for a moment.

"What's the problem?"

"If we're staying, I'd like to get my hair cut."

"Okay?" He said it tentatively, waiting for a point.

"I don't have any money." I gave him a sheepish smile.

"Your name's on the traveler's checks. You signed the signature card on our debit card and our checking account. What do you mean, you don't have any money? You've got plenty of money."

"I don't feel right spending your money. Could you just loan me a little cash?"

He smiled as I turned back to the telephone to leave a message on a machine. I asked Mallory to call us.

"Jancy, there is no more *your* money." Jim produced his billfold and thumbed through currency. "Why didn't you say something?" He took out several bills, closed the wallet, stepped over in front of me, and smiled. "Here."

"I only need thirty dollars," I said as he filled my hand with several denominations of bills.

"There's eighty-five bucks." He stared at me in disbelief. "Write checks. Use the debit card or traveler's checks. Spend what you want where you want. You don't have to ask. Buy whatever you need whenever you need it."

"But this is your money," I objected again, my conscience nagging.

He pretended a grimace. "Didn't you pay attention at the church? I pledged all my worldly possessions. Like I just said, there is no more *your* money or *my* money. Now there's only *our* money."

"But I feel awful using *this* money to get my hair done."

He laughed. "Okay." He narrowed his eyes and gazed into my face. "Would you feel better about spending money you've earned?"

I half-smiled, half-frowned as I met his dark, dark eyes. "For doing what?"

He rubbed his chin with his fingers and pretended to be thinking as he glanced around the room.

"Maybe you could sell me your clothes." He shook his head at his own suggestion. "No. I really don't have a use for those, or for any of your cosmetics or your curling iron or other stuff." He snapped his fingers as if he had an idea. "You do provide a certain valuable service, however. How about if I take it out in trade?"

I couldn't stop a staccato little laugh twittering from my own throat.

"I guess when you come down to it, my body is about the only thing I've got to sell, the only thing that's of any value to you anyway." I pretended to be sorrowful.

"Now we haggle. How much do you charge for, say, showering together? I suppose you'll demand payment for services already rendered, like our communal bath this morning. Compute our activities there to cash. What's the damage?"

I sidled toward him, warming to the game. "What's a little back scrub worth to you, big boy?"

"I'd have paid fifty bucks to get you in there. I can think of a minute or two when you could have cleaned me completely—no pun intended."

I fingered the cash he put in my hand. "What exactly do I have to do for eighty-five?"

"Credit it to my account. We'll think of something."

CHAPTER TWENTY-SEVEN

Prison records showed Jeremiah Doyle was released from the Texas Department of Corrections in 1997, only to return eighteen months later. He died during an hour in the exercise yard on March 15, 2001, stabbed with a shiv, a spoon whose handle had been honed to a knifelike blade. No charges were filed in the matter.

According to prison records faxed to Ernie Udouj, Doyle had been an administrative snitch, but he had refused to comply either with prison regulations or with the cons' more stringent, certainly more strictly enforced, rules.

Notice of his death, sent to his wife Cletis at her last known address in 2001, had been returned unclaimed. Officials had no idea of the whereabouts of Doyle's wife or the sons he bragged about. Doyle did not receive much mail.

A notation in his file showed a cellmate remembered Doyle spent his months of freedom searching for his family. The cellmate thought Doyle had found his wife, who had married again without bothering to divorce him first. She had given Doyle money to keep him quiet and to help get him on his feet, the cellmate thought, then waffled and couldn't decide if that was Doyle's story or someone else's. He couldn't be sure.

Doyle's body was buried in the prison cemetery, a desolate outpost near Huntsville.

"What do we do now?" I stood close beside Jim in the formal living room in Mrs. Berry's home where our little group gathered at midmorning Saturday to assess information provided by both Lieutenant Udouj and Detective Grimm.

Jim and I had swapped our tickets on the noon flight to Dominion. Unable to reserve space for Sunday or Monday, New Year's Eve and New Year's Day, we were able to get seats on an afternoon flight Tuesday, January second.

"What do we do now?" Jim repeated my question. "I'd say we have to decide who might be next and try to protect that person."

Puckering, I nodded sagely, then cast a puzzled look at his face, provoking a laugh.

"Well, who do you think it might be?" he asked.

"Who?"

Jim glanced at Mrs. Berry. The mental cloud cleared, quickly replaced by an even darker cloud.

"Won't his mother have to surface first?"

"No. She told us there's a provision in her will, remember, that authorizes the lawyer to search for her siblings after her death. She even set aside money to pay for it. Denim will probably just stand back and observe the process. If they hit a snag, I imagine he'll provide a helpful clue here or there."

"But we know what he's done." I couldn't seem to keep the anguish off my face or out of my voice.

"She's watching you," Jim cautioned, keeping his voice low. "We don't want to alarm her, do we?"

I shook my head, making a conscious effort not to look in Mrs. Berry's direction.

Mrs. Berry looked thoughtful as she raised her voice, speaking to us. "I was just thinking." She stood, picked up her cane, and began walking our way. "I live alone. Perhaps you would consider staying here with me. There's plenty of space. I have a very nice guest room two doors down from my own suite. I always rest better when someone else is in the house. Would you please do me this favor?"

I thought first about the importance of our privacy, of having Jim all to myself, locked away in our honeymoon suite. Of course, with the holiday, the hotel was crowded. We might have trouble extending at the Regency. I hadn't thought about that. We hadn't asked about keeping the room until the second.

Also, Mrs. Berry seemed to subsist almost entirely on butter cookies, gingersnaps, and hot tea. Staying in the house probably would mean no more lavish dining—certainly no room service— less privacy, and, of course, no more skiing. Maybe it was selfish of me, but I was eager to ski again and continue our honeymoon.

Conscience dictated, however, that I sacrifice my wants if it meant saving a person's life. The food and the skiing were two important considerations, but I could pretty well rationalize my way around those. Then, of course, there was the other.

I was not as willing to sacrifice the intimacy, the giving and receiving of passion and pure sexual pleasure, the leisurely touching, the sensuous bathing, the raucous, rough-and-tumble activity we enjoyed. I'd gotten bold—eager, even—about touching my willing husband's beautiful body. I had just become uninhibited enough to coo and moan, experimenting with the sounds of love. I couldn't bear the thought of giving up all that.

Suddenly I looked into the steady gaze of Ernie Udouj. The woman was waiting for my response to Mrs. Berry's question. I hoped none of what I was thinking showed. Looking around, I realized Mrs. Berry and Jim and even Dale Grimm all were regarding me peculiarly. Had I said anything? Muttered? Made any sound at all? I didn't think so. Then what? I looked to Jim for input and, as I turned to him, his eyes shifted to our hostess.

"That's very gracious of you, Mrs. Berry," he said evenly. "We'd be happy to stay, if you're sure it's not too much trouble."

Mrs. Berry brightened noticeably and I realized how much

the older woman wanted us to accept what had seemed a casual invitation.

"No trouble at all," she assured us.

I drew a deep breath, actually relieved that I hadn't had to make the decision. In the scheme of things, Jim and I should have years of intimacy in front of us. I could afford to give Mrs. Berry a couple of days—three nights, to be exact—reminding myself that our gesture might actually save the older woman's life.

The guest room was in fact a suite, two rooms and a private bath. There was a sitting room with a small, worn, stiffly formal Victorian sofa facing a fireplace fitted with gas logs and an enormous bedroom that appeared even larger with its twelve-foot ceiling and sparse furnishings: a four-poster bed, a clothes butler, and an oak wardrobe in lieu of a closet. Like the sitting room, the bedroom had a fireplace fitted with gas logs. Both rooms also had radiators, which stood mute and cold to the touch.

There was no shower in the bathroom, only a large porcelain bathtub with great claw feet sitting squarely in the middle of the room, a freestanding basin on one wall, and a matching toilet on the other. All of the fixtures appeared to have been original with the house.

The bathroom floor of tiny black and white ceramic tiles radiated the cold. A small gas stove was mounted on one tile wall. I opened the tall, white metal cabinet that contained bed linens and worn towels and washcloths—all of which smelled musty—and shivered. The winter chill permeated all three rooms.

Still, there was something agreeable about the wooden floors and the smells wafting through the sitting room and bedroom. I smiled approval at Jim, whose eyes followed my every movement.

"Okay?" he asked tentatively. I nodded. Looking perplexed, he snorted. "Would you rather stay here or go with me to the hotel to pick up the luggage?"

"Will Mr. Grimm and Lieutenant Udouj be here for a while?"

"No, they're leaving."

"Maybe I'd better stay, then. Do you think you can manage without my help?"

Jim laughed. "You're not dealing with one of your little brothers."

"Well, after you've gotten everything out of the room, will you go back through once more to double-check?"

"Yes." He eyed me suspiciously. "Jancy, you haven't gotten sentimental about the Regency, too, have you?"

"When you say 'sentimental, too' do you mean like you have?"

"No. I mean sentimental like you felt about our first hotel room in Dominion."

"Well, all these places hold special significance for me."

"Me, too, but if we get sentimental about every place we have sex, we may be soft on the whole country before we're through."

"So, you think we'll be through someday?"

My pretended concern prompted a laugh. "No, baby. I can see myself chasing you around the nursing home in my wheelchair someday, still in a lather."

At that mental picture, I couldn't help giggling. "I'll probably look like Mrs. Berry by then, a little droopy."

"I think she's kind of cute, in her own little septuagenarian way. And she's not you."

"True. Now get going."

"Do you really expect me to leave here before we initiate the bed?"

"Jim, we'll have to put sex on hold while we're here."

"The hell you say. If that's the case, honey, we ain't staying."

"Jim, we can't . . . behave like that . . . here."

He raised his eyebrows and put his finger to his lips. "We'll be vewy, vewy quiet," he whispered, doing a respectable Elmer Fudd. "We'll even twy it in that gweat big bathtub."

"And what if Charlie Denim slips in and slits our throats while we're carrying on?"

Elmer Fudd gave way to Jimmy Durante. "I'll die with a smile on my face." He chuckled at my affected tremors.

Lieutenant Udouj, Dale Grimm, and Jim all left together after devising a plan to park in the alley two doors down from the house and reconvene at four o'clock. Udouj would provide backup. Grimm thought Jim might be of help since he had actually seen Denim once and could identify him. Jim did not tell Grimm that I, too, had seen Denim in person in San Diego.

Shortly after they drove off, a small blue Geo pulled up in front of the house across the street. The driver, fair and slim, with a hawkish nose, unfolded himself and strode confidently to Mrs. Berry's front door.

CHAPTER TWENTY-EIGHT

Thad Bias' look of astonishment again mirrored my own when I answered Mrs. Berry's front doorbell.

"We've got to quit meeting like this," I said, laughing as Thad stood staring and stammering and trying to collect his wits.

"Thad, you just missed Lieutenant Udouj. I'll bet you haven't even met her yet, have you?" Bias didn't speak. "Or maybe you have. Oh sure, I guess you must have talked to her on the phone. She probably sent for you, didn't she?"

His head moved up and down, but he remained mute.

"Come on, Bias, get a grip." I backed up, indicating he should step inside. "Come on in and meet Mrs. Berry."

Bias hesitated before crossing the threshold. "Where's your husband?" The corner of his left eye seemed to have developed a tic. He scanned the foyer.

"He ran over to the hotel. He'll be back in a little while."

Thad drew a deep breath, stepped inside, and pushed the door closed behind him, effectively closing out the icy north wind at his back. A funny thing: the tic in his eye seemed to relax.

"Come on." I motioned for him to follow. Regarding me oddly at first, he slowly relinquished that disarmingly boyish grin I liked so well, and reached out to take my beckoning hand. I smiled but felt a little uncertain. Then, reminding myself this was my old buddy Thad, I closed my hand around his and drew him through the house and beyond the kitchen into the intimate little breakfast room reserved for close friends.

Mrs. Berry glanced up and immediately answered Thad's winsome smile with one of her own.

"Mrs. Berry," I announced, "this is my very good friend, Thad Bias."

Releasing my hand, Bias wrapped both of Mrs. Berry's hands with both of his as he murmured some standard greeting with surprising affection. I felt both puzzled and pleased by Mrs. Berry's eager response.

After the initial exchanges, Mrs. Berry suggested I take Thad on a tour of the house to familiarize him with the layout, a suggestion that met with his immediate approval.

Still puzzled by something I couldn't quite identify, I agreed. Thad placed his hand on the small of my back and applied a little pressure as if guiding me, retracing our steps through the kitchen.

I prattled nervously. "I'm really glad you're here."

Thad's hand moved casually around my back and clasped my forearm on the other side. It wasn't that I felt threatened, exactly, more like awkward and terribly self-conscious. He seemed different.

In both the formal living and dining rooms, Thad released me and stooped to examine the gas log inserts, twisting the knobs on both to turn the gas on, then off, I supposed checking to see that they actually worked. I didn't bother asking his reason. It had been my experience that law enforcement types were insatiably curious and often scrutinized things when they were formulating theories. I waited patiently while he brushed his hands over the tops of each radiator.

As we climbed the stairs, I asked how he liked Colorado now, the altitude, the people. I think I was trying to regain the easy camaraderie that had developed between us in San Diego. Again Thad slid his arm around my waist and grasped my opposite forearm. It was a controlling type of grip, but I didn't want to object to what he probably perceived as a friendly gesture. He was probably trying to make me feel more secure.

He inquired about our skiing and expressed surprise that we had been on the slopes only twice during our entire stay.

Upstairs, Thad wandered into the rooms and showed particular interest in the gas logs, the radiators, and the wall stoves in the bathrooms on the second floor.

I purposefully avoided looking at the beds in the various bedrooms.

"And is this Mrs. Berry's room?" he asked, arching a brow and looking from me to the ornate antique bed and back at me. I fidgeted and his smile broadened. Annoyingly, I failed to quell the rising heat of my old, reliable blush.

Twice he walked ahead of me to a doorway, then waited. Both times I had to brush past him, breathe the sweet, mingling fragrance of him, feel his touch or his breath on my face or my neck or my body as I squirmed by.

Instead of being irked at him, I grew more and more annoyed with myself with each close encounter, especially when I glanced back to see Thad watching me, the familiar smirk playing at the corners of his mouth. He seemed to be teasing me. He was well aware I was married, but that didn't seem much of a deterrent.

Moving quickly through the remote third story, I scurried, not allowing Thad to linger or move into the doorjambs ahead of me or to maneuver too close.

Back in the breakfast room with Mrs. Berry, I relaxed a little when Thad accepted my offer, sat down, and let me serve him a cup of our hostess's very strong coffee.

"We haven't seen the basement," Thad said, flashing me a taunting look. I ignored the suggestion and the look. He turned his attention to Mrs. Berry. "Is there a boiler down there to heat your house through the radiators?"

The older woman smiled. "I suppose it still works, but it hasn't been fired up in years. I live here alone. It hardly seems worth the fuel and trouble to heat the whole place just for me. The fireplaces and little gas stoves heat the three rooms where I spend most of my time. They keep me quite comfortable."

Thad guided the conversation skillfully but always brought it back to me. "I must have misunderstood," he said. "I thought you and your husband were leaving today."

"We were, but when Charles Denim called Mrs. Berry and told her he would like to visit her this afternoon, we decided to stay an extra day."

"Why?"

I eased into a chair across from him and propped one elbow on the breakfast table. "Curiosity, mostly. He ran us a merry chase in San Diego. I wanted to see what the rascal looks like."

"I thought you'd already seen him."

"Just glimpses, in The Town Tavern that night, his reflection in a storefront once, and on a bus as he rolled by leering at me. I want to see him close up and personal. He just doesn't look smart enough to plan and execute such an elaborate scheme of burglaries."

"You think he's devised a brilliant plot of some kind?"

" 'Brilliant' might be overstating it a bit."

"Appearances can be deceiving. You know that."

I nodded uncertainly. "What do you mean?"

"Your husband's a good example. Truth is, I didn't take a hard run at you in San Diego because I thought your guy back home was probably someone special."

"Oh?"

I didn't know if Mrs. Berry didn't hear well or if she were only pretending to be unaware of our exchange. She appeared to be engrossed in removing a speck from her teacup. Thad continued.

"He's strong looking, I suppose, if you go for the beefy type, but while you and I were waiting, holding out, Jancy, I think it's obvious he was helping himself to more than his share of women." Thad's face was solemn. "I'd waited all my life for you." His voice was husky, just above a whisper.

I knew my expression reflected shock before I averted my eyes, not knowing where to begin defending Jim.

"I'll bet he's hairy, isn't he?" Thad said, lowering his voice still further. "Hairy like an ape? Does it feel like you're suffocating when he's on top of you, Jancy? Does he sweat and smell disgusting, like a wet animal? Does he . . . ?"

"Stop it," I ordered. Mrs. Berry jumped at the command, which came out louder than I intended. "Who are you, anyway?" I stood there, fists clenched. "What have you done with my friend Thad Bias, an honorable man? A man I trusted. A man I confided in. Where is that man?"

He suddenly was on his feet. He put up both his hands, palms forward, and sputtered. "Wait, wait, Jancy. Don't get your panties in a wad. I'm . . . I'm . . . well, I guess you could say I'm disappointed in you for settling for someone so . . ."

My eyes narrowed to slits. If I'd ever struggled not to take a swing at someone, it was at Thad Bias at that moment. He took a step back, watching me closely.

"He's not the man for you, Jancy. You've probably figured that out by now. Oh, I suppose he probably has average intelligence, but he wasn't smart enough to catch Charlie Denim in San Diego and he didn't have enough evidence to charge the man with a crime, much less convict him, even if he had been able to catch him."

The insight I got right then was a powerful relief.

"I get it. The old green-eyed monster has taken a bite out of you. You're jealous. Jim was in California for two days and figured out the whole thing. You and O'Brien had been chasing your tails for weeks. It took Jim to get you on track. No wonder. This tirade of yours has nothing to do with me. It's Jim. You're jealous of him." I sat down again.

Thad's expression darkened. "It's not like you to play dumb. Is that what he told you, that he solved those insignificant little burglaries single-handedly?"

I puffed up, sitting straighter in the chair. "Whose side were you on, Bias? Were you so eaten up with jealousy that you'd complain about the one man who was able to help you and your superior?" I chose that word knowing it would hit him where he lived: in his ego.

He slumped into his own chair, suddenly pretending to be cowed by my charges, but there was something phony in his look and his demeanor.

"I didn't mean to make you mad or put you on the defensive," he said. "I mean, well, I figured you knew the man's shortcomings when you married him. I was only voicing my observations, things you've probably already found totally distasteful about him. I happen to agree with your assessment. The guy's a big disappointment." He captured my eyes as I turned on him, shocked at what he was saying. "It's not too late, though, Jancy. I can get you out of this mess. I can rescue you, like any ordinary super hero."

I smiled, thinking he was kidding, but his expression was hard. Leaping to my feet, I stalked to the sink, turned on the faucet, and washed my hands, rubbing them together briskly. In the window over the sink, I saw Thad wink at Mrs. Berry before he ducked his head trying to hide the smirk. When we heard the distinct sounds of men's voices approaching the house, Thad was suddenly on his feet again.

"I guess I'd better be going," he said and it occurred to me he was taking the coward's way out. "It looks like I've done everything I can do here for now. I'll go out the back. I want to take a look at the lock on that basement door."

"Don't want to face him, do you? Shall I tell Lieutenant Udouj you'll be back for the briefing at four?" I liked how indifferent my voice sounded as I turned away from the sink.

Thad nodded and his eyes delved straight into mine. "I'll be anywhere you want me, anytime you say."

Big talk. I managed a tolerant smile. Thad's laugh sounded artificial as he turned on his heel and disappeared out the back door.

I looked first at the floor, then into Mrs. Berry's face as the older woman peered into mine.

"A handsome man," Mrs. Berry said. "Awfully bright. Quite charming, really."

Not wanting to endorse Mrs. Berry's words, I shrugged and remained mute. Surely the woman was a better judge of character than that. She probably just hadn't heard our nasty little exchange.

The doorbell startled me from my musings as I rinsed cups and saucers and loaded them in the dishwasher. Mrs. Berry, who had again buried herself in the morning newspaper, looked up.

"I'll get it." I grabbed a tea towel and dried my hands as I hurried toward the front of the house. I saw Jim clearly through the sheer drapes, which provided only a thin veil over the glass panes of the front door. Hairy animal, indeed!

He swept inside on a gust of wind, carrying three suitcases. "Good idea, keeping the door locked." He strode straight to the stairs and up without even pausing to say hello. That went all over me. It was the first time we had been miles apart in days and here we were, reunited, and he didn't even take a minute to give me a kiss or ask how I'd been.

CHAPTER TWENTY-NINE

I know he realized something was wrong. I tried to make pleasant conversation, but failed miserably. I was preoccupied and felt restless and out-of-sorts. Throughout the four o'clock briefing, I paced to the windows and into the foyer to peer out the front door over and over again.

"What's the matter?" Jim's whispered question startled me. I didn't realize he'd come up behind me or that he'd asked what was wrong when other people were present.

"I thought Thad would be here."

"Why did you think that?" he asked.

"When he stopped by this afternoon, I told him about this meeting and suggested he come."

"Thad Bias was here? In this house? With you and Mrs. Berry? This afternoon? When?" Jim was intense.

"You hadn't been gone long when he knocked on the door. I assumed Udouj had contacted him and that she had brought him up to date about what was going on."

Jim motioned to Udouj, who stopped speaking to one of her officers and hurried to Jim's side. He didn't mince words.

"Have you talked to Thad Bias?"

"No, I couldn't locate him."

I tried to ignore the inner alarm that buzzed inside me. "He came here to the house this afternoon. I naturally assumed you had gotten hold of him, and that's how he knew about Mrs. Berry. That he'd gotten her address from you."

Udouj's pleasant expression dissolved to a frown. "No, and my people have strict orders regarding the confidentiality of this matter. They know any information at all has to come directly from me."

"But he . . ."

"He what?" Jim asked, a warning look preventing additional comment from Udouj.

"He seemed to know all about the situation," I said. "He met Mrs. Berry. She thought he was charming and," I shot Jim a haughty glance, "very nice looking."

"What else?"

"He wanted to look around, check out the house. I didn't see any harm in giving him the cook's tour."

"What . . ." Udouj piped up.

"What did you all talk about?" Jim asked, interrupting.

I darn sure wasn't going to tell him Thad made a play for me and that was what dominated our conversation. "Not much. He thought you and I were leaving today and wondered why we stayed. I told him Denim's meeting today with Mrs. Berry would be our chance finally to see Charlie Denim face to face and I wasn't going to miss that."

"What else did he say or do?"

"He just roamed around looking at things like you cops always do."

"Did he see every room?"

"Probably not every room."

"But he was gone by the time we got back."

"Well, he wasn't completely gone. He went out the back way. That was after you drove up."

"He didn't want to hang around and meet the lieutenant?"

"No, I guess he thought he'd meet her when he came back this afternoon at four."

Udouj peered at me through unbelieving eyes. "He didn't

show up at four."

"I guess he couldn't make it," Jim said, regarding me with a suspicious frown. I didn't attempt to offer an explanation. I had no idea why Thad had failed to appear.

After Udouj drifted off to converse with Mrs. Berry, Jim's frown continued.

"Bias talked to you about us—you and me—didn't he?"

I shrugged, not wanting to get into it right then.

"He planted some poison seeds in that fertile little imagination of yours, didn't he?"

"No."

"Did he express opinions about your poor choice in spouses?"

"Maybe."

"Remember who the players are here, Jancy. How long have you known me? How well? You've seen me in a hundred different circumstances, not all of them pleasant. You know me. Now, think of how long and how well you've known Bias and under what circumstances. Think, honey. He's been a no-show before when he told you he'd be someplace, and I suspect he probably had similar reasons those times, too."

"You don't know him, Jim."

"Yeah? Well, neither do you, sweetheart. Now chew on that for a while."

We were all in position by four-thirty, poised to greet Mrs. Berry's five o'clock caller. Udouj and two unmarked cruisers were positioned in neighbors' driveways, strategically located to cover the doors to Mrs. Berry's home. Jim and I were posted on the ground floor inside the house watching the front and back. We'd sent Mrs. Berry upstairs for a little rest and relaxation. We waited, and waited.

At five-twelve, a rental car rolled by slowly, the driver scanning house numbers. He nearly stopped in front of Mrs. Berry's house, then stepped on the accelerator and peeled off down the street. The police officer with the best vantage point described the driver as "slight" with "a pointed, weasel-like face."

"That was him," I pronounced. "He has good instincts. He knew something wasn't right. We blew it."

Later, in private, Jim admonished me as I repeated the accusation.

"Jim, I know that was Denim."

"No, you don't know that."

I turned on him angrily.

"Cut the dumb act, Jim. We stayed here for nothing. You had him practically in your clutches and you missed him . . . again!"

"What?"

Avoiding his astonished look, I started out of the room. He was right behind me.

"We may have saved a life here today, Jancy. I consider that a hell of a lot more than nothing."

I didn't respond as I stormed down the hall.

Udouj posted security guards in front of the house for the night. Acting on Mrs. Berry's advice, Jim ordered dinner in—Chinese food for Mrs. Berry, himself, and me—from a nearby carryout. I couldn't bear to look at Jim. Every time I did, I thought about how many women he'd had before me, and the thoughts almost made me ill.

We sat at the kitchen table after dinner and Mrs. Berry recounted vague memories of her childhood. Finally, at nine-thirty, she apparently had held out as long as she could, excused herself, and went upstairs.

Jim cleared the table, occasionally glancing at me. I avoided eye contact. "What did Bias say to you this afternoon?" he asked casually.

"It's none of your business," I blurted, then blushed furiously.

"Was Mrs. Berry with you while he was here?"

"Most of the time. If you don't believe me, why don't you ask her?"

"I'd rather get it from you."

I looked at him, brooding. "Jim, have you had sex with a lot of other women?"

He leaned back against the sink, crossed his arms over his chest, and eyed me skeptically. "Not many."

How many was "not many," I wondered, but I just didn't want to pursue it. Jim folded and hung up a tea towel and snapped off the light. I followed him toward the stairs. We both snapped off lamps and gas jets in the converted fireplaces as we went, both preoccupied with our own thoughts.

"How many?" I asked as I started up the stairs well ahead of him.

"I don't know. It's not significant."

"Not a significant number, you mean, or the women themselves were not significant?"

"Both."

"But they slept in your bed—in our bed—in Bishop, right?"

He didn't answer as he trailed me through the door into our rooms.

Fires blazed cheerfully in the gas logs in both our sitting room and bedroom. He'd apparently turned them on earlier to warm the area and make things cozy, but I darn sure wasn't ready to let go of the subject vexing me. In the sitting room, I turned to face him squarely.

"How many, Jim?"

He didn't flinch. "You knew I had experience. It's probably a good thing one of us had, don't you think?"

"What's that supposed to mean?"

"You know exactly what it means. Now who's playing dumb?"

I glowered at him, my mind and my jaw set.

He continued watching me closely. "Do you want to take a bath before bed?"

"No." Indignant, I grabbed some clothes out of the suitcase Jim earlier had positioned and opened on a luggage stand he'd found in the wardrobe. Then I marched into the bathroom, warmed by the little gas wall heater, and slammed the door behind me.

Jim stared after her a long moment before he began removing his clothes. Moving methodically, he turned the flames in the gas logs down, but not off, turned out the lights, and slipped between the chill sheets.

I scurried out of the bathroom in my granny gown, shivering, and lay down on my side, putting my back to him. When Jim put his hand on my waist, I shifted away from him.

"Jancy, how long have you known me?" His words sounded quiet in the dark stillness of the bedroom.

"Sixteen months."

"In that time, you've learned to trust me? My judgment? My integrity?" I didn't speak. "And you have some idea of how much I love you, haven't you?"

"Hmm," I hummed, my attitude softening.

"And what exactly do you know about Thad Bias?"

"This has nothing to do with Thad. This is strictly between you and me."

"The guy is a snake, Jance. Surely you can see the treachery, the misery gnawing away in him. You've seen people like him before, damaged folks who want to inflict their pain on everyone around them."

I rolled onto my back and stared straight up at reflections of the fire dancing on the ceiling.

"Women I knew in the past never concerned you before you

talked to him today, did they?"

I remained silent.

"Well, did they?"

I rolled my face toward him, studying his features in the flickering light. "Will you tell me about them?"

"No," he said quietly.

"Don't you trust me?"

"Honey, I don't even want to think of other women, much less discuss them."

"Because they were so much better at sex than the amateur you wound up with?"

"Sweetheart, you're too stressed to have this conversation tonight. Let's get some sleep."

I flopped onto my side facing him and pushed his near shoulder with both hands. "I want you to get out of my bed."

As if he hadn't felt a thing, Jim rolled onto his side, turning his back to me.

"I said I want you to leave." I began pushing his back.

"No," he said, and didn't budge.

"You have to sleep somewhere else. I can't stand for you to be here in this bed with me. I gag at the thought of your touching me."

"Tough."

"You have to go. I can't bear to have you lying here next to me."

"This is my bed, Jancy. It's warm and I'm comfortable."

"I want you to leave."

"You're the one who's mad, not me. I have no desire to be anywhere else and I'm not leaving."

"I can't stand the sight of you. I won't lie in bed beside some . . . some filthy womanizer."

"Okay." He obviously understood, but he didn't move.

"If you don't leave, then I'll have to. Do you want me to

sleep somewhere else?"

"No, I don't."

"Then go."

"No."

Livid, I scrambled out of the bed, taking my pillow and stripping off the bedspread in flight. I flounced into the sitting room, angrier than I'd ever been, and did a full turn looking for a place to light. The pinched little Victorian divan, decrepit as it was, looked the most promising.

The upholstered seat was smashed and worn thinner at the front. I lay down and lapped the spread over me. Curling, I tried to position my body to fit the divan's abbreviated length. It felt like I might slide onto the floor if I relaxed. My anger escalated. I closed my eyes, but thoughts of Jim's obstinacy and my own discomfort made me angrier.

What was the biblical admonition? Don't allow the sun to go down on your anger? What was the upshot? I strained to remember, at the same time struggling to keep it beyond my conscious thought.

Jim had always seemed like a gentleman, yet here he was kicking me out of my own bed. I seethed. When he realized I wasn't coming back, he would come after me, and he'd better be damned contrite, that's all I knew. I lay there furious, smoldering, waiting. I couldn't relax. The flickering of the flame in the gas logs of the sitting room, rather than soothing, annoyed me. Struggling out of my cocoon, I got up and turned up the gas jet. If the flame were going to annoy me, it might as well warm the room a little more.

But it wasn't enough. With the temperature outside plunging into the teens, I got colder and colder until my hands and feet felt like popsicles, my nose frozen.

I strained to hear some sound, but there was only silence from the bedroom. The only noise I did hear was the wind whistling around the sitting room windows.

I changed position, tried putting my back to the room and curling around my arms and legs, which were crushed between my torso and the back of the divan, trying to generate some warmth.

Why didn't he come? Was he intentionally letting me suffer? Was he lying there in our warm bed, battling his own stubborn pride?

I remembered the rest of that biblical admonition. Going to sleep angry allows the devil to get a foothold. Jim should come straighten this out.

But he didn't.

Shivering and exasperated, I kicked free of the bedspread, tiptoed to the open bedroom door, and listened. There was only one sound: a snore.

I stood a long time in that doorway, clutching the bedspread, trembling, cold, and fuming. Why should I be punished? Rationalizing my way to a decision, I tiptoed to the side of the bed and stared down at him. There was no pretense. He was genuinely sound asleep.

Without making a sound, I laid the spread across the foot of the bed, eased the sheet and quilts back, and slid my frozen body under the covers. I shivered at the warmth. Stretching, I nestled my back as close to Jim as I dared, trying to glean some of his body heat.

Jim rolled to cover my chilled shoulder with one warm, massive arm. He slipped his hand over my breast to settle in the middle of my stomach and pulled me snugly into the heated curve of his body. I shivered again, the shiver almost a spasm.

"I love you," he whispered.

Nestling, I sighed and immediately slept.

I was accustomed to Jim's moving around in the early morning.

We frequently made love in the predawn hours. But these movements were different, abrupt, jerky, and annoying.

He spoke, but I couldn't understand his words. Nor could I identify the awful smell. Dreamily I decided that the pungent odor was causing the vile headache.

Jim yanked me out from under the covers into the cold blackness of the room. Struggling against him, I grabbed for the lost blankets. Had he gone berserk? We needed to stay in the warm bed, comfortable, except for the headache that increased its intensity with every movement. He picked me up as I snatched at the bedspread.

What was he doing? Wrestling at this hour? It wasn't even light yet. He sat me on the side of the bed, wrapped the bedspread around me, then tossed me over his shoulder. I thought my head would split wide open. I dangled from his shoulder like a side of meat, but I couldn't get awake enough to fight him. My head pounding, I clung to the bedspread. My mind refused to wake up.

"Jim, turn up the heat, please. I'm cold. No, no, no. Honey, don't open the windows."

Running, stumbling, then righting himself, he raced down the hall. Jostled, I slid from his grasp as it felt like we fell down the stairs. He stopped long enough to pull me back onto his shoulder, then drew a deep breath, as if he were diving under water. He took off again, running straight out the front door. High-stepping in the snow, he bounded down the walk to our rental car.

I felt him fumbling with keys before he finally opened the passenger door and lowered me onto the seat.

The front of my forehead felt as if it might shatter. My throat burned. There was a terrible taste in my mouth. My blood seemed to race through my veins, creating thunder behind my ears. I coughed. Lord, that hurt, but I coughed again. Then I couldn't seem to stop coughing, although it made my head throb and my throat feel like the flesh inside was being stripped away. I couldn't stop coughing. Someone heaped the trailing length of the bedspread into my lap. At least that made me warmer. I was sitting there in the car, the door open, exposed to the world, in my nightgown. Lucky for me it was the flannel granny gown. Why in the world was I wearing that?

I heard voices, people gathering around us. Someone stuck a bottle of water in my face. I grabbed it and drank, swallowing several times. The water stopped my coughing and soothed my raw throat, though it did nothing for the awful headache. Trying to capture a thought, I realized the crowd was composed of the security guards Udouj had posted.

I tried to look at Jim, but my eyesight was skewed. The predawn darkness added to my confusion. Besides all the other problems, my eyes would only open to slits. Dimly I could see his outline leaning against the car, against the fender right in front of me. Why was he outside in the cold, wearing only boxer shorts, talking to people?

Unable to wrap my mind around his standing there nearly naked in that brutal cold, I tried to formulate a question, but my brain refused to function, to translate thought to words. People in uniforms bombarded me with questions, with words I couldn't assimilate.

"What?" was the only word I seemed able to utter and I kept directing that at Jim, who either ignored or couldn't hear me over the other conversations.

Finally, he came to me and ducked his head below the door frame. He flashed a silly smile and patted my shoulder. I opened my arms. He sat on the edge of the floorboard and wrapped his arms around my waist and hips. Leaning into him, I put both hands on the back of his head and pulled, forcing his face into my lap. His nose had to be cold and I wanted to warm it.

More bystanders asked more questions, but I didn't care. All that mattered was that Jim and I were holding each other.

Then I heard sirens wailing in the distance, assaulting my headache.

Suddenly Jim tore loose and took off. He galloped into the house and up the stairs, his wild flight visible from the driveway. Two or three police officers ran in after him, yelling, their shouts hammering my poor old head.

Moments later, Jim reappeared wearing jeans and carrying a body swaddled in bedding over his shoulder. I scooted into the center of the front seat, giving him room to deposit the bundle in the passenger seat warm from the heat of my body.

Arranging his load on the seat, Jim stripped one of the bed covers from the clump and tossed it over me. Then he secured the remaining blankets around the new arrival, unveiling her face.

It was Mrs. Berry.

An ambulance whined up the street and stopped in front of the house. A fire truck followed. Two wide-eyed paramedics elbowed their way to the side of the rental car to examine Mrs. Berry first, then me.

Hazel Doctorman Berry gasped for air, then began wheezing and coughing uncontrollably. She twisted, flailing her hands, fighting the oxygen mask the paramedics attempted to place over her nose and mouth. They easily overcame her frail resistance.

Unable to speak, the older woman tried to force her eyes to open to more than slits. I already knew her eyesight would improve, but she couldn't force it. Failing in her attempts, Mrs. Berry's head lolled back to rest against the seat. She seemed content for the moment to gulp the clean mixture available through the mask.

Jim was off again. He trotted back into the house, followed

by two of Udouj's security guards.

Several firemen bounded off the fire truck. Two, their hands full of equipment, tromped double-time into the house. They had just disappeared inside when a police cruiser containing Ernie Udouj herself rolled into the circle drive. Before she could get out of her vehicle, a little blue Geo pulled in behind her.

Thad Bias's face looked twisted with concern as he leaped out of his car and ran toward the house, shoving Udouj aside without a word. Thad glanced toward the rental car, saw me, did a double-take, and stopped dead in his tracks.

Erratically, Thad sidestepped his way back to the car, looking neither right nor left as he advanced. Watching him dreamily, I squinted, wondering at the look on his face and his peculiar behavior. He stopped to open the driver's-side door and slid into the car. He reached out and his hand looked as if it were swimming toward me. When his fingers touched my face, he drew a deep breath.

"What are you doing here?" he asked, his eyes bright, his stare intense. "Why aren't you at the hotel? You weren't supposed to be here."

"She invited us," I said, speaking deliberately. The words formed slowly in my head and seemed to take forever to come out of my mouth.

Thad looked almost ill as he began rubbing my hands briskly. "I'm sorry." He bowed his head, moaning, "I'm so sorry. If I'd known. Oh, Jancy, I'd never let anything happen to you."

"What?" I felt as if I were in a stupor because I couldn't figure out what he meant.

Thad started to say more, but stopped short. Instead, he stroked my face with his fingertips.

Wrapped in the blanket Jim had provided, I'd freed my shoulders and arms. When I tried again to see Thad, I was surprised to find his eyes fixed on the unbuttoned neckline of my granny gown.

Ignoring him, I looked back at the house.

Despite the cold, police and firemen inside appeared to be throwing open every window in Mrs. Berry's huge home.

"What are they doing?" I asked.

Thad's eyes shifted. "It looks like they're airing the place out."

"Gas fumes," one of the paramedics attending Mrs. Berry said. "Almost asphyxiated everyone in the place."

Thad looked beyond me to see Mrs. Berry, whose skin looked ashen. "Is she gone?"

I looked at the older woman beside me. She was pale, slack-jawed, and unmoving, and her eyes were closed.

The medic shook his head no. "She's tough. It will take a lot more than a little gas to ice this one."

Mrs. Berry's eyes popped open and the medic grinned. Seeing her eyes crinkle at the corners, I realized she was returning the medic's smile from behind her oxygen mask.

"So, how'd you ladies wind up out here?" Thad's intensity seemed to melt as he got out of the car.

"Jim." I produced the answer more quickly. I seemed to be recovering. "He hauled me out over his shoulder. It wasn't pretty."

Thad chuckled dutifully and his blue, blue eyes feasted on my face. "I owe him big time for this." His next words were almost inaudible.

I hid my confusion behind a smile. I didn't know what he meant. My head still throbbed and the cold air seemed to draw the fiercest pain to my frontal lobe.

When the gas was cleared from the house, the paramedics carried Mrs. Berry and me both back inside. They wouldn't allow either of us to walk and refused Thad's offer to help. Mrs. Berry insisted we be put on couches in the formal living room where we could monitor the ongoing activity.

Having checked our vital signs several times, the medics grudgingly allowed that neither Mrs. Berry nor Jim nor I required hospital care.

Still afraid to light any open fires, they bundled Mrs. Berry and me in additional blankets and left us perched on the living room sofas, still accompanied by an attentive Thad Bias. We were there for probably half an hour before Jim strode in from the kitchen, fully clothed. He glanced at me and scowled at Thad, who had made me sit up so he could sit right beside me on the sofa. Jim walked briskly over to hunker beside Mrs. Berry, who was still stretched out on her couch.

"How do you feel?" he asked, studying her soberly.

She smiled. "Thankful. You saved my life, you know. No, no, don't try to be modest or deny it. That's what the medics said. Oh, Jim, what a terrible, terrible accident. It is so lucky for me that you were here."

Jim's pleasant expression lapsed for a moment, then revived as he stood and looked at me. In the light of his full attention, I yielded a slow, meaningful smile. He smiled back.

"And how are you?" he asked, quickly closing the space between us to kneel in front of me.

"Fine, thank you." I smiled into his eyes and freed my arms from under my covers to reach for him.

As if he were completely unaware of Thad, next to me on the couch, Jim put his hands on either side of my knees and traced the blankets up the outline of my legs. His hands moved to my hips. I placed my hands on his head like a priest giving a blessing as he turned his head to one side to lay his face on my lap.

Thad huffed noisily and stood, looking furious. I wondered what part he thought he played in this scenario. His behavior seemed bizarre, but then I was not altogether myself yet.

CHAPTER THIRTY

"What happened?" I asked Jim later when he finally sat beside me on the sofa. Holding my hand, he leaned back, sighed, and rolled his head toward me. I sat erect, studying his face.

Thad Bias apparently had gone.

Mrs. Berry had finally submitted to the paramedics' repeated suggestions and allowed herself to be carried upstairs to finish out her night's sleep, even though it was eight-thirty in the morning. Having settled Mrs. Berry, the medics loaded their equipment back in their ambulance and left. Firemen tromped in and out, tidying up equipment they had dragged in and strewn about earlier.

Udouj was debriefing her security people outside. Their astonishment at finding their charges spilling out of the house they were guarding at four in the morning indicated they had not seen anyone prowling around, but the embarrassed lieutenant was not satisfied with their stammered explanations.

Jim and I were momentarily alone in the living room.

"We left gas stoves burning to keep the temperature up in the house," he said. "There are indications someone turned off the gas at the meter. The flames went out. Then that someone apparently turned the gas back on. I suspect that person tried to asphyxiate us."

"Is there evidence to make you think it was done intentionally? Couldn't it have been a fuel surge in the line or something that accidentally snuffed the flames?"

Jim solemnly rolled his head back and forth against the sofa, indicating a negative answer. "They used a wrench to turn the spigot on the gas line. There are fresh scratches on the valve. Also, there were footprints in the snow at the meter. Several sets lead from the street to the back of the house. There are two distinctive sets actually at the meter.

"One of those sets, a man's size eleven shoe, not a fireman's boot, comes out the back door of the house, down the wooden steps off the porch, and to the gas meter where he stopped. Apparently he stooped to examine the line from the meter to the house, his weight thrown forward onto his toes. Then the tracks move to the basement door, where he stopped again. From there they go around to the front on the driveway and got obliterated by all the other pedestrian traffic."

"Those tracks were probably Thad's," I said, "but I don't know why he would have stopped at the gas meter."

"Say again." Jim straightened, alert.

"I told you Thad was here yesterday, before the strategy meeting with Udouj." Jim nodded but didn't speak, encouraging me to continue. "We were in the kitchen. He left just as you got back from the hotel. He went out the back door because he wanted to look at the lock on the basement door, to make sure it was secure."

Jim nodded somberly. "Yeah, I remember your saying he slipped out the back."

"What about the second set of tracks?"

"A man's size nine. It looks like he came up the driveway, around the house directly to the gas meter where he did some tramping around, then straight back down the drive and, again, lost in the crowd."

"Oh." My breath became thready. "That seems like a lot of foot traffic in a place where there are security people keeping an eye on things, doesn't it?"

Jim didn't answer. The room was silent, movement and voices in other parts of the house muted for the moment. The phone rang in the kitchen. Someone answered it on the first ring.

"Jancy?" It was Lieutenant Udouj. "You have a call. Can you come?"

"Sure." Unexpectedly, I wobbled as I stood, still wrapped in the blanket. Making sure I had my sea legs, I shuffled toward the hallway, but stopped.

"What woke you?" I asked, turning to look back at Jim.

"You did. Crying in your sleep. I was only vaguely aware that something was wrong. I didn't know what. Then I recognized the smell. My first and only reaction was to get you out of there. I grabbed you and we were gone. I didn't think of Mrs. Berry until the fresh air cleared my head a little."

"I was dreaming." My memory seemed hazy. "In the dream, I was inside a balloon. Someone was blowing it up. It was stuffy and the smell gave me a headache. I wanted to get away from the smell but I didn't want to wake up. Then you were shaking me and the next thing I knew, I was upside down, bouncing as you ran down the stairs." I shot him an accusing look. "By the way, over someone's shoulder is not a very comfortable way to travel."

He smiled indulgently. "No, I guess not."

"Thanks."

"No trouble."

Mallory's baritone exploded over the telephone. "I had a hell of a time tracking you down. You people need to tell me when you move around like that."

I smiled, but I didn't feel like explaining, so I endured several moments of his chastising me like a Dutch uncle before I interrupted his tirade to ask if there were any reason for his call other than to shout complaints at me the first thing in the morning.

"Yeah. I got a call this morning from the Reverend John Wesley Lincoln out of Branch, Texas. It seems he's at a meeting in Denver. He wanted to know if you and Jim were still in Colorado. I told him I didn't think so, but I'd find out. I didn't know you'd decided to stay over. When did that happen?"

"When Charles Denim called Mrs. Berry and asked to come for a visit yesterday afternoon at five."

"Were you there?"

"We were. He wasn't. He didn't show."

"So, now what?"

"I don't know yet." I turned around, looking for Jim. "We had a little mishap last night. Jim and I stayed overnight here at Mrs. Berry's. She has a bunch of gas stoves and artificial logs for heat. Someone apparently was able to get around the security guys watching the house and turn the gas off. Then, when all the fires were out, he turned it back on."

"That doesn't sound good."

"No, it was pretty nearly permanently bad . . . for us."

"Jancy, you need to quit screwing around with this Denim guy. Why don't you pack it up and go on home. Leave that worthless piece of trash to the law up there. Dead is no way to start a marriage."

"He's too darn slick, Mallory. And we've got a history with him now. It's like we know him pretty well. These people are brand new acquaintances. Were you ever able to get a mug shot?"

Mallory cleared his throat, a habit that was his early warning to the wise before he lost his temper. "No, but I'll sure as hell get one today or take it out of O'Brien's hide. Then I'm hand-carrying it to you. I'll be on the first flight out."

"It's the holidays, Mallory. The airlines are booked solid."

"Don't you worry about that. Where does the old lady live?"

I gave him Mrs. Berry's address. "Did you have something else to tell me about Reverend Lincoln?"

"I'm going to call him back and tell him to meet us at that address you just gave me as soon as he can get there."

"Right." That was just what this honeymoon needed: more people.

I hung up and shuffled back to the living room to find Jim gazing out a front window, deep in thought.

"Mallory's coming this afternoon," I said. "And he's invited Reverend John Wesley Lincoln who just happens to be in Denver."

Jim turned, his face reflective. "Oh? That's good, I guess. Is Lieutenant Udouj still here?"

"In the breakfast room."

Jim nodded absently, then walked slowly toward the back of the house. Curious, I followed.

"Is Thad Bias helping you?" Jim asked the lieutenant, not bothering with preliminaries.

Standing at the back door watching a forensics team work the area around the gas meter, Udouj turned to look at him as if making sure he was speaking to her before she shook her head. "Your wife asked me that, too. Like I told her, I was never able to find him."

"Do you know where he's working?"

"No, my dispatcher called around but couldn't even get that. Personally, I haven't really made much effort. I've been busy, you know."

Jim nodded.

Udouj glanced at me, then back at Jim. "Why?"

"Just curious."

"Or jealous?" Udouj asked.

Jim regarded her oddly.

"I hear he's a good-looking guy," she explained. "You worried about the competition?"

Jim didn't answer. I was puzzled about several aspects of the conversation.

"What do you mean, you heard he was a good-looking guy?" I asked. "What did you think when you saw him?"

"I haven't seen him." Udouj eyed me like she wasn't sure if I had it together or not.

I glared back. "Yes you have. This morning. He pulled into the driveway behind you, passed within a foot of you coming to the house."

"Was he that long, tall drink of water?" Udouj looked surprised. "I wondered who that guy thought he was, shoving me out of his way like he did." Udouj again turned her attention to Jim. "He might be worth worrying about, Wills. Not that he's so great looking, but I saw the way he eyeballed your wife. The guy's obviously got a burn."

I groaned as Jim nodded. Cops were paid to be suspicious.

"Where is he, anyway?" Udouj asked, looking around at the empty breakfast room.

"I don't know," Jim said when I shrugged. "He took off after things quieted down."

The lieutenant studied Jim a moment before she said, "So, what exactly are you thinking?"

"I'm not sure. I find it a little uncanny that Candlesticks, Denim, and Bias were all in San Diego at the same time and now they all three seem to have turned up here, together. No matter how I put two and two together, it keeps adding up wrong."

"Do you think Candlesticks is after Thad too?" I asked. "Do you think he followed Thad here?"

"Not exactly. But my idle thoughts are beginning to form a theory, a possible picture of what this puzzle is supposed to look like."

Udouj cleared her throat to draw everyone's attention. "Would you care to share?"

"Not yet. Right now I'm just entertaining random thoughts bouncing around in my head. But sometimes my idle thoughts line themselves up like ducks in a row. I'm just now beginning to get a glimmer."

He suddenly looked directly at me. "When did Mallory say we could expect Reverend Lincoln?"

I shrugged.

Jim looked me up and down and I realized I was still in my nightgown under the blanket.

"Maybe you'd better go get dressed."

I glanced down, smiled at Jim, then shuffled back through the kitchen. As I left, I overheard Jim ask Lieutenant Udouj to send a man to locate Thad Bias and ask him to join us here as soon as he could. He described the blue Geo and even dictated a license tag number.

Bathed, shampooed, and fully clothed, I made up our bed feeling incomplete. It was the first bed we'd slept in since we'd been married that we hadn't initiated. Bummer. I sorted through the clothing in my suitcase, putting dirty items in one area of the weekender bag and the few remaining clean pieces in a separate single stack. Inspired, I transferred excess items from my purse to the suitcase to lighten my load. Among those items was the envelope full of snapshots I'd picked up at the one-hour photo service but hadn't taken time to view.

Holding my open purse on my lap, I sank onto the edge of the bed to examine its contents, looking for other items to move into the suitcase. I thumbed the envelope of snapshots and negatives and opened it.

"Awesome," I sighed, admiring the Aspen-covered Rockies looming high beyond Jim posing in the foreground.

"Me or the scenery?" Jim asked. Noiselessly, he had slipped into the bedroom behind me.

"You, of course." I smiled up at him, then back at the picture in my hand. "The mountains are craggy and old. They make you look handsome. What are you doing?"

When he didn't answer, I glanced at his face. "Oh, no." I giggled, arching my eyebrows, recognizing the look.

"It's been eighteen hours. Did you think a little distraction like someone trying to kill us could make me forget your wifely charms?"

"You have a one-track mind." I shifted and glanced anxiously behind him toward the open bedroom door.

"When you're involved, I'm afraid so."

"Is this a good time, with people milling through the house and a bedroom with no lock on the door?"

"I can prop a chair under the knob."

We heard footsteps coming up the stairs moments before Ernie Udouj appeared in the doorway, a sheet of paper in her hand. "Could I see you for a minute?" She looked at Jim, then at me. "I need both of you."

Udouj looked around the bedroom and smiled awkwardly. "Let's talk downstairs. We don't want to disturb Mrs. Berry."

I put the envelope of negatives on top of the clothing, closed the lid of the suitcase, and stood, absently sliding the snapshots, loose in my lap, into my purse to show to Jim later. As usual, I hoisted the purse strap over my shoulder.

Jim waited until I fell into step behind the lieutenant before he placed his hands on my hips just below my waist and followed in lock step. As we proceeded through the hall and down the stairs, his hands moved in a familiar way, riding easily as I walked. Teasing him, I exaggerated the sway of my hips, then looked back at his face and grinned broadly.

He glowered. "You're going to pay for that, wife. You'll get yours, I promise."

"I'm counting on it," I said, giggling.

Udouj led us to the breakfast room, where the three of us sat around the breakfast table. She laid the sheet of paper in front of us.

It was a faxed copy of a mug shot. The distorted likeness depicted the narrow face with beady eyes set a little too close together and the beak-like protuberance, which I easily recognized as Rat Face, alias Charles Denim.

"Do you know this guy?" Udouj asked.

Jim looked at me and I nodded without any hesitation. "That's Charlie Denim."

"Maybe." Udouj frowned. "But Texas penal records identify him as Lloyd Doyle, also known as Lloyd Thatcher."

"Lloyd Doyle?" I looked at Jim. He gazed back vacantly. He appeared to be thinking.

"Denim's brother?" I asked, desperate for Jim to retrieve the information stored so much more clearly in his organized memory than in my cluttered recollections.

"Reverend Lincoln said they were once placed in the same foster home," I reminded him, trying to jog his memory. "They got into so much trouble, they had to be separated."

I took hope when Jim's expression brightened. Udouj looked from one of us to the other expectantly.

Suddenly, however, I felt deflated. "Have we been looking for the wrong Doyle all this time?" I slumped, making my purse strap slide off my shoulder. Annoyed, I tossed my darn purse onto the table. The magnetic closure popped loose and the flap flopped open, freeing the bag's contents, which slid across the slick surface of the table. Distracted, I put the items back in my purse one at a time.

The doorbell rang.

"That may be Thad Bias," Udouj said. "I've had two people

trying to run him down. I think we really may be able to use his help straightening out this mess.

"Jancy, didn't you tell me he had also seen Doyle or Denim or whoever, that Bias can identify him, too?"

"Yes." The three of us stood at the same time and trooped single file to the front door.

But the form visible beyond the sheer drapes covering the glass in the front door definitely was not Thad Bias. The visitor appeared to be taller, thinner, more stooped, and noticeably older.

Lieutenant Udouj was first to the door. "What can I do for you?" she asked, opening it.

The man had a gentle look. "How do you do. I am John Wesley Lincoln and I'm here to see . . .." But he didn't get to finish the sentence as I darted by Ernie Udouj and grabbed his hand.

"Reverend Lincoln!" I smiled broadly. "I'm Jancy Dew . . . Wills. It's wonderful to see you, here, in person. I'm so glad you remembered we might be here."

Lincoln's broad smile reflected mine as I tugged him into the house and continued pumping his hand.

Lincoln had a thin, craggy face with watery blue eyes. He wore a dated black suit over a shirt that was frayed at the collar and cuffs, a somber necktie, and run-over, brown wing-tipped shoes. The joy in his face overshadowed his drab appearance.

Ushering him inside, I quickly introduced him to Ernie Udouj and Jim, then invited him to join us in the front living room.

After polite inquiries about Reverend Lincoln's trip and about the meeting that fortuitously had brought him to Colorado, Udouj asked him to give her a description of Charles Denim.

"She means Carl Donnan . . . Chester Doyle . . . you know," I explained when Lincoln appeared confused by the question. I turned to Udouj. "He knew Denim by other names."

"How do you know we're even talking about the same person,

then?" Udouj asked.

I started to speak, but Jim shot me a warning look before I remembered he had obtained that information surreptitiously from documents that had been sealed, adoption proceedings that were not matters of public record.

I bit both lips as I rethought my answer. "Just trust me on this, Ernie. My source is very reliable."

Udouj looked as if she might want to pursue the question of my reliable source when Jim interrupted.

"He was born Chester Doyle, became Carl Donnan, Jr., and has used the name Charlie Denim. Those are just a few of the names we've run across so far. He seems to stay with those same initials."

"Always?" Udouj asked.

"Looks like it."

"Why?"

"Maybe they're on a suitcase or monogrammed on his shirts. I don't know."

"Maybe it's to retain some semblance of his true identity," Lincoln guessed. "He was a very bright boy. I'm sure he has his reasons. I don't know that it matters."

I surveyed the group. "We may have made a mistake, Reverend. We may not be dealing with Chester/Carl/Charlie at all. It may be his brother, Lloyd Doyle, that we're after. Jim," I said, turning to him, "where's the fax?"

Ernie looked back toward the kitchen. "We left it on the table in the breakfast room."

Reverend Lincoln leaped to his feet as Udouj rose. "Do I smell coffee?" he asked.

The lieutenant nodded. "Sure enough."

"Might I prevail upon you for a cup, if you are going anywhere in the vicinity of the coffee pot?"

Udouj smiled but waited to speak as Jim, too, stood. "We

might as well all go. We can talk back there as comfortably as we can in here."

As we walked into the kitchen, I glanced at the contents of my purse scattered over the tabletop. "Just push that stuff out of your way," I said.

Lieutenant Udouj caught one corner of the faxed mug shot and lifted it from beneath my strewn belongings.

Lincoln frowned down at the distorted likeness.

Reaching in front of him, I gathered the contents of my purse, trying to stuff them back in my bag.

Lincoln shook his head slowly. "That's not Carl." He sounded definite, even though he hadn't seen either of the men in years.

"Is it Lloyd?" I asked, but Lincoln's attention had strayed. Suddenly he put two fingers on one of the snapshots, suspending my effort to clear the table.

"There he is," Lincoln said triumphantly. "There's Carl. See there, it's like I told you, he did make a fine-looking man, just like I thought he would. Well, I'll be jiggered."

I stared down at the snapshots as Ernie and Jim both crowded in to see the person Lincoln had identified.

The picture the cleric singled out was the one of Thad and me standing in front of the ski shop at the Regency Hotel. Reverend Lincoln ecstatically tapped a finger directly on Thad's face.

"Yes, sir, that's him all right. I'd have known him anywhere."

CHAPTER THIRTY-ONE

"I thought you wanted me to identify Carl for you," John Wesley Lincoln said, obviously puzzled by my sullen reaction.

I remained mute, the wheels in my brain spinning without gaining traction, trying to reconcile this startling new development. Totally stressed, I looked to Jim for an explanation. He stared at the floor, nodding, smiling slightly before he looked at Reverend Lincoln.

"Do you recognize the faxed mug shot at all?" he asked, taking an entirely different track than I expected.

Lincoln picked up the picture of the man I referred to in my own heart and mind as "Rat Face," frowned down at it for a long moment, then gave Jim a queer glance.

"I didn't think I did at first, but yes, I believe I do." He looked apologetic. "I believe this may very well be Lloyd, Carl's brother."

Feeling ill, my gaze swung from Jim to the preacher and back. How could my good friend Thad have fooled me so completely? How could I have been so gullible?

"Did you say they were in foster homes together for a while but had to be separated because they became incorrigible?" I wanted to hear the preacher verify what he'd told me before.

"I only saw him once or twice," he said, not really answering my question, "but I'm pretty sure this is Lloyd Doyle."

I again looked to Jim for more. "Thad worked two full-time jobs?"

"Actually two-and-a-half. He was sufficient as a cop, convincing as an R.N., and an almost uncatchable thief." He snorted as if annoyed with himself. "What a guy."

Reverend Lincoln and Lieutenant Udouj sifted idly through the collection of pictures, but neither joined the conversation.

"That's why the patients at St. Simeon's described Denim as nice looking," I breathed, ignoring Jim's sarcasm. "All the time, I thought they were talking about Rat Face. I couldn't figure how people could describe Denim as 'nice looking.' I kept thinking it had to be because he was kind to them. You know, 'beauty in the eyes of the beholder'?"

Jim frowned at me. "And you consider Thad Bias 'nice-looking'?"

Udouj's inquisitive eyes suddenly locked on me, waiting for my answer. Although I doubted anyone else would recognize it, I heard the taunt in Jim's voice. As I returned his look, I arched my eyebrows.

"Very."

He snorted his disdain and relinquished a grin. "Touché."

Udouj looked relieved.

Watching Reverend Lincoln thumb through the pictures, I fell back to brooding. "Thad is the Candlesticks burglar?" I said, then repeated, trying to grasp the truth of it. "I can't seem to wrap my brain around that."

Jim's voice emerged in a low tone. "Possibly a murderer, too, Jance. While you're entertaining new ideas, you might want to consider that one, too."

I couldn't help the tears that formed and slithered down my face. "No, Jim. The deaths had to be accidents . . . or Rat Face's doing. Thad . . . that is, Denim . . . can't be involved in murder."

"Thad Bias being Charlie Denim is the one explanation that makes everything in this cockeyed deal fit, finally." Jim kept nodding his head.

I stared at the pictures for a long time. As I looked, reviewing in my mind the burglaries in San Diego, I knew. It was true. Had to be. Thad always knew what the police were doing in the burglary investigations and about the incidental deaths.

"Oh, Jim," I sighed, exhaling deep, deep disappointment and struggling to keep the tears in check. "I know Thad. He's a kind, gentle, sensitive guy. He couldn't have murdered those two lovely old ladies." The statement sounded more like a question, and a whine, at that.

"Three lovely ladies and two lovely gentlemen, allegedly," Jim corrected. "And don't forget the demise of Edwin Prophet."

"What you're saying is the hound they had for supper story . . . that was about Thad too, I suppose."

"And we don't know. Perhaps Mr. Prophet was not your boy's first. There may have been others, before and after."

My shoulders drooped. "Sometimes when Thad was out of the loop, I was the one who kept him up to speed on the investigations. I fed him information." I stared at Jim, trying to understand, trying to absolve myself of helping a thief, maybe even a murderer.

Jim returned my look. "You knew him as a cop, Jancy. You thought he could help."

"And he did come up with some good ideas."

Jim couldn't contain the caustic note in his voice. "I'll just bet he did."

I turned my back to him and wrapped my arms around myself. "Am I just plain stupid? I thought running into him here was one of life's weird little coincidences. Things like that happen to me all the time. How was I supposed to know our running into him here was significant?"

When he didn't answer, I looked back at him over my shoulder. Jim's gaze softened as our eyes met.

Reverend Lincoln picked up the picture of Thad and me

again and smiled. "This is an awfully good picture."

Jim stepped closer to look. "We can fax copies to the funeral home people in Bocco and that Kansas City suburb, see if they can identify Thad as the nephew who ordered the bodies of those two Doctorman heirs cremated."

"Knowing that Bias is Denim, can we stop him?" I asked, genuinely troubled.

Jim shook his head. "Not without some hard evidence and/or witnesses. He's been slick. He was a legitimate relative of the folks in Bocco and Kansas City—actually is a nephew—had the authority, maybe even the responsibility, of seeing to their final rites. He'll probably claim he was looking for his long-lost relatives and was bereaved to find them too late."

"Jim," I pressed, beginning to take hold of these new, totally bizarre circumstances, "I don't see how he managed to be both Thad Bias and Charlie Denim in San Diego."

All eyes turned to Jim, waiting for his explanation.

"Well, Thad worked regular days as a police detective. What days was he off?"

"Sunday and Monday," I remembered.

"Detectives do a lot of their work outside the office," Jim went on. "He probably moved around pretty freely, even when he was on duty. Charlie Denim worked the four P.M. to two A.M. shift at St. Simeon's Sunday through Wednesday."

I bit my lips, staring into space remembering. "He was always coming on to me. I figured he didn't ask me out because I was engaged. Actually, it was probably because he didn't have time for anything else."

"It was a nice setup," Jim said, pulling us back to theorizing from personal recollections that might get some of us feeling tender toward our perp. "Even Denim's neighbors couldn't describe him, knew he was a day sleeper, didn't bother him. He kept his two identities entirely separate. Bias didn't share so much as his car with Denim, or his wardrobe, probably."

". . . or even his Social Security number," I added. "But how did he have time to go to Bocco, Texas, or Kansas City or . . ."

"I imagine when we check San Diego P.D. travel records, we'll find Thad Bias made trips on police business at those times, to pick up or deliver prisoners or records or run some other errands."

"Why would the San Diego police send a man to Bocco, Texas?"

"They might have sent him to Houston. Bocco's north of there. It wouldn't have been hard to arrange side trips to conduct his personal business. Of course, this is just conjecture at the moment."

"But how could Denim be away from St. Simeon's?"

"He was off every day and three nights a week. It was probably just a matter of arranging for Bias to be gone when Denim was off."

"That would be some juggling act."

"It was only temporary. Once the San Diego contingent of Doctorman heirs was eliminated, he planned to move on."

Reverend Lincoln, who had been listening intently as we spoke, cleared his throat. It appeared he had a thought to interject.

"I may have mentioned, Carl was awfully smart, clever actually. Also, the boy had that peculiar sense of humor. What you describe is just the kind of scheme Carl might have enjoyed cooking up and executing, as much for the challenge and his own entertainment as for the money. He enjoyed putting people in awkward situations and watching them react."

"I thought he genuinely liked me," I said, thinking aloud. I know I sounded dejected.

"What?" Jim snapped.

Suddenly aware again of the people around us, I rolled my

eyes. "Not that I liked him back, exactly . . . at least not that way."

Watching Jim, both Lincoln and Udouj laughed.

"Vanity, vanity . . ." Jim said, shaking his head.

"Jim, it really is hard for me to think about sweet, thoughtful, harmless Thad Bias murdering those lovely people."

"Those lovely people?" Jim rounded on me. "How about the lovely Mrs. Berry and you and me, her lovely house guests?"

"But he didn't know we were staying here."

"And he was 'sincerely sorry' that he almost iced us along with his intended victim, is that it?" Jim sounded testy.

Another memory sent me down another avenue. "He sent me the bloody finger in the mail . . . and made those awful phone calls and threats. Why did he do that?"

Jim glowered. "When we have the opportunity, sugar, we'll ask him."

"And telling me all that crap about your not being smart enough for me and talking about your vast experience with other women. What was that about?"

Looking suddenly enlightened, Jim shook his head and merely looked at me. "A lot of people are going to have a lot of other questions for him, Jancy, before we get down to those."

"But we won't catch him now." My statement evolved into more of a question. "He's long gone, isn't he?"

Jim crossed his arms over his chest and slowly shook his head. "I don't think so. He's come a lot of miles and buried a lot of people chasing the pot of gold at the end of this rainbow."

"Can he risk claiming it? Reverend Lincoln says he's smart. Isn't he too smart to try?"

Jim looked offended. "People have been describing Candlesticks as 'smart' all along, including Reverend Lincoln here." Jim shot a look at the reverend, and Lincoln nodded. " 'Smart' is a relative term, Jancy. 'Smart' for a Doctorman or a Doyle may not be all that smart compared with the general population. Prisons are full of smart guys who screwed up, overreached, overlooked things, even obvious things." Jim seemed to be lecturing himself along with the rest of us.

"Yeah, I think he'll stick with this project. He's got too much invested in it to walk away now. And what's he got to lose? There are no witnesses, no hard evidence against him."

"But now we know his real identity. Doesn't that change things?"

Jim puckered his lips and gave me a studious look. "Ah, but he doesn't know that we know."

"Does that matter?"

"Actually, he's not put himself in any jeopardy, as far as I can tell. We've got no witnesses, no evidence, no case. I doubt he's dragging loot from any of the burglaries around with him, evidence we could use to convict him.

"We've just barely identified his victims. All of them have been rather neatly dispatched. He doesn't know we've made contact with Reverend Lincoln. As far as Bias is concerned, he only has one deterrent, at this point."

"What's that?" I asked.

Jim gave me a thoughtful frown. "You."

"Why am I a problem for him?"

"Because I think he has a heartfelt soft spot for you."

"With the bloody finger in the mail in San Diego and the calls, scaring me out of my wits?"

"He may have anticipated you'd turn to him for help."

I could tell by the look on Jim's face that he was warming to his own theorizing as he continued.

"In San Diego he probably didn't anticipate you would call me or that I would fly thirteen hundred miles to defend you from some assailant you might only have imagined."

"That's crazy."

"Crazy?" Jim said. "Do you mean me or him?"

I saw the twinkle in his eyes, heard the teasing in his tone. "Both of you." I pretended a grimace. "Now what do we do?"

"What was it we were doing here in the first place? Do you remember?"

"We're supposed to be on our honeymoon," I said softly, embarrassed to have to be reminded.

"Then, my love, perhaps we should get back to it."

"So, you think Candlesticks' siege is over?"

"No, I don't think it's over. The guy's got a lot of gall. My guess is he'll reveal his true identity, ingratiate himself with Mrs. Berry as her long-lost nephew, and try to bluff the thing through."

Reverend Lincoln, who had been quiet through our give and take, continued gazing fondly at the picture of Thad Bias. "I would really like to see the man this boy grew into, but I think I would be more help by beating it out of here before he finds out I've talked with you."

Jim looked like he agreed. "When this is over, you'll have ample opportunity to get reacquainted. Either you can visit him regularly in the lockup or, if he gets away with it, you can tap him for charitable contributions to your church. If he pulls this off, he'll be able and maybe even willing to give you substantial donations, probably regularly."

Lincoln did not seem pleased with either of those prospects. Having lost the good-natured countenance so noticeable at his arrival, he strolled slowly toward the front of the house.

"Will we see you again?" I asked, trailing him and breaking his reverie.

Lincoln looked at me and shook his head. "I will drive straight back to the conference now." He heaved a heavy sigh. "You know, I saw real potential in Carl years ago. I can't help feeling disappointed. And I feel a certain measure of responsibility for all this."

We walked him to the front door, where he hesitated and turned back to face us.

"The real shame of it is, even if he is able to get away with the whole of Mrs. Berry's fortune, he will learn a dismal lesson. No matter how much it is, money is never enough."

With that, he opened the door, said his goodbyes, and left.

Jim suggested we pretend to settle in for another night.

"And then slip out?" I chided. "Are you afraid of the big bad wolf?"

"I'm about to set a bear trap for this wolf, but you're not going to be bait. Like I said, he's got a lot of gall and may try to bluff it through, especially if you're not here; if he doesn't have to face those big brown eyes and disapproving pout."

"I'm not going anywhere without you."

"Yes, you are." His voice dripped with certainty. "You and Mrs. Berry are going to take a trip out of harm's way."

I pinched my face into my best scowl. "Jim, this is supposed to be my honeymoon. Mrs. Berry is a sweetheart, but she isn't you. Where are we going and for how long?"

"To Dominion, to my folks' house, with my family to guard you and under the watchful eyes of law enforcement people I know and trust."

"No!" I was getting mad. "I'm not going home without you."

Jim grabbed my chin and squared my pouting face with his. "This is not a debate."

"I'm not taking orders from you," I said, setting my feet, ready to argue this one good and proper. "This is a marriage of equals. You are not the boss."

"No, ma'am, but right now I am going to tell you what to do and you are going to do it. First, because this is my field; second, because you could put all three of us—you, Mrs. Berry, and me—in serious danger if you stay; third, because I need someone I trust to get Mrs. Berry away from here.

"Our marriage is going to have a lot of different faces, Jance. For the moment, it's a benevolent dictatorship with me as boss, and you as obedient underling."

"You, Tarzan; me, Jane?"

He smiled glibly but showed no sign of relenting. "This is one time we are going to do it my way."

"We always 'do it' your way." I smiled, proud of my spontaneous double meaning.

He shook his head. "Cute won't work either."

"I've already lost the power?" I flashed him a sidelong look. Jim ignored the plea and pulled an envelope from his inside coat pocket.

"The schedule is written down here." He indicated the outside of the envelope. "At three A.M., you and Mrs. Berry get into our rental car and drive to Boulder, to the bus station. You catch the early ride to Denver, rent a car there at Jiffy Travel, which is in the same block as the bus station. You drive to Colorado Springs, turn in that rental, walk three blocks to the Quick Trip Travel, and rent another car, which you will drive to Dominion."

"Where did you get this information?"

"I had Udouj line it up. I didn't want to risk someone listening on these telephones."

"Why the cloak and dagger routine?"

"Because it'll slow him down, if he tries to follow you. Also, because it mimics his methods and he'll understand that we're onto him."

"Do I put all these rentals on a credit card?"

Jim shook his head and opened the envelope to reveal several hundred-dollar bills. "Cash only. No plastic. If you get tired, pull into a motel someplace, use other names and cash, and you'll be awfully hard to track even for a guy who's had experience and can get his hands on a computer."

I fingered the envelope, frowning, for a long moment. "Jim?" I had a couple of questions before I agreed to his plan. "How could Bias have known about Mrs. Berry's will in the first place?"

Jim smiled, a genuinely happy expression for the first time. "I couldn't figure that out until we drove by the bank this morning. Mrs. Berry's bank. I called to ask Mrs. Berry what lawyer had drawn her will, then I called his office. Her will includes a testamentary trust."

I couldn't help interrupting. "Did the lawyer just give you that information?"

"The fact that the will includes a trust probably isn't all that confidential, but he talked to Mrs. Berry, got her permission before he would discuss it with me.

"Anyway, as a matter of form, he had taken that part of the will that pertains to the trust over to the bank to let them file it in their records for future reference. That was back in 2000. I had Lloyd Doyle's mug shot.

"It was hard to find anyone who still worked there who remembered temporary employees from that long ago. An old guy in customer service fingered Lloyd from the mug shot. It seems that some time ago, Lloyd worked for the janitorial service that cleaned the building at night."

I walked over to a chair and perched on its edge. "What does all that have to do with what's going on here now?"

Jim smiled indulgently. "The Doyle brothers were traveling around the country back then locating their birth relatives."

"Why?"

"Looking for someone they could mooch off of, someone to blackmail, a windfall."

"And it paid off when they found Mrs. Berry?"

Jim nodded sagely. "I'll bet they thought they'd hit the mother lode. They probably studied her long and hard, trying to figure out the best scam to run on her."

I was beginning to get it. "And they discovered when they found her that she was actually looking for them. But why all the cloak and dagger? She would have been tickled to pieces if they'd just walked up on her porch, rung the doorbell, and asked for money."

"Where would the challenge have been in that? Besides, they didn't want to share. The document gave distributive shares of her estate to those of her lost siblings who survived her, however many there were. It specified proportions, but not amounts."

"How did the brothers know her estate was worth going after?"

"Poor folks don't usually need trusts." Jim smiled. "Also, working in and around the bank, Lloyd probably managed to get some idea of her assets. His record indicates he was a fair hand on computers in prison. He had had some accounting. I imagine the information he was able to turn up got the brothers pretty excited."

I slumped. "You think Thad was involved from the beginning?"

"I don't know, but somebody had to concoct their plan. Maybe Lloyd scoped it out and then invited his brother into the deal. However it happened, shortly after the brothers found out about her estate, Mrs. Berry's heirs began to turn up . . . dead."

"They must have been awfully good detectives to find her heirs when Mrs. Berry's trained investigator couldn't."

"Mrs. Berry's investigator did find them," Jim argued. "He was just always a little bit late."

Chapter Thirty-Two

Jim sat stiffly erect on the living room sofa as Thad Bias pulled his blue Geo to the curb in front of Mrs. Berry's home on New Year's night. Jim had paced, read, paced, and pondered.

Not having seen Thad Bias in two days, he worried that the man might have followed Jancy and Mrs. Berry, but they had called that afternoon to report their safe arrival at the home of Jim's parents in Dominion, Oklahoma. They had driven straight through.

Bias waited as an unkempt, shabbily dressed woman struggled out of the passenger side of his car. All but ignoring the woman, Bias strode briskly to the door and rang the bell. Jim opened the door and smiled politely.

"We'd like to see Mrs. Berry," Bias said.

The woman trailing him hobbled up the walk, her head down, her matted hair plastered by hairpins. The hem of her worn coat was uneven and the wrap was buttoned wrong. She reeked, a mingling of scotch whiskey, dog, and body odor. Jim could smell her before she set foot on the porch.

The woman was a vivid contrast to her companion, who carried himself haughtily and was well turned out, freshly shaved and wearing a sport coat, tie, and camel-hair overcoat.

"Mrs. Berry's out of town for a day or two," Jim said, indicating Bias should come inside.

Thad looked unpleasantly surprised and took two steps inside before he spoke to the woman. "Wait in the car."

She turned around without looking up and started back down the porch steps, muttering to herself. Bias moved further into the house and closed the door against the bitter cold. "I understood Mrs. Berry was practically housebound."

"No. She's actually pretty spry, mentally and physically. Agile, I'd say, considering her age."

Bias stared at Jim as if thinking. "Well, then, I'd like to speak to Jancy."

"Gone, too. I guess this just isn't your day."

"Not yours either, I'd say." Bias looked a little smug. "Pretty tough honeymooning without a bride, isn't it?"

"Brides get emotional. Jancy is strong-willed, wants her own way a lot."

Bias appeared genuinely pleased. "So, where is she?"

"She needed a little time away."

"Did you have a tiff? A lover's spat?"

"I'm sure things will get straightened out, given time and distance."

"She went home to her mama?" Thad chortled.

"I didn't say that."

"Wills, I know Jancy." Thad looked victorious. "I may know her a lot better than you even guess. My only surprise is that when she ran, she didn't come to me."

"Maybe she didn't know where to find you."

Bias's triumph melted as he pursed his mouth and nodded, frowning.

Jim motioned him into the living room and indicated he should sit. Bias followed but remained on his feet. When his guest didn't sit, Jim strode to the window, leaned his back against the cold radiator, and propped his hands on either side of him on the sill.

"So, if both ladies are gone," Bias said, obviously not convinced, "why are you still here?"

"I waited to see you."

"Why's that?"

"Mrs. Berry and I discussed my theory of your scheme, yours and Lloyd's."

Bias stared at Jim. "I don't know what you're talking about."

"I told Mrs. Berry all about her birth siblings and their recent, unexpected deaths. We discussed how convenient those deaths were to a survivor anticipating an inheritance."

"You have no proof of any such thing."

Jim crossed his arms over his chest and studied his glowering companion. "Oddly, Mrs. Berry didn't require proof. We had a long talk. I provided details, filled her in on the particulars. She was quite interested, asked a lot of questions, showed a lot of insight. Of course, I had to guess at some of the answers, but I gave her my best suppositions. She seemed satisfied. Of course, you helped verify my speculation when you called to ask to speak with her. Your call sort of confirmed what I had been telling her. That's when she decided to go away to think things over."

"How did Jancy react to these allegations of yours?"

"Jancy likes to think the best of people. She insisted you were not capable of cold-blooded murder."

"Are you implying you were able to convince her?" Bias's voice oozed disbelief.

Watching his face, Jim bit the corner of his mouth. "She didn't take to it right away. She thought you were too smart or too honorable or had too much integrity or something. She didn't think you had homicidal tendencies. She'll get used to the idea."

"I don't believe you." Bias's voice quavered and the blood left his face. "I think that's why Jancy ran, to get away from you and your vile accusations and your raging jealousy."

He glanced toward the stairs. "And I think Mrs. Berry is still right here, tucked away upstairs someplace. You're trying to keep us apart, but it won't work. The outcome is set. There's nothing you can do to change it. Mrs. Berry is my aunt. We are blood. No wild speculations can change that. She's spent years searching for me." His face grew placid, comforted by his own words, and he gazed lovingly at the rooms and the furnishings. "All that time she wanted to bring me home, to this house, to establish me in my rightful place. I wish I'd known." He drew a deep breath. "People have been trying to keep us apart all my life, denying me my heritage. Now there is nothing and no one to stand in our way."

"There are still some obstacles for you to overcome."

"Name one."

"Me," Jim said quietly. "And law enforcement people from San Diego to Texas."

Bias smiled, then snorted. "There aren't any charges against me in any of those places. I'm clean as a newborn babe—born again, you might say."

Jim eyed Bias suspiciously. "You keep talking about yourself. What about Lloyd? And that woman out there? I guess you're going to try to palm her off as your mother, Mrs. Berry's long-lost sister. Are you planning on those two moving in here with you, just one big, happy family?"

"Lloyd who? What woman?"

"Lloyd, your brother, and Mary Queen of Scotch, there in the car. What term did you use? Blood kin. Queenie there is the actual heir, if she can prove her identity. She, not you, is the true heir. She gets the whole enchilada. If she proves out, when she finds out how rich she is, she may just decide to ditch you . . . again."

"Don't be a fool."

"Why shouldn't she? She abandoned you before, didn't she? Do you think she's just now feeling the belated stirrings of maternal love? If she should decide to share her wealth, a conscience would require that she give to each of you equally, you and your brother.

Bias's eyes grew bright, riveted on Jim, and he shook his head. "I don't know who you're talking about. I've got no other relatives, only my Aunt Hazel. I'm an orphan, alone in this world, looking for someone to love. I've got a lot of love to give." His eyes darted back to Jim's face. "Ask Jancy. She can tell you the passion that burns in my soul."

Jim's knuckles tightened around his biceps, but he remained still, regarding Bias with no change of expression.

"Oh, that's right," Thad continued, "Jancy's gone. Well, we all saw that coming. You saw how she looked at me that day at the ski shop. We have a special relationship, Jancy and I. It started the day we met.

"We were alone there in San Diego while you were back home playing hero. She and I got to know each other intimately, nights out on the warm sand. You were fighting crime and winter weather while I was on the beach boffing your woman, nearly every night. She begged me for it, told me over and over how much she loved me."

Jim's dark eyes narrowed and shot darts through Thad Bias, but he didn't flinch. Finally, when several seconds had passed, Jim smiled grudgingly. "I see."

Bias sneered. "I was her first. She'd saved it all that time just for me." Again Jim nodded. "And after things are settled with my Aunt Hazel, I'm going to get Jancy back. Count on it."

Still looking hard at Bias, Jim suddenly smiled. "What do you mean 'when things are settled' with Mrs. Berry?"

"You're so damn proud of your suppositioning, you figure it out." Bias started toward the door, eyeing Jim carefully but Jim didn't move until the visitor was gone.

★   ★   ★   ★   ★

At Mrs. Berry's insistence, I took her to Fry and Fritch, the law firm where Jim had spent his short-lived career in private practice. While I sat twiddling my thumbs in the reception room, Mrs. Berry went behind closed doors with an estate attorney.

Phil Demopolis, well known for his unbreakable trusts, objected at first to drawing a new trust and will for Mrs. Berry.

"You need to have that done in Colorado, the state where you reside," he explained patiently.

Sitting across the desk from him, Mrs. Berry indicated she understood. "I am coming back here to live, close to my friends and family. I will be comfortable here, knowing my estate will pass to people other than those responsible for the deaths of my brothers and sisters."

Without knowing the particulars of her comment, Demopolis began jotting notes on a legal pad.

"I want sixty-five percent of my estate to go to the charities I have named on this sheet in the proportions indicated." She handed him a piece of notebook paper from her purse.

"I want thirty percent divided between the surviving children of my natural siblings, except, of course, for Chester and Lloyd Doyle, who saw fit to make an attempt on my life. Here's a list, complete with their current contact information.

"The other five percent I want to give to Jancy and Jim Wills for their diligent efforts in my behalf. Jancy's the young woman waiting in your reception room, the one who brought me here. I would not be alive today if it were not for those two young people."

Demopolis finished his notes. "I will need an inventory of your assets so we can fund this trust. I will draw a pour-over will to cover any assets that, through some oversight, do not make it into the trust. I'll need copies of deeds, car titles, account numbers and locations of all bank accounts, things like that."

"Yes, well, I will send that along later, after I have returned to Colorado. I don't have time to piddle with all that right now. I have some young people to meet, people who are hopefully carrying the best parts of my genetic makeup into future generations."

Back in Colorado, convinced that Thad Bias was gone, Jim hired Dale Grimm to house-sit Mrs. Berry's home and he flew back to Dominion.

At the airport on January third, I leaped into his arms, nearly bowling him over. Laughing out loud, Jim set his carry-on bag aside and endured my enthusiastic welcome with rousing good cheer.

A week later, having executed her new trust, Mrs. Berry flew to San Diego, where Duke Mallory arranged for quarters at the Chestnut Hotel. Duke himself insisted on squiring her around.

"Hell, she fusses over me like a clucking hen," he complained to us long distance. "She grouses about the food I eat, chastises me when I smoke, and I may have to give up drinking altogether, at least until Carrie Nation leaves town."

I rocked, laughing out loud. "I can't believe you're putting up with reform, Duke. How did she get her bluff in on you?"

"She nags with a kind of Old World charm."

I couldn't help being mystified at the bonding of those two unlikely companions.

Jim and I settled down to routine married life in his condo. I called Riley Wedge to discuss possible assignments.

"The only things I've got are junkets, a couple of weeks here or there, but you say your lord and master doesn't want you to make extended trips."

"He doesn't like me to be away too long."

"Give me the straight of it, honey, have you even mentioned any of these opportunities to him?"

"No," I said quietly.

I maintained contact with Lieutenant Udouj. She'd seen no sign of either Thad Bias/Charlie Denim or of his brother, Lloyd Doyle Thatcher.

"I guess they've given up on glomming onto Mrs. Berry's estate," I speculated over dinner at home one evening.

"I guess so," Jim agreed, and we both frowned, neither looking certain. "I wonder what new mischief they're hatching."

"Maybe they've decided to go straight," I offered.

Jim laughed derisively. "Nah." His expression darkened each time we mentioned Thad, like he was carrying a grudge.

"Jim, do you have a personal vendetta going with Thad?" I had asked that question before. Each time he dodged.

"Woman, thy name is vanity."

"Hold it right there, fellow," I ordered as Jim emerged from the bathroom the next morning, wrapped in a towel. Propped in our bed, I leered at him.

"What's the trouble?" He tensed.

"Put your hands on your head and keep 'em where I can see 'em."

He locked his hands behind his head.

"Now turn around. Slowly."

He complied and I saw him swallow a grin.

"Again," I ordered. He did another complete turnaround. "Looks to me like you're carryin' a concealed weapon there, buddy." He looked down at the front of him, realizing I was referring to the bulge beneath his towel.

Jim arched his eyebrows as he glanced at me. "Not very well concealed."

"I'm going to have to pat you down, son. This situation may

call for a strip search."

He puckered his lips. "You going to do that yourself, ma'am?"

Sucking in my cheeks to waylay the smile, I narrowed my eyes and tried to look menacing.

"If you're going to do it, screw, then do it," he prodded.

Still in my very sheer black nightie, I struggled out from under the bed covers and padded over to stand squarely in front of him. Then I yanked the gown up and over my head. Without lowering his hands, he leaned into a kiss.

"Don't give me your smart mouth," I murmured.

"It's the only one I've got," he said, catching my face in his hands and planting wet kisses all over it as he strong-armed me back to the bed.

"Did Thad try to sabotage us?" I asked as we lay sated from the lovemaking.

"He tried. Did it work?"

I gave him a suggestive, throaty laugh. "Not with me. How about you?"

"Action speaks louder than words." He slipped his hand under the covers and began fondling my breasts again.

Late Tuesday morning, my birthday, Jim was off to work and I had just finished making our bed when the doorbell rang. I jogged down the stairs and peered out the peephole into a vast bouquet of flowers. I flung open the door.

"Happy birthday!" a man's voice sang out from behind the foliage. I stepped out onto the stoop and reached for the offering as he shoved the flowers forward into my outstretched arms.

The face behind the bouquet was grinning from ear to ear.

It belonged to Thad Bias.

CHAPTER THIRTY-THREE

Looking into Thad's face, I shivered even as I took the bouquet from his hand. His arms, which he'd opened as if expecting me to step into them, slowly lowered to his sides when I declined his unspoken offer. Eager anticipation drained from his face. "I thought you'd be happy to see me." He sounded injured. "Aren't you glad I'm here?"

I recovered enough presence of mind to force a smile. "Darn right." I delivered the words with all the enthusiasm I could muster. "I'm just shocked. Where in the world have you been?"

There was an awkward silence as he surveyed my face. "You aren't afraid to ask me in, are you?"

Shifting the enormous bouquet to one arm, I patted his forearm with my free hand and tried for a genuine smile. "Of course not." I was pleased that my voice sounded so natural when inside, my nerves were pinging like popcorn. "Come on in."

Following me inside, Bias looked around. "So this is the home of the great Jim Wills."

"Sit," I ordered, pointing him toward the living room as I hurried through to the kitchen to get a vase for the flowers.

"Mr. and Mrs. Jim Wills live here," I corrected, calling to him over my shoulder. "This is our home." I ran water into the flower-laden vase. Turning around, I was startled to find Thad planted in the doorway, directly in my path. He looked serious.

I flashed him another forced smile. "Excuse me." I waited for him to clear the doorway.

"What lies has that animal you're married to told you about me, Jancy? What's made you afraid of me?"

I struggled to maintain the smile, and shook my head as if I had no idea what he was talking about.

His voice became a soothing croon, like a carnival worker trying to lure a country rube into his game. "Honey, you don't ever need to be afraid of me. I love you. I loved you before I ever saw you."

My smile wavered. "Thad, you and I are friends. We . . ."

"Friends? No, darlin', we are a whole lot more than friends."

I shifted the vase to prop it on my hip. It was getting heavy.

"Can we go in the other room to talk?" Again I was pleased my voice stayed calm in spite of an escalating inner turmoil.

He backed out of the doorway. As I passed, he reached for me, but I shot him a stern warning look and he dropped his hands back to his sides.

I placed the vase in the center of the glass coffee table, the focal point for seating in the living room, then regarded him casually. "Thad, what happened to your brother?"

His smile deteriorated. "He's around." He set his eyes on the flower arrangement.

I sat tentatively on one of the side chairs and leaned forward, giving my full attention to rearranging the flowers, clipping an occasional stem with my thumbnail. Neither of us spoke. I did not want to initiate the next conversation and was content to wait for Thad to choose a subject.

"I want you always to call me by that name," he said.

"Thad? That's familiar. I don't care much for your other names, or the way those guys behave."

"It's okay. I'm going to be Thad Bias from now on. He is who I am in my heart. Thad is the man I always knew I was, the one I always wanted to be, really. And you . . ." He hesitated, gazing at the floor before he raised his eyes to capture mine. "I want you to go with me, Jancy. Be with me. Now, I mean. Today."

"Why?" It seemed a reasonable question.

"Wills isn't right for you. You're just another cunt to him. You're everything to me. He doesn't understand about you, about who you really are. Jancy, the guy'll be a millstone around your neck. You'll drown trying to carry him. Oh, you're putting up a good front. I can see the determination in you, struggling to make the best of a bad situation. I've been in your place a lot of times. You can't stay with him.

"Honey, I'm about to be a very rich man. I'm willing to share it—everything I have and inherit, all of it—with you."

"With me and your brother, you mean?"

"We're talking about us here, Jancy, not parasite husbands and brothers."

"I don't think either one of them would appreciate your referring to them as 'parasites.'"

"They're losers, Jancy. They've got a death grip on us, like they're expecting us to haul them everywhere we go. We're the smart ones. They're drones. We don't need them."

"And just how do you plan to get rid of Lloyd?"

"That's almost a done deal."

"Are you paying him off?"

"I have a plan. And I'm going to do Wills the same way."

"I thought you just wanted me?"

Thad shook his head. "We have to get rid of him." He sounded resigned to the inevitability of what he'd said. "He wouldn't leave us alone. If he found us, he'd just tell you more lies about me, maybe even get you believing them. I want you to want him out of our lives. I want you to tell me to get rid of him."

I stood slowly and looked around the living room. Things in Jim's condo had changed just in the days since I had moved in.

Drapes and shutters usually kept closed were open, inviting bright sunlight in to bathe the room. Wedding gifts and bric-a-brac were strategically placed. A tablecloth and centerpiece adorned the dining table. There was new, colorful artwork on the stark white walls. And there were the smells and sounds of someone at home during the day: laundry humming in the washer, dinner's roast beef in the oven, the slight aroma of the birthday cake I'd baked early to celebrate the day.

"I don't want to go anywhere," I said frankly without looking at him. "I like it here. I'm happy. This is where I belong."

"Not with him." Thad's voice cracked with what sounded like pent-up emotion. "I lie awake at night sweating bullets thinking of you, of him touching you with his filthy hands." As he paused, his face twisted piteously. "I imagine him making love to you. The pictures in my head are disgusting. They make me crazy." Thad's face became distorted. "How could you do that with him? How could you let him touch you like that? It's degrading and disgusting."

I wheeled to stare into Thad's face. "As disgusting as Edwin Prophet's wife?" I cringed as his blue eyes became ice. I knew I had said too much. Rage changed his expression. We stood there, stalemated, glaring into each other's faces until Thad's gaze wavered.

"She hated him," Bias murmured finally, quietly, speaking to the floor. "He whipped her, treated her worse than an animal. He didn't have the balls to whip me. He knew if he tried to do it again, I'd kill him. I would have enjoyed doing it. He beat her to keep me in line.

"I ran off. I thought if I was gone, he would stop. But I sneaked back to see about her. She was nothing to me, except, well, except she was the first woman I ever had." He shot me a guilty look. "I wasn't ever going to tell you about her because she meant nothing to me.

"The day I ran off and came back, I heard her crying and moaning before I got to the house. I sneaked up close and peeked in the bedroom window.

"He had her skinny little wrist lashed to the bedpost with his big, old leather belt. She was naked, crumpled there on the floor beside the bed, all bloody and beat up, the worst I'd ever seen her. She was mostly quiet right then, whimpering, whining like a dog beat up in a fight.

"Then I saw him, sitting off in a corner, rocking in the rocking chair, humming to himself and watching her. She was looking at the floor or down at her poor, old battered body. He started to stand up and she got on her knees and reared backwards, exposing all her best nakedness. She begged him not to touch her. That got him grinning from ear to ear.

"I probably would have stood for it if he hadn't smiled. Something snapped inside me when he did that.

"I ran down to the shed, got a rope, and looped it. He was standing over her when I busted down the bedroom door. It probably wasn't even locked, but I wanted to catch him by surprise. I bulldogged him, knocked him down. He was too surprised to fight me.

"I put that noose around his neck and gave it a yank.

"He started screaming, but his voice came out in this high-pitched whisper. He tried to tell me it was a game they played. He was gurgling. Said they played it all the time. Said she liked it. You only had to look at her to know that couldn't be true.

"I trussed him up like a hog ready to load, tied his arms and legs behind him so if he moved much, he'd choke himself to death. I left him gagging, wobbling around on his knees trying to support himself against the side of that bed.

"I untied her. I asked her what she wanted to do with him. She didn't care. We left him there that night and all the next day. When we went back to see about him, he was choked dead.

It wasn't anyone's fault, except his own."

My knees went weak and I eased back down onto the side chair, keeping my eyes on Thad. He sat on the chair directly across the glass coffee table from me.

"And you buried him," I said simply.

He nodded.

"Then you left. Why? Why did you leave then, after he was out of the picture?"

"I was going to stay. No one knew he was dead. We figured to let the Veterans and the Social Security keep sending his checks to the bank every month to take care of us." He paused and I waited, but he apparently needed prodding.

"Then, something happened," I said. It was a statement rather than a question. After I said it, I promised myself I wouldn't talk anymore, so I watched and waited until he continued.

"She got well pretty quick and she started showing a lot of interest in me, sexually. I'd fooled around with some girls, kids, but I'd never had a woman before her."

"How old were you then?"

"Thirteen or maybe fourteen. No one fussed over my birthday and I didn't know exactly when it was, to be honest. I could have had it by then. I'm not sure."

"Go on."

"Well, I was flattered and happy to accommodate her." He looked apologetic. "I didn't know much then. It was after that when I started dreaming about you, planning how it would be with us, even before I ever laid eyes on you."

Something about his speech pattern had changed with his recollections. He sounded more country and far less sophisticated than the Thad I had known. But I didn't question it, I just sat quietly and listened to him reminisce.

"Then one night she came in and handed me the buggy whip." He got an odd look on his face. "She said she'd been bad and she needed whipping. I didn't want to do it. I'd been whipped when I was a little kid moving from one place to another and one family and all. I wasn't going to inflict that on anyone. She said it would be easier for her if I tied her up so she couldn't get away because if I didn't, she'd try to run, not from me but from the beatin'. She said she particularly liked being tied to the bed because it was handy for later, when we were both pretty well lathered up. I didn't want to beat her. That's when I ran.

"I'm telling you all this to show you that no matter how bad you ever were, Jancy, I would never hurt you."

I nodded solemnly, trying to look convinced, but there was a madness glittering in those blue eyes of his and I didn't trust his words.

When the telephone rang, I reached to answer the cordless on the side table before Bias could react. He got to his feet, went to the telephone on the desk, and picked it up to listen.

"I was just thinking of you, Birthday Girl." It was Jim. "How's your day going?"

I said, "Fine. You don't have to apologize, Jim. I've forgiven you. My lip didn't even swell this time." Jim didn't say a word for a minute and I knew he was getting the message. Thad looked at me. I stuck out my bottom lip and tapped it lightly with my index finger. He frowned and nodded that he understood.

"Glad to hear it." Jim words were measured. "I may be a little late tonight. Patsy Leek sent some papers over for me to serve, but the guy doesn't get home until five."

I drew a deep breath. Oh, yeah, we were on the same frequency mentally. Patsy Leek, once a dispatcher for Sheriff Dudley Roundtree, had been in the state mental hospital for the past year.

"Will you be all right until I get there?" he asked.

"Yes, I'll be fine."

"See you about six. I won't be late. I love you."

I choked and cradled the phone without attempting a response. I just ran smooth out of nerve.

"Take everything," Thad said, looking around. "We've got plenty of time. He won't be here until six. Pack it all."

"Thad, I'm not leaving."

He flew around the coffee table, grabbed my arm with one hand, and slapped me across the face with the other. Mine was the knee-jerk reaction of a woman who is not accustomed to abuse. A knee to the groin sent him stumbling back two or three paces before he crumpled onto the sofa.

I stepped toward him uncertainly. "Oh, Thad, I'm so sorry. I've never been slapped before."

He flashed me an accusing look. "How'd you get the busted lip, if you haven't been slapped?"

"Jim? That was an accident. He would never have hit me . . . intentionally," I said, stammering, trying to cover the gaffe. "You heard him apologize."

"Sure, all wife beaters apologize. They usually promise it'll never happen again."

I looked hard at Thad Bias. "But you hit me, and you did it on purpose."

"You weren't listening to me." He pushed himself upright on the couch. "You have to understand and do what I say. That's all that was, just a reminder."

"Even if what you commanded was not what I wanted?"

"You'll figure out I know what's best for you."

"You are a jerk. I decide what's best for me. That's what I'm doing here in this house, married to this man. Now get out of here."

The words were barely out of my mouth when the front door burst open and Jim strolled in, followed closely by the hulking

Sheriff Dudley Roundtree, his hand on the gun in the unsnapped holster at his side, and Deputy Gary Spence, whose weapon was already drawn.

CHAPTER THIRTY-FOUR

Bias was arrested, but I didn't want to sign a formal complaint against him. I was relieved when he left our house, drove away, and virtually vanished. As far as Jim and the sheriff knew, Thad had done nothing illegal. He insisted he had only stopped by to see an old friend and we'd had words, like friends do.

Later, when we were alone, Jim insisted on the unabridged account of Thad's visit. He became furious when I told him Thad had slapped me.

"We should have filed assault charges against the bastard," Jim railed, "busting into my home, assaulting my wife."

I spoke quietly to calm him. "I didn't tell you about the slap earlier because I didn't want to file a complaint. He's not stable, Jim. He's lived a hellish life. Who knows how we might have turned out if we had grown up like he did? I only wanted to get him out of our lives.

"Come on, let's settle down now and enjoy that fairytale happily-ever-after we've heard so much about."

Jim caught my face between his hands to examine it carefully. Apparently convinced there were no marks, certainly no permanent damage, he calmed down gradually, but he remained watchful. Wednesday morning, he didn't want to leave me in the house alone, which I told him was ridiculous. Thad hadn't broken in, after all. I had opened the door and invited him inside. Besides that, I genuinely doubted he would be back. His ego took a beating every time he and I tangled.

"I'm pretty sure we've seen the last of Thad Bias," I said, brimming with confidence.

Jim was less certain, which only proved how important I was. I was pretty sure no one else valued me as highly as my husband did, including Thad.

Valentine's Day turned blustery and cold. I had worked in the wire service bureau in Dominion all week, getting home later each night.

Logs blazed in the fireplace and a pot of stew simmered on the stove by the time I blew through our front door on a stiff north wind.

Jim was there immediately, took my coat and gloves, and nudged me toward the fireplace. "You ready to eat or do you want a bath first to warm up?"

Shivering, I sat on the raised hearth to warm my backside and consider those two delicious options. The telephone rang. We didn't have caller ID, but I was tired and wanted to hide out from the rest of the world.

"Please don't answer it," I pleaded, but my words stopped him only until the next ring. As he picked up the receiver, I said, "Tell whoever it is we can't go outside anymore tonight, no matter who it is. Please, Jim."

He smiled reassurance. He said hello, responded to the caller with four quick yeses, then hung up and turned around to frown at me.

I pleaded with a look and with words. "Please tell me we are locked in this cozy, warm place alone for the whole night."

"It's up to you." He sat tentatively on the edge of the coffee table facing me. "That was Lloyd Doyle Thatcher." He hesitated.

I immediately sat straighter and shifted uncomfortably on the hearth. "What did he want?"

"He's at University Hospital. He's been shot. The police

found him early this morning crying and bleeding behind Sweet Leona's."

"What was he doing in Dominion?"

"I don't know. He says his brother shot him and left him for dead."

My heart fell into my stomach.

"He said his dad predicted he'd wind up dead in an alley behind some bar someday. Lloyd thinks his brother's been planning to kill him ever since they started playing for Mrs. Berry's estate."

I got up and moved from the hearth to the couch where I slouched against the pillow back and clasped my hands in my lap. Jim swiveled on the coffee table, keeping his eyes on me. Avoiding his gaze, I stared at the fire.

"Maybe now," I said, "at long last, you can actually charge Thad or whatever his name is with a crime." I felt bad, festering with guilt that if I'd pressed charges against Thad, he might not have been free to shoot his poor, rat-faced brother.

"Maybe. We'll need a witness, a weapon—some hard evidence. I don't believe we can do it on the uncorroborated word of a victim who is, himself, a convicted felon." He looked at my face. "Don't get all eaten up with guilt, sweetheart. Thad's slippery as an eel. Has been all along. Even if we can put together a decent case, we may have a tough time locating him again."

I tried to smile. "I don't think you'll be able to dangle me as bait anymore. So, why did Rat Face call here?"

"He wants to see you . . . tonight."

"Is his injury life-threatening?"

"No."

"Could we wait until morning?"

Jim smiled. "Yes, we could. I'll call back, leave a message for him at the nurses' station. He doesn't have a phone in his room."

With a huge sigh of relief, I stood and smiled at my marvelous husband. "Good. I think I'll have a quick bath."

Jim grinned. "Don't make it too hot. I'll make that call, turn down the heat on supper, and join you."

Looking back over my shoulder, I gave Jim a slow, sexy smile. I unbuttoned my blouse as I climbed the stairs, removed it, then let it float to settle softly on the step behind as I glided on, stepping right out of my shoes.

Having finished his chores and chuckling evilly, Jim picked up the discarded blouse and shoes, her slacks at the top of the stairs, her bra at the bedroom door, and her stockings and panties just outside the bathroom.

CHAPTER THIRTY-FIVE

Lloyd Doyle Thatcher was dead when Jim and I got to the hospital shortly before nine A.M. They didn't tell us immediately. As soon as we asked at the desk for his room number, the receptionist called the floor supervisor, who asked us for photo IDs. Curious, but not alarmed, we complied.

"Mr. Thatcher expired," she said after she was satisfied with our identification. "It appears he suffocated."

I didn't waste questions on her, simply turned to Jim. "Who . . . ?" He knew what I wanted to know and also understood when I clouded up and couldn't get the rest of my question out.

He arched his eyebrows. "It's a short list."

"We should have come last night. If I'd had any idea . . . why?"

Jim slid his arm around me and pulled me close, but his eyes remained on the nurse. "Are the police here?"

"Not yet. We didn't call them. We weren't exactly sure it was a police matter."

Jim leaned over the counter, picked up the phone with his free hand, pressed "9" for an outside line, and dialed the Bishop Police Department.

"Didn't you have a monitor of some kind on him?" he asked as he waited for the detective division to answer.

"No. He didn't really need to be admitted. He could have been treated and released directly from the emergency room. It was his idea to stay. He had only a flesh wound. The nurse assigned to his room said he threw a fit—was terribly angry when he got the message you weren't coming last night. He tried to call you at home several times after that but got no answer."

I had unplugged the telephones to guarantee our evening was uninterrupted.

I tapped my knuckles against my mouth. Jim watched me as he gave the detective on the other end of the phone information and asked them to send a unit. He hung up, keeping one arm tightly around me, and turned back to the nurse.

"What name was he using?"

"Lloyd Doyle Thatcher is the name the police gave us when they brought him in."

"Did he tell anyone what was so urgent?"

"Not anyone on this shift. You'll have to ask the night floor nurse. She went off duty at two. I'll give you her home number. She sleeps late. You might want to wait until after lunch to call her."

"Are his personal effects still in his room?"

"He's there too," she said. "I'm afraid you probably should authorize an autopsy." She shot a wary look at me. "He listed you, Mrs. Wills, as the person to notify in case of an emergency."

Exhaling did not relieve any of the guilt as I buried my face in Jim's shoulder. I closed my eyes trying to blot out the mental pictures of Rat Face dead, practically at my hand. The man had annoyed and then frightened me. His very appearance made me squeamish. Yet he considered me the closest thing he had to next of kin. It was ludicrous, at the same time gruesome, almost ghoulish.

"We'll need your approval for an autopsy," the nurse prattled, interrupting my dark thoughts. Summoned down the hall to tend a patient, the nurse said she would call downstairs, have the business office prepare a release for my signature.

I couldn't cry over him, but I felt terrible, sick that he'd died, particularly that he had when his last wish had been to talk to me.

Jim took us to the waiting room and sat with me until the police arrived. I assured him I was fine so he could accompany the investigative team to the scene and to help them inventory Lloyd Doyle Thatcher's possessions.

I waited nearly an hour, watching people come and go and trying to think of anything I knew that might have any bearing on this . . . this . . . event. Eventually, the shift supervisor appeared with the release. I signed it and a short time later watched two orderlies wheel an empty gurney into Thatcher's room, emerge with a covered body, and roll by me to the staff elevators. With the body gone, I sauntered down the hall and peered into the room.

Jim, one of three men talking together inside, looked up. "Just finishing." He said something else to the men, walked over to take my arm, turned me around, and guided me down the corridor, onto and off of the elevator and out into bristling sunlight that cheered the cold, windswept day.

He drove us to Cheerie's Cafe in Bishop for coffee. "How do you feel?" he asked.

"Guilty as sin. Did you realize that while we enjoyed our marathon lovemaking, a man was dying?"

"It was bound to happen sooner or later," Jim said. "We did not contribute to the guy's end. He made his own bed, so to speak, and we made ours."

What a dreadful time for a pun. I wouldn't have smiled if he hadn't looked like a naughty kid who'd just gotten away with his first cuss word.

"Jim," I chided, but he grinned.

"I just can't feel sad that when he's six feet under, we're still going to be romping and fooling around in our bed. Rat Face was nothing to us but a nuisance. Now, come on, lighten up or I'm taking you home for some more fun."

Again, I couldn't help smiling. My former good friend Thad would no doubt be the prime suspect in his brother's death, too.

"How could I have been so wrong about Thad?" I murmured.

"You're a cockeyed optimist, baby. And you always give people the benefit of the doubt. In your opinion, everyone's good until proven bad."

"That makes me sound stupid."

"No, but it maybe makes you naive. The funny thing is, people pretty well behave the way a person expects them to behave. You expect people to be nice and they almost always are on their best behavior with you. It's one of those things I love most about you, that you bring out the best in the worst of us."

He looked sincere and I couldn't help taking his comment as a compliment. "It's a gift."

He laughed and tapped my nose with an index finger, and suddenly I was ravenous.

"We were supposed to go out for breakfast after we talked to Rat Face . . . I mean, Lloyd Thatcher," I reminded him.

"And here we are," Jim said brightly. "It's only eleven-forty and, lucky for us, Cheerie's serves breakfast all day long."

My spirits improved dramatically after we ate. I insisted on accompanying Jim to the SBI office to telephone the night nurse for her account of Thatcher's last night. I listened on an extension telephone to Jim's interview.

They had already called from the hospital to notify the nurse that Thatcher was dead, that the police were investigating and would be contacting her. She was precise, her voice clipped and devoid of emotion. Even without a chart or records in front of her, she recalled in detail Thatcher's arrival and his nervousness.

"He became particularly anxious at not being able to speak with Mrs. Wills," she said. "The last time I opened his door, about midnight, he asked me not to turn on the lights, to leave him alone and let him sleep. His voice sounded muffled, like he might be yawning.

"He was only there at his insistence, not even for observation. I had sick people who actually needed my care. I made a note that Mr. Thatcher was not to be disturbed."

As they concluded the interview, the night nurse agreed to call Jim if she thought of any other information that came to light during her conversations with Thatcher.

"By the way," she said before they hung up, "Would you mind asking Mrs. Wills something . . . well, the janitor noticed Mr. Thatcher's shoes, ankle-high boots, expensive ones. He asked if I had the chance, if I would ask Mrs. Wills if she had plans for the shoes."

Jim looked and sounded excited. "What?"

"Mr. Thatcher listed Mrs. Wills as his next of kin. He even signed a power of attorney form we provide. I don't mean to sound unfeeling about your loss, that is, Mr. Thatcher's death, but . . ."

"I'll ask her."

"He gave me his power of attorney," I repeated, shaking my head, still not believing the nurse's statement.

Jim raised his eyebrows and nodded solemnly, obviously as baffled as I.

"Is there any reason the janitor shouldn't have the shoes?"

"No, I guess not," he said, "though a power of attorney is no good after a person's dead. I doubt anyone will object to your giving away the shoes, but maybe we should look them over first, along with his other possessions and apparel, everything he brought to the hospital with him."

"You and the police have already been through all of his personal effects, haven't you?"

"Not thoroughly. Before you gift anything, I think you and I might make one more trip through his belongings, if it's okay with you. Are you too tired? I know this has been a strain. I can take you home for a while."

"Drop me off?"

"No. I'll stay too."

I shivered with relief. I just didn't feel like being alone right then. "No. I feel fine. I want to go."

We went to the police department evidence room, where the officer on duty gave us two trash sacks containing Thatcher's belongings. Jim gave the boots a thorough going-over.

"Nice," he said, turning them. "Good dancing shoes. All leather soles and uppers." He reached inside and ran his hand all the way into the toe of one and withdrew a piece of paper.

"Wadding," he said, as if answering my questioning look. "Maybe they were too big." He smoothed the paper out on the table. Words, written in pencil and smeared, were barely legible. Jim and I scanned it together.

Chet is deturmened to rap and kill Jancy. Tell her.

As soon as he had figured out the misspelling, Jim folded the note and shoved it deep into his pocket, but he was too late. I had already figured it out.

" 'Chet' being Chester?" I guessed. "He was wrong." I regarded Jim earnestly. "I don't think Thad would actually harm me."

I could tell the expression on my face belied my words.

Jim looked very grim and very determined. "We're not going to give him an opportunity to harm or kill you. As we discussed, you tend to be generous in assessing people's character. From now on, I'm assigning myself to you, round-the-clock surveillance." He grinned. "It's a dirty job, but . . ."

My smile of relief was genuine.

The forensics people lifted three clear fingerprints from the newly unwrapped I.V. tube used by his assailant to restrain Lloyd Doyle Thatcher's hands while he died, smothered by a plastic-protected hospital bed pillow. Jim began an eager search for Thad Bias's fingerprints as a match. He turned up some in Branch, Texas, where Carl Donnan had been printed as a juvenile. The identification would be complicated, though. Jim would have to prove that the myriad identities belonged to one and the same person. Thad had pretty well muddled his tracks over the years.

Jim explained the situation to Sheriff Dudley Roundtree. By using names like Carl Donnan, Chester Doyle, Charlie Denim, and whatever other aliases Bias had adopted and then discarded along the way, he'd gotten lost in a maze.

There followed for Jim and me three uninterrupted days of personal surveillance. Jim took his assignment literally. It was one of those periods a person might have orchestrated, if she had been able to imagine it.

"Lovers sometimes play sex games," I said, initiating conversation the third evening, after a long lull. Jim was on the sofa, his feet propped on the coffee table, reading the *Dominion Evening News.* A fire blazed in the fireplace and sleet peppered the windows.

He flipped down a corner of the newspaper to see me standing by the stairs in jeans, a sweatshirt, and fluffy house shoes. He smiled slightly and nodded. "I've heard that."

"Sometimes they use handcuffs. Have you ever played sex games using restraints?"

"No, I never have."

It was my turn to provide the mysterious smile. "Want to?"

"That depends."

"On what?"

"Who's playing?"

I turned around with a sweep of my hand. "Everyone."

"You mean everyone who's here?"

I grinned. "Yep."

"Do you know the rules?"

"I'll make some up as we go. Will that make you nervous?"

"Yeah." He laid the newspaper aside, stood, and walked slowly as I began backing up the stairs. His steps quickened. I whirled and bolted, giggling. He slowed and took his time, removing his shirt as he followed, moving deliberately.

When he stepped into the bedroom, I was standing by the closet holding the belt from my terry cloth robe. I had placed a red scarf over the lone table lamp, giving the bedroom an eerie, rose-colored glow.

"I want you to go in the bathroom," I said, enunciating, but speaking quietly, "take off all your clothes and wrap a towel around you, then come back in here and lie down on your stomach on the bed. And don't say a word."

Nodding, he obediently disappeared into the bathroom.

I heard water running. He was gone several minutes, time I used to lace the terry cloth sash through the middle rungs in the headboard, leaving lengths at either side.

When Jim emerged from the bathroom clad as instructed, he looked at me, at the bed, back at me, and arched his eyebrows, asking a mute question.

"Lie down on your stomach, please. Cross your arms above your head. I'm going to tie your wrists. Okay?"

Without a change of his expression, he did as he was told.

"Relax your legs. Don't be stiff."

Again he obliged.

The ends of the tie were thick. I was barely able to knot them once, but pulled them tightly to secure his wrists. He turned his head on the pillow and watched intently as I took off my sweat-shirt and skimmed out of my jeans.

Slowly, provocatively, I arched my back, sucked my stomach against my ribs, and removed my bra, shimmying, making its straps slide down my arms before it dropped to the floor.

I fondled my breasts, pushing them forward, up and down and from side to side, careful not to look at Jim or to acknowl-edge his presence.

Revolving, I slid my panties down, rubbing my thighs and splaying my hands over my stomach and hips as I pivoted. The panties gone, I stretched up on my tiptoes, reached high over my head, and oscillated, like a fan sweeping from side to side in the dim light. Jim breathed heavily.

I placed one knee on the bed beside him, threw the other leg over to straddle him, and lowered the length of my torso to his back. He strained a little against the restraints, flexing his marvelous biceps, warming to the game.

I stroked his muscled shoulders, murmuring how beautiful they were, how magnificent he was. I shivered before I ran my fingernails down his bare back. The pelt between my legs rasped as I moved.

"Oh, it's a massage," he said. "A cunt rub."

The term momentarily distracted me. "Jim, what's a 'cunt'?"

"Tell you later. I'm not supposed to talk."

I leaned forward and touched my lips to the back of his ear, at the same time allowing my nipples to titillate him before I scrubbed my breasts against him. His biceps strained harder against the restraints and he tightened his hips, the muscles there stimulating my lower body until I began to writhe and twist.

"Stop it," I whispered, running my tongue along the rim of his ear. "This is my game."

"When do I get to play?"

"Later. I want to touch you and kiss you all over. It's my duty, to 'know you fully,' in the biblical sense."

"Oh. Is this supposed to be a religious experience?"

"Sort of," I said. "Be quiet."

My fingers and hands, my lips and my mouth traced the lines of him as the rest of my body scrubbed against him carelessly. As I worked on his legs, he groaned and flexed.

When my caressing reached the towel, I hesitated. He was breathing heavily, taking in deep draughts.

I shifted, kneeling on the bed beside him to concentrate on the pads on the bottoms of his feet. He didn't flinch.

I massaged each leg, kneading his calf muscles, producing the expected flex, then the backs of his thighs. Warming as I wended my way up his legs, my breathing quickened. My hands grew hot and moved more urgently and I murmured sweet words. "You have such perfect legs, so firm, so muscular, so very strong. My hands reached the towel, where I hesitated before sliding my fingers to investigate his manhood.

"And what have we here?" I wheezed. "A canvas marble bag, you say . . . I love touching . . ." I stammered, my murmuring interrupted by nervous inhalations. "I have other work to do . . .

"Turn over," I commanded, a little breathlessly. Still straddling him, I rocked up on my knees to give him room to turn, and I clasped my hands and bit my lips, struggling to maintain control. Jim raised his head to see which way to turn to keep from knotting the tie restraining his wrists, then complied.

Stretched on his back, he eyed me somberly. Unable to meet his gaze, I rocked forward and buried my face in his neck. Neither of us moved for a long moment before I began to tighten and relax my legs, lifting and settling me up and down over him, the towel an annoying obstacle between us.

Carefully, I brushed the hair on his chest. He flexed his

pectoral muscles as I brushed the mat of hair toward the center of his stomach. I trailed the natural trough down the middle of his stomach, beyond his belly button to the edge of the towel. Again my breath caught and my legs flexed, lifting, then settling. Snatching the towel, I tossed it aside, revealing the power of his man's body, engorged, that most important muscle flexed and ready.

Frantically, I slid down to fit the most intimate part of me to the most intimate part of him and eased down, impaling myself. Too far gone, I squirmed and lay down to rub his naked body with my own, crushing my breasts to his chest, aligning my thighs with either side of his.

When he didn't move, I gasped. "Come on. Jim, please. Help me."

My mouth was hot as it covered his. Begging and pleading, I kissed him wildly. I sucked his tongue ruthlessly but he remained unmoving beneath me.

"What is it?" I wailed, finally. "Come on. You have to do it. Now."

"I can't," he said, speaking into my mouth covering his.

"What? Why?" I lifted my flushed face from his and he shot a glance at the tie still holding his wrists. I lunged to one side, grabbing that tie with both hands. I yanked and tugged, but it wouldn't come loose. Flustered, I swung to the other side, not caring that Jim captured and suckled my breasts in his mouth as they brushed within his reach. I attacked the second binding, clawing and scratching, but it, too, held fast.

Tears blinded my frenzied efforts and I came completely undone.

"Help me," I blubbered, frustrated, overwhelmed, and not able to control my own passion. I blinked hard, trying to clear my eyes, to focus on his face. I stroked his captive wrists, groaning, defeated.

"It's all right, baby." His voice sounded husky, but controlled. With no effort at all, he slipped one hand free, then the other. He had been playing with me, pretending to be bound when he could have gotten free anytime he pleased.

"Damn you," I hissed and scrambled to dismount, but he was quicker. Before I could get my bearings, he had flipped us, putting himself on top, catching my fists, quieting my mouth with his own, nudging my legs apart and sliding between them. He entered smoothly and began to pump. Gradually my physical, emotional, and mental thrashing stilled as he methodically soothed and placated me with the familiar intimacy of our bodies. He worked our mutual magic, comforting, and eventually satisfying me, as smoothly as if my tantrum had never happened.

When the tumult had passed, I lay quietly beside Jim, naked and flushed despite the chill of the room.

"How many times can you do that?" I asked.

"What do you mean?"

"In a twenty-four-hour period, how many times can you, ah, perform?"

"I don't know."

I rolled onto my side and propped my head on a hand to look at him. "Why don't you know?"

"I never needed to know. I never screwed competitively."

I swallowed my chagrin, then snickered as he smiled. "I wonder if there's a competition like that somewhere. I mean, the same people who bring us wet T-shirt contests surely have devised a similar competition among males."

His laughter mingled with mine. "Not that I know of, but if there were, we could probably qualify."

I became serious. "Jim, what's a 'cunt'?"

He smiled in the rosy half-light provided by the scarf covering the lamp. "It's a private word, Jancy. Where did you first hear it?"

"Thad. He said I was just another cunt to you, and that I was more than that to him. I'd never heard that word before. I didn't know what it meant."

Jim's expression darkened, but when he looked back to evaluate my puzzlement, he smiled again. "Your cunt, Jancy, is the dark sweetness that lures me inside you. It doesn't just call, it sings to me. Has, ever since the first time I laid eyes on you."

I was more confused than ever and it must have shown.

"Is it an anatomical part? Is it my vagina?"

He shook his head.

"Is it the sex act itself?"

"No. It's where the sex act takes place for a woman, but it's more than that. It's that private part of you that signals your desire." He stoked the recently sensitized area between my legs. "It's your place of longing that needs filling. With us, it's you pulling me inside you, like you did tonight."

I remained puzzled.

"The Avon lady comes to the door," he said, expanding. "You are reserved but polite. A good friend from high school stops by. You're more cordial to her, invite her for dinner. It's a stronger feeling than you expressed toward the sales lady. And you are even more cordial when you welcome family or loved ones.

"This may be an oversimplification. But the call of your cunt is the most compelling—the height of all the hospitality you have to offer. And you, Jancy girl, extend that invitation exclusively to me, and no one else.

"Bias mistakenly thought you were inviting him. With his background and his insanity, he misinterpreted your kindness as a more intimate interest. Now do you understand?"

I wondered if Jim thought I had misled Thad. I shrugged.

"Well, I get it well enough to know Bias had a lot of gall using that word to me. Anyway, I need a shower. How about it?"

"Together? I don't know if I'm up to an encore."

Stroking him down to and over his belly button, I giggled. "Come on and let's see what develops."

Jim pretended to wince, but got up and trailed along behind me grinning.

The morning of the fourth day, Jim received a call from Mrs. Teeman in his office. The district attorney in Dominion needed his testimony in a drug matter, testimony vital to the prosecution's case. The Dominion Police Department would send a unit to guard me and our house while he was gone. Jim needed to appear at two. The prosecutor could interview him during the lunch break. They would have a team on the street in front of our house before eleven.

"I'll be back before dark," Jim said as I assured him, again, that I welcomed the prospect of a little time alone. I needed to do laundry, vacuum, and take care of some personal chores. That's how I happened to be at home alone when the phone rang at twelve-fifty P.M.

Jim had suggested more than once that I use a laundry basket to collect clothing from the upstairs hamper. Just as often I explained that if I failed to bring a basket upstairs, I didn't want to make an extra trip down to get one.

Juggling an armload of dirty laundry, I dropped several pieces, then dumped the rest on the floor and scurried to answer the phone on our bedside table.

"What are you doing?" a pleasant voice asked.

"Not much." I tried to place the caller's voice without having to ask. It was a man's voice, but I had to run through a process of elimination. It was not one of Jim's brothers or mine or either of our dads or Kellan Dulaney, or any of our other usual male callers. Still, it might be any one of a dozen law enforcement people or prosecutors I had met recently.

"Is Jim around?"

"No, but he'll be back shortly. Can I take a message?" Suddenly a form loomed in the bedroom doorway. Startled, I looked up into the angry face of Thad Bias.

"No," Thad crooned from the doorway, a cell phone in his hand, "no message." He was wearing latex gloves.

Chapter Thirty-Six

"Convenient to find you waiting for me in the bedroom," Thad said. His blue eyes glittered brighter than usual, ogling me in an unpleasantly suggestive way.

Standing beside the bed looking into Thad's face, I wondered how I had ever considered him handsome. I supposed his outward kindness and boyish charm had fooled me into thinking his pale, freckled features with the thatch of straw-colored hair attractive. The eyes of the beholder found him comely. Of course, usually he flashed the winsome smile that displayed his marvelous teeth. There was no sign of the smile now. The bones in his face seemed more pronounced, his temples and cheeks sunken, his beak of a nose more angular than before.

"We'll do it all," he said. "You and I will, right here in this room." He stared straight into my face as if thinking he could intimidate me, subdue me with his will. "Right here in his bed."

I had no idea what was going to happen before Thad left this time, but having sex with me was not on my agenda, regardless of what he thought.

He tossed the cell phone onto the bed and watched it bounce. "If you're good to me, I might let you live." He looked from the bed to my face and frowned. "To be honest, it'll be hard for me to kill you, Jancy. I will if I have to, of course, but I don't want you to think I'll like doing it. It's important to me for you to know that."

He didn't move any closer, so I stood still and silent.

"Actually, it'll be better punishment for you and for him, too, if I don't. That way neither one of you will ever be able to forget me. You'll never be able to come into this room, to get into this bed, without thinking of me. In a way, what I do here this afternoon could make me immortal." He continued watching me and paused as if giving me a chance to speak, but I had nothing to say.

"I guess it'd be overly optimistic to think you might be trying to get pregnant right now, that you're off the pill or whatever. If that was the case, you and I could really make me immortal."

I didn't move or speak. I didn't want to incite him, so I remained still, as if I were frozen, the bedroom phone still in my hand. Slowly I lowered the receiver into its cradle.

I glanced down at the dirty clothes I had dropped on the floor, then I stooped and gathered the laundry as if it were the most normal thing in the world. Concentrating on my task, ignoring Thad Bias completely, I moved slowly, hoping to confuse him. My actions seemed to have exactly that effect.

When I had picked up the last sock, I straightened.

Keeping my eyes firmly set on the hallway, I walked toward the door. Baffled and standing slightly to one side, Bias made no effort to deny me the path.

I forced myself to move in slow motion, steadily, predictably to the stairs. I had started my descent before he reacted.

The doorbell rang.

I threw the armload of clothing on the stairs and flew down the remaining steps to the front door, turned the knob, and yanked. It held. *Deadbolt,* I thought. *Key.*

Someone pounded on the front door.

"Help!" I screamed.

Bounding like a cat tired of stalking its prey, Bias leaped over the clothing scattered on the stairway, grabbed a handful of my ponytail from behind, and slapped his other hand over my mouth. I thrashed and elbowed him to free my arms. His long, strong fingers locked on either side of my face, sealing the hand firmly over my lips.

Spinning, lunging, I couldn't see clearly enough to know where we traveled as we struggled. My plan was to get back to the front door. On the other side was help. I raked my hands over the knob, fumbling with latches and locks before I realized the deadbolt key was missing. The lock, intended to secure the occupants from intruders, now served only to keep me the intruder's prisoner.

With a fierce yank, Thad locked his long arms around me, effectively pinning my arms to my sides. Doing so forced him to release my mouth. I needed an advantage. Maybe the element of surprise. Suddenly I went very still, holding myself stiffly against him. We were both panting from our struggle and probably were both reconnoitering.

I felt his nose in my hair. His arms tightened and his body trembled while I held stiff and unyielding.

"Come on," he coaxed in a breathless whisper, "you know me. You've always liked me. I know you trust me. I know what's right for you. You do like me, don't you, Jancy?"

I forced my body to relax. "I used to like you. I don't anymore."

His arms tightened again, this time to inflict pain. I gritted my teeth to keep from crying out. I didn't want to give him that satisfaction, or any other. He dug his fingers into my upper arms and turned me, forcing me to face him. When I finally allowed my eyes to meet his, I jutted my jaw and tried to let him see my seething hate and rage.

"Come on," he ordered angrily, his fingers digging deeper into my arms, pinching and inflicting as much pain as he could. "We're going back upstairs."

"No."

He raised a hand to strike me. It took everything I had, but I glared at him without flinching.

"You are a spineless, shitless excuse for a man," I hissed, the ugly words barely audible. Bias stared at me in disbelief. Then his jaw tightened and he swung that upraised arm, catching my jaw with the back of his hand. I reeled, but marveled that the blow didn't hurt nearly as much as I'd expected it to.

"Upstairs!" he shouted, yanking me so hard, I stumbled. It took a minute to get my feet going as he shoved me toward the stairway. I staggered, then dug deep and veered toward the living room before he realized I was foiling his plan.

"I want you in the bedroom," he screeched, his voice, like his body, going out of control. He shoved me again, hard, back toward the stairs.

"Why? You sniveling weasel. You won't be able to perform in Jim's bed. Surely you know that." Again my words hit home and he waffled. "I'll tell you a secret," I pressed, hoping to keep him staggering emotionally. "Jim is magnificent in that bed. I tingle just thinking of his body poised over mine. He has a man's regal chest with a lion's mane of black hair. The muscles in his arms ripple when he lowers himself into me. He's so amazing, I'm scarcely able to breathe."

I lowered my voice to a sneer. "I can just imagine you, simpering, groveling, whining your way through the sex act, your stringy little arms and your concave, hairless little chest. The thought of you dangling over me like a buzzard makes me sick."

I narrowed my eyes and dropped my voice to a rasping whisper. "I've seen your fear of people and things, especially that you're frightened to death of him. I understand your cowardice. He's bold and brave and all those things you can never be. Jim strides through life facing the world with courage and confidence. You skulk, darting in and out of the shadows, hiding, frightened of everything, quivering like the gutless little quisling you are. You're even a gutless killer, ambushing your victims, hitting them from behind, even old, helpless people."

With that, I got a sudden insight. "You're even afraid of the dark, aren't you?"

His face became ashen. I'd struck a nerve, a very raw, exposed one. Could what I was thinking be fact? I scoured his face, reading the vulnerability so clearly visible.

"Candlesticks." I whispered, amazed by the sudden truth.

He didn't move.

"You're afraid of the dark! Of course. Someone, sometime, locked you in the dark to punish you, didn't they? You learned to carry a candle and matches. You had to have them for light.

"You worked at night, in well-lighted places, and slept in the daytime, while the sun lit the world." I stared at him in disbelief. "You're a grown man who's still afraid of the dark."

As if my accusation ignited him, Bias grabbed the collar of my shirt and threw me toward the stairs. I stumbled on the bottom step and fell. Grabbing a handful of hair, he yanked me up.

I threw an elbow that caught him in the solar plexus. He let go of my hair, but grabbed at my clothes as he dropped, gasping for air. I kicked his shins and drove a heel into his foot, not quite able to get away from his grasping hands. When he tried for a new hold on my hair, I clawed his arm, shredding his shirtsleeve.

In spite of my fighting like a tiger, he caught me around the middle and half-carried, half-shoved me up the first few steps.

Getting a new idea, I let my legs go limp and dropped, suddenly dead weight. He followed me down, then grabbed the front of my blouse with both hands and yanked.

Concentrating, I forced myself to remain limp. The fabric and buttons gave and my shirt flapped open. I grabbed at the two sides, pulling them back together. He snatched the front of my slacks and tried to rip them the same way. The corduroy, however, was tougher and did not yield.

I pummeled his head with my fists and kicked furiously, trying desperately to knee him in the groin as he attacked the closure on my slacks while trying to protect himself from the blows of my flying hands and feet.

Nearly free, I half stood and lunged forward into him, the tackle driving him back down the stairs and sending us both sprawling onto the floor. He grappled, trying to secure my flailing fists as I continued battering him.

Then, to my everlasting joy, I heard glass shatter somewhere in the house.

Monitoring the Wills's telephones, the police dispatcher was surprised. He radioed the surveillance team. A telephone call currently in progress apparently originated on a cell phone and was answered in the house.

"Maybe she's testing a new phone or ringer or something," one officer suggested. They discussed it at length, speculating about the mysterious call.

"Won't hurt to check," the other said.

"I hate to be a nuisance."

"Well, I'm not going alone. Come on."

"My coffee will be cold by the time we get back."

"Okay, finish it. We'll check on her before you pour the next one."

Eventually both officers got out of their parked cruiser and ambled to the front door of the Wills's condo. They rang the doorbell. No one answered, so they rang again.

"Did you hear something?" one asked. Neither was certain. They pounded on the door. Still no response.

"We know she's here," one assured the other.

"Might be in the bathroom. Better wait a minute or two and see."

Minutes passed. Growing concerned, one officer walked around the perimeter of the house looking for an unlocked window or door. It was the second man who noticed a window in the utility room missing a pane. When he tried to raise the window, it yielded quietly.

Again the partners discussed possibilities. The windowpane could have been broken for a while. Hadn't they been right in front of the house since before eleven? Few cars and no pedestrians had entered or left this block. They would swear to it. But could they risk having overlooked something?

"Give me a boost," the first officer said, indicating he wanted a closer look at the utility room window. Leaning over the sash, he saw broken glass on the floor. He slipped and stuck a fist through a second pane before he climbed inside. His partner ran back to the police cruiser to report a possible break-in.

When I heard muffled noises in the utility room, I got a second wind. Help was on the way. That gave me hope, and hope gave me new strength. I broke free of Thad's grasp and darted to the kitchen. When he caught me, I unleashed a renewed assault, but he no longer made any effort to handle me gently. Wrenching my arm, he wrestled me to the floor and leered at my open shirt as he dropped to his knees.

I heard the dead bolt turn, the front door open, then voices and running feet. Looming over me on the kitchen floor, Bias struggled to subdue me, oblivious to other people surging through the front and sweeping through the house.

Two large, thick hands caught the back of Bias's jacket and lifted him from his knees to his feet. More figures peopled the kitchen doorway. I couldn't see well enough to recognize anyone.

I heard Sheriff Roundtree's baritone before I actually saw him. He was yelling, struggling with Jim, trying to wrest Thad's limp body from Jim's determined clutches. I tried to get to my feet, but my body didn't respond. I did well to pull my shred-ded shirt closed.

Roundtree shouted, "Give him to me, Jimbo. We've got him dead to rights this time; plenty of evidence, a whole slew of eyewitnesses. He's nailed. Come on, son, let me put the cuffs on him."

Choking back sudden, uncontrollable sobs, I couldn't speak. The next best thing seemed to be to get up. I got to my hands and knees and reached for Jim, tugging at his pant leg. Looking down, he suddenly dropped to the floor and caught me up in his arms.

When he was able to withdraw a little from my death grip, Jim pushed me to arm's length to look me over. Drawing a tis-sue from his pocket, he blotted blood at the corner of my mouth before he caught my face gently in both his large, thick hands. The right side of my bottom lip protruded so much I could see it in my peripheral vision. When I attempted a reassuring smile, Jim's expression fell and his dark, dark eyes glittered with menace.

"It's just that I've never been punched on purpose," I tried to explain, tapping my fingers carefully on my swollen lip.

He groaned as if he were in agony. "I'm sorry. Oh, honey, I never should have let this happen. I should have been here. I thought you were safe." Putting an index finger under my chin, he tilted my head back to examine it more closely. "Is this the worst of it?"

I nodded, continuing the crooked smile, an effort to assure him I was all right and to maybe entertain him as well.

"He didn't . . ." he began, again looking alarmed.

"Don't be ridiculous."

Jim studied my face a long minute, then laughed ruefully. "Of course he didn't. Stupid bastard didn't have time. Getting into your pants takes months of diligent planning and strategy and finally, commitment. I ought to know."

Burying my forehead against his shoulder, I laughed while, at the same time, complaining loudly at the discomfort my euphoria was causing my poor busted lip.

CHAPTER THIRTY-SEVEN

"Thad was hoping we were trying to have a baby," I said. I was stretched across the bed on my stomach watching Jim shave. He wore only his boxers and was definitely the sexiest man I had ever seen. I loved watching his body language as he went about his morning ritual. I enjoyed admiring his arms and his chest, savoring the moments when even the muscles in his legs flexed as he drew the safety razor down his face.

His eyes met my reflection in the mirror. "Why was that?"

"The implication was that he would father my offspring and thus become immortal."

"I assume you were not receptive."

"Fought like a banshee."

"If you start thinking about getting pregnant, you will talk to me, right?"

I nodded but turned my face from his scrutiny.

Jim finished, rinsed the excess lather, and patted his face dry. Still carrying the hand towel, he eased onto the bed beside me. He slid one spaghetti strap of my nightgown off my shoulder and kissed my warm skin, which grew warmer with his attention.

"Would you like to have a baby?" he asked.

I rolled my eyes toward him and looked at him a long moment before I answered. "Someday."

He said, "We can do it whenever you're ready."

"What if I can't?"

"You mean what if we can't conceive?"

"No, not that. What if I can't endure childbirth?"

"Women have been doing it for thousands of years, including your mom and mine."

"Thank goodness for them, but they are both a lot braver than I am. What if I can't stand the pain?"

Jim smiled tolerantly, stood up, and started back to take his shower. "You know it's perfectly okay with me if we don't have kids. I didn't marry you because I thought you'd be good breeding stock, although I'm sure you will be. I want to spend the rest of my life with you, not a swarm of rug rats. Kids come and go. They're sort of temporary, when you think about it."

A little offended for our hypothetical offspring, I swung my legs around to perch on the side of the bed. "Don't call our children rug rats."

When he looked around and saw I was serious, Jim appeared to be confused. "What difference does it make what I call our theoretical children, which you may decide not to have any of?"

"Well, if I do decide to have a baby someday, I don't want it to find out you referred to it as a 'rug rat.' That might make it feel unwanted."

Jim rolled his eyes and turned his back, but I saw his shoulders shake.

He turned on the shower, removed his shorts, and stepped under the spray. Before he could pull the shower door closed, I tossed off my nightgown and joined him.

Our communication in the confines of the shower consisted entirely of physical manipulations, the result of which was that we both emerged feeling sated and clean as we toweled each other.

"Maybe we could practice our parenting skills on a dog," Jim suggested after he was ready for work and pouring coffee.

"Too confining."

"Good point. Same goes for kids."

"Jim, you're twenty-nine. Should we be concerned about our biological clocks?"

"I understand men can father children until they're seventy and beyond."

"But I'm probably only good into my forties."

"Yeah, definitely cause for concern. That only gives us twenty years or so."

I cleared our cereal bowls.

"Are you working today?" Jim asked.

I yawned and stretched from side to side. "I can go or not."

"You're bored, is that it?"

"Jim, I worked hard to get hired by the wire service. Now it hardly seems like it was worth the trouble. With Candlesticks caught, I'm fresh out of projects worthy of my vast skills and abilities."

"So, give yourself a couple of days off. Stop by the paper. Talk to Melchoir. You'll be a shot in the arm for him and maybe he'll be a dose for you. Come by the office. I'll take you to lunch."

He grinned, patted my backside, grabbed his briefcase, and strode through the utility room and out the door to the garage.

He was all the way out when he turned around and stuck his head back in the door. "By the way, don't look for your birth control pills. I flushed 'em. We're on our own."

My first errand that morning was a stop at the drugstore for more pills. Jim might be a benevolent dictator, but there are some things a woman wants to decide for herself.

Besides that, I'd been reading and getting worked up about toxic waste dump sites.

People in Washington, D.C., apparently thought Oklahomans had plenty of unused space and with the right monetary motivation might be willing to turn our state into a giant trash can.

My second stop was the *Bishop Clarion*. I wanted to talk to Managing Editor Ron Melchoir about a little investigative reporting by a nosy reporter who happened to have a little time on her hands and sources primed and ready to pump.

Jancy Dewhurst . . . that is, Jancy Wills . . . had more important things to do than reproduce, at least for the time being.

ABOUT THE AUTHOR

A voracious reader, **Sharon Ervin** loves mysteries, but prefers them laced with a little romance. "Since that's what I like to read," she says, "that's what I write.

"I wrote my first novel in 1982. Through seventeen years of rejections on seven manuscripts, I wrote what I liked best. It looked like I would be the only one reading them anyway.

"When a publisher offered on my eighth manuscript, I thought it was a scam. But it was for real."

Since then, other of Ervin's manuscripts have been published. *Candlesticks* is the ninth.

A former newspaper reporter, Ervin has a degree in journalism from the University of Oklahoma. She is married, has four grown children, and lives in McAlester, Oklahoma. Her website is sharonervin.com.